THE WRATH OF ANGELS

John Connolly

THE WRATH OF ANGELS

HODDER &
STOUGHTON

For Professor Ian Campbell Ross

First published in Great Britain in 2012 Hodder & Stoughton
An Hachette UK company

1

A CIP catalogue record for this title is available from the British Library

Hardback ISBN 978 1 444 75644 9
Trade Paperback ISBN 978 1 444 75645 6
ebook ISBN 978 1 444 75646 3

Typeset in Sabon LT Std by Palimpsest Book Production Limited,
Falkirk, Stirlingshire

Printed and bound by Clays Ltd, St Ives plc

Hodder & Stoughton policy is to use papers that are natural, renewable
and recyclable products and made from wood grown in sustainable
forests. The logging and manufacturing processes are expected to
conform to the environmental regulations of the country of origin.

Hodder & Stoughton Ltd
338 Euston Road
London NW1 3BH

www.hodder.co.uk

I

I prefer winter and fall, when you feel the bone structure of the landscape – the loneliness of it, the dead feeling of winter. Something waits beneath it, the whole story doesn't show.

Andrew Wyeth (1917–2009)

1

At the time of his dying, at the day and the hour of it, Harlan Vetters summoned his son and his daughter to his bedside. The old man's long gray hair was splayed against the pillow on which he lay, glazed by the lamplight, so that it seemed like the emanations of his departing spirit. His breathing was shallow; longer and longer were the pauses between each intake and exhalation, and soon they would cease entirely. The evening gloaming was slowly descending, but the trees were still visible through the bedroom window, the sentinels of the Great North Woods, for old Harlan had always said that he lived at the very edge of the frontier, that his home was the last place before the forest held sway.

It seemed to him now that, as his strength failed him, so too his power to keep nature at bay was ebbing. There were weeds in his yard, and brambles among his rose bushes. The grass was patchy and unkempt: it needed one final mow before the coming of winter, just as the stubble on his own chin rasped uncomfortably against his fingers, for the girl could not shave him as well as he had once shaved himself. Fallen leaves lay uncollected like the flakes of dry skin that peeled from his hands, his lips, and his face, scattering themselves upon his sheets. He saw decline through his window, and decline in his mirror, but in only one was there the promise of rebirth.

The girl claimed that she had enough to do without worrying about bushes and trees, and his boy was still too angry to perform even this simple service for his dying father, but to Harlan these things were important. There was a battle to be fought, an ongoing war against nature's attritional impulse. If everyone thought as his daughter did then houses would be overrun by root and ivy, and towns would vanish beneath seas of brown and green. A man had only to open his eyes in this county to see the ruins of old dwellings suffocated in green, or open his ears to hear the names of settlements that no longer existed, lost somewhere in the depths of the forest.

So nature needed to be held back, and the trees had to be kept to their domain.

The trees, and what dwelled among them.

Harlan was not a particularly religious man, and had always poured scorn on those whom he termed 'God-botherers' – Christian, Jew or Muslim, he had no time for any of them – but he was, in his way, a deeply spiritual being, worshipping a god whose name was whispered by leaves and praised in birdsong. He had been a warden with the Maine Forest Service for forty years, and even after his retirement his knowledge and expertise had often been sought by his successors, for few knew these woods as well as he. It was Harlan who had found twelve-year-old Barney Shore after the boy's father collapsed while hunting, his heart exploding so quickly in his chest that he was dead within seconds of hitting the ground. The boy, in shock and unused to the woods, had wandered north, and when the snow began to descend he had hidden himself beneath a fallen tree, and would surely have died there had Harlan not been following his tracks, so that the boy heard the old man calling his name just as the snow covered the traces of his passing.

It was to Harlan, and to Harlan alone, that Barney Shore told the tale of the girl in the woods, a girl with sunken eyes, and wearing a black dress, who had come to him with the first touch of snow, inviting him to follow her deeper into the woods, calling on him to play with her in the northern darkness.

'But I hid from her, and I didn't go with her,' Barney told Harlan, as the old man carried him south upon his back.

'Why not, son?' said Harlan.

'Because she wasn't a little girl, not really. She just looked like one. I think she was very old. I think she'd been there for a long, long time.'

And Harlan had nodded and said, 'I think you're right,' for he had heard tales of the lost girl in the woods, although he had never seen her himself, unless dreams counted, and he prayed to his god of air and tree and leaf that he might always be spared the sight of her. There was a time, though, when he had felt her presence, and he had known as he was searching for the boy that he was once again drawing close to her territory.

He shuddered, and thought carefully before he spoke.

'If I were you, son, I wouldn't mention the girl to anyone else,' he said at last, and he felt the boy nod against him.

'I know,' he said. 'They wouldn't believe me anyway, would they?'

'No. I reckon they'd think you were suffering from shock and exposure, and they'd put it down to that, most of them.'

'But you believe me, don't you?'

'Oh yes, I believe you.'

'She was real, wasn't she?'

'I don't know if that's the word I'd use for her. I don't reckon that you could touch her, or smell her, or feel her breath upon your face. I don't know that you could see her footprints indented in the snow, or discern the stain of sap and leaf upon her skin. But if you'd followed her like she asked then I'd never have found you, and I'm certain that nobody else would ever have found you either, alive or dead. You did well to keep away from her. You're a good boy, a brave boy. Your daddy would be proud.'

Against his back began the convulsions of the boy's sobs. It was the first time he had cried since Harlan had discovered him. Good, thought Harlan. The longer it takes for the tears to come, the worse the pain.

'Will you find my daddy too?' said the boy. 'Will you bring him home? I don't want him to stay in the woods. I don't want the girl to have him.'

'Yes,' said Harlan. 'I'll find him, and you can say goodbye to him.'

And he did.

Harlan was already in his seventies by then, and he had a few more years left in him, but he was no longer the man he once had been, even though he, and he alone, had found Barney Shore. Age was part of it, that was for sure, but so too were the losses he had endured. His wife, Angeline, had been taken from him by a cruel alliance of Parkinson's and Alzheimer's one year before Barney Shore spoke to him of predatory girls. He had loved her as much as a man can love his wife, and so nothing more need be said.

The loss of his wife was the second such blow that Harlan would receive in less than a year. Shortly after she passed away, Paul Scollay, Harlan's oldest and closest friend, had sat on a bucket in the little woodshed at the back of his cabin, put his shotgun in his mouth, and pulled the trigger. The cancer had been nibbling at him for a while, and now had got a taste for him. He put an end to its feeding, as he had always told his friend that he would. They had shared a drink earlier in the day: just a beer or two at the pine table beside that very woodshed with the sun setting behind the trees, as beautiful an evening as Harlan had seen in many a year. They had reminisced some, and Paul had seemed relaxed and at peace with himself, which was how Harlan had known that the end was near. He did not remark upon it, though. They had simply shaken hands and Harlan had said that he would see Paul around, and Paul had replied, 'Ayuh. I guess so,' and that was the end of it.

And though they spoke of many things in those final hours,

there was one subject upon which they did not touch, one memory that was not disinterred. They had agreed years before that they would not talk of it unless absolutely necessary, but it hung between them in the last of their time together as the sun bathed them in its radiance, like the promise of forgiveness from a god in whom neither of them believed.

And so it was that at the time of his dying, at the day and the hour of it, Harlan Vetters summoned his son and his daughter to his bedside, the woods waiting beyond, the god of tree and leaf moving through them, coming at last to claim the old man, and he said to them:

'Once upon a time, Paul Scollay and I found an airplane in the Great North Woods . . .'

2

Fall was gone, vanished in wisps of white cloud that fled across clear blue skies like pale silk scarves snatched by the breeze. Soon it would be Thanksgiving, although it seemed that there was little for which to be thankful as the year drew to its close. People I met on the streets of Portland spoke of working second jobs to make ends meet, of feeding their families with cheap cuts of meat while their savings dwindled and their safety nets fell away. They listened while candidates for high office told them the answer to the country's problems was to make the wealthy wealthier so that more crumbs from their table might fall into the mouths of the poor, and some, while pondering the unfairness of it, wondered if that was better than no crumbs at all.

Along Commercial Street some tourists still wandered. Behind them a great cruise ship, perhaps the last of the season, loomed impossibly high over the wharves and warehouses, its prow reaching out to touch the buildings facing the sea, the water supporting it invisible from the street so that it seemed a thing discarded, marooned in the aftermath of a tsunami.

Away from the waterfront the tourists petered out entirely, and at the Great Lost Bear there were none at all, not as afternoon melted into evening. The Bear saw only a small but steady stream of locals pass through its doors that day, the kind of familiar faces that ensure bars remain in business even during the quietest of times, and as the light faded and the blue of the sky began to darken, the Bear prepared to ease itself into the kind of gentle, warm mood where conversations were hushed, and music was soft, and there were places in the shadows for lovers and friends, and places, too, for darker conversations.

She was a small woman, a single swath of white running through her short black hair like the coloring of a magpie, with an 's'-shaped scar across her neck that resembled the passage of a snake over pale sand. Her eyes were a very bright green, and, rather than detracting from her looks, the crow's feet at their corners drew attention to her irises, enhancing her good looks when she smiled. She looked neither older nor younger than her years, and her makeup was discreetly applied. I guessed that most of the time she was content to be as God left her, and it was only on those rare occasions when she came down to the cities for business or pleasure that she felt the need to 'prettify' herself, as my grandfather used to term it. She wore no wedding ring, and her only jewelry was the small silver cross that hung from a cheap chain around her neck. Her fingernails were cut so close that they might almost have been bitten down, except the ends were too neat, too even. An injury to her black dress pants had been repaired with a small triangle of material on the right thigh, expertly done and barely noticeable. They fitted her well, and had probably been expensive when she bought them. She was not the kind to let a small tear be their ruination. I imagined that she had worked upon them herself, not trusting in another, not willing to waste money on what she knew she could do better with her own hands. A man's shirt, pristine and white, hung loose over the waist of her pants, the shirt tailored so that it came in tight at the waist. Her breasts were small, and the pattern of her brassiere was barely visible through the material.

The man beside her was twice her age, and then some. He had dressed in a brown serge suit for the occasion, with a yellow shirt and a yellow-and-brown tie that had come as a set, perhaps with a handkerchief for the suit pocket that he had long ago rejected as too ostentatious. 'Funeral suits', my grandfather called them, although, with a change of tie, they served equally well for baptisms, and even weddings if the wearer wasn't one of the main party.

And even though he had brought out the suit for an event that was not linked to a church happening, to an arrival into or departure from this world, and had polished his reddish-brown shoes so that the pale scuffing at the toes looked more like the reflection of light upon them, still he wore a battered cap advertising 'Scollay's Guide & Taxidermy' in a script so ornate and curlicued that it took a while to decipher, by which time the wearer would, in all likelihood, have managed to press a business card upon you, and inquire as to whether you might have an animal that needed stuffing and mounting, and, if not, whether you felt like rectifying that situation by taking a trip into the Maine woods. I felt a tenderness toward him as he sat before me, his hands clasping and unclasping, his mouth half-forming slight, awkward smiles that faded almost as soon as they came into existence, like small waves of emotion breaking upon his face. He was an old man, and a good one, although I had met him for the first time only within the hour. His decency shone brightly from within, and I believed that when he left this world he would be mourned greatly, and the community of which he was a part would be poorer for his passing.

But I understood too that part of my warmth toward him arose from the day's particular associations. It was the anniversary of my grandfather's death, and that morning I placed flowers upon his grave, and sat for a time by his side, watching the cars pass by on their way to and from Prouts Neck, and Higgins Beach, and Ferry Beach: locals all.

It was strange, but I had often stood by my father's grave and felt no sense of his presence; similarly for my mother, who had outlived him by only a few years. They were elsewhere, long gone, but something of my grandfather lingered amid the Scarborough woods and marshes, for he loved that place and it had always brought him peace. I knew that his God – for each man has his own God – let him wander there sometimes, perhaps with the ghost of one of the many dogs that had kept him company through his life yapping at his heels, scaring the birds from the rushes and chasing them for the joy of it. My grandfather used to say that if God did not allow a man to be reunited with his dogs in the next life then He was no God worth worshiping; that if a dog did not have a soul, then nothing had.

'I'm sorry,' I said. 'What did you say?'

'An airplane, Mr Parker,' said Marielle Vetters. 'They found an airplane.'

We were in a back booth of the Bear, with nobody else near us. Behind the bar, Dave Evans, the owner and manager, was wrestling with a troublesome beer tap, and in the kitchen the line chefs were preparing for the evening's food orders. I had closed off the area in which we sat with a couple of chairs so that we would remain undisturbed. Dave never objected to such temporary changes of use. Anyway, he would have more significant worries that evening: at a table near the door sat the Fulci brothers with their mother, who was celebrating her birthday.

The Fulcis were almost as wide as they were tall, had cornered the market in polyester clothing that always looked a size too small for them, and were medicated to prevent excessive mood swings, which meant only that any damage caused by nonexcessive mood swings would probably be limited to property and not people. Their mother was a tiny woman with silver hair, and it seemed impossible that those narrow hips could have squeezed out two massive sons who had, it was said, required specially-built cribs to contain them. Whatever the mechanics of their birth, the Fulcis loved their mother a lot, and always wanted her to be happy, but especially so on her birthday. Thus it was that they were nervous about the impending celebrations, which made Dave nervous, which made the line chefs nervous. One of them had already cut himself with a carving knife when informed that he was to be solely responsible for looking after the Fulci family's orders that evening, and had requested permission to lie down for a while in order to calm his nerves.

Welcome, I thought, to just another night at the Bear.

'You mind me asking you something?' Ernie Scollay had said, shortly after he and Marielle had arrived and I'd offered them a drink, which they'd declined, and then a coffee, which they'd accepted.

'Not at all,' I replied.

'You got business cards, right?'

'Yes.'

I removed one from my wallet, just to convince him of my bona fides. The card was very simple, black on white, with my name, Charlie Parker, in bold, along with a cell phone number, a secure email address, and the nebulous phrase 'Investigative Services'.

'So you got a business?'

'Just about.'

He gestured at his surroundings.

'Then how come you don't have a proper office?'

'I get asked that a lot.'

'Well, maybe if you had an office, then you wouldn't get asked it so much,' he said, and it was hard to argue with his logic.

'Offices are expensive to keep. If I had one, I'd have to spend time in it to justify renting it. That seems kind of like putting the cart before the horse.'

He considered this, then nodded. Maybe it was my clever use of an agricultural metaphor, although I doubted it. More likely it was my reluctance to waste money on an office that I didn't need, in which case I wouldn't be inclined to pass on any associated costs to my clients, one Ernest Scollay, Esq., included.

But that was earlier, and now we had moved on to the purpose of the meeting. I had listened to Marielle tell me of her father's final days, and her description of the rescue of the boy named Barney Shore, and even though she had stumbled a little as she told of the dead girl who had tried to lure Barney deeper into the forest, she had kept eye contact and had not apologized for the oddness of the tale. And I, in turn, had expressed no skepticism, for I had heard the story of the girl of the North Woods from another many years before, and I believed it to be true.

After all, I had witnessed stranger things myself.

But now she had come to the airplane, and the tension that had been growing between her and Ernie Scollay, the brother of her father's best friend, became palpable, like a static charge in the air. This, I felt, had been the subject of much discussion, even argument, between them. Scollay appeared to pull back slightly in the booth, clearly distancing himself from what was about to be said. He had come with her because he had no choice. Marielle Vetters planned to reveal some, if not all, of what her father had told her, and Scollay had known that it was better to be here and witness what transpired than to sit at home fretting about what might be said in his absence.

'Did it have markings?' I asked.

'Markings?'

'Numbers and letters to identify it. It's called an "N-number" here, and it's usually on the fuselage, and always begins with the letter "N" if the plane was registered in the United States.'

'Oh. No, my father couldn't see any identification marks, and most of the plane was hidden anyway.'

That didn't sound right. Nobody was going to fly a plane without registration markings of some kind.

'Are you sure?'

'Very. He said that it had lost part of a wing when it came down, though, and most of the tail was gone.'

'Did he describe the plane to you?'

'He went looking for pictures of similar aircraft, and thought that it might have been a Piper Cheyenne or something like it. It was a twin-engined plane, with four or five windows along the side.'

I used my phone to pull up an image of the plane in question, and what I saw seemed to confirm Marielle's statement about the absence of markings. The plane had its registration number on the vertical fin of its tail: if that was gone, and any other markings were on the underside of the wing, then the plane would have been unidentifiable from the outside.

'What did you mean when you said that most of the plane was hidden?' I asked. 'Had someone tried to conceal its presence?'

Marielle looked at Ernie Scollay. He shrugged.

'Best tell the man, Mari,' he said. 'Won't be much stranger than what he's heard already.'

'It wasn't a person or people that did it,' she said. 'My father told me that it was the forest itself. He said the woods were conspiring to swallow the plane.'

3

They would never even have found the airplane had it not been for the deer; the deer, and the worst shot of Paul Scollay's life.

As a bow hunter, Scollay had few equals. Harlan Vetters had never known a man like him. Even as a boy, he'd had a way with a bow, and with a little proper training Harlan believed that Paul could even have been an Olympic contender. He was a natural with the weapon, the bow becoming an extension of his arm, of himself. His accuracy wasn't merely a matter of pride to him. Although he loved hunting, he never killed anything that he couldn't eat, and he aimed to despatch his prey with the very minimum of pain. Harlan felt the same way, and for that reason he had always preferred a good rifle with which to hunt; he didn't trust himself with a bow. During archery hunting season in October he preferred to accompany his friend as a spectator, admiring his skill without ever feeling the need to participate.

But as Paul grew older, he came to prefer the rifle to the bow. He had arthritis in his right shoulder, and in a half dozen other places too. Paul used to say that the only major part of his body in which he didn't have arthritis was the one place where he would have appreciated a little *more* stiffness, if the good Lord could have seen His way to answering that kind of prayer. Which, in Paul's experience, He never did, the good Lord apparently having better things with which to occupy Himself than male erectile dysfunction.

So Paul was the better shot with a bow, and Harlan the

superior hunter with a rifle. In the years that followed, Harlan would muse upon the likelihood that, had it been he who took the first shot at the deer, none of this business, for good or bad, would have happened.

But then they had always seemed opposites in so many ways, these two men. Harlan was softly spoken where his friend was loud, dry where he was obvious, driven and conscientious where Paul often seemed aimless and unfocused.

Harlan was thin and wiry, a fact that had sometimes led drunks and fools to underestimate his strength, even though only a strong man could have carried a grief-stricken boy for miles across rough, snow-covered ground without stumble or complaint, even in his seventies. Paul Scollay was softer and fatter, but it was padding over muscle, and he was fast for a big man. Those who did not know them well had them pegged for an odd couple, two men whose diverse personalities and appearances allowed them to form a single whole, like two matching pieces of a jigsaw. Their relationship was much more complex than that, and their similarities were more pronounced than their differences, as is always the case with men who maintain lifelong friendships with each other, rarely allowing a harsh word to pass between them, and always forgiving any that do. They shared a common outlook on the world, a similar view of their fellow man and their obligations toward him. When Harlan Vetters carried Barney Shore home on his back, the beams of flashlights and the raised voices guiding him at the last to the main search party, he did so with the ghost of his friend walking by his side, an unseen presence that watched over the boy and the old man, and perhaps kept the girl in the woods at bay.

For after Barney Shore had spoken of her, Harlan had become aware of movement in the trees to his right, a roving darkness obscured by the falling snow, as though the mere mention of her existence had somehow drawn the girl to them. He had chosen not to look, though; he feared that was what the girl wanted, because if he looked he might stumble, and if he stumbled he might break, and if he broke then she would fall upon them both, boy and man, and they would be lost to her. It was then that he called upon his old friend, and he could not have said if Paul had truly come to him or if Harlan had simply created the illusion of his presence as a source of comfort and discipline. All he knew was that a kind of solace came over him, and whatever was shadowing them in the forest had retreated with what might have been a disappointed hiss or just the sound of a branch surrendering its weight of snow, until at last it was gone from them entirely.

And as he lay on his deathbed, Harlan wondered if the girl had remembered him, if she had recalled him from that first day, the day of the deer, the day of the airplane . . .

They had started late. Harlan's truck had been acting up, and Paul's was in the shop. They'd almost not headed out at all, but it was beautiful weather and they had already made their preparations: their clothing – their checked Woolrich jackets, their wool pants from Reny's, and their 'union suits', the one-piece garments of underwear that would keep them warm, even when wet – had been stored overnight in sealed bags of cedar to mask their human scent, and they had eschewed bacon and sausage patties in favor of oatmeal for breakfast. They had food in sealed containers, and each carried a bottle in which to pee as well as a flask from which to drink. ('Don't want to go getting those two mixed up,' Paul would always say, and Harlan would laugh dutifully.)

So they had pleaded like children for Harlan's daughter to allow them to use her car, and she had eventually relented. She had recently returned to live with her parents following the break-up of her marriage, and spent most of her time mooning around the house, as far as Paul could tell. He had always considered her to be a good kid, though, and thought her an even better one after she handed over her car keys to them.

It was already after three when they parked the car and entered the woods.

They spent the first hour or so just jawing and giving each other the pickle, heading for some old clearcut that they knew which now had second growth timbers beloved of deer: alders, birches, and 'popples', as men of their age tended to call poplar trees. They each carried a Winchester 30-06, and moved softly on their rubber-soled LL Bean boots. Harlan had a compass, but he barely glanced at it. They knew where they were going. Paul carried matches, a rope to drag the carcass, and two pairs of household gloves to wear while dressing the animal and to protect against ticks. Harlan had the knives and shears in his pack.

Harlan and Paul practiced what was known as 'still hunting': not for them the use of stands, or canoes, or groups of men to drive the deer onto their guns. They relied solely on their eyes and their experience, seeking traces of buck sign: the rubs where the bucks were drawn to smooth-barked aromatic trees like pine and balsam and spruce; the deer beds where they lay down; and the desire lines that the deer used to traverse the shortest distance between two points in the woods, thereby conserving their energy. As it was now afternoon, they knew the deer would be moving to low ground where the cold air would drive scents down, so they walked parallel to the ridge lines, Harlan seeking trace on the ground while Paul kept an eye on the surrounding woods for movement.

After Harlan came upon red hairs caught on some blades of grass, and signs of big deer rub on a mature balsam, both men grew silent. The hunt drew on, the urgency of it growing as the light dimmed, but it was Paul who caught first sight of the deer: a big nine-point buck, probably weighing close on two hundred pounds. By the time Paul spotted him the buck's tail was already raised high in alarm, and it was preparing to run, but it was only thirty feet away from him, if that.

Paul went for the shot, but he rushed it. He saw the deer falter and stumble as the bullet struck, and then it turned and fled.

It was such a spectacular miss that he would scarcely have believed it if he hadn't witnessed it with his own eyes, the kind of misfire he usually associated with neophyte hunters from away who fancied themselves as wilderness men even while their fingers still bore the inkstains of their office jobs. He'd known more than one guide who'd been forced to finish off a wounded animal after his client, or 'sport', had failed to find the mark, the sport lacking the energy, the guts, or the decency to follow the trail of the wounded animal in order to put it out of its misery. Back in the day, they'd kept a blacklist of such sports, and guides were discreetly warned of the risks of accompanying them into the woods. Hell, Paul Scollay himself had been among those who'd been forced to track a wounded deer and finish it off, hating the suffering of the beast, the waste of its life force, and the stain that the slow manner of its dying was destined to leave upon his soul.

But now he had become just such a man, and as he watched the agonized buck vanish into the dark woods, he could barely speak.

'Jesus,' he said at last. 'What the hell was that?'

'Ham shot,' said Harlan. 'Can't be sure, but he could go far.'

Paul looked from the rifle to his fingertips and back again, hoping that the blame for what had transpired might be found in damage to the sights, or a visible weakness in his own hand. There was nothing to be seen, and later he would often wonder if that was the sign, the moment when his body began to fail, when the process of contamination and ruination commenced, as though the cancer had sprung into being in the seconds between squeezing the trigger and firing the bullet, and the error had been caused by his body spasming minutely in sudden awareness of the first cell being turned against itself.

But all that came later: for now, all Harlan and Paul knew for sure was that they had caused a mortal injury to an animal, and they had a duty to end its suffering. A pall had been cast over the day, and Harlan wondered how long it would be before Paul went hunting again. Not that season, certainly. It wasn't in Paul's nature to return to the woods and prove that the miss had been a one-off. No, he would brood over it, and consider his gun, and practice some on the range at the back of his house. Only when he had racked up bull after bull would he consider aiming once again at a living animal.

The buck left a clear trail for them to follow, dark red blood and panic excrement splashed on bushes and leaves. They moved as fast as they could, but both were older men now, and the pace quickly wore on them. The buck, disoriented and in agony, was not cleaving to any known trail, and it seemed to be making no attempt to cut behind them to familiar ground. Their progress slowed. Soon they were bathed in sweat, and a low branch gave Harlan a bad scratch to his left cheek that bled into the collar of his shirt. It would need stitches, but Paul pulled a couple of adhesive strips from the first aid pack to hold the cut together, and eventually it began to clot and the bleeding stopped, although the pain made Harlan's eyes water, and he thought that there might be a splinter buried in the wound.

The woods grew darker, the branches meeting above their heads to cut off the sunlight. And then the clouds came, and what little light there had been was suddenly obscured, and the air grew colder around them, all warmth now gone so quickly that Harlan could feel the sweat cooling upon him.

He examined his compass. It told them that they were moving west, but the last known position of the sun gave the lie to it, and when he tapped it again the needle shifted position, and west became east, and after that the needle didn't spin exactly, not like it did in those fantasy films that they showed at the movie theaters in summer, but it refused to remain fixed.

'You keep that with your knife?' asked Paul. A knife could throw off the magnetism of a compass.

'No, I never do.' As if he'd make that kind of amateur error.

'Well, something's up with it.'

'Ayuh.'

Harlan and Paul knew that they were heading north, though. Neither of them suggested that they should turn back and leave the buck to its fate, not even as the day died, and the foliage became denser, the trees older, the light dimmer. Soon it was dark, and they resorted to flashlights to guide them, but they did not give up on the animal. The blood was not drying out, which meant the injury was fatal, and the buck was still suffering.

They would not leave it to die in pain.

Ernie Scollay interrupted the tale.

'That was my brother's way,' he said. 'Harlan's too,' he added, although it was clear that his focus was on his late brother. 'They weren't going to give up on the buck. They weren't cruel men. You have to understand that. Do you hunt?'

'No,' I said, and I watched as he tried to hide a kind of smugness, as though I had confirmed a suspicion he had of me and of my innate city softness. Then it was my turn to add something – 'Not animals.' – and maybe it was petty, but there was some small pleasure to be derived from watching his expression change.

'Anyhow,' he continued, 'my brother never wanted to see a living thing suffer, animal or human.' He swallowed, and his voice broke on his next words. 'Not even himself, at the end.'

Marielle reached out her right hand and placed it gently upon Ernie Scollay's knitted fingers.

'Ernie is right,' she said. 'You should know, Mr Parker, that they were both good men. I think they did the wrong thing, and their reasons for doing it weren't wholly justified, not even to themselves, but it was uncharacteristic of them.'

I said nothing, because there was nothing to be said, and they were moving ahead of themselves. They were no longer talking about the buck, but what came after. All I would have by which to judge these two dead men was the tale itself, and that was not yet ended.

'You were telling me about the buck,' I said.

It was standing at the edge of a clearing, swaying on its legs, blood and froth at its mouth, the lower part of its hide soaked in red. Harlan and Paul couldn't figure out how it had kept going for so long, yet it had barely slowed until the last mile or so, when they at last started to catch up with it, and now here it was, seemingly dying where it stood. But as they drew closer it inclined its head toward them, and then back in the direction of the clearing. The trees were so thick at either side of it that, if it had the strength to do so, it could only go on or come back in their direction, and it seemed torn between the two choices. Its eyes rolled, and it sighed deep in itself and shook its head in what Harlan thought was almost resignation.

With the life that was left to it, the buck turned and ran at them. Harlan raised his gun and blasted the animal in the chest. Its momentum took it onward even as its forelegs collapsed beneath it, and it came to rest barely inches from its killers. Harlan thought that he'd never felt worse about an animal, and he hadn't even fired the original errant shot. The buck's strength, its desire to survive, had been enormous. It had deserved to live, or at least to die a better death. He looked to his friend, and saw that his eyes were wet.

'It came right at us,' said Harlan.

'But it wasn't charging us,' said Paul. 'I think it was trying to run away.'

'From what?' asked Harland. After all, what could be worse than the men who were trying to kill it?

'I don't know,' said Paul, 'but it's the damnedest thing.'

'The damnedest thing,' agreed Harlan.

But it wasn't the damnedest thing.

It wasn't at all.

4

Ernie Scollay excused himself and headed to the men's room. I went to the bar to retrieve the coffee pot in order to freshen our cups. Jackie Garner walked in while I was waiting for the coffee to finish brewing. Jackie occasionally did a little work for me, and he was a bosom buddy of the Fulcis, who looked up to him the way they did to the handful of people whom they considered saner than themselves without being square. He was carrying a bunch of flowers, and a box of fudge from the Old Port Candy Company on Fore Street.

'For Mrs Fulci?'

'Yeah. She likes fudge. Not almond, though. She has an allergy.'

'We wouldn't want to kill her,' I said. 'It might cast a pall over the celebrations. You okay?'

Jackie looked flustered, and distracted. 'My mom,' he said.

Jackie's mother was a force of nature. She made Mrs Fulci look like June Cleaver.

'Acting up again?'

'Nah, she's sick.'

'Nothing serious, I hope.'

Jackie winced. 'She doesn't want people to know.'

'How bad is it?'

'Can we talk about it another time?'

'Sure.'

He slipped past me, and there were cries of delight from the Fulcis' table. They were so loud that they made

Dave Evans drop a glass and reach for the phone to call the cops.

'It's okay,' I told them. 'That's their happy sound.'

'How can you tell?'

'Nobody got hit.'

'Oh thank God. Cupcake Cathy's made her a cupcake birthday cake. She likes cupcakes, right?'

Cupcake Cathy was one of the Bear's waitstaff. She had a sideline in baking the kind of cupcakes that led strong-willed men to propose marriage in the hope of ensuring a regular supply, even if they were married already. They figured their wives would probably understand.

'She likes cake, as far as I know. Mind you, if there are nuts in it, it could kill her. Apparently she has an allergy.'

Dave paled. 'Jesus Christ, I better check.'

'Can't hurt. Like I told Jackie Garner, hard to see the evening recovering from the death of the birthday girl.'

I took the coffee pot to the table, refilled our cups, then gave it to one of the waitresses to bring back. Marielle Vetters sipped delicately from her cup. Her lipstick left no mark.

'It's a nice bar,' she said.

'It is.'

'How come they let you use it for . . . this?'

Her left hand drifted lightly through the air, her index finger raised, a gesture that contained both elegance and amusement. Something of it was in her face too: the faintest hint of a smile despite the nature of the story that she was engaged in telling.

'I work the bar sometimes.'

'So you're a part-time private investigator?

'I prefer to think of myself as a part-time bartender. Anyway, I like it here. I like the staff. I even like most of the customers.'

'And I guess it's different, right? Different from "not hunting animals".'

'That's right.'

'You weren't just kidding either.'

'No, I wasn't.'

The smile came again, a little uneasier this time. 'I've read about you in the newspapers, and on the Internet. What happened to your wife and child – I just don't know what to say.'

Susan and Jennifer were gone, taken from me by a man who thought that, by spilling their blood, he could fill the emptiness inside himself. The subject of them frequently came up with new clients. I had come to realize that whatever was said came with the best of intentions, and people needed to mention it, more for their own sakes than for mine.

'Thank you,' I said.

'I heard – I don't know if it's true – that you have another daughter now.'

'That's right.'

'Does she live with you? I mean, are you still, you know . . .'

'No, she lives with her mother in Vermont. I see her as often as I can.'

'I hope you don't think that I was prying. I'm not a stalker. I just wanted to find out as much as I could about you before I started sharing my father's secrets with you. I know some cops in the County,' – nobody in Maine ever referred to it as Aroostook County, just 'the County' – 'and I was tempted to ask them about you as well. I figured they might be able to tell me more than I could find online. In the end, I decided it would be better to say nothing and just see what you were like in person.'

'And how's that working out?'

'Okay, I guess. I thought you'd be taller.'

'I get that a lot. Better than "I thought you'd be slimmer," or "I thought you'd have more hair."'

She rolled her eyes. 'And they say women are vain. Are you fishing for compliments, Mr Parker?'

'No. I figure that pond is all fished out.' I let a few

26

seconds elapse. 'Why did you decide not to ask the police about me?'

'I think you know the answer already.'

'Because you didn't want anyone to wonder why you might need the services of a private investigator?'

'That's right.'

'Lots of people hire investigators, for lots of reasons. Cheating husbands—'

'I'm not married anymore. And, for the record, I cheated on him.'

I raised an eyebrow.

'Are you shocked?' she asked.

'No, I just wish he'd had my card. Business is business.'

It made her laugh.

'He was a jerk. Worse than a jerk. He deserved it. So why else do people hire you?' she said.

'Insurance fraud, missing persons, background checks.'

'It sounds dull.'

'It's safe, for the most part.'

'But not all the time. Not for the kind of investigation that ends up with your name in the papers, the kind that ends with people dying.'

'No, but sometimes investigations start out as one thing and mutate into another, usually because someone tells lies right from the start.'

'The client?'

'It's been known to happen.'

'I won't lie to you, Mr Parker.'

'That's reassuring to hear, unless that itself was a lie.'

'My, the world has taken its toll on your idealism, hasn't it?'

'I'm still idealistic. I just keep it safe behind a carapace of skepticism.'

'And I don't want you to hunt anyone down either. At least, I don't think so. Not in that sense, anyway. Ernie may disagree with me on that one.'

'Did Mr Scollay try to dissuade you from coming here?' I
asked.

'How did you know that?'

'A trick of the trade. He's not very good at hiding his feelings. Most honest men aren't.'

'He believed that we should keep quiet about what we knew.
The damage was done, in his view. He didn't want his brother's
memory besmirched in any way, or my father's either.'

'But you didn't agree.'

'A crime was committed, Mr Parker. Maybe more than one.'

'Once again, why not go to the police?'

'If everyone went to the police, you'd be a full-time
bartender and a part-time private investigator.'

'Or no private investigator at all.'

Ernie Scollay was returning from the men's room. He
removed his baseball cap as he walked and ran his fingers
back through his thick white hair. If I was conscious of a
tension between him and Marielle, I was more conscious of
the fact that Ernie was frightened. So was Marielle, but she
hid it better. Ernie Scollay: the last of the honest men, but
not so honest that he didn't want to keep his brother's secrets
hidden. He glanced at Marielle and me, trying to ascertain if
we had been discussing anything that we shouldn't have while
he was absent.

'Where were we?' he asked.

'At the clearing,' I said.

Paul and Harlan looked to the clearing. The buck lay dead
at their feet, but the fear it had emanated was still with them.
Harlan tightened his grip on his rifle; there were four bullets
left in his magazine, and Paul had the same. Something had
spooked the buck, perhaps drawn by the smell of its blood,
and they didn't want to face a bear with their hands hanging
or, God forbid, a mountain lion, because they'd both heard
stories about the possible return of big cats to the state.

Nobody had seen one for certain for the best part of twenty years, but they didn't want to be the first.

They stepped around the remains of the buck and advanced on the open space. It was only as they drew nearer that they smelled it: dampness, and rotting vegetation. A body of still black water lay before them, so dark that it was more pitch than liquid, with the promise of a viscosity to match. Staring into it, Harlan caught only the barest reflection of his own face. The water appeared to absorb more protons than it should have, sucking in the beams of their flashlights and what little illumination filtered through the branches above, allowing almost nothing of it to escape. Harlan took a step back as he felt his sense of balance faltering, and he bumped into Paul, who was standing directly behind him. The shock caused him to teeter, and for a moment he was about to fall into the pool. The ground seemed to tilt beneath his feet. His rifle fell to the ground and he raised his arms instinctively and flapped them at the air, like a bird striving to escape a predator. Then Paul's hands were on his torso, pulling him back, and Harlan found a tree against which to lean, circling its trunk with his arms in a desperate lover's embrace.

'I thought I was going in,' he said. 'I thought I was going to drown.'

No, not drown: suffocate, or worse, for just because he was certain that no living thing moved through its depths (Certain? Certain how? Certain north was north, and east was east? But such certainties did not apply in this place; of that, at least, he *was* convinced.), it did not mean that the pool was empty. It stank of malevolence, of the possibility that something more than the sucking power of its mass might drag you down if you fell into it. Harlan was suddenly aware of the silence of this place. He was conscious too that night was coming on quickly: he could see no stars in the sky, and the damn compass was gone all to hell. They could be stuck out here, and he didn't want that to happen, not one damn little bit.

'We ought to leave,' said Harlan. 'This place feels wrong.'

He realized that Paul had not spoken since they found the pool. His friend stood with his back to him, the muzzle of his gun now pointing at the ground.

'You hear me?' said Harlan. 'I think we should get out of here. It's bad. This whole damned place is—'

'Look,' said Paul. He stepped to one side and shined his flashlight across the expanse of the pool, and Harlan saw it.

It was the shape that marked it out, although the forest had done its best to obscure its lines. At first glance, it looked only like the trunk of a fallen tree, one much larger than those that surrounded it, but a portion of one wing protruded from the foliage, and the flashlight made parts of the fuselage glitter. Neither of the men knew much about airplanes, but they could see that it was a small twin-engine prop, now minus the starboard engine, lost during the crash along with most of that wing. It lay on its belly to the north of the pool, its nosecone hard against a big pine. The forest had closed over the path that it must have torn through the trees upon its descent, although that in itself was not so remarkable. What was strange, and what gave the men pause, was that the plane was almost entirely covered with vegetation. Vines had wrapped their tendrils around it, ferns had shaded it, shrubs had masked it. The very ground itself appeared to be slowly absorbing it, for the plane had sunk some distance into the earth, and the lower portion of the port engine was already lost. The plane must have been here for decades, Harlan thought, but the portions of it that were visible through the greenery did not appear that old. There was no rust, no obvious decay. As he would tell his family during his final days, it was as though the forest were absorbing the plane, and had accelerated its growth accordingly so that this end might be more rapidly achieved.

Paul began walking toward the wreckage. Harlan released his hold on the tree trunk, and gave the pool a wide berth as he followed his friend. Paul used his rifle butt to test the earth around the slowly sinking plane, but the earth was hard, not moist.

'It'll soften during the spring thaw,' said Harlan. 'That might explain the way the plane is going down.'

'I guess,' said Paul, but he did not sound convinced.

All the windows of the plane were covered with ivy, including those at the cockpit. For the first time, Harlan acknowledged the possibility that there might still be bodies in there. The thought made him shudder.

It took them a while to find the door, so thick was the cloak of vegetation. They used their hunting knives to hack at the ivy. It came away reluctantly, coating their gloves with a sticky residue that gave off a sharp, caustic odor. Paul got some of it on his exposed forearm, and he would carry the burn scar that it left until the day that he took his own life.

When they had exposed the shape of the door, they found that the sinking of the plane had left an inch or more of it beneath the earth, so they had to hack at the ground to make enough space for the door to open out a little. By that time the blackness was upon them.

'Maybe we ought to come back when it's light,' said Harlan.

'You think we'd even be able to find this place again?' asked Paul. 'It's not like any part of the woods I've ever seen.'

Harlan took in their surroundings. The trees, a mix of tall evergreens and huge, misshapen deciduous, were older here. This area had never been logged. Paul was right: Harlan couldn't even have said where they were, exactly. North: that was all he knew, but this was Maine, and there was a lot of north to go around.

'We can't find our way back in the dark anyway,' said Paul,

'not with the compass on the fritz and no stars to guide us. I figure we got to stay till first light.'

'Stay here?' Harlan didn't like the sound of that at all. He glanced at the black pool, its surface smooth as a plate of obsidian. Vague memories of old horror movies came to him, B-features in which creatures emerged from ponds just like that one, but when he tried to put a name to the films he found that he could not, and he wondered if he had made up those images all by himself.

'You got a better idea?' said Paul. 'We have supplies. We can light a fire. Wouldn't be the first time we spent a night in the woods.'

But not in a place like this, Harlan wanted to say, not with a pool of not-quite-water calling to us, and the wreck of a plane that might well be a tomb for anyone still inside. If they could get far enough away from it then the compass might begin to function properly again, or, if the sky cleared, they could navigate their way home by the stars. He tried to find the moon, but the clouds had smothered all, and there was not even the faintest glow to be seen.

Harlan looked at the plane once again. Paul had his hand on the exterior handle of the door.

'You ready for this?' he said.

'No,' said Harlan, 'but I reckon you'd best go ahead anyway. We've come this far. We may as well find out if there's anyone left in there.'

Paul turned the handle and yanked at the door. Nothing happened. Either it was stuck fast, or it was locked from the inside. Paul tried again, his face contorted with effort. There was a grinding sound, and the door came free. Harlan raised his hand to his face, expecting the smell of dead, but there was only the musty odor of damp carpets.

Paul poked his head inside and passed the flashlight's beam around the interior. After a couple of seconds, he climbed in.

'Take a look at this,' he called to Harlan.

Harlan steeled himself, and followed his friend into the plane.

The empty plane.

'Empty?' I said.

'Empty,' said Marielle Vetters. 'There were no bodies, nothing. I think that helped. It made it easier for them to keep the money.'

5

The money was in a big leather holdall behind what Harlan figured was the pilot's seat. In every film he'd ever watched the pilot sat on the left, and the copilot sat on the right, and he had no reason to believe that this plane would be any different.

Harlan and Paul stared at the money for a long time.

Beside the holdall was a canvas satchel containing a sheaf of papers sealed in a plastic wallet for further protection. It was a list of names, typewritten for the most part, although some had been added by hand. Here and there sums of money had been included, some small, some very large. Also, again sometimes typewritten and sometimes handwritten, notes had been added to some of the entries, mostly words like 'accepted' and 'declined', but occasionally just a single letter 'T'.

Harlan couldn't make much sense of it so he turned his attention back to the money. It was mainly in fifties, used and nonconsecutive, with some twenties thrown in for variety. Some of the wads were held together with paper wraps, others with elastic bands. Paul picked up one of the bundles of fifties and did a quick count.

'That's five thousand dollars, I reckon,' he said. The flashlight picked out the rest of the money. There were probably forty similar bundles of cash in there, not counting the twenties. 'Two hundred thousand, give or take,' he concluded. 'Jesus, I never seen so much money.'

Neither of them had. The most cash Harlan had ever held in his hand was $3,300, which he'd got from selling a truck years before to Perry Reed up at Perry's Used Autos. Perry had screwed him over on that truck, but then nobody ever went to Perry the Pervert for a fair deal: they went to him because they were desperate and needed money fast. Having that much cash was the closest Harlan had ever come to feeling rich. He hadn't felt wealthy for long, though, because the money had gone straight to servicing his debts. Now Harlan knew that both he and Paul were thinking the same thing:

Who would know?

Neither would have considered himself a thief. Oh, they'd shaved a few dollars here and there from the IRS, but that was your duty as a taxpayer and an American. Someone had once told Harlan that the IRS factored cheating into their calculations, so they kind of expected you to do it, and by not holding out on them you messed up their system. You caused more trouble by not cheating on your taxes than you did by smudging your return, the fella said, and if you looked too square then the IRS would start thinking that maybe you were hiding something, and next thing you knew they had their claws in you and you were scouring the attic for receipts for ninety-nine cents just to stay out of jail.

But now they weren't talking about a hundred dollars here and there kept back from Uncle Sam's purse; this was potentially a serious criminal enterprise, which raised the second question:

Where had it come from?

'You think it's drug money?' asked Paul. He watched a lot of TV cop shows, and immediately associated any cash sum too large to be kept in a wallet with drug dealing. It wasn't like drugs weren't a thing here, either: they flowed across the border like driven snow, but they mainly came in by truck and car and boat, not by plane.

'It's possible,' said Harlan. 'I don't see no drugs, though.'

'Could be they sold them already, and these are the

proceeds,' said Paul. He flipped through the bills with his index finger, and seemed to like the sound they made a lot.

A larger object in the cash bag caught Harlan's eye, and he pulled it out. It was a copy of the *Gazette* out of Montreal, dated July 14, 2001, just over one year earlier.

'Take a look at that,' he told Harlan.

'It's not possible,' said Harlan. 'This plane has been here longer than that. It's almost part of the woods.'

'Well, unless the *Gazette* delivers to crash sites, she hit the ground sometime around July fourteenth,' said Paul.

'I don't remember hearing nothing about it,' said Harlan. 'A plane goes down, you figure somebody is going to notice and come asking, especially if it went down with a couple hundred thousand dollars on board. I mean—'

'Hush!' said Paul. He was trying to remember. Something about a reporter, except . . .

'I think someone did come asking,' he said at last.

A moment later, Harlan caught up.

'The magazine woman,' he said, then grimaced as Paul added, 'And the man who came with her.'

Ernie Scollay shifted in his seat. His unease was more obvious now. It was the mention of the man and the woman that had provoked it.

'Did she have a name?' I asked.

'She gave *a* name,' said Marielle, 'but if it was her own then she never wrote for any newspaper or magazine that my father could find. She called herself Darina Flores.'

'And this man you mentioned?'

'He wasn't the kind to give a name,' said Ernie. 'They came separately, and didn't keep each other's company, but Harlan saw them talking together outside the woman's motel. It was long after dark, and they were sitting in her car. The interior light was on, and Harlan thought they might have been arguing, but he couldn't be sure. Harlan already thought there was something hinky about them both. That just confirmed it for him. The next day they were gone, and the woman didn't come back again.'

The woman didn't come back again.

'But the man did?' I said.

Beside him, Marielle trembled slightly, as though an insect had crawled across her skin.

'Oh yes,' she said. 'He came back for sure.'

Darina Flores was as beautiful as any woman Harlan had ever seen. He had never been unfaithful to his wife, and each had given up their virginity to the other on their wedding night, but if Darina Flores had offered herself to Harlan – a possibility as unlikely as any that Harlan could imagine short of his own immortality – then he would have been sorely tempted, and might somehow have found a way to live with the guilt. Her hair was chestnut brown, her face olive complected, and there was a hint of Asian to her eyes, the irises so brown that they shaded to black in a certain light. It should have been disconcerting, even sinister, but instead Harlan found it alluring, and he wasn't alone: there wasn't a man in Falls End – and perhaps a couple of women too – who didn't go to bed at night with impure thoughts of Darina Flores after meeting her. She was the talk of the Pickled Pike from the moment she arrived, and probably the talk of Lester's too, although Harlan and Paul didn't frequent Lester's because Lester LeForge was an asshole of the highest order who had played loose with Paul's cousin Angela when they were both nineteen and had never been forgiven for it, although Harlan's son Grady drank in Lester's whenever he came back to Falls End, just to spite his father.

Darina Flores took a room at the Northern Gateway Motel on the outskirts of town. She told folk that she was putting together a magazine feature on the Great North Woods, an attempt to capture something of their grandeur and mystery for the kind of people who not only subscribed to glossy travel magazines, but had the money to visit the places described therein. She was, she said, particularly interested in stories of disappearances both recent and not-so-recent: early settlers, any Maine equivalents of the Donner Party, hikers who might have vanished . . .

Even airplanes, she added, because she'd heard the woods were so dense that planes had come down in them and never been found.

Harlan wasn't sure how stories of folk going missing or resorting to cannibalism would appeal to well-heeled travelers with a lot of disposable income, but then he wasn't a journalist, and, anyway, the dumbness of people had long ago ceased to surprise him. So he and Paul and Ernie and a few others recycled all the old tales they could recall for the delight of Darina Flores, embellishing the details where required, or making them up entirely where necessary. Darina Flores dutifully noted them down, and bought rounds of drinks on her expense account, and flirted outrageously with men who could have been her grandfather, let alone her father, and as the night drew on, she gradually brought the conversation back to airplanes.

'You think she might have a, you know, a *thing* for airplanes?' Jackie Strauss, one of the town's three resident Jews, had asked as he and Harlan stood side by side in the men's room, making space in their bladders for more beer and, by extension, more time with the divine Darina Flores.

'Why, you hiding an airplane that I don't know about?' asked Harlan.

'I was thinking maybe I could borrow one, and offer to show her around.'

'You could join the Mile High Club,' said Harlan.

'I got a fear of flying,' said Jackie. 'I was hoping we could just stay on the ground and do our business there.'

'Jackie, how old are you?'

'Seventy-two next birthday.'

'You got a dicky heart. Any business you did with that woman would probably kill you.'

'I know, but it's how I'd like to go. If I survived, my wife would kill me anyway. Better I go in the arms of a woman like that than give my Lois the pleasure of beating me to death after.'

And so the men fed Darina Flores tales both real and fantastic, and she in turn fed their fantasies, and a pleasant night was had by all except Ernie Scollay, who wasn't drinking at the time because he was on medication, and who had noticed that Darina Flores barely sipped at her vodka tonic, and her smile rose no further than her upper lip, never even coming close to those extraordinary eyes that grew darker as the night drew on, and she had long ago stopped writing and was now listening yet not listening, just as she was smiling yet not smiling, and drinking yet not drinking.

So Ernie tired of the game before the others, and he excused himself and left. He was walking to his truck when he saw April Schmitt, who owned the town's other motel, the Vacationland Repose, standing outside the motel office, smoking a cigarette in a manner that could only be described as distracted. April didn't smoke much, Ernie knew, this knowledge based upon the fact that he and April were content to share a bed when the mood struck them, each of them being generally inclined to solitude yet still requiring a little company on occasion. April only smoked when she was unhappy, and Ernie preferred April to be happy as that state of mind was more conducive to bed-sharing, and Darina Flores, falsely affable or not, had put him in the mood for some female company.

'You okay, hon?' he asked, laying a hand gently on the small of her back, the heel of it resting upon the swell of her still fine buttocks.

'It's nothing,' she said.

'You're smoking. It's never nothing when you're smoking.'

'There was a guy came asking for a room. I didn't care for the look of him so I told him we were full up.'

She took a drag on the cigarette, then looked at it in disgust before throwing it to the ground, still only half smoked, and stamping it out. She wrapped her arms across herself and shivered, even though it was a warm evening. Tentatively, Ernie put an arm around her shoulders, and she leaned into him. She was shaking, and April wasn't a woman who scared easily. Her fear drove any carnal thoughts from his mind. April was a frightened woman. Ernie loved her in his quiet way, and he did not wish her to be frightened.

'He asked me why the "Vacancy" light was on if we were full,' said April. 'I said that I'd forgotten to turn it off, was all. I could see him looking at the lot. I mean, there are only four cars in it, so he knew that I was lying. He just smiled, the ugly piece of shit. He smiled, and his fingers moved, and it was like he was stripping the clothes from my body, and the flesh from my bones. I swear, I felt his fingers on me, *in* me, in my . . . in my private parts. He was hurting me, and he wasn't even touching me. Christ!'

She started to cry. Ernie had never seen her cry before. It shocked him more than what she had said, the swearing included, because April didn't swear much either. He held her tighter, and felt her sobbing against him.

'Fat, bald son of a bitch,' she said, gasping the words out. 'Piece of shit bastard, touching me like that, hurting me like that, all over a fucking motel room.'

'You want me to call the cops?' asked Ernie.

'And tell them what? That a man looked at me funny, that he assaulted me without laying a hand on me?'

'I don't know. This guy, what did he look like?'

'Fat. Fat and ugly. He had a thing on his throat, all swollen like a toad's neck, and he had a tattoo on his wrist. I saw it when he pointed at the sign. It was a fork, a three-pronged

40

fork, like he thought he was the devil himself. Bastard. Miserable rapist bastard . . .'

'What?' Ernie had stopped talking. 'What is it?'
   He had seen the look on my face. I could not hide it.
   I know who he was. I know his name.
   After all, I killed him.
   'Nothing,' I said, and he caught the lie, but chose to set it aside for now.
   Brightwell. Brightwell the Believer.
   'Go on,' I said. 'Finish the story.'

Darina Flores left after two days with little to show for her efforts but a hole in her expense account, real or imagined, and a store of old tales that were barely on nodding terms with reality. If she was disappointed, she didn't show it. Instead she passed around some cards with her phone number printed on them, and invited anyone who remembered anything useful or pertinent to her article to call her. Some of the more optimistic men of the town, strengthened by a beer or three, tried calling the number in the days and weeks after she left but got through only to an answering service on which Darina Flores's dulcet tones invited them to leave a name, number, and message, with a promise to get back to them as soon as possible.
   But Darina Flores never called anyone back, and over time the men grew tired of the game.
   Now, squatting in the wreckage of a plane in the Great North Woods, Harlan and Paul thought back on Darina Flores for the first time in years, and once the floodgates of memory were opened a torrent of related incidents followed, each inconsequential in itself but suddenly meaningful when taken as a whole in the light of what they had just found: city men and women who hired guides for hunting or hiking or, in one unlikely case, bird-watching, but who seemed to

41

have little interest in nature while being very clear on the areas that they wished to explore, to the extent of marking them carefully in the form of grids on their maps. Harlan recalled Matthew Risen, a guide since deceased, talking to him of a woman whose skin was a virtual gallery of tattoos that seemed almost to move in the forest light. She had not spoken a single word to him during the long hours of a deer hunt that ended with a single desultory shot at a distant buck, a shot that might possibly have scared a squirrel who was halfway up the tree struck by the bullet but posed no danger to the deer itself. Instead, her partner did all of the talking, a garrulous man with red lips and a pale waxen face who reminded Risen of an emaciated clown and never even unslung his rifle, chatting and joking even as he gently overruled his guide's choice of direction, moving them away from any deer and toward . . .

What? Risen had not been able to figure that out, but now Harlan and Paul thought they knew.

'They were looking for the plane,' said Paul. 'All of them, looking for the plane, and the money.'

But it was Harlan who wondered if it was less the money that interested those strangers than the names and the numbers on the papers in the satchel, as he and Paul Scollay sat by the fire that they had made, the barest flicker of it reflected on that black water. He kept coming back to the list of names even as they discussed the cash and those who had come to seek it. The list made him uneasy, but for no reason that he could figure out.

'You could use the money,' said Paul. 'You know, what with Angeline getting sick and all.'

Harlan's wife was showing the first signs of Parkinson's. She was already in the middle stage of Alzheimer's and Harlan was finding it harder to take care of her needs. Meanwhile Paul was always being chased by some bill or another. There would be hard times ahead as old age tightened its hold on them and theirs, and neither man had the kind of funds that would permit any difficulties to be handled with ease. Yes, thought Harlan, I could use the money. They both could. That still didn't make it right.

'I say we keep it,' said Paul. 'It stays out here much longer and it will sink into the ground along with that plane, or it'll be found by someone even less worthy of it than we are.'

He tried to make a joke of it, but it didn't quite work.

'It's not ours to keep,' said Harlan. 'We ought to tell the police about this.'

'Why? If this was honest money then honest men would have come looking for it. It would have been all over the news that a plane had gone down. They'd have been scouring the woods looking for wreckage or survivors. Instead, what did we get but some woman pretending to be a reporter, and a swarm of creeps who were no more hunters or birders than the man in the moon?'

The bag lay between them. Paul had left it open, probably deliberately, so that Harlan could see the money inside.

'What if they find out?' said Harlan, and his voice almost cracked as he spoke. Is this how evil is done, he asked himself, in small increments, one foot after the next, softly, softly until you've convinced yourself that wrong is right, and right is wrong, because you're not a bad person and you don't do bad things?

'We use it only as necessary,' said Paul. 'We're too old to be buying sports cars and fancy clothes. We just use it to make the years that are left a little easier for ourselves and our families. If we're careful, then nobody will ever find out.'

Harlan didn't believe that. Oh, he wanted to, but secretly he didn't. It was why, in the end, though they took the money, he chose to leave the satchel where it was, with its lists of names intact. Harlan sensed their importance. He hoped that, if the plane was eventually found by those who had been seeking it, they would accept his offering as a form of recompense for their theft, an acknowledgment of what was truly important. Perhaps if the papers were left for them, they wouldn't come looking for the money.

That had been a long, long night. When they weren't talking about the money, they were talking about the pilot or pilots. Where had they gone? If they had survived the crash, why hadn't they taken the money and the satchel with them when they went to look for help? Why leave them in the plane?

It was Paul who went back inside, Paul who examined one of the passenger seats and found that its arms had been broken, Paul who found two pairs of handcuffs discarded beneath the pilot's seat. He showed all that he had discovered to Harlan.

'Now how do you suppose that happened?'

And Harlan had sat in the seat, and gripped the broken armrests, pulling them up. Then he'd examined the handcuffs, each set with the key still in the lock.

'I think someone was cuffed to this chair,' he said.

'And they got free after the crash?'

'Or before. Could be they even caused it.'

They both stepped out of the plane then, and the blackness of the pool was mirrored in the blackness of the forest, and the beams of their flashlights were swallowed up by both. Somehow they managed to sleep, but it was an uneasy rest, and while it was still dark Harlan woke to find Paul standing over the embers of the fire, his rifle in his hand, his aged body tensed against the night.

'What is it?' said Harlan.

'I thought I heard something. Someone.'

Harlan listened. There was no sound at all, but still he reached for his rifle.

'I don't hear anything.'

'Someone's out there, I tell you.'

And every hair on Harlan's body seemed to stand on end at that moment, and he got to his feet with the alacrity of a man a third of his age, because he *felt* it. Paul was right: there was a presence out there among the trees, and it was watching them. He knew it as surely as he knew that his heart still beat, and the blood still coursed through his veins.

'Jesus,' whispered Harlan. His breath was catching in his chest. A sense of profound vulnerability washed over him, and in its wake he was engulfed by a terrible despair. He felt its hunger, its need. If it was an animal out there, then it was like none that he had ever encountered.

'Can you see it?' asked Paul.

'I can't see nothing, but I can *feel* it.'

They stayed that way, Harlan and Paul, their weapons ready, two frightened old men facing an implacable presence in the dark, until both sensed that whatever was out there had departed, but they still agreed to alternate watches until dawn. Paul dozed first while Harlan stayed awake, but Harlan had been more tired than he thought. His eyes began to close, and his shoulders sagged. He would experience flashes of dreaming before he jerked awake, and in those moments he dreamed of a little girl dancing through the woods, although he could not see her face clearly. She approached the fire, peering through the smoke and the flames, examining the two old men, growing bolder in her approaches until, in the final dream, she was reaching out a hand to touch Harlan's face, and he could see that some of the nails were broken and the rest were filled with dirt, and he smelled the rotting of her.

He stayed awake after that. He stood to keep sleep at bay. Sleep, and the girl.

Because that stink had still been there when he woke up.

It was real.

But they took the money. In the end, that's what it came down to. They took the money, and they used it to make their lives a little easier. When the cancer began flipping Paul's cells like the tiles on an Othello board, turning them from white to black, he discreetly pursued a range of treatments, some orthodox, some not, and he never lost hope, not even when he put his gun in his mouth at last, because for him it was not an act of ultimate despair but the embracing of his last, best and surest hope.

And Harlan Vetters' wife was looked after in her own home as the Parkinson's quickly combined with the Alzheimer's to create critical mass, and he was forced to move her into residential care. It was the best facility that he could find within easy reach of Falls End. She had her own room flooded with light and a view of the woods, because she loved the woods as much as her husband did. Harlan visited her every day, and in summer he would put her in a wheelchair and together they would head into town for ice cream, and there were days when she would remember who he was for a few moments, and she would hold his hand in her own, and his strength would seem to still the trembling. For the most part, though, she would stare vacantly ahead of her, and Harlan could not decide if that absence was better or worse than the fear that would occasionally animate her features, when everything was strange and terrifying to her: the town, her husband, even herself.

When Paul Scollay's sister found that her husband had gambled away their savings, her brother stepped in, and money was put into a high-yield account to which only she had access. Her husband, meanwhile, was encouraged to seek treatment for his addiction, spurred on by a conversation that he'd had with Paul during which Paul's shotgun was conspicuous by its presence.

And because they lived in a small town, they knew when someone was hurting – a job lost, an injury suffered, a child yielded up to the care of grandparents because the mother couldn't cope – and an envelope would be placed on the doorstep during the night, and a little of the pressure would be anonymously relieved. In that way they salved their consciences, although both men remained haunted by the same strange dreams, visions in which they were pursued through the forest by an unseen entity, ending up at last before the black pool where something was rising from the depths, always threatening to surface but never appearing before they woke.

Rarely, too, did a day pass during those years without Harlan and Paul fearing that the plane would be discovered, and some trace of their presence at the wreckage would be revealed. They were not sure which they feared more: the law, or those who might have a personal interest in the plane and its contents. But those fears faded, and the nightmares came less frequently. The money was gradually spent until only a little of it remained, and Harlan and Paul had started to believe that they might just have committed a victimless crime when the man with the distended neck returned to Falls End.

6

It was a cold January afternoon in 2004 when the man known as Brightwell – if man he truly was – reappeared.

Harlan Vetters had always hated these winter months: they'd been bad enough when he was a young man with stamina and muscle tone and strong bones, but now he had significantly less of all three and had grown to dread the first fall of snow. His wife used to find it amusing when he began railing at the photographs in the winter catalogs that started turning up in their mailbox in August, or at the glossy store advertisements tucked inside the *Maine Sunday Telegram* as summer ended, all of them depicting happy, grinning people wearing warm clothing and holding snow shovels, as if three or four hard months of winter was just about the best damn thing that could be imagined, and even more fun than Disneyland.

'Nobody in this state posed for those photos, I tell you that,' he would say. 'They ought to fill these things with pictures of some poor bastard up to his knees in snow trying to dig his truck out with a spoon.'

And Angeline would pat him on the shoulder and say, 'Well, they wouldn't sell too many sweaters that way, would they?' and Harlan would mutter something in turn, and she'd kiss him on the crown of his head and leave him to his business, knowing that later she would find him in the garage, checking that the plow attachment for his truck was undamaged; that the flashlights worked, and there were batteries to spare; that the backup generator was in working order, and the woodshed was dry, and this before the first leaves had even begun to drop from the trees.

In the weeks that followed he would make a list of all that was needed, both food and equipment, and then he would set out early one morning to the big suppliers in Bangor or, if he felt like the ride, Portland, returning that same evening with tales of bad driving, and two-dollar cups of coffee, and donuts that weren't as good as the ones Laurie Boden served at the Falls End Diner, don't know why, after all how hard could it be to make a donut? She would help him to pack his purchases away, and there would always be hot chocolate mix, more than a whole town could ever drink in the longest winter imaginable, because he knew that she loved hot chocolate and he didn't want her to be without.

And there would be some small treat for her at the bottom of the box, something that he had chosen himself in a boutique and not in one of the big department stores. It was the real reason why he drove so far, she knew, so that he could find her something that wasn't available locally: a scarf, or a hat, or a small item of jewelry, with maybe a box of candy or cookies thrown in with it, and often a book, some big hardback novel that would keep her going for a week when the snow settled upon them. It amused and touched her to think of him in a fancy women's clothing store, fingering varieties of silk and wool and interrogating the saleswoman on issues of quality and price, or browsing the aisles of a bookstore with his notebook open to a page filled with titles he had jotted down over the preceding months, a list of books that she had mentioned in passing, or novels about which he had read himself and thought she might like. She knew that he would have spent as much time, if not more, on choosing those gifts for her as he did on buying all of his winter supplies, and he would glow with delight at the pleasure she derived upon discovering what he had brought for her.

Because here was the thing: while her friends sometimes

complained at their husbands' absence of taste and their seeming inability to buy anything appropriate for Christmas or birthdays, Harlan always chose right. Even the smallest of his gifts spoke of the consideration he had given to their suitability, and, over their many years together, she came to understand that he thought of her a great deal, and she was always with him, and these small tokens were simply occasional physical expressions of her deep and abiding presence in his life.

So, on the day of the great expedition, she in turn would have a hot meal waiting for him, and a pie she had baked that day: peach or apple, not too sweet, the crust slightly burned, just the way he liked it. The two of them would eat, and talk, and later they'd make love, because he had never stopped loving her.

He loved her still, even though she no longer always knew who it was that loved her.

There was ice on the road that day, black and treacherous, and Harlan was forced to drive to the nursing home at a pace barely above walking, even for an old timer like himself. He experienced a profound sense of relief at the sight of the redbrick building looming against the pristine blue of the sky, the fairy lights still illuminated on the bushes and trees, the tracks of birds and small mammals crisscrossing the compacted snow. Lately, the imminence of his own mortality had begun to press upon him, and he had found himself taking more care than usual when driving. He did not wish to predecease his wife. Oh, he was certain that his daughter would care for her if that happened, because Marielle was a good girl, but he knew that, in her infrequent moments of clarity, his wife found some reassurance in the routine of his visits and he did not wish to add to her fears by his absence. He had to be careful, as much for her sake as for his own.

He stomped the snow from his boots before entering the

reception area, and greeted Evelyn, the pretty young black nurse who worked the desk from Monday through Thursday, and every second Saturday. He knew all of their schedules by heart, and they in turn could set their watches by the times of his arrival and departure.

'Good afternoon, Mr Vetters. How you doin' today?'

'Still fighting the good fight, Miss Evelyn,' he replied, just as he always did. 'Cold one, huh?'

'The worst. Brrrr!'

Harlan sometimes wondered if black people felt the cold more than white people, but he was too polite to ask. He figured it was one of those questions that was destined to remain unanswered for him.

'How's the old girl?'

'She had a troubled night, Mr Vetters,' said Evelyn. 'Clancy sat with her for a while and calmed her down, but she didn't sleep much. Last time I checked she was napping, though, so that's good.'

Clancy worked only nights. He was a huge man of indeterminate race with sunken eyes and a head that looked too small for his body. The first time Harlan had met Clancy he'd been coming out of the home in his civvies, and Harlan had briefly been in fear of his life. Clancy looked like an escapee from a maximum security jail, but as Harlan had got to know him he'd discovered an immeasurably gentle soul, a man of seemingly infinite patience with his elderly patients, even those who, like Harlan's wife, were often scared of their own spouses and children. Clancy's presence worked like a sedative, with fewer negative side effects.

'Thanks for letting me know,' said Harlan. 'I'll go through and see her now, if that's okay.'

'Sure, Mr Vetters. I'll bring some hot tea and cookies in a while, if you and your wife would like that.'

'I'm sure we'd like that just fine,' said Harlan, and the young woman's genuine solicitude caused a tickle in his throat, just as it always did whenever one of the staff showed some small kindness like this. He knew he was paying for their services, but he appreciated the fact that they went the extra yard. He'd heard horror stories about even the most expensive care facilities, but nobody here had ever given him the slightest cause for complaint.

He trotted down the warm hallway, aware of the pain in his joints and a dampness in his left shoe. The leather was coming away from the sole. He hadn't noticed it before. A couple of stitches would see it repaired, though. He lived frugally, mostly out of habit but also to ensure that his wife could spend the rest of her days in this place. He hadn't wasted a dime of the money from the plane, although the thought of it never failed to cause his stomach to tighten. Years later, he was still awaiting the hand upon his shoulder, or the knock on the door, and the voice of authority, flanked by uniforms, telling him that they wanted to talk to him about an airplane . . .

He seemed to be the only visitor that afternoon. He supposed that the state of the roads had kept a lot of people at home, and he passed patients napping, or watching TV, or simply staring out of the windows. There was no conversation. It had the silence of a cloister. There was a separate secure wing, accessed by a keypad beside the doors, for those who were more troubled than the rest, more likely to wander when they got confused or frightened. His wife had been there for a couple of years, but as the Parkinson's got worse her capacity for roaming was reduced, and now she was not even able to leave her bed without assistance. In a way, he was happier that she was in the general area: the secure wing, for all its comforts, felt too much like a prison.

The door to his wife's room was slightly ajar. He knocked gently upon it before entering, even though he had been told that she was sleeping. He was more conscious now than ever before of maintaining her privacy and her dignity. He knew the distress that a sudden invasion of her space could cause her, particularly if she was having one of her bad days when she failed to recognize him at all.

His wife's eyes were closed when he entered, her face turned to the door. He noticed that the room was cold, which surprised him. They were very careful about ensuring that the patients did not get too cold in winter or too warm in summer. The main windows were kept locked and could only be opened with special keys, mostly to prevent the more disturbed patients from climbing out and injuring themselves, or running away. The smaller top windows could be opened slightly to let some air in, but Harlan could see that they were all sealed shut.

He stepped further into the room, and the door slammed behind him. It was only then that he smelled the man. When Harlan turned he was standing against the wall, smiling a dead smile, the swollen purple goiter at his throat like a huge blood blister waiting to burst.

'Take a seat, Mr Vetters,' he said. 'It's time we had a talk.'

It was strange, but now that the worst had happened, Harlan found he was not afraid. Even as he hoped that it might not be true, he had always known that someone would come, and sometimes, in those dark dreams, a man had appeared on the periphery of the pursuit, his profile deformed by his own obesity and a terrible growth that distorted his already bloated neck. This was the form that vengeance would take when it came.

But Harlan was not about to confess, not unless he was given no other option. He assumed the role that he had always determined he would play if this moment came: the innocent. He had practiced it well. He could not have said why, but he believed it was important that this man did not discover the location of the airplane in the Great North Woods, and not just because of the money that Harlan and Paul had taken. The ones who had come looking for it over the years – because, once he and Paul had come to understand their purpose, they grew better at spotting them, better at recognizing them from the tales told by bemused guides – bore no resemblance to one another: some, like Darina Flores, were beautiful and some, like this man, were profoundly ugly. Some looked like businessmen or schoolteachers, others like hunters and killers, but what they all had in common was a sense that they meant no good for God or man. If they wanted something from that plane (and Harlan had a fixed memory of those papers with their lists of names) then it was the duty of right-thinking men to ensure that they didn't get it, or so Harlan and Paul told themselves in an effort to make some small recompense for their larceny.

But neither were they so naive as to believe that their theft of the money might be allowed to go unpunished, that, if they revealed what they knew of the plane's location to Darina Flores or someone like her, the truth would be enough to buy them peace in their final years. Even the knowledge that the plane existed might be enough to damn them because they'd both examined that list, and some of those names were fused in Harlan's brain. He could recite them, if he had to. Not many of them, but enough. Enough to see him dead.

Then again, if the man was here, it was probably because of the money. The money would have drawn him. Perhaps Harlan and Paul had not been as careful as they thought.

'What are you doing in my wife's room?' he asked. 'You're not supposed to be here. It's for family and friends only.'

The man wandered over to where Harlan's wife lay, and stroked her face and hair. His fingertips trailed across her lips, then parted them obscenely. Angeline mumbled in her sleep, and tried to move her head. A pair of pale fingers entered her mouth, and Harlan saw the tendons flexing in the man's hand.

'I told you to sit down, Mr Vetters. If you don't, I'll tear out your wife's tongue.'

Harlan sat.

'Who are you?' he asked.

'My name is Brightwell.'

'What do you want with us?'

'I think you know.'

'Well, sir, I don't. I want you gone from here, so I'll do my best to answer any questions you might have, but you'll have had a wasted trip by the end.'

The sleeve of Brightwell's coat fell back from his arm as he continued to stroke Angeline's hair, and Harlan saw the mark upon the man's wrist. It looked like a trident.

'I understand that your wife has Parkinson's *and* Alzheimer's?'

'That's right.'

'It must be very difficult for you.'

There was no trace of sympathy in his voice.

'Not as difficult as it is for her.'

'Oh, I don't believe that's true.'

Brightwell glanced down at the sleeping woman. He removed his fingers from her mouth, sniffed them, then licked at their tips with a tongue that was almost pointed. In texture and color it reminded Harlan of a piece of raw liver The man allowed his other hand to rest on Angeline's brow. Her mutterings grew louder, as though the pressure of his hand troubled her, yet still she did not wake.

'Look at her: she barely knows who she is anymore, and I guess that, most of the time, she doesn't know who you are either. Whatever you loved about her once is long gone. She's just a shell, a hollow burden. It would be a mercy for you both if she simply . . . slipped away.'

'That's not true,' said Harlan.

Brightwell smiled, and his hard, dark eyes looked at and into Harlan, and they found the place where Harlan hid his worst thoughts, and even though Brightwell's lips did not move, Harlan heard the word 'liar' whispered. He could not hold Brightwell's gaze, and he felt shame as he bent his face to the floor.

'I could make it happen,' said Brightwell. 'A pillow over the face, a little compression on the nose and mouth. Nobody would ever know, and then you'd be free.'

'You stop talking like that, mister. You don't dare say that again.'

Brightwell tittered. It was a strangely effeminate sound. He even covered his mouth with his free hand while he did so.

'I'm just playing with you, Mr Vetters. To tell you the truth, somebody would find out if she died under, um, unusual circumstances. It's easy to murder, but it's harder to get away with murder. That, of course, is true of most crimes, but particularly so with killing. You know why that is?'

Harlan was keeping his head down, and his focus fixed on his shoes. He was afraid that this man might stare into his eyes again, and see his guilt. Then he began to feel concerned that this might be taken as the aspect of a guilty man, that he was, in effect, admitting the crime before he had even been accused of it. He composed himself, and forced himself to look up at this loathsome intruder.

'No,' said Harlan. 'I don't know.'

'It's because murder is one of the few crimes that is rarely committed by practiced criminals,' said Brightwell. 'It's a crime of rage or passion, and so is usually unplanned. Murderers make mistakes because they've never done it before. They have no experience of killing. That makes them easy to find, easy to punish. There's a lesson to be learned from that: crime, of any kind, is a pursuit best left to professionals.'

Harlan waited. He tried to keep his breathing under control. He was grateful for the cold in the room. It stopped him from sweating.

'Such sacrifices you've made for her,' said Brightwell, and his hand began stroking Angeline's hair again. 'You can't even afford new shoes.'

'I like these shoes,' said Harlan. 'They're good shoes.'

'Will you be buried in them, Mr Vetters?' asked Brightwell.

'Are those the shoes you'll want peeping out of your casket when they come by to mourn you? I doubt it. I reckon you probably have a pair in a box in your closet for just that eventuality. You're a careful man. You're the kind of man who plans ahead: for old age, for illness, for death.'

'I don't think it'll make a difference to me one way or another how I'm tricked out when I'm dead,' said Harlan. 'They can put me in a dress for all I care. Now would you mind taking your hand off my wife. I don't like it, and I don't believe she does either.'

Brightwell's hand left Angeline's skin, and Harlan was grateful. She grew calmer, and her breathing deepened.

'This is a nice place,' said Brightwell. 'Comfortable. Clean. I bet the staff are kind. No minimum wage employees here, right?'

'I guess not.'

'No whore nurses stealing small change from the lockers, taking the treats left by little children for Grandma,' Brightwell continued. 'No bored deviants slipping into rooms in the dead of night, fingering the patients, giving them a little something to remember, a relic of the good times. You never know, though, do you? I don't like the look of that man Clancy. I don't like the look of him at all. I can smell the badness on him. Like knows like. I've always trusted my instincts when it comes to deviancy.'

Harlan didn't reply. He was being baited here, and he knew it. Best to remain silent, and not get angry. If he became angry, he might give himself away.

'Still, no harm done, right? Your wife wouldn't remember anyway. She might even enjoy it. After all, it's probably been a while. Let's give old Clancy the benefit of the doubt, though. Looks can be so deceptive, I find.'

He grinned, and fingered the growth at his throat, exploring its wrinkles and abrasions.

'To return to the matter in hand, what I'm saying is that

it must cost more than small change, this kind of ongoing care. A man would have to work long hours to make the payments. *Loonnnng* hours. But you're retired, aren't you, Mr Vetters?'

'That's right.'

'I guess you put the pennies aside for a rainy day. Like I say, a careful man.'

'I was. Still am.'

'You were part of the warden service, weren't you?'

Harlan didn't bother asking how the man knew so much about him. The fact of the matter was that he was here, and he'd done his research. Harlan shouldn't have been surprised, and therefore he wasn't.

'I was.'

'Did it pay much, being a warden?'

'Enough, and then some. Enough for me, anyways.'

'I accessed your bank account details, Mr Vetters. It never seemed like you had more than nickels and dimes in your accounts, relatively speaking.'

'I never trusted banks. I kept all of my money close by.'

'*All* of your money?' Brightwell's eyes opened wide in mock astonishment. 'Why, just how much of it was there? All: that could be quite a lot. That could be thousands, even tens of thousands. Was it, Mr Vetters? Was it tens of thousands? Was it *more*?'

Harlan moistened his mouth and throat. He didn't want his voice to crack. No weakness: there had to be no frailty in front of this man.

'No, there was never very much of it. It was only the sale of my parents' house after my momma died that left me with a cushion, you might say.'

Something that might have been doubt flickered across Brightwell's face.

'A house?'

'They lived over by Calais,' said Harlan. He pronounced

it 'Callas', like the singer, the way everyone did in the state. 'Me being the only child, it came into my possession. Fortunate, given what happened to Angeline.'

'Fortunate indeed.'

Now Harlan met Brightwell's gaze. 'I told you at the start, sir: I don't know what you came looking for here, but I warned you that you wouldn't find it. I'd be grateful to you if you'd leave us now. I've had enough of your company.'

At that moment, Angeline opened her eyes. She stared at Brightwell, and Harlan expected her to start screaming. He prayed that she wouldn't because he didn't know how the intruder would react. He was capable of killing to protect himself, of that Harlan was sure. He could smell death on the man.

But Angeline did not scream: she spoke, and the sound of it brought tears to Harlan's eyes. She spoke in a voice that Harlan had not heard for so long, in the soft, beautiful tones of her middle years, yet there was another voice behind hers, one deeper than her own.

'I know what you are,' she said, and Brightwell looked at her in surprise. 'I know what you are', she repeated, 'and I know what lies imprisoned within you. Soul-keeper, binder of lost men, hunter of a hidden angel.'

Now it was her turn to smile, and it seemed to Harlan more terrifying even than any expression he had yet seen on Brightwell's face. Angeline's eyes were bright, and her tone was mocking, almost triumphant.

'Your days are numbered. He is coming for you. You'll think that you've found him, but it's he who will have found you. Leave here. Hide while you can. Dig yourself a hole and cover your head with dirt, and maybe he'll pass you by. Maybe . . .'

'Bitch,' said Brightwell, but his voice was uncertain. 'Your dying mind is spewing inanities.'

'Old hateful thing, trapped in a rotting body,' said Angeline, as if he had not spoken. 'Pathetic soulless creature, stealing the souls of others for company. Run, but it will do you no good. He'll find you. He'll find you and destroy you, you and all the others like you. *Fear him.*'

The door to the room opened, and the nurse named Evelyn appeared, carrying a tray on which she had placed two cups, and a plate of cookies. She stopped short at the sight of Brightwell.

'Who are you?' she asked.

'Get help,' said Harlan, rising from his chair. 'Now!'

Evelyn dropped the tray and ran. Seconds later, an alarm began to sound. Brightwell turned to face Harlan.

'This isn't over,' he said. 'I don't believe what you told me about that money. I'll be back, and maybe I'll steal what's left of your wife and carry her in me, once I've finished with you.'

With that he swept by Harlan, Angeline's bell-like laughter following him. Although the home had instantly been locked down no trace of him was found in the building, or the grounds, or in the town.

'The police came,' said Marielle, 'but my father said that he didn't know what the man wanted. He'd simply entered my mother's room and found this Brightwell leaning over her. When the police tried to question my mother, she was already gone, and she never spoke again. The end came quickly for her after that. My father told Paul about what had happened, and they kept waiting for Brightwell to return. Then Paul died and it was just my father who was left to face him. But Brightwell never came back.'

'Why are you telling me this?'

'Because the last word that my mother whispered to my father after that man fled was your name – "When it comes down, tell the detective. Tell Charlie Parker." – and that, in turn, was the last thing that he whispered to me after he told us the story of the plane in the woods. He wanted you to hear this story, Mr Parker. That's why we came. And now you know.'

Around us music played, and people talked, and ate, and drank, but we were no part of it. We were cocooned in our corner, surrounded by the silk-wrapped forms of the dead.

'You knew who this man Brightwell was, didn't you?' said Ernie. 'I saw it on your face the first time we described him to you.'

'Yes, I've met him.'

'Will he be coming back, Mr Parker?' asked Marielle.

'No,' I said.

'You seem very certain of that.'

'I am, because I killed him.'

'Good,' said Marielle. 'And the woman? What about the woman?'

'I don't know,' I said. 'With luck, maybe somebody killed her too.'

7

South, south: down Interstates and winding roads, past cities and towns, hamlets and scattered houses, across rivers and open fields, to a car on a lonely, dark stretch, to a woman leaving home, a woman who, if she could have heard the tale being told in a quiet bar in the Port City, might well have said, 'I know of these things . . .'

Barbara Kelly had just left home when she saw the red SUV. A woman perhaps a decade younger than herself was hunched over the right front tire, struggling with a lug wrench. When the headlights found her she looked frightened, as well she might. This was a dark, relatively unfrequented stretch of road, used mainly by residents making their way to and from the houses at the top of the narrow laneways that fed into Buck Run Road like tributaries. On a night like this, with clouds gathering and a brisk breeze making it feel colder than it was, there would be even fewer cars on the road than usual. Sunday evenings tended to be quiet around there at the best of times, as the residents resigned themselves to the end of the weekend and the imminent resumption of the weekly commute.

The lanes all had names inspired by the natural world – Raccoon Lane, Doe Leap Lane, Bullfrog Lane – a decision made by the developers without any apparent reference to the reality of their surroundings. Barbara had never seen a doe here, leaping or otherwise, had never heard a bullfrog, and the only raccoons she ever saw were dead. It didn't matter much, in the end. She had not raised the subject with her neighbors, or with anyone else. She had grown used to blending in. It made it easier for her to conduct her business.

Now here was an SUV with a flat tire, and a woman in trouble. A child stood beside her, a boy of five or six. He was wearing black shoes and blue jeans, and a blue windbreaker was zipped up to his chin.

The rain began to fall. The first drop landed with a loud *pop* on Barbara's windshield, and her view became almost entirely obscured before she had time to hit the wipers. She saw the boy huddle into himself under a tree to escape the downpour. He pulled up the hood on his windbreaker while the woman doggedly continued trying to change the wheel. She seemed to have managed to get one of the lug nuts loose, and wasn't about to stop now. Barbara admired her gumption, even though she could see how clumsily the woman was handling the wrench. Barbara herself would have done a better job. She was good with her hands.

She slowed down just as the jack slipped, the woman stumbling back as the SUV came down heavily on the damaged tire. She put her hands out behind her to stop herself from striking her head. Barbara thought that she heard her swear, even above the noise of the rain and the engine. The boy ran to her. His face was contorted, and Barbara guessed that he was crying.

Under ordinary circumstances Barbara would have driven on. She was not prone to helping others. It was not in her nature. Quite the opposite, in fact. Her life had, until recently, been devoted to their slow ruination. Barbara was an expert in the small print that taketh away, the legalese in contracts that permitted them to be manipulated in favor of the creditor but not the debtor. Then again, this assumed that the contracts she negotiated were available to be read and examined, which was only sometimes the case. The particular contracts in which Barbara Kelly dealt were largely verbal in nature, except when it was advantageous to have them otherwise. Sometimes they involved money, or property. Occasionally they involved people. For the most part, they were promises of assistance made and accepted, favors to be called in at opportune moments. Each was a small cut to the soul, another footstep on the path to perdition.

Her work had made her wealthy, but it had also sapped most of her humanity. True, she would sometimes choose to engage in random acts of philanthropy, both small and significant, but only because there was a power in pity. Now, as she drew to a halt beside the woman and the child, she felt something of that power, mingled with an element of sexual excitement. Even tired and wet, the woman was clearly beautiful.

The surge of desire was both unexpected and welcome. It had been a long time since Barbara had felt it, not since the lump had appeared in her armpit. It hadn't even hurt at first, and she'd dismissed it as just one of those things. She'd never been hypochondriacal by nature. By the time it was diagnosed as lymphoma, her lifespan was already being counted in weeks and months. With the diagnosis came fear: fear of pain, fear of the effects of treatment, fear of mortality.

And fear of damnation, for she understood better than anyone the nature of the bargain that had been struck. Voices had begun to whisper to her in the night, sowing seeds of doubt in her mind. They spoke of the possibility of redemption, even for one such as her. Now here she was, slowing down for a stranded woman and child, a warmth spreading from between her legs, and she did not yet know if she was stopping for reasons of goodwill or self-interest, or so she told herself.

Barbara rolled down the window.

'You look like you're in trouble,' she said.

The woman was back on her feet. Because of the headlights and the rain, she hadn't been able to tell if it was a man or a woman at the wheel of the approaching vehicle, but now the relief showed. She came forward, the rain streaming down her face. Her mascara had run. Combined with her dark dress and coat, it made her look like a mourner at the end of a particularly difficult funeral, but one radiant in her grief. The boy hung back, waiting until his mom told him that it was okay to approach. No, it wasn't just that: Barbara was very good at picking up on the responses of others, and there was something in the boy's reaction that went beyond obedience to his mother, or a child's innate caution. He was suspicious of Barbara.

Clever boy, thought Barbara. Clever, sensitive boy.

'Damn tire blew,' said the woman, 'and the jack doesn't seem to be worth shit. Do you have one I can use?'

'No,' Barbara lied. 'Mine gave out a couple of months back, and I never got around to replacing it. I tend to wait for a helpful cop when I get into trouble, or I just call Triple A.'

'I don't have Triple A, and I haven't seen any cops, helpful or otherwise.'

'Haven't you heard? They melt in the rain.'

The woman tried to smile. She was already soaked through. 'They may not be the only ones.'

'Well, this is down for a while, and it's not such a good idea for you to wait with your car,' said Barbara. 'There have been a lot of accidents at the bend in the road just ahead. People take it too fast, especially in bad weather. If someone hits you, you'll have bigger worries than a flat tire.'

The woman's shoulders sagged.

'What do you suggest I do?'

'I live just up the road from here. You can almost see my house from that big pine back there. Come up, get dry, and I'll call Roy, my neighbor, when the rain stops.' Once she had told the lie about her own jack, she could hardly offer to change the tire herself. 'He lives to help out damsels in distress. He'll have that tire changed in no time. In the meantime, you and your son can have a warm drink and wait in comfort. He is your son, isn't he?'

There was an odd pause before the woman answered. 'Oh yes, of course. That's William. Billy to me, and to his friends.'

That pause was interesting, thought Barbara.

'I'm Barbara,' she said. 'Barbara Kelly.'

'I'm Caroline. Hi, pleased to meet you.'

The two women shook hands slightly awkwardly through the open window. Caroline gestured to the boy. 'Come here, Billy, and say hello to the nice lady.'

Reluctantly, or so it seemed to Barbara, the boy came forward. He was not a good-looking child. His skin was very pale, and Barbara wondered if he was ailing. If this woman was really his mother, and there was already some doubt about that, then there was little of her in him. The boy seemed destined to grow into an ugly man, and something told her that he was not a child with many friends.

'This is Barbara,' Caroline told him. 'She's going to help us.'

The boy didn't speak. He simply stared at Barbara with those dark eyes, like raisins set in the dough of his face.

'So,' she said, 'hop in.'

'You're sure we're not imposing?'

'No, not at all. I'd just be worrying if you insisted on staying out here, so I'll be happier if I know that you're safe. You need anything from the car?'

'Just my purse,' said Caroline. She turned away, and left Barbara and the boy alone. With his hood up, and his windbreaker zipped, he looked older than his years. He reminded her uncomfortably of a doll come to life, or a homunculus. He regarded her balefully. Barbara did not let her smile waver. She had all kinds of medicines in her house, and she could easily put a child to sleep.

His mother too, if it came to that, for she could almost taste Caroline, and the warmth had begun a slow, insistent throbbing.

Repentance could wait.

The two women chatted as they drove to the house. It seemed that Caroline and William had been on their way to visit friends in Providence, Rhode Island, when the tire blew. Barbara tried to figure out where they might have been coming from to have found themselves in her neck of the woods. When she asked, Caroline said that she had taken a wrong turn somewhere, and Barbara did not pursue the matter further.

'You been to Providence before?' asked Barbara.

'Couple of times when I was a student. I was a Lovecraft fan.'

'Yeah? I never really got Lovecraft. He was too hysterical for my liking, too overblown.'

'That's not an unfair criticism, I guess,' said Caroline. 'But perhaps he was that way because he understood the true nature of the universe, or thought he did.'

'You mean ancient green demons with weird stuff covering their mouths?'

'Hah! Not like that, although who knows? No, I mean the bleakness of it, its coldness, its absence of mercy.'

The word 'mercy' struck at Barbara like a blade. She could almost feel the infected lymph nodes responding to the stimulus of the word, a painful counterpoint to the demands of her lower body. I'm like a walking metaphor, she thought.

'Cheerful,' said Barbara, and the woman beside her laughed.

'A puncture in the rain will do that to a girl,' she said.

Barbara signaled right, and they turned into the short drive that led to her house. The lights were on inside. It looked warm and welcoming.

'I never asked,' said Caroline, 'but where were you going when you found us? We haven't taken you away from anything urgent, I hope.'

A church, Barbara almost replied. I was going to a church.

'No,' said Barbara, 'it was nothing important. It'll wait.'

She showed them into the living room. She brought them towels with which to dry themselves, and invited them to remove their shoes. They both did so, although the boy seemed reluctant. Nevertheless, he insisted on keeping his windbreaker zipped, and the hood raised. It made him look even more like a malevolent dwarf. Barbara could see that he was overweight. Perhaps he was embarrassed by his appearance. The woman smiled at him indulgently, then followed Barbara into the hallway as she hung up her coat to dry.

'He's very much his own man,' she said. 'Sometimes I wonder who is really in charge in our home.'

Barbara glanced at the woman's ring finger. She wore no wedding band. Caroline knew where she was looking, and waved her left hand.

'Still free and single,' she said.

'The father?'

'He's not around anymore,' said Caroline, and although she spoke lightly an undertone made it clear that any further questions on the subject would not be welcomed. 'What about you? You married?'

'Only to my job.'

'What do you do?'

'I'm a consultant.' It was her standard reply to the question.

'That sounds very vague.'

'I advise on contracts and negotiations.'

'You're a lawyer?'

'I have legal training.'

Caroline laughed. 'I'll let it drop,' she said.

'Sorry,' said Barbara, and laughed in turn. 'My work isn't very interesting.'

'Oh, I'm sure that's not true. You seem too smart a person to end up doing a job that's dull.'

'Another one deceived,' said Barbara.

'Such modesty. So, you may be married to your job, but do you fool around on the side?'

Barbara caught a glimpse of herself in the hallway mirror, and turned away. She did not consider herself attractive. Her hair was lank and dull, her face unremarkable. She could count her sexual partners on one hand, with fingers to spare.

'No,' she said. 'I don't fool around much at all.'

Caroline looked at her quizzically.

'Do you prefer women to men?'

The bluntness of the question surprised Barbara.

'Why do you ask?'

'Just a vibe. It's not a judgment or anything.'

Barbara let a couple of seconds go by.

'Yes,' she said. 'I prefer women to men. In fact, I've only ever dated one man. I was young. It didn't take. I've always been sexually attracted to women.'

Caroline shrugged. 'Hey, I've been with women. I prefer men, but I was wild in my youth.'

She winked at Barbara. Jesus, thought Barbara, this one is really something. She's perfect. It was almost as if she were—

An offering. The word was both unexpected, and apt. Could they have known the direction of her thoughts? Could they have sensed the doubts that assailed her? Was this their way of keeping her with them: a gift, like a fly cocooned in silk presented to the spider who stalked the web? It was not beyond the realms of possibility. After all, that was how they worked. That was how *she* worked. Still, the idea troubled her. She wanted a minute or two alone to consider it. The woman's presence was somehow overpowering, and the boy was an enigma. He watched them both with a knowingness, his eyes unblinking in that desolate, bleached face.

'Would you like something to warm you up?' asked Barbara. 'Coffee, or tea?'

'Coffee would be fine.'

'What about William, or Billy?'

'Oh, he'll be okay just as he is. He has a sensitive stomach. It's been acting up this trip. Better to just leave him be.'

Barbara went to the kitchen. After a minute, during which Barbara could hear her speaking softly to the boy, Caroline followed. She leaned against the counter while Barbara poured water into the coffee machine, and the slow trickle began. Her presence was starting to make Barbara uneasy. Perhaps it had been a mistake to invite her in, but then, if she had been sent by them, why had she not come directly to the house?

Unless she had been on the way to the house when her tire was punctured.

'You have a lovely home,' said Caroline.

'Thank you.' Barbara realized that she sounded abrupt. 'I mean, it's nice of you to say. I decorated it myself.'

'You have very good taste. By the way, I didn't mean to be insensitive back there. You know, about your sexuality. I just think that it's better to be clear on these things, before we go any further.'

'Are we going further?' asked Barbara.

'Would you like to?'

Barbara looked out of the kitchen window. The falling rain resembled static on a TV screen, obscuring the picture so that she could not follow the unfolding narrative. Only the woman named Caroline was clear to her, her reflection apparent in the glass like a waning moon.

I'm right about her, thought Barbara. I *feel* that I'm right. All traces of desire, of lust, were gone now. It was the disease, Barbara realized. It had debilitated her more than she thought. In the past, she would have been alert to a trap like this, having set so many of them for others. They'd been watching for her, waiting for her. They knew. They *knew*.

'What is your name?' Barbara asked.

'I told you: my name is Caroline.'

'No,' said Barbara. 'What is your real name?'

The reflection of the woman's face flickered in the glass, like an image projected from a faulty instrument. For a few moments, she even seemed to disappear, and there was only darkness where once she had been.

'I have many names,' she said, as her face was slowly illumined back into existence, lit from within, except that it was different now. Even in the rain-slicked glass, Barbara could tell that she had changed. She was more beautiful, yet also more terrifying.

'But which is the true name? Which is closest to what you truly are?'

'Darina,' said the woman. 'You can call me Darina.'

Barbara shuddered. Her legs felt weak, and she was grateful that she had the kitchen sink to support her. She suddenly wanted to feel cool water on her face. At worst, it would hide her tears if she began to cry.

'I've heard of you,' she said. 'They send you after those who renege. You're the shadow in the corner, the blood on the glass.'

Another, smaller face joined the woman's. The child had come.

'Why are you here?' asked Barbara. 'Were you sent as a temptation? As a reward?'

'No, I am neither of those.'

'Then why?'

'Because you have already been tempted, and we fear that you may have succumbed.'

'Tempted? By what?'

'By the promise of salvation.'

'I don't know what you mean. Who is the boy? Is he really your son?'

In the stories Barbara had heard of this woman, there had been no mention of a child. Sometimes, when it suited her ends, she had worked with others, but they were similar in nature to herself. Barbara had encountered one of them many years before, a bloated imp of a man, his neck swollen by a filthy goiter, an outward manifestation of his spiritual pollution. The sight of him, the stench of him, had provided her with the first true insight into the nature of those whom she served, and of the price that would ultimately have to be paid. Perhaps, she now thought, that was the moment when the seed of doubt had been sown, and the lymphoma had been the final stimulus she had required to act, a reminder of the greater torment to come.

But that man was dead now, or so they said, the ones like Barbara who whispered behind their masters' backs but had never gone as far as she had, had never resorted to betraying them.

'Yes, he is my son,' said Darina, approaching Barbara from behind. 'My son, and so much more.'

She reached out and laid her hand on Barbara's shoulder, forcing her to turn, to look her in the face. Her eyes had gone completely black, no distinction between pupil and iris, twin eclipsed suns suspended against pristine whiteness. Beside her, the boy stared unblinkingly at Barbara. There was something familiar about him, she thought, but then the woman's hand moved from Barbara's shoulder to her armpit, languidly brushing against her left breast along the way. Her fingertips found the swollen lymphs, and Barbara felt a coldness seeping through her system.

'How did you think you could keep this hidden from us?' she asked.

'I've kept it hidden from everyone. Why should you be any

different?' Barbara replied, and she was briefly astonished at her own bravado. Even Darina appeared surprised, and the boy scowled in disapproval. Darina's fingers pressed harder into Barbara's flesh, and a pain shot through her that was unlike any she had experienced before. It was as though the woman had reached out to each individual cancer cell, and they had responded to her touch. The strength went out of Barbara's legs at last, and she sank to the floor, the woman and child standing over her now as tears sprang from her eyes, the pain that had flared throughout her system slowly reducing to a dull, awful glow.

'Because we *are* different,' said Darina. 'We could have helped you.'

'How? How could you have helped me? I am dying. Can you cure cancer?' She laughed. 'That would be the kind of joke you'd appreciate: the capacity to prevent pain and misery held back from those who need it.'

'No,' said Darina, 'but we could have brought your pain to an end. It would have been as if you had fallen asleep, and when you woke all pain would be gone. A new world would be waiting for you, your reward for all that you had done for us.'

And in the blackness of her eyes, Barbara saw the furnace flames, and smelled the smoke on the woman's breath, and tasted burned flesh. Lies, all lies: any rewards were received in this life, not the next, and they were dearly bought. The price of them was the loss of peace of mind. The price of them was endless guilt. The price of them was the betrayal of strangers and friends, of lovers and children. Barbara knew: after all, she had looked for those who might be exploited, and formulated the agreements to which they appended their names and signed away their futures, in this world and the next.

'But instead,' the woman continued, 'you began to doubt. You were frightened, and you looked for a way out. That I understand. I cannot condone it, but I can understand it. You felt fear and distress, and you sought a means to assuage them. But to confess? To repent? To betray?' She grasped Barbara's face in her hands, her fingers digging into the skin below her cheeks. 'And all for what? For the promise of salvation? Here: let me whisper to you. Listen to my truth. There is no salvation. There is no God. God is a lie. God is the name given to false hope. The entity that brought this world into being is long gone. We are all that remain, here and elsewhere.'

'No,' said Barbara. 'I do not believe you.'

She kept a gun by her nightstand, but she had never had cause to use it. She tried to figure out a way that she might get to it, then realized there was no way the woman would fall for any trick. Whatever she planned to do, she had to do it here, in the kitchen. Her eyes began to cast about for potential weapons: the knives on their magnetic rack, the saucepans hanging from their ornate hooks above the kitchen island . . .

Behind her, the coffee pot was bubbling. The plate had started to overheat a week ago. She'd meant to have it fixed or replaced when it began to act up, but she hadn't managed to get around to it. Instead, she'd simply started using instant for herself, afraid that the glass on the pot might crack if she didn't keep an eye on it.

'We are the only hope of immortality,' said Darina. 'Watch, and I'll prove it to you.'

But Barbara had no intention of watching anything. The car keys were on the table in the hall. If she could make it to her car, she'd find her way to safety. She had already reached out to those who might be in a position to help her. They could hide her, shelter her. They might even be able to find a place for her to rest, a bed in which to die in peace as the disease had its way with her.

Sanctuary: that was the word. She would seek sanctuary.

Darina sensed the threat as Barbara rose, although she could not pinpoint its source. She simply knew that the cornered prey was about to strike back. She moved quickly, but not as fast as her intended victim.

Barbara grabbed the coffee pot and threw its contents into the woman's face.

8

A chorus of 'Happy Birthday' rang out from the direction of the Fulcis' table. I went over to join in with it, and we sang around a candlelit heap of cupcakes while the Fulcis smiled proudly at their mother, and Mrs Fulci beamed with love for all, and Dave Evans somehow found the strength to sing a couple of words while praying that no stray almonds had found their way into the cupcake mix. The candles were blown out, cupcakes were passsed around, and Mrs Fulci didn't die. Jackie Garner prepared to leave, and took two cupcakes with him, one for his girlfriend and one for his mother. I made a mental note to ask him more about his mother's health when the opportunity presented itself, then returned to the booth at the back where Marielle Vetters and Ernie Scollay were exchanging words. It looked like Marielle was trying to convince Ernie that they'd done the right thing by talking to me, and Ernie was reluctantly agreeing.

'So: that's our story,' said Marielle Vetters. 'What do you think?

'You want something stronger than coffee now?' I asked. 'Because I do.'

Ernie Scollay consented to a small whisky, and Marielle accepted a glass of Cab Sauv. I had the same, although I barely sipped it. I just liked having it in my hand. There was also the fact that Ernie hadn't relaxed for a single moment since he'd entered the bar. He may not have been much of a drinker, by his own admission, but now that the story was told he clearly felt that he'd earned a glass for his efforts. Some of the tension went out of his body with the first sip.

He leaned back in the booth and tuned out of the conversation, his thoughts elsewhere, perhaps with his dead brother, standing beside Paul's closed casket.

'What do you want me to do?' I asked.

'I don't know,' said Marielle. 'We felt that we had to tell you what happened: both of my parents mentioned you before their deaths.'

'Why didn't he come to me himself after his wife spoke of me?' I said.

'He told me that he didn't think it would do any good, and Paul Scollay counseled him against it too. They were always frightened about the money. They were afraid that, if they came to you, then you'd report them to the police. But you were supposed to hear about what my father did, which was why he waited until the law could do nothing to him before he spoke to me of you. As for me, I guess I wanted you to advise us. We were afraid that man Brightwell might come back, but if what you say is true there's no chance of that.'

My hand tightened involuntarily on my wine glass. Marielle was wrong. I had been warned not to kill Brightwell: he was supposed to be taken alive because there were those who believed that the entity that animated him, the dark spirit that kept his decaying body moving, would depart at the moment of his death and migrate to another form. Only the host body died: the infection remained. Frankly, I didn't think there was enough whisky and wine in the world to make Ernie Scollay and Marielle Vetters happy to hear that. Anyway, it might not even be true. After all, who would be foolish enough to believe such a thing?

'No, no chance,' I said. *Little* chance. Perhaps.

'How did you first come across him?' said Marielle.

'I encountered him in the course of a case a few years back. He was –' I searched for the right word, but couldn't find it, so I settled for 'unusual.'

'My father had served in Korea. He didn't think anything

could frighten him more than hordes of Chinese coming at him over the brow of a hill, but Brightwell did.'

'He had that capacity. He terrified. He tortured. He murdered.'

'No loss to the world, then.'

'Precious little.'

'How did he die?'

'That doesn't matter. It's enough to know that he's dead.'

Ernie Scollay came back to us from wherever his thoughts had taken him. He worried at the base of his tie, rubbing it between his fingers as though trying to remove a stain. Eventually, he said: 'What would happen if the police found out about what Harlan and Paul did?'

Ah. There it was.

'Are you still worried about the money, Mr Scollay?'

'It's a lot, at least for a man like me. I never had that much money in my life, and I sure don't have it now. Could they make us pay it back?'

'It's possible. Look, let's be straight with one another here: an act of theft was committed out there in the woods. The money wasn't theirs to take, but you weren't aware of the source of the money until Harlan Vetters confessed on his deathbed, right? Your brother never spoke of this to you, did he, Mr Scollay?'

'No,' he answered, and I believed him. 'My brother wasn't above doing some poaching, when it suited him, and I know that he used to smuggle liquor and tobacco too, once upon a time. I got used to him having money in his pocket one day and none the next, but I chose not to ask him how he came by whatever he had.'

Marielle looked at him in surprise.

'Paul was a smuggler?'

Ernie shifted awkwardly in his seat. 'I'm not saying he was a master criminal or nothing, but he wasn't above engaging in illegalities.'

It was a wonderful turn of phrase. I was starting to like Ernie Scollay more and more.

'Did my father know about Paul's smuggling?' asked Marielle.

'I guess so. He had eyes in his head.'

'But he didn't—?'

'Oh, no, no. Not Harlan.' Scollay caught my eye, and a corner of his mouth rose mischievously, making him look decades younger. 'Not that I know of, anyway.'

'It's an evening of revelations,' I said. 'As far as the money is concerned, any potential criminal action died when those men died. A civil action, well, that's another matter. If you were to go to the police and tell them what you know, and someone came forward with proof of ownership of that money as a consequence, then it's possible that an attempt could be made to seek restitution from the estates of the deceased men. I'd have to seek advice on that, though. I'm just speculating for now.'

'And if we remain silent?' said Marielle.

'Then that plane stays where it is until someone else discovers it, assuming that ever happens. Who knows about it? Just you two?'

Marielle shook her head. 'No, my brother was there when my father told his story. He knows most of what I do.'

'Most': that was an interesting choice of word.

'Why "most"?'

'Grady is a troubled man. He's had problems with alcohol and drugs. My father's dying hit him hard. They'd always fought, and even on my father's deathbed they struggled to make up. I think Grady felt angry at my dad, and guilty for what he'd put my dad through by acting like a douche for most of his life. He found it difficult to be in the same room as him. The story my father told, he told to us over the space of two days. Sometimes he'd fall asleep, or lose his concentration. He'd become anxious or frustrated, and we'd have to calm him down and let him rest, but he always came back to the tale. But by then Grady wouldn't always be around. He was hooking up with old buddies, reliving his youth. It wasn't quite a party for him, but sometimes it sure seemed that way. In the end, he wasn't even there when my father finally passed away. One of my dad's friends had to go drag him from a bar before the body went cold.'

'Can you trust him to keep his mouth shut?'

Her shoulders sagged. 'I couldn't even trust him to stay sober for the funeral.'

'You have to make the possible consequences of loose talk clear to him. Did your father leave much in his will?'

'Hardly anything at all: the house, a little money in the bank. Most of his savings –' she paused at the word, smiled resignedly, and continued – 'went to caring for my mother.'

'Who gets the house?'

'Everything was split evenly between us. Even with all of Grady's problems, my father didn't want to be seen to favor one child over another. I'm trying to secure a bank loan to buy out Grady's half of the house. He doesn't want to live up in the County again, and he certainly doesn't want to be tied to Falls End. There aren't enough bars for him, and his exes are mostly married, or overweight, or gone to Texas. The novelty of being back in Falls End wore off about the same time that my dad died.'

'Do you want me to speak to your brother?'

'No. I imagine you can be quite persuasive, but it's better if I talk him around myself. We get on okay, Grady and I. His beef was with our father, not with me.'

'Well, make sure he understands that, if he talks, the house itself may be at risk, and in that case nobody will get anything. And you, Mr Scollay? Did your brother bequeath you anything when he died?'

'Just his truck, and even then he still owed payments on it. He was only ever renting his house. Money went through my brother's fingers like sand. I'm just glad that he held onto

enough of that forest cash to make fighting his sickness easier
for him, but it was all pretty much spent by the time he died.
I guess that's as it should be. That money was tainted from
the moment they found it, and I'm glad I don't have to worry
about any of it now. In conclusion, I got no interest in anybody
else hearing about that plane in the woods. In an ideal world,
you'd forget we ever told you anything at all.'

And that seemed to be that, as far as they were concerned.
Marielle asked me about payment for my time, and I told her
that all I'd done was listen to a story over coffee and wine
in a bar. That hardly counted as billable hours. Ernie Scollay
looked relieved. He probably didn't believe that anyone down
in the cities did anything for nothing. He asked Marielle if
she was ready to go, and she said that she'd follow him in a
few minutes, just as soon as he brought the truck around.
He looked a little reluctant to leave, as though fearful that
there might be further disclosures.

'Go on now, Ernie,' said Marielle. 'I just need a moment
or two with Mr Parker here about a private matter. I'm not
going to speak out of turn.'

He nodded, shook my hand, and headed out into the
evening.

'A private matter?' I said.

'Private enough. This Brightwell: who was he really? None
of that bullshit about him being unusual or nothing. I want
to know the truth.'

'You could say that he was a member of a cult. They called
themselves "Believers". That trident symbol on his wrist was
an identifying mark.'

'For whom?'

'For others like himself.'

'And what did they believe in?'

'They believed in the existence of fallen angels. Some of them
even believed that they were angels themselves. It's not an
uncommon delusion, although they took it to a rarefied level.'

'Did Brightwell believe he was a fallen angel?'

'He did.'

She considered what I had just said.

'What did my mother mean when she spoke of a "hidden angel"?'

There were two possible meanings. The first was a legend arising out of the great banishment of the rebel angels, and their fall from heaven to earth: that one repented and, even though he believed he had no hope of forgiveness for his transgressions, he continued to make recompense, turning his back on his angry, despairing brethren, eventually concealing himself amid the great sprawling mass of humanity.

But I shared with Marielle the second possibility. 'Brightwell believed that he was the servant of twin angels, two halves of the same being. One had been found by its enemies a long time before and imprisoned in silver to prevent it from roaming, but Brightwell and the other angel had continued to search for it. They were consumed by their need to free it.'

'Jesus. And did he find what he was looking for?'

'He died finding it but, yes, he thought that he did, at the end.'

'That woman, Darina Flores, could she have shared the same beliefs?'

'If, as it seems, she was with Brightwell when he came to Falls End, then it's possible.'

'But she didn't have a mark like that, I asked my father.'

'It might have been hidden. I've never heard of Darina Flores until tonight.'

She sat back and stared at me.

'Why was Brightwell so interested in that plane?'

'Are you asking me to find out?'

She considered the question and then some of the tension released itself from her.

'No. I think you're right, and Ernie is too. We should just stay quiet, and leave the plane where it is.'

'In answer to your question, Brightwell wasn't interested in money, or not as an end in itself. If he was curious about that plane, it was because of something else. If your father was right about a passenger being on that plane, cuffed to a seat, then it's possible this individual was the object of Brightwell's curiosity; that, or the papers your father saw. Those names had meaning. They're a record of some kind. So the cash was only a means to an end for Brightwell. He confronted your father at your mother's rest home because he and, presumably, the Flores woman were looking out for unusual spending patterns. The cost of your mother's care qualified.'

'Do you think Brightwell accepted my father's lie about the source of the funds?'

'Even if he didn't, he never had the chance to pursue the matter. He died in the same year that he confronted your father.'

Again, she gave me the stare. She wasn't a fool. Ernie Scollay might principally have been worried about the police, or someone coming after him for money that he didn't have, but Marielle Vetters had deeper concerns.

'You called them "Believers", plural. Even if the woman wasn't one, that still implies that there are more of them out there, more like him.'

'No,' I said, 'there were never any others like him. He was unpleasant in ways that you can't even begin to imagine. As for the Believers, I think they've been wiped out. But this Flores woman may be something different. That's why it's better if you and Mr Scollay keep a lid on this. If she's still out there, you don't want to bring her down upon yourselves.'

A horn tooted in the parking lot. Ernie Scollay was growing impatient.

'Your ride's here,' I said.

'Ernie knew about the plane before I did,' said Marielle. 'His brother told him the story before he died, and it was only when I came to him with the rest of it that he felt compelled to seek advice. He'll stay quiet now. He's a good man, but he's no fool. I'll work on my brother too. He can be an idiot, but he's a self-aware idiot. He won't want to put easy money at risk.'

'And you're not going to say anything either.'

'No,' she said. 'Which just leaves you.'

'I'm not bound by issues of client confidentiality since, strictly speaking, you're not a client, but I know what these people are like. I'm not going to put you, your family, or Mr Scollay at risk.'

She nodded in understanding, both at what I had said and its subtext, and rose.

'I have one last question, Mr Parker,' she said. 'Do you believe in fallen angels?'

I did not lie to her.

'Yes, I think I do.'

From her bag she produced a sheet of paper. It looked old, and had clearly been unfolded and refolded many times. She placed it by my right hand.

'What is it?' I asked.

'My father left the satchel on the plane, but he took from it one sheet of names. He couldn't say why. I think he saw it as some form of additional security. If something happened to him or to Paul, then this might have provided a clue to the identity of those responsible.'

She rested her hand on my shoulder as she passed.

'Just don't mention *our* names,' she said, and then she was gone.

In the pristine kitchen of a Connecticut house, Barbara Kelly was fighting for what little life she had left.

Darina Flores took an instant to react to the pain as the coffee struck her face. She screamed and raised her hands, as though she could simply wipe the liquid from her face. Then it began to burn, and her shrieks rose in pitch as she stumbled back against the kitchen island. Her legs tangled under her, and she fell to the floor. The boy's mouth formed a silent 'o' of shock. He froze, and Barbara pushed him aside so hard that the back of his head hit the marble countertop with a hollow, sickening sound that set her teeth on edge. She didn't look back, not even when she felt Darina's nails raking at her ankle. Barbara almost lost her footing, but she held her nerve and kept her eyes fixed on the hall stand, and her car keys, and the front door.

She grabbed the keys in passing, yanked the door open, and found herself out in the pounding rain, the car parked a few feet away in the drive. She clicked the 'unlock' button on the fob, the lights came on, and the car beeped its welcome. She already had the driver's door fully open when something landed on her back, wrapping its legs around her belly as its hands tore at her hair and eyes. She turned her head and saw the boy's face close to the left side of her own. His mouth opened, revealing nasty, rodentlike teeth, and he bit hard into her cheek, tearing at the flesh until a chunk of it came away; now it was Barbara's turn to scream. She reached behind her, pulling at his windbreaker, trying to yank him off. He held on tightly, and now his jaws were coming in for a second bite, this time at her neck.

She slammed him hard against the body of the car, and felt the wind go out of him. She did it again, and this time she followed through with the back of her head. His nose broke against her skull, and he released his grip on her, but he knocked the keys from her hand as he fell. He slumped to the ground, one hand protecting his ruined nose. She turned on him and aimed a sharp kick at his ribs. God, her face hurt! She could see her reflection in the glass, a jagged red hole the size of a silver dollar in her cheek.

She looked to the gravel and found the keys. She bent to pick them up, and when she stood again Darina was behind her. Barbara had no time to react before the knife sliced at her left leg, cutting the tendons behind the knee. She went down hard, and the full weight of the woman struck her, followed by more pain as the second sweep of the blade disabled Barbara's right leg. Now she was the one being kicked as the woman forced her onto her back, forced her to gaze upon what Barbara had done to her looks.

Darina would never be beautiful again. Most of her face was a deep, scalded red. Her left eye was red and swollen. From the way she held her head, Barbara could tell that she was now blind in that eye.

Good, thought Barbara, even as she writhed in agony against the hard gravel, her legs on fire.

'What have you done to me?' said Darina. Only the left side of her mouth moved, and then just slightly, slurring the words.

'I fucked you up, you bitch,' said Barbara. 'I fucked you up good.'

Darina raised her ruined face to the heavens, allowing the cooling rain to fall upon it. The boy appeared beside her. His nose had swollen and was streaming blood.

'Where is your three-headed god now?' asked Darina. 'Where is your salvation?'

She pointed at the boy.

'Show her,' she said to him. 'Show her the meaning of true resurrection.'

The boy lowered his hood, exposing an uneven skull that was already balding, wisps of hair clinging to it like lichens to rock. Slowly, he unzipped his jacket, revealing his neck to her, and the purple goiter that was already swelling there.

'No,' said Barbara. 'No, no . . .'

She put her hands out, as though they might have the power to ward him off, and then her arms were being grasped, and she was being pulled back into the house, her screams lost against the thunder and the rain, her blood spilling then vanishing, washed away just as surely as hope and life were about to be.

She began to whisper an Act of Contrition.

II

What beck'ning ghost, along the moonlight shade
Invites my step, and points to yonder glade?

'Elegy to the Memory of an Unfortunate Lady',
Alexander Pope (1688–1744)

9

North again: north of New York, north of Boston, north of Portland. North, to the last places.

They were lost. Andrea Foster knew it even if her husband wouldn't admit it: he never admitted his failings if he could avoid it, but she could tell that he wasn't sure of where they were. He kept looking at his map as if its neat details of hills and trails bore any relation to the haphazard reality of the forest around them, and consulting his compass in the hope that, between paper and instrument, he might be able to find his bearings. Still, she knew better than to ask if he had any idea where they were, or where they were going. He'd just snap, and sulk, and an already irksome day would deteriorate further.

At least they'd remembered to bring the 100 percent DEET spray so the insects were being kept at bay, although probably at the cost of some kind of long-term damage to brain cells. If it came down to a choice between being eaten alive in the woods right now and a deterioration of her mental functioning somewhere down the line, she'd take her chances with brain death. He'd assured her that insects wouldn't be a problem at this time of year, but here they were: small flies mostly, but she'd also had to fight off a wasp, and that had bothered her more than anything else. Wasps had no business being alive in November, and any that survived would be in a foul mood. She'd killed the wasp by swatting it with her hat and then crushing it beneath her boot, but she'd seen others since then. It was almost as if, the deeper they went into the woods, the more of the insects there were. There was still some repellent in the dispenser, but it was running disturbingly low. She wanted to get back to civilization before it ran out entirely.

It was warm too. Logic said that the shade of the trees should have cooled them some, but that didn't seem to be the case. She had found herself struggling for breath on occasion, and her thirst never seemed to be slaked no matter how much water she drank. She usually liked day hikes, but after this one she'd happily spend a couple of days in a nice hotel, drinking wine, taking long baths, and reading a book. Once today was over and they were back in Falls End, she'd talk to Chris about heading up to Quebec or Montreal a little earlier than they'd planned. She'd had enough of the great outdoors, and she suspected that, secretly, he had as well. He was just too stubborn to admit it, just as he was too stubborn to hold up his hands and confess that, if they weren't quite up shit creek, they could smell it from where they were.

She'd only reluctantly agreed to this trip. Pressure of work meant that Chris had been forced to cancel his summer vacation plans, so she and their daughters had joined her sister and her kids in Tampa for ten days while Chris stayed in New York. It was the downside of being self-employed: when the work was there you had to take it, especially with times being so tough. But he loved the Maine woods: they reminded him of his childhood, he said, when friends of his parents would offer them the use of their camp at The Forks for a couple of weeks each summer. So this was a nostalgic trip for him, particularly since his mother had passed away in January, and Andrea could hardly have refused to accompany him. She had been a little reluctant to go traipsing through the woods during hunting season, but he assured her that they'd be fine, especially decked out as they were in reflective orange.

Orange was not her color.

Orange was not anybody's color.

She looked to the sky. There was an oppressive clouding to it, which concerned her. There might even be rain coming, although she couldn't recall it being forecast.

'Damn it,' said Chris. 'There should be a stream around here. If we follow it, it'll take us back to town.'

He looked left and right, hoping for some glimmer of silver, listening for the sound of running water, but there was nothing, not even the song of a bird.

She so badly wanted to shout at him: I don't hear a stream. Do you hear a stream? No, because there's no fucking stream here. We're lost! How long have you been leading us in the wrong direction? How fucking hard can it be to distinguish between north, south, east, and west? You're the great outdoorsman. You have the compass and a map. Come on, Tonto, figure it out!

He turned to look at her, as if she'd screamed so loudly in her head that some atavistic part of his brain had picked up on it.

'It should be here, Andrea,' he said. 'I've been heading east, following the compass.'

He sounded bewildered, and he looked like a small boy. Some of her anger at him diminished.

'Show me,' she said.

He handed over the compass, and pointed a manicured finger at the map. He was right: they seemed to be heading east, and at their rate of progress they should have been at the Little Head Stream by now. She tapped the compass, more out of habit than anything else.

Slowly, the needle turned 180 degrees.

'What the hell?' said Chris. He took the instrument back from his wife. 'How can it be doing that?'

He jabbed at the compass with his own finger. The needle didn't move.

'Could we have been going west all this time?' asked Andrea.

91

'No. I can tell east from west. We were heading east. I think.'

For the first time, he sounded genuinely worried. They had an emergency kit, and some food, but neither of them had any desire to spend the night out in the woods without the proper equipment. In fact, they weren't fans of sleeping outdoors at the best of times. Both of them liked their creature comforts, and a long day's hike was made worthwhile by the promise of a little luxury and a good meal at the end of it.

She looked up at the sky again, but there were only glimpses of it to be seen between the trees. They were thicker here, and more ancient. Some of them must have been centuries old, their trunks distended and tumorous, their branches like broken limbs that had been set wrongly. The terrain was rocky in places, and there was a stench on the air. It smelled like old stew made with innards.

'Maybe you could climb a tree and get our bearings,' she said, and giggled.

'That's not helpful,' said Chris.

He scowled at her, and she giggled again.

She didn't know why she was laughing. They were lost, and while it wasn't as bad as being adrift in the woods when snow was falling and there was a chance that they might freeze to death, their cell phones had no signal, they still only had limited supplies, and the temperature was bound to fall once darkness came. Nobody knew that they were out here, either. They'd checked out of their motel in Rangeley shortly after dawn, just in case they found somewhere more interesting along the way north, and their car was now parked on the main street of Falls End. It might be days before someone noticed that it hadn't moved. She'd told Chris that they should have made a provisional booking somewhere in Falls End, but he'd replied that it was too early to start thinking about that, and the town seemed quiet anyway, and if they made a start on the hike they'd be back by late afternoon. That was one of his other faults: he hated committing to anything in advance, even a motel room in a small town. When they went out to dinner in a new city, he would walk her from restaurant to restaurant examining each menu in turn, always looking for the perfect food in the perfect place. There had been evenings where they had walked and debated for so long that everywhere good was either closed or full by the time Chris made a decision, and they'd ended up eating burgers in a bar, her husband simmering at missed opportunities.

'And what's that stink?' said Chris.

'It smells like cheap meat was boiling in a pot, and then it went off,' she replied.

'It might mean that there's a house nearby.'

'Out here? I didn't see any road.'

'You notice how thick the trees are? There could be a four-lane highway a stone's throw from here, and we wouldn't know about it until we heard a truck.'

There's no highway out here, she wanted to say. There isn't even a hiking trail. We lost that when you decided to 'explore', and now look at the mess we're in. She remembered a cartoon she'd seen in a magazine once, depicting a family in the wilderness surrounding a father who was examining a map. The caption read: 'What matters isn't so much where we are as who we blame for it.'

'If there's a house, there may be a phone,' Chris went on. 'At the very least we can ask for directions back to town.'

Andrea supposed that he was right, although she wasn't sure how much time she wanted to spend dealing with someone who lived so deep in the Great North Woods. Anyone who had come this far to find some solitude wasn't necessarily going to welcome two lost city dwellers smelling of sweat and DEET into his lovely, secluded home.

'There!' said Chris. He was pointing to his right.

'What?'

'I saw someone.'

She looked, but could see nothing. The branches of the trees moved, creating a faint rustling. Odd: she had felt no breeze.

'Are you sure?'

'There was a man among those trees. I'm sure of it. Hey! Hey! Over here! We're lost. We need a little help.' He put his hand to his forehead to shade his eyes. 'Sonofabitch. I think he's heading away from us. Hey! Hey!'

Andrea still couldn't see anyone, but she joined in with her husband's shouts, just in case the man was concerned at the presence of a solitary male on his territory.

'Please,' she called. 'We don't mean any harm. We just need to get back on the trail.'

Chris folded the map and stuffed it into his rucksack.

'Come on,' he said to her.

'Come on where?'

'We're going after him.'

'What? Are you crazy? If he doesn't want to help us, that's his business. Chasing after him isn't going to make things better.'

'Jesus, Andrea, there has to be some kind of code of the forest, right? It's like the law of the sea. You don't leave people stranded when they're in trouble. All we're looking for is directions.'

Andrea had never heard of a code of the forest, and she was pretty sure that none existed. Even if it did then, just as with the law of the sea, there would be those who did not abide by it. She didn't know what the forest equivalent of a pirate might be, and she didn't want to find out. People went missing in these woods, and some of them were never found again. They couldn't all have been eaten by bears, could they?

'What if he has a gun?' she said.

'*I* don't have a gun. Why would he shoot me? You know,

94

Deliverance was just a movie. Anyway, that was somewhere in the South. They're different down there. This is Maine.'

He set off after the man only he had seen. Andrea trailed after him. She had no choice. The woods were thick, and she didn't want to lose sight of her husband. The only thing worse than being in their current situation would be to find herself in it alone. He was setting a fast pace now. That was Chris all over. Once he eventually got an idea fixed in his head, he'd pursue it full speed to its conclusion. Like a lot of men she knew, he couldn't follow more than one clear line of thought for any length of time, but he had a determination that she sometimes lacked.

'Wait up, Chris,' she said.

'We'll lose him.'

'You'll lose *me*.'

He paused, his left hand outstretched to her from the top of a small incline while he continued to look ahead.

'Is he still there?'

'No. Hold on, he's back again. He's staring at us.'

'Where?' She strained her eyes, squinting into the forest gloom. 'I still can't see him.'

'I think he's raising his arm. He wants us to follow him. Yep, that's definitely it. He's showing us the way.'

'Are you sure?'

'What else would he be doing?'

'Uh, leading us *deeper* into the woods?'

'Why would he want to do that?'

Because people are just bad, sometimes. Because he means to hunt us.

'I don't know. He might want to steal from us.'

'He wouldn't have to lead us deeper into the forest to do that. He could just hold us up right here.'

Chris had a point, but she still felt uneasy.

'Let's just be careful, okay?'

'I'm always careful.'

'No you're not. That's how I got pregnant with Danielle, remember?'

He flashed that grin at her, the one that had attracted her back at college, the one that had made her climb into bed with him the first time, and she responded in kind with that sly, sexy smile that always caused the hairs on the back of his neck to rise up, and other parts of him to rise too, and both of them made the same wish: that they were in bed together with a bottle of wine half-drunk beside them, and the taste of it on their lips and tongues as they kissed.

'It's going to be okay,' he said.

'I believe you,' she replied. 'But no more hiking for a while after this, promise?'

'Promise.'

She took his hand, and he squeezed it. As she stood beside him she saw the man for the first time. Perhaps it was the cloud cover combining with the natural gloom of the forest, but it seemed to her that he was dressed in some kind of a cloak. He wore a hood over his head, so that she could not see his face. He was clearly beckoning to them, though. Her husband had been right about that.

She felt an ache in her stomach, a cold pain. She'd always had a good sense about other people, although Chris just tended to smile indulgently when she spoke of it. Men were different. They were less attuned to their own potential vulnerability. Women needed that added awareness of the dangers that surrounded them. She'd passed it on to their girls, she hoped, attuning them to it. This man meant them some harm: she was sure of it. She was just glad that the girls were safe with her parents in Albany and not out here in the woods. She tried to speak, but then Chris's hand slipped from hers, and he was moving again, following the slowly waving figure, following him deeper and deeper into the woods.

And she followed after.

10

I t was the day after my meeting with Marielle Vetters and Ernie Scollay.

The month of November was set to die a sticky death, it seemed. A snowstorm had hit early in the month, presaging a long, cold winter, but no further snows had followed, and slowly the temperature had climbed until there were days when a sweater seemed too much to wear, and nights when the bars let their doors stand open to allow a little air to circulate. Now there was at least a north wind blowing, and from the window of my office at home I watched the cordgrass of the Scarborough marshes perform delicate dances at the breeze's call.

On my desk before me was the typewritten list given to me by Marielle. It consisted of seven names: six men and one woman. Beside four of those names were sums of money, ranging from $3,000 to $45,000. The other three names each had the word 'Contacted' handwritten beside them, followed by 'Accepted' in two cases, and 'Refused' in one. Just one of the names was familiar to me, and then only after I had cross-checked a box number to make sure that it was the same person: Aaron Newman was a reporter with one of the New York newspapers, a political writer with what appeared to be extremely good sources. His profile had risen recently following a series of articles exposing a married congressman's contacts with a pair of nineteen-year-old boys whom he may or may not have paid for sexual favors. Naturally, the congressman's career had immediately gone down the toilet, and his wife had helped to flush the bowl by failing to appear at any of his teary-eyed press conferences. The flock is easily led: show them a penitent with a forgiving spouse and they'll consider forgiving too, but give them a penitent alone on a platform and they'll start looking for rocks to throw. Newman's name did not have a sum of money beside it, only the word 'Accepted.'

The name of a second man, Davis Tate, rang a bell somewhere, and the miracle of Google did the rest. Tate was a talk radio shock jock, a minor celebrity on the extreme right, the kind who gave a bad name to ordinary conservatives who didn't immediately hate on sight anyone who wasn't like them in race, creed, or sexual orientation. Tate's name had a letter 'A' handwritten after it, along with three asterisks. Either he was a very good student or Davis Tate had accepted, or been accepted, with more than usual enthusiasm.

One of the others, a woman called Solene Escott, had a twelve-digit number beside her name, but it didn't work as a telephone number, and when I tried an Internet search on it I came up with nothing, even when I included her name alongside. A further trawl produced a handful of Solene Escotts, including a banker, a writer, and a housewife who had died in a car accident in October 2001 somewhere north of Milford, New Hampshire.

I looked again at those twelve digits beside Solene Escott's name, which, unlike the others on the list, was typed in red, then separated them into two six-digit numbers. The first set ended in '65', the second in '01'. The first numbers conformed to the date of Solene Escott's birth, according to her obituary, and the second set matched the date on which she died. But according to the newspaper found in the plane, it had gone down in July 2001, three months before Solene Escott perished. Either someone connected to that plane had a direct line to God, or Solene Escott's death had been planned well in advance.

The obituary also gave me the name of Solene Escott's

husband. Solene had kept her own name when she married. Her husband's name was Kenneth Chan, apparently known to his friends and associates as Kenny. His name was typed above Solene's on the list.

Beside it was written the word 'Accepted'.

It took me another hour to come up with a possible identity for one further name on the list, and again it was Solene Escott who provided the link. The only person with 'Refused' beside his name was one Brandon Felice. A Brandon Felice had been killed in a gas station robbery outside of Newburyport, Massachusetts in March 2002. There was no apparent reason for his death. According to an eyewitness, a salesman who had been drinking coffee in his car across the street when the robbery occurred, Felice had been pumping gas into his Mercedes when two masked men pulled up in a Buick, both armed with pistols. One of the men ordered the attendant to empty the register while the other forced Felice and a woman, Antonia Viga, who had been putting air in the tires of her minivan, to lie on the ground. When the first raider emerged with the cash, having first shot and seriously wounded the attendant, the second walked to where Felice and Viga were lying and shot both of them in the back of the head. The men then drove off, and the Buick was later found burned out off Route 1. The Buick had been stolen earlier from Back Bay in Boston. The raiders netted a total of $163 in the course of the robbery, and were never found.

Brandon Felice was linked to Solene Escott through her husband, Kenny Chan. Felice, Escott and Chan had been involved in a software start-up company, Branken Developments Inc., in which each of them held a one-third share. Felice had not been married and had no children. Upon his death, his share was acquired by a company named Pryor Investments. Meanwhile, Solene Escott's share in the company had passed to her husband following her fatal accident.

I'd never heard of Pryor Investments, but another search

revealed a little about the company. It was a very discreet operation, working on behalf of clients who preferred that their business dealings should remain as anonymous as possible. The only time that Pryor made the news was when something went wrong, most recently in 2009 when it was found to have 'inadvertently' broken an embargo on new investment in Burma. One of Pryor's junior partners appended his signature to a contract from what was ostensibly a foreign-incorporated and headquartered subsidiary of a shelf company in Panama, but which was traced back to Pryor's offices in Boston. Pryor had received a $50,000 fine following an investigation by the Treasury Department's Office of Foreign Assets Control, and the junior partner had been punished with the equivalent of an hour on the naughty step. Garrison Pryor, the company's CEO, described it as 'an isolated incident' and 'an error of detail', whatever that meant.

Branken Developments, meanwhile, had specialized in security algorithms for the defense and weapons industries, and became a significant player in its field. In 2004, the company had quietly ceased trading, its operations were folded into a subsidiary of the Defense Department, and Kenny Chan had retired, reputedly a very wealthy man. Pryor Investments was once again involved: it had brokered the deal for a percentage of the profits from the sale.

The twist to the tale lay in the fate of Kenny Chan: in 2006 he was found dead in his own safe, surrounded by share certificates, various forms of gold currency, and about $20,000 in cash. The safe was big, but not big enough to take Kenny Chan comfortably, so someone had broken his arms and legs to make him more malleable. It was some time before his body was discovered, and it was unclear whether he had suffocated or choked to death on the Swiss gold franc found lodged in his throat.

So Kenny Chan's wife died in a car accident that appeared to have been planned in advance, and his business partner was shot for no reason during a gas station robbery a few months later. Kenny Chan subsequently made a killing by selling his accumulated shares in his company before someone made a killing of a more literal kind on Kenny Chan, with robbery apparently not the motive. At the very least, Mr Chan had led an interesting, if relatively brief, life. Solene Escott's death was treated by police as an unfortunate accident; the investigation into Brandon Felice's death appeared to have dried up with no resolution; and Kenny Chan's demise remained quite the mystery.

The other two names on the list meant nothing to me, although I discovered obituary notices for any number of people who might have been them. Without something more than the names in isolation, it seemed that I wasn't likely to get any further with the list.

And all the time I kept coming back to Brightwell: Brightwell, a killer of men and women; a harvester and repository of souls; a being whose image had appeared in photographs from the Second World War, hardly different from the face of the man who had still been murdering for his cause sixty years later, and who bore a startling resemblance to a figure in a centuries-old painting of a battlefield, fighting alongside a fallen angel. I had killed him, and yet I had been led to doubt whether one such as he could ever be dispatched with a bullet or a blade. I still heard whispers of creatures reborn, of the transmigration of spirits, and had witnessed the consequences of vengeance pursued through generations. Brightwell, and those like him, were not of the order of men. They were Other.

So what had drawn Brightwell to the town of Falls End, and how was the list connected?

That afternoon, I began clearing my desk of other work. There wasn't very much to clear. Business had picked up some in the last few months, but it still didn't amount to a whole lot. The previous year, the case of a missing girl, with which I'd become involved through my lawyer, Aimee Price, had attracted a lot of attention, and it had led to offers of similar work. I'd turned down all but one. A man named Juan Lozano, a Spanish academic and translator who had married an American woman from the northern Maine town of Harden, had hired me to find his wife. They'd had an argument over sex, he told me, and she'd left him. Sexual relations between them had virtually ceased over the previous two years and he had accused her of having an affair. They'd had a shouting match, he'd stormed out, and when he returned she was gone. He just wanted to know that she was okay, he said, nothing more. I'd accepted his money because I thought that finding her would be easy: her credit cards were still being used, and withdrawals had been made from ATMs in the DC area using her bank card in the two days prior to my first meeting with Lozano. Beatrice, his wife, was either alive and well, or someone was using her cards and being careless about it.

I flew down to DC and rented a car. It took me less than a day to find Beatrice Lozano. She was holed up in a motel called the Lamplighter in a small town near Chesapeake Bay, the battered rental she had picked up a week earlier from a firm that wasn't giving Hertz and Avis any headaches about competition parked directly outside the room. When I knocked on the door she didn't bother to put the security chain in place before opening it. The room was dark, but even when she stepped into the sunlight I couldn't tell if she was plain or pretty. She was in her mid-thirties and spreading slightly. Her face was pale, her short hair greasy and plastered to her skull, her skin dotted with pimples. There were fresh open cuts to her arms and hands. As we spoke, the thumb and index finger of her right hand moved to her left, and the nails began to dig into the flesh, creating a new wound for her to explore.

Her eyes were dead, and the skin around them was so dark that it looked like she'd been beaten.

'Did he send you to look for me?' she asked, after I told her who I was.

'If you're talking about your husband, then, yes, he did.'

'Are you going to take me back to him?'

'Do you want to go back?'

'No.'

'Then I won't.'

'But you'll tell him where I am?'

'He hired me to find out if you were okay,' I said. 'If it's what you want, I'll inform him that I saw you, and you seemed fine. It'll be a lie, but that's what I'll tell him.'

'A lie?' She frowned.

'You're tearing holes in your skin. You're not sleeping or, if you are, you're having bad dreams. You've been moving from motel to motel, but you haven't planned what you're doing well enough to avoid using credit cards. Your husband didn't seem too familiar with your wardrobe, but he was pretty certain that you hadn't taken many clothes with you when you ran, so it was a snap decision on your part. You haven't run away with anybody because I can see only one suitcase in the room behind you, and no sign of a man – or another woman – sharing the room. And if you had run away with someone, I think you'd probably be paying more attention to your appearance. No offense meant.'

'None taken.' She managed to raise a smile. 'You sound like Sherlock Holmes.'

'Every private detective wants to be Sherlock Holmes, except maybe without the gay undertones.'

We were still standing outside her room. It didn't seem like the best place to discuss the intimate details of her life.

'Do you mind if we sit down somewhere to talk about this, Mrs Lozano? It doesn't have to be your room, if you'd rather keep that private or if you're concerned about admitting a stranger. We can find a quiet diner, a coffee shop, a bar, whatever you prefer. If you're worried about your safety with me, you shouldn't be. I'm not going to do anything to harm you, and if you want to call the police at any time, you can do that and I'll stay with you until they come. I can also give you the name of a couple of cops in Maine and New York who'll vouch for me.' I reconsidered. 'Well, maybe not New York, and possibly just one in Maine. He might also swear some when you mention my name.'

'No,' she said. 'No police.' She stepped back into her room. 'We can talk in here.'

Despite the 'No Smoking' sign beside the TV, the room smelled strongly of old tobacco. There was no closet, just a rail from which hung three empty wire coat hangers. There were two beds separated by a single nightstand on a carpet the color of pea soup, and one of the skirting boards was coming away from the wall. Mrs Lozano's case lay on the floor beside the bed on the right. It contained a pitiable array of clothes, some cheap toiletries, and a paperback book. She sat on the edge of one bed, and I sat facing her on the other. Our knees almost touched.

'Why did you leave, Mrs Lozano?' I asked.

Her face crumpled. She began to cry.

'Did your husband hurt you?'

She shook her head. 'No, he's a good man, a sweet man.'

I took a paper tissue from the box on the nightstand and handed it to her.

'Thank you,' she said.

'Do you love your husband, Mrs Lozano?' I asked.

'Yes, I love him very much. That's why I ran away. I wanted to protect him.'

'From what?'

She gagged, as though the words she wanted to say had to be vomited up, not spoken. It took her three tries to produce them.

'I'm protecting him from my brother,' she said.

'Why? What does your brother do?'

This time she did vomit. She put her hand to her mouth and puked bile into the palm.

'He rapes me,' she said. 'My brother rapes me.'

Beatrice Lozano's maiden name was Reed. Her older brother was a man named Perry Reed who sold used cars to people who didn't know what they were buying, and crystal meth, OxyContin, and Canadian prescription medicines to people who did. He also ran a couple of titty bars with dancers who qualified as hookers if you examined the fine print closely enough. Perry Reed was slick, plausible, sociopathically violent, and had begun raping his sister when she was fourteen. It stopped when she was in her late teens and left for college, occurred sporadically during her twenties, and had resumed with some intensity shortly after she got married. Perry would come to the house when her husband was away, although sometimes he would summon her to the auto dealership, or to one of the apartments he owned in and around Harden if it wasn't being rented at the time. She always went because he had warned her that he'd kill her husband if she ever refused him, or if she spoke a word to him or anyone else about what they did together in their private moments. When her husband accused her of having an affair, something had broken inside her. She'd run away because she couldn't stay in Harden, and she couldn't talk to her husband about what her brother did to her. All this she told me, a stranger, in her bedroom in the Lamplighter Motel.

'Perry has men who work for him,' she said. 'They're as bad as he is. He told me that even if he couldn't get to Juan, they would, and then Alex Wilder would haul me into the woods, and he and his friends would take turns raping me before burying me alive. And I believe my brother, Mr Parker. I believe him because nobody knows him as well as I do.'

'Who is Alex Wilder?'

'He's my brother's right-hand man. They share everything.

They've even shared me sometimes.' She swallowed. 'Alex is rough with me.'

I gave her another tissue. She blew her nose in it.

'Aren't you going to ask me why I've put up with it for so long?' she said.

'No.'

She stared at me for a long time. 'Thank you,' she said.

After we had spoken for a while longer, I went outside and called her husband. I told him that his wife was safe, and I asked him to pack some clothes in a bag for her and take it to the offices of the lawyer named Aimee Price in South Freeport. I then called Aimee and shared much of what I had heard, leaving out only names and locations.

'Will she testify?'

'I don't know. And it's appalling, but her brother could always claim it was consensual. It would be her word against his.'

'I don't think so. In cases like this, the victim's testimony is crucial. That's immaterial for now. She needs immediate help. I know some people in DC, if she wants to stay down there for a while. Convince her to talk to a counselor. Do you know anything about this Perry Reed?'

'Just rumors, but I plan to find out more.'

That evening I drove Beatrice Lozano to a sexual trauma specialist in Prince George's County, and she was immediately admitted to a shelter for abused women. One week later, her husband came down to visit her, and she spoke to him of what she had endured. But there remained the problem of Perry Reed, because Beatrice Lozano refused to testify against him. Something had to be done about him.

Something had been done. Two gentlemen of my acquaintance had taken the matter in hand while I was speaking with Marielle Vetters and Ernie Scollay in the Great Lost Bear.

Perry Reed, I heard, was going to lead this evening's news.

11

Chris put his hands on his knees and paused for a breath. The air was so damn still, and it tasted foul. That stink of rotting food was stronger now, and he had lost his bearings entirely. He thought that they'd been following the unknown man northwest, but he could be wrong. He had, it seemed, been wrong about everything else that day. Now the stranger had disappeared from sight, and as far as Chris was concerned they were even more lost, if there was such a thing as gradations of being lost. The flies had grown more persistent too: even the DEET spray wasn't keeping them away, and he'd been stung on the back of the neck by a wasp, which hurt like hell. He'd killed it under his hand, which gave him some satisfaction. He'd have to look up the life cycle of wasps when he and Andrea got home. Wasps in November was just plain bizarre.

The light had changed as the sun began to set. The lines of the trees were already less clearly defined, as though someone had dropped gauze across the landscape. He no longer had any concept of time. When he looked at his watch, he found that it had stopped. They were trudging through a darkening fairytale world, and he was ashamed to admit that he was afraid.

He looked back. Andrea was struggling. She indulged his amateur's taste for outdoor pursuits, but she had never really embraced them. She suffered through them because he enjoyed them, and also for the promise of luxury at the end of a day in the wild. Maybe it was the Catholic in her. She was the religious one. She still went to church on Sundays. He'd given up on his faith a long time ago; in a way, the child abuse scandals had provided him with an excuse to feel better about himself and his reluctance to sacrifice an hour of his weekend to the religion of his childhood. He did occasionally feel a lapsed believer's pang of guilt, and was not above making the odd plea for assistance in times of trouble. Now, as he watched his wife drink thirstily from her water bottle, he offered up a prayer for their safe return to Falls End, or anywhere that even resembled a settlement.

'Lord, I can't say that I'm going to return to church, or that I'm even going to be much of a better man, but we need some help here,' he whispered. 'If not for my sake, then for hers, please: get us safely back to civilization.'

As if in answer to his prayer, their guide – if that was what he was – appeared among the trees again. He lifted his arm, enjoining them to follow him.

'Hey, where are we going?' Chris called to him. 'Talk to us. We can't keep doing this. We're tired. Jesus.'

Andrea joined him. She pulled down the collar of his jacket to expose the wasp sting, and hissed in sympathy.

'That looks bad,' she said.

She slipped her pack off and found the tube of antiseptic lotion in the small first-aid kit. Carefully she applied it to the sting.

'You're not allergic to wasp stings, are you?'

'You know I'm not. I've been stung before. They don't affect me badly.'

'Uh, this one is really big, and it seems to be spreading.'

'I swear, I can feel it in my spine.'

'I have some lorazepam in my suitcase,' she said. 'That should help. You might need to see a doctor if it doesn't start going down.'

In the distance, one more thin shape among the trees, she could see the man watching them.

'How long have we been following him?'

'I don't know. My watch has stopped.'

'Stopped?'

'Yeah.'

'Mine too.'

They compared watches. The time on Andrea's watch showed five minutes later than her husband's, but Andrea always set her watch five minutes fast. Both watches had stopped at the same time.

'That's weird,' said Chris.

'This is all weird,' said Andrea. 'And it's going to be dark soon.'

Her voice cracked slightly on the word 'dark'. She was holding it together, but only barely.

'We could go back the way we came, but what good would that do?' he said. 'We'd be back in the same position that we were in earlier. We have to trust him.'

'Why?'

'Because that's what people do when they have no choice.'

'He means us harm.'

'Come on, not this again . . .'

'I'm telling you. And I'd swear he's leading us in circles.'

'You don't know that.'

'I don't *know* it, but I *feel* it.'

She saw the stranger's head tilt slightly, as though he had heard what she said. She couldn't get over how dark his silhouette was. Even when the light had been good, she'd been unable to tell how he was dressed, or discern the lineaments of his face. He was like a shadow given life.

'What's he doing now?'

The man's gestures had changed. He was pointing to his right, jabbing a finger in that direction. Once he was sure that they'd seen what he was doing, he raised the same hand and waved them farewell, then disappeared into the trees, away from whatever he had been pointing at.

'He's leaving,' said Chris. 'Hey, where are you going?'

But the man could no longer be seen. The shadow had been absorbed by the greater shade of the forest.

'Well,' said Chris, 'we may as well go see what he was pointing at. Could be a road, or a house, or even a town.'

Andrea adjusted her pack on her back and followed her husband. Her eyes kept returning to the patch of darkness into which the stranger had vanished, straining to penetrate it. She wanted him to be gone, but she was not certain that he was. She sensed him waiting in there, watching them. It was only when her husband spoke that she realized she had stopped walking. She willed her feet to move, but they wouldn't. She wondered if this was how vulnerable animals reacted when faced with a predator, and if that was why they died.

'He's gone,' said Chris. 'Wherever he was taking us, we're almost there.'

The hairs on the back of her neck were standing on end. Her skin prickled. He isn't gone, she wanted to tell him. We can't see him, but he's still out there. He's led us somewhere, but it's nowhere that we want to be.

The slightest of breezes arose. It was almost a blessing until they smelled the stench carried upon it. There were birds in the air now: crows. She could hear their cawing. She wondered if crows were attracted by dead things.

'It's stronger now,' said Chris. 'It smells like a rendering plant. You know, paper mills smell real bad. That could be what's causing it: a paper mill.'

'Out here?'

'Out *where*? We don't even know where here is. We were so lost we could have traveled to Canada and not realized it. Come on.'

He reached out for her hand again, but still she did not respond in kind.

'No,' she said. 'I don't want to go.'

'Fine,' he said. 'You stay here, and I'll go see what's up there.'

He moved away from her, but she grabbed at his pack, holding him back.

'I don't want to be left here alone.'

He smiled. It was his other smile, the indulgent, patronizing one that he gave her when he thought she was failing to grasp something very simple, the one that made her feel about nine years old. She thought of it as his 'man smile', because only men ever used it. It was ingrained in their DNA. This time, though, it didn't make her angry, just sad. He didn't understand.

Chris came to her, and gave her an awkward hug.

'We'll see what he was pointing at, then make our decision, okay?' said Chris.

'Okay.' Her voice sounded tiny against his chest.

'I love you. You know that, right?'

'I know.'

'You're supposed to tell me that you love me too.'

'I know that as well.'

He gave her a playful poke in the ribs.

'Come on, I'll buy you a drink.'

'A cocktail. With champagne.'

'With champagne. *Lots* of champagne.'

Hand in hand, they walked to the rise.

12

As predicted, the evening news bulletin contained a lot of information about Perry Reed and his activities, both business and personal. At 10.40 p.m. the night before, while I was still mulling over what I had just been told of airplanes and lists, Henry Gibbon and Alex Wilder, two close associates of Reed, king of the far Northeast's used auto dealers, were stopped by police and DEA agents as they drove their respective vehicles from the parking lot of a biker bar ten miles east of Harden. When the cars were searched, the trunks were found to contain a combined total of $50,000 worth of OxyContin and heroin, which came as a surprise to Gibbon and Wilder as a) they were not heroin dealers; and b) the trunks had been empty when they parked the cars. In addition, Wilder's car contained substantial quantities of child pornography on a number of USB drives, and a cell phone with more than a dozen suspected providers of child prostitutes among its saved contacts. Both cars were registered to one Perry Reed of Harden, Maine.

At one a.m., a fire swept through the auto lot at Perry's Used Autos in Harden, aided by high winds and thirty gallons of ethyl alcohol as accelerant, destroying his entire inventory, all of the buildings on the lot, and the titty bar adjacent to it.

At 3.30 a.m., Perry Reed was arrested following a search of his house that produced a large quantity of discs and USB drives containing twenty-five thousand pornographic images of children, and a cell phone programmed with numbers identical to those found on the phone in Alex Wilder's car.

In addition, police discovered an unlicensed Llama pistol with pearl grips and a chrome finish, a pistol that would, following examination, be found to have been used in the shooting dead of two men in an apartment in Brooklyn the previous year, and possibly the severe beating of their female companion whose head injuries had left her in a persistent vegetative state. Their numbers, too, would be found on both Wilder's and Reed's cell phones, and Perry Reed's prints would be found on the weapon, having been lifted from a coffee mug in his office and transferred to the gun before it was planted, a fact that was obviously unknown to the police and, indeed, to Perry Reed.

One of the detectives was later heard to comment that Perry Reed was officially in more trouble than any other single human being he'd ever encountered in the course of his entire career, closely followed by Alex Wilder, with Henry Gibbon a distant third. The arrests were credited to an anonymous tip-off, and everyone seemed pretty satisfied with a good night's work, with the possible exception of Perry Reed who was pleading innocence and demanding to know who had burned down his auto lot and titty bar, but since Perry Reed was now facing the likelihood of a lifetime in prison, nobody cared very much what he thought.

'Very unfortunate for Perry,' I said to Angel later that night, as he and Louis sat in a booth at the back of the Great Lost Bear, the same booth in which I had spoken to Marielle and Ernie the night before. Both men were drinking Mack Point IPA from the Belfast Brewing Company, and making Dave Evans feel uneasy for reasons that he couldn't quite put his finger on. Angel and Louis were from New York, although that wasn't why they made Dave nervous; neither was it their homosexuality, Dave welcoming anybody to the Bear who didn't spill beer, insult the staff, or try to steal the bar's bear head mascot.

But Louis killed people, and Angel sometimes helped him, and, if they didn't openly advertise this particular service, then the air of potential lethality that hung around them both was usually enough to convince the more sensible of citizens to keep their distance. I sometimes wondered how like them I was becoming: they had set up Reed and his associates, but I had formulated the plan. A moral philosopher might have said that I was becoming like those whom I fought, but he would have been wrong. I was my own unique form of monster.

'It was almost like the man wanted to go to jail,' said Louis, as he mused upon the fate of Perry Reed.

'He did seem to be trying very hard,' I agreed. 'I wonder where all of those drugs came from?'

'We borrowed them from some bikers,' said Angel.

'"Borrowed"?'

'Well, it was more of a permanent loan.'

'Drugs, and a gun, *and* child pornography,' I said. 'Some people might call that overkill.'

'Other people might call it making sure,' said Louis.

'Well, that's what I paid for.'

'Remind me how much we're getting again?' asked Angel.

'You want another beer?'

'Yeah, I want another beer.'

'Then you can consider it a one hundred percent bonus,' I said. 'I don't quibble. It's not my style.'

I called for another round. When it arrived, I drank their good health and passed them a bulging brown envelope. Beatrice Lozano's husband had delivered it to my door earlier that afternoon. He didn't speak, didn't say thank you, didn't give any sign that what had occurred in Harden might be linked in any way to what had happened to his wife. He just handed me the envelope and walked away.

'I know you don't need the money, but it's nice to be appreciated,' I said.

'Better to have it and not need it.' Angel slipped the money into his pocket.

'Aimee Price say anything to you?'

'About what happened to Reed? Nope.'

'Smart woman. Eventually she'll cut you loose, you know that?'

'Possibly. Possibly not.'

'No possibly about it. She strikes me as one of those strange lawyers who seem concerned about the law.'

'Not as concerned as you might think when it suits her needs.'

'Maybe she's not so strange after all.'

'Maybe not. You want to hear something really strange?'

'From you? If you think it's strange we should call the *National Enquirer*, get them to sit in.'

I took a sip of my beer. 'It's about an airplane . . .'

And as we spoke, Andrea Foster lay dying. There was blood in her mouth, blood on her hands, blood in her hair. Only some of it was her own.

She lay still, reliving the events of the last days and hours of her life. She hovered above herself and her husband, saw them ascending the incline, making their way toward whatever it was that the stranger had been pointing at. She watched them pause, heard Chris's exclamation of surprise, then shock. She saw fallen idols – a shattered image of the Buddha, Ganesh covered with blood and filth, a *pietà* from which the sculpted heads had been removed and replaced with those of dolls. She saw a wall of wood. She saw shadows intersecting: two crosses, the remains of the men who had died upon them now reduced to bones, with more bones piled at the foot of each cross. She saw dead birds hanging by their feet from branches. She saw Chris's mouth open to say something, his panic clear, and a long tongue erupted from his jaws, a tongue with a point and barbs, and as Chris fell forward she saw the arrow that had pierced him, its shaft a bright yellow, its fletching red and white. He spasmed at her feet, and she held him as the light left his eyes. She had not even had a chance to cry before she heard footsteps behind her, approaching fast, and two blows to the head took away all of her pain for a time.

Now she lay against timber, the sky above her lit by a pale yellow moon: no roof here, and only the barest shapes of trees. The wall opposite her was pasted with pages torn from books of worship: Bibles and Korans, texts in English and Hindi and Arabic, in symbols and letters both familiar and unfamiliar. All of the pages had been defaced with pornographic pictures. The pages were further smeared with dark stains, some recent, some old, and she knew it to be blood.

There was an immense pressure on her head, as though her brain was swelling inside her skull. Perhaps it was. Was that what happened if you were hit hard enough on the head? She couldn't move her legs. She couldn't speak. She was a trapped soul, but soon she would be freed.

A shape appeared at the door. He was still only a dark silhouette, a being of blackness. She had not yet seen his face, but his skull was curiously misshapen: warped, like his spirit. If she could have spoken to him, what would she have said? Spare me? Sorry?

No, not sorry. It was not their fault. They had done nothing wrong. They had simply become lost, and in doing so they had become prey. He had lured them deeper into the forest with the unspoken promise of safety and rescue, and then had turned upon them, his arrow bringing her husband down, and his fists and his blade doing the same for her.

Chris. Oh, Chris.

She tried to reach for the silver cross around her neck, a present from her mother on the occasion of her Confirmation, but it was gone. He had taken it from her, and in the moonlight she saw it shining among the pages on the wall close by her head, and she picked out the droplets of fresh blood upon it.

Now she could hear the stranger breathing, and interspersed with his exhalations were her own failing breaths, until the final one caught in her throat, and she began to shudder. Death advanced on her, and the stranger followed, racing to keep up.

13

There were no falls at Falls End, and the principal endings there were those of civilization, ambition and, ultimately, lives. Sensibly, the founding fathers of the town had decided that, even in its earliest incarnation, a name like Civilization's End, or Ambition's End, or Dead End, might have hobbled the community's chances of progress, and so an alternative identity was sought. A stream was found to feed into Prater Lake, and that stream began its life on a patch of rocky high ground known as The Rises, cascading down in a manner that might loosely be said to resemble a waterfall, as long as nobody had seen an actual waterfall against which to measure it. Hence Falls End, with no possessive apostrophe to trouble it on the grounds that such additions smacked of pretension, and pretension was for the French across the border.

That particular stream no longer flowed into Prater Lake. It had simply ceased burbling past the outskirts of the town some time at the start of the last century, and an expedition of the curious and the concerned, aided by a couple of local drunks who fancied some air, discovered that water no longer tumbled from the top of The Rises. Speculation as to what might have caused the blockage included seismic activity, a redirection of water flow due to logging, and, courtesy of one of the drunks, the actions of the devil himself. This latter suggestion was quickly discounted, although it later gave its name to a local phenomenon known as the 'Devil of the Rises' after it was pointed out that, seen from a certain angle, some of the rocks appeared to form the profile of a demonic figure if one was prepared to squint some, and discount the fact that, seen from a slightly different angle, it resembled a rabbit, or, if one moved along just a bit farther, nothing at all.

The town's proximity to the Great North Woods, and the area's reputation for fine hunting, meant that Falls End was, if not thriving, then surviving, which was good enough for most people, especially those who were aware of the difficulties being faced by similarly sized but less fortunately situated towns elsewhere in the County. There were a few modest motels that stayed open year-round, and a slightly more upscale lodge that opened from early April to early December, offering both intimate cabins and stylish rooms to hunters and leaf-peepers with money to burn. Falls End also had a pair of restaurants, one fancier than the other and in which locals ate only on special occasions such as weddings, graduations, anniversaries, or lottery wins.

Finally, Falls End boasted a grand total of two bars: one, named Lester's Tavern, that stood on the town's western edge, and another, The Pickled Pike, that lay at the center of the narrow strip of stores and businesses that constituted Falls End's beating heart. These included a bank, a coffee shop, a grocery-cum-drugstore, a taxidermist's, a lawyer's office, and Falls End Bait & Fish. The latter stocked hunting and fishing equipment, and had recently discovered a lucrative sideline selling fly-fishing feathers to hairdressing salons for use on women who thought it exotic to add rooster feathers to their hair, a development that had occasioned some discussion in Lester's Tavern, since there were a great many people, in Falls End and elsewhere, who felt that fly feathers had no business being anywhere other than at the end of a line, and should adorn nothing more unusual than a hook, although Harold Boncoeur, who owned Falls End Fish & Bait, had been known to remark that he found the thought of a woman with feathers in her hair wicked sexy. He had not mentioned this to his wife, though, for Mrs Boncoeur favored blue rinses and perms, and thus was not a likely candidate for feathering, nor was she likely to listen with any great understanding to such fantasies on the part of her husband.

So it was that there were worse places to live than Falls End. Grady Vetters had lived in a couple of them, and was in a better position to judge than most of his peers, including Teddy Gattle, with whom he had been friends since childhood, a friendship that had remained firm even during the long periods of Grady's absence from town. In the manner of such friendships, Grady and Teddy simply picked up their conversation each time from where they had previously left off, regardless of months or years spent apart. It had been that way between them ever since they were boys.

Teddy felt no resentment toward Grady for leaving Falls End. Grady had always been different, and it was only natural that he should try to seek his fortune out in the wider world. Teddy just looked forward to Grady's return, whenever that might be, and the stories he would bring with him of the women in New York, and Chicago, and San Francisco, places that Teddy had seen on television but which he had no desire to visit, the size and scale of them being frightening to him. Teddy was already a little lost in the world: he held on to his life in Falls End the way a drunk holds on to his bed when his head is spinning. He could not imagine what it would be like to be set adrift in a big city. He thought that he would surely die. Better that Grady should be the one to negotiate the wider world like the explorers of old, and leave Teddy to Falls End, and his beloved forest.

And what of Grady's efforts to make his mark in that world of skyscrapers and subways? Teddy couldn't and wouldn't have said it, mainly because he didn't allow himself to dwell too long on the matter, but it was possible, just possible, that Teddy was secretly pleased Grady Vetters hadn't become the big shot artist he had always hoped to be, and the women he screwed in those faraway cities remained the stuff of stories and were not there in the flesh to stoke the secret fires of Teddy's envy.

Now here they were, Grady and Teddy, together once more, smoking cigarettes out back of Lester's, sitting at the bench tables placed there for precisely that purpose, and the starlight flickering through pinpricks in the night sky. Grady had told Teddy that you couldn't see the stars in some cities, so bright were their own lights, and Teddy had shuddered. He loved these cloudless nights, loved to pick out the constellations, loved to navigate his way through the woods by their position in the heavens. He saw no contradiction in his fear of the immensity of cities and his comfort with the vastness of the universe. He watched a shooting star cross the sky, burning itself out in the atmosphere, and he looked at his best friend and thought that Grady Vetters was the closest thing to a shooting star he had ever encountered close up, and just like one of those stars he was destined to burn out to nothing.

The barest of breezes stirred the fairy lights that adorned the back of the bar but not, strangely, the front, a circumstance dictated by a town ordinance that Teddy did not understand, since it wasn't as if Falls End was so pretty that it couldn't do with a little more color along its main street. On the other hand, it lent the back of Lester's a vaguely magical air. Sometimes when Teddy was returning to town from one of his trips into the forest, whether as a guide or as a solitary hunter, or simply because he wanted to be away from people for a time, he would glimpse the lights of Lester's twinkling through the branches, and it was a sight that he always associated with comfort, and warmth, and belonging. For Teddy, the lights of Lester's meant home.

Grady didn't like Lester's as much as Teddy did. Oh, he'd always have a good time there on his first night back in town, shooting the breeze with familiar faces and joshing with old Lester, who had a fondness for Grady because Lester was something of a frustrated artist himself whose godawful watercolors hung on the walls of the bar and were always for sale, although Teddy couldn't recall anyone ever taking Lester up on that offer, no matter how low he priced them. The paintings changed a couple of times a year, mostly to give the impression that somebody, somewhere was cornering the market in the primitive, unique vision of Lester LeForge, instead of the reality, which was that Lester's paintings now took up so much space in his garage that he had to park his car in the drive. To Lester, Grady Vetters was a success: he'd exhibited his work in minor galleries, and had even been reviewed in a Friday edition of the *New York Times* back in 2003 as part of an 'emerging artists' show somewhere in SoHo. Lester had carefully cut out the review, plasticized it, then stuck it behind the bar beneath a hand-lettered sign that read 'Local Boy Makes It in the Big Apple!'

That was as good as it had ever got for Grady Vetters, and now it seemed to Teddy that his friend was less an emerging artist than a submerging one, gradually sinking beneath the weight of his own failed expectations, his inability to hold down a job of any kind, his ongoing love affairs with booze, pot, and inappropriate women, and his hatred for his father, which hadn't eased any despite the old man apparently making Grady's fondest wish come true by dying at last.

Everybody believed that Grady Vetters was smarter than Teddy Gattle, even Teddy himself, but he knew that for all Grady's talk about old Harlan and how much of a hard-ass he was, and how he had meant nothing to his only son, and vice versa, Grady was worse off than ever now that his old man was gone. Despite everything, Grady had wanted to impress his father, and any success he had made of his life was largely down to that desire. Without him, Grady had nothing to aim for because he didn't have enough self-respect and self-motivation to pursue his painting and drawing for the love of the thing itself. He was also destined, Teddy thought, to carry through life the knowledge that his father had died unreconciled with his only son, and at least fifty percent of the blame for that, and maybe a good deal more, lay with the younger party.

But, Jesus, Grady was in a foul mood tonight. Kathleen Cover was in Lester's with her husband, and some of his buddies and their wives. Kathleen and Grady had enjoyed a fling a couple of years back while Davie Cover was off fighting the ragheads in some place that Davie couldn't even spell, and certainly couldn't have found on a map before he was sent there. It might have been considered low, and even unpatriotic, to fuck a man's wife while he was off serving his country, except that Davie Cover was a bedbug on the ass of life, and the president of the United States himself would have felt duty-bound to fuck Kathleen Cover as a way of spiting her husband had he ever been forced to spend any time in Davie's company. Davie Cover was a bully and – naturally, since the two went together – a coward, a man with the social skills of a scorpion and the higher intellectual functions of one of those insects that could keep existing on a basic level even if their heads were cut off. He'd joined the National Guard because he craved the veneer of authority offered by a weekend warrior's uniform, and the official sanction for his actions that it implied. Then airplanes had started flying into buildings, and suddenly the US was seemingly at war with every country that was more than half sand, except maybe Australia, and Davie had found himself separated from his wife of six months and the mother of his child, Little Davie, the fact of their marriage not being unconnected to the existence of that child. Most everyone in Falls End, possibly including some of Davie's blood relatives, felt a sense of profound relief at Davie Cover's departure, and waited hopefully for the appearance of his name in an obituary column.

Surprisingly, though, Davie Cover had thrived in the army, in no small part because he was put on a prison detail, and therefore spent most of his time in uniform tormenting semi-naked men by alternately beating them, boiling them, freezing them, and pissing in their food. He'd liked it so much that he'd stayed on for an extra nine months, and he might still have been there had his enthusiasm for the uncontracted aspects of his job not brought him to the attention of superiors with a conscience and, more to the point, a desire to protect their own reputations, and Davie Cover had found himself quietly discharged.

By that time, Grady Vetters and Kathleen Cover had been conducting a discreet but passionate affair for almost a year, and Grady had even considered asking Kathleen to run away with him. She could bring Little Davie along too, because he was a cool kid, especially as his father wasn't around to make him otherwise. But then Davie Cover came home, and Kathleen dropped Grady like he'd brought crabs to her bed, and when he persisted with his attentions she threatened to tell her husband that Grady had come on to her repeatedly while he was away, and had once even tried to rape her out back of Lester's. Grady had left Falls End again shortly after, and had not returned for more than a year. He just didn't understand what happened at the end between Kathleen and him, and, judging by his mood tonight, he still didn't.

But Teddy did, because in some things he was much smarter than his friend would ever be. Teddy knew that Kathleen Cover had Falls End in her veins. She was never going to leave that place, for the wider world frightened her almost as much as it frightened Teddy. Kathleen and her husband had more in common than Grady could ever have imagined, and Grady had just been a way to kill time until Davie's return. Grady had believed himself to be something exotic, something more than her husband could ever be, and maybe he was, but secretly Kathleen Cover despised him for it, and Teddy suspected that her happiest moment in the relationship had come when she'd dumped Grady and taken her husband back into her bed. If she could, she'd have made Grady watch

Davie humping her while she smiled back at him over her husband's hairy, boil-spattered shoulder.

So that was why they were out back of Lester's, smoking and spitting, with Grady staring off into the woods, raging silently, and Teddy beside him, keeping him company, waiting for Grady to make a decision about what to do next, just the way that it had always been. Teddy had already paved the way for a possible departure from Lester's, and the memory of Kathleen Cover, by telling Grady about a party at Darryl Shiff's place, and Darryl knew how to throw a good party. He had a nice sideline in distilling his own alcohol using a pair of five-gallon oil cans, two pressure cookers, and some scavenged plastic and copper tubing. Darryl was classy too: he oak-aged the alcohol by adding to it a little wood, smoked and charred so that the natural sugars caramelized. It lent his moonshine a distinctive color and taste, and the batch he was offering for tasting tonight had been aging for over a year.

So there'd be free booze at the party and, it was rumored, some out-of-town women too. Grady needed a woman even more than Teddy did, which was saying something given that Teddy perpetually walked around town with something in his pants resembling the state of Florida in miniature.

Grady blew a smoke ring, then another and another, trying to fit each between the dissipating dream of the last. Teddy slapped at a bug on his neck, then wiped the smeared remains of it on his pants. It looked like a big bitch too. If this went on any longer, they'd find his withered remains beside this bench in the morning, every drop of his blood now residing in the digestive systems of half the female mosquitoes in Maine. Overwintering mosquitoes were rare this far north, and the rest should all have been dead. Teddy wondered if there might not be something in all of this global warming shit after all, although he kept it to himself: in Falls End, coming out with pronouncements like that was tantamount to Communism.

'How much longer we going to stay out here, Grady?' he asked. 'I just squashed a bug looked like a jet plane.'

'You want to go back inside?' said Grady. 'You do, you can just go right ahead.'

'I don't unless you want to. Do you? Want to go back in, I mean.'

'Not so much.'

Teddy nodded.

'I guess there's no point in telling you she ain't worth it.'

'Ain't worth what?'

'All this mooning, all this aggravation.'

'You ever been with her?'

'God, no.' Teddy said it with some feeling, and Grady seemed to take it as meaning that Kathleen Cover was out of Teddy's league, which was true. On the other hand, Teddy wouldn't have climbed into the sack with Kathleen Cover if God Himself had sent the Archangel Michael down with entry instructions and a diagram. The woman was such bad news she should have arrived with a pastor in tow and a letter of condolence from the government. Teddy would rather take his chances with the mosquitoes. At least with them he had a chance of not being sucked completely dry.

'She was fine,' said Grady. 'Very fine.'

Teddy wasn't about to argue, so he let a couple of beats go by, and another bite. Damn, but he'd be swollen in the morning. It really was beyond understanding.

'How is your sister doing?' asked Teddy. Teddy thought that Marielle Vetters was fine, very fine; not that he'd ever done anything about it, not with Grady still living and breathing, and assuming Marielle might even be willing to consider him, which Teddy doubted. Teddy had been around the Vetters family for so long that he almost counted as blood, but it wasn't just his longstanding proximity that might have given Marielle pause. Teddy wasn't an attractive man: he was short, and overweight, and had started balding almost as soon as adolescence hit. He lived in his childhood home, left to him by his mother in her will along with $525 and a fourth generation Oldsmobile Cutlass Supreme. His garage and yard were littered with bike and automobile parts, some acquired legally and some not so legally. He did custom jobs when asked, and regular repairs to keep the roof above his head. Teddy was good enough at his work that some of the bikers had been known to use him, paying him hard cash along with a little weed or blow, and sometimes one of the hookers they ran as a sweetener if they were particularly pleased with what he'd done. He still had some of their weed stored away; he'd been saving it for a special occasion, but now he was considering offering to share it with Grady if it would just get them away from Lester's.

'She's okay,' said Grady. 'She misses my old man. They were always tight.'

'You hear any word yet on what's coming to you?'

Teddy knew that Harlan Vetters had split his worldly wealth evenly between his children. There wasn't much money in the bank, but the house would be worth something, even in these hard times. It was a big old rambling place with a lot of land adjoining it, land that bled into the forest on three sides so that there was little chance of anyone building nearby. Harlan had kept it nice too, right until the end.

'Marielle talked to the bank about taking a loan to buy me out, with the house as security.'

'And?'

'They're still talking,' said Grady, and his tone made it clear that it wasn't a subject he wished to pursue.

Teddy took a long drag on his cigarette, right down to the filter. He'd heard whispers about this because his old buddy Craig Messer was engaged to a woman who worked as a teller at the bank, and this woman had said that Rob Montclair Jr, whose father managed the bank, didn't care none for Grady Vetters, and was doing his damnedest to ensure that the bank didn't go lending money to his sister. The reasons for his hatred were lost in the mists of high school, but that was the way of small towns: little hatreds had a way of lying dormant in their soil, and it didn't take much to make them germinate. Marielle could go someplace else for a loan, but Teddy felt sure that the first thing she'd be asked was why she wasn't talking to her own bank about this, and then someone from the second bank would call Rob Montclair Jr. or his poppa, and the whole sorry business would start over again.

'You know, Teddy, I hate this place,' said Grady.

'I figured,' said Teddy. He wasn't resentful. Grady just saw Falls End differently. He always had.

'I don't know how you can stand to stay here.'

'I ain't got nowhere else to go.'

'There's a whole world out there, Teddy.'

'Not for people like me,' said Teddy, and the truth of it made him want to die.

'I want to go back to the city,' said Grady, and Teddy understood that this wasn't a conversation between equals. Grady Vetters wasn't just the center of his own universe, but a planet around which men like Teddy orbited adoringly. As far as changes in the direction of Grady Vetters' conversation went, the best that his friend could hope for would be, 'Enough about me, what do you think of me?'

'Which city?' said Teddy. Only a little of his resentment showed, not that Grady noticed.

'Any city. Any place but here.'

'Why don't you, then? Go back to what you were doing and wait for the money to come.'

'Because I need the money *now*. I got nothing. I been sleeping on couches and floors these past six months.'

This was news to Teddy. Last he heard, the whole art business had been paying well enough for Grady. He'd sold some paintings, and there were more commissions in the pipeline.

'I thought you was doing okay. You told me that you'd sold some stuff.'

'They didn't pay much, Teddy, and I was spending it as soon as it came in. Sometimes *before* it came in. I had it bad for a while.'

This Teddy did know about. Heroin scared the shit out of him. Blow you could take or leave, but with heroin you were a full-blown, living-out-of-Dumpsters-and-selling-your-sister-for-quarters addict, although Teddy would have paid more than quarters for Marielle Vetters.

'Yeah, but you're all good now, right?'

'Better,' said Grady.

There was a frailty to how he said it that made Teddy fear for him.

'Better than I was.'

'That's something,' said Teddy, not sure what else to say. 'Look, I know Falls End ain't for you, but at least here you have a roof over your head, and a bed to sleep in, and people who'll look out for you. If you got to wait a while for the money to come through, better here than on someone's floor. It's all relative, man.'

'Yeah, all relative. Maybe you're right, Teddy.'

He gripped the back of Teddy's neck and smiled at him, and there was such sadness in his eyes that Teddy would have given a limb to make it go away, any residual anger at Grady's selfishness now forgotten, but he just said 'So you want to go over to Darryl's? There's no percentage in staying here.'

Grady tossed his cigarette butt. 'Sure, why not? You got any weed? I couldn't listen to Darryl's shit with my head straight.'

'Yeah, I got some. I don't want to bring it to Darryl's, though. Shit'll be gone before I got time to find my rolling papers. Let's go back to mine, pick up some beers, have a smoke. When your head's in the right place, we can join the party.'

'Sounds good,' said Grady.

They finished their beers and left them on the bench, then scooted round the side of the bar so they didn't have to see Kathleen Cover and her shitbird husband again. They got bitten some more on the way to Teddy's truck, so back at the house Teddy hunted down a bottle of calamine while Grady put on some music – CSNY, *Four Way Street*, couldn't have been more mellow if Buddha himself was on backing vocals – and then Teddy produced the Baggie of weed, and it was very good weed, and they never did make it to Darryl Shiff's party but instead talked long into the night, and Grady told Teddy things that he had never told anyone before, including the story of the airplane that his father and Paul Scollay had found in the Great North Woods.

'That's it,' said Teddy, through a fug of smoke. 'That's how you do it.'

He stumbled to his bedroom, and Grady heard closets being searched, and drawers being emptied on the floor, and when Teddy returned he was holding a business card in his hand, grinning like it was a winning Powerball ticket.

'The plane, man. You tell them about the plane . . .'

That night, a message was left on the answering service for Darina Flores, the first time any such message had been received in many years.

It had begun.

14

In her dark bedroom, Darina Flores drifted in and out of consciousness. The painkillers disagreed with her, causing tremors in her legs that tore her from sleep. They also provoked peculiar dreams. She couldn't have called them night terrors, for she was herself virtually without fear, but she experienced sensations of descent, of falling into a great emptiness, and she felt the absence of grace with a pain that was unfamiliar to her. The god she served was a pitiless one, and there was no consolation from him in times of distress. He was the god of mirrors, the god of form without substance, the god of blood and tears. Trapped in her misery, she understood why so many chose to believe in the Other God, to follow Him even though she saw in Him only a being as heedless of suffering as her own. Perhaps the only true difference was that her god took pleasure in agony and grief; at least, one might argue, he had a sense of involvement.

She had always considered herself to have a high tolerance for pain, but she had a fear of burns, and a reaction to them that was disproportionate to the severity of the injury. Even a minor burn – the careless brushing of a candle flame, a match held for too long – caused blistering to her skin, and a fierce throbbing that found an echo deep inside her. A psychiatrist might have speculated on childhood trauma, an accident of youth, but she had never talked with a psychiatrist, and any mental health specialist would have been forced to travel further back than distant memories of her childhood to find the source of her terror of burning.

Because her dreams were real: she had fallen, and she had burned, and somewhere inside she was still burning. The Other God had made it so, and she hated Him for it. Now her inner pain had its most ferocious external manifestation yet, the extent of it hidden from her by dressings and the refusal to allow her a mirror.

Barbara Kelly had surprised her in the end. Who could have guessed that she would prove to be so weak and yet so strong, that she would seek to save herself at the last by turning to the Other God, and in doing so would inflict such damage on the woman sent to punish her? My beauty, she thought, now gone; temporarily blind in one eye, with the possibility of lasting damage to her vision caused by the old grounds in the coffee pot sticking to her pupil. She wanted to shed her body like a snake slews off its skin, or a spider leaves its old carapace to wither. She did not want to be trapped in a disfigured shell. In the darkness of her agonies, she feared that it was because she did not wish to see the corruption of her spirit reflected in her outer form.

Each time she woke the boy was there waiting, his ancient eyes like polluted pools against the pallor of his skin. He still had not uttered a word. As an infant he had rarely cried, and as a boy he had never spoken. The doctors who examined him, chosen for their trustworthiness, their commitment to the cause, could find no physical defect to explain the boy's silence, and his mental functions were adjudged to be well above average for his age. As for the goiter upon his neck, that troubled them, and there had been discussions about removing it. She had demurred. It was part of him. After all, that was how she had known it was him. She had thought that it was possible when she felt him kicking in her womb. A sense of his presence had suffused her as though she were enveloped in his embrace, as though he were inside her more as a lover than a developing child, and it had grown in intensity throughout her second and third trimesters so that it became almost oppressive to her, like a cancerous growth in her belly. Expelling him from herself had come as a relief. Then she had looked upon him as he was placed in her arms, and her fingers had traced his lips, and his ears, and the delicacy of his hands, and had paused at the swelling upon his throat. She had gazed into his eyes, and from the blackness of them he had looked back at her, an old being resurrected in a new body.

And now he was beside her, stroking her hand as she moaned upon the sweat-dampened sheets. While they were finishing with Barbara Kelly, Darina had summoned help, but their nearest tame physician was in New York and it took time for him to reach her. Strangely, there was not as much pain as she might have anticipated, not at first. She attributed it to her rage at the bitch who had turned upon her, but as Kelly's life slowly seeped from her beneath blades and fingers, so too the torment in Darina's face seemed to increase, and when Kelly at last died it screamed into red life with her passing.

Deep second-degree burns: that was how they described them. Any more severe and there would have been serious nerve damage, which would at least have numbed the pain, she thought. There was still the possibility that grafts might be necessary, but the doctor had decided to hold off on that decision until a degree of healing had occurred. Some scarring was inevitable, he said, particularly around her injured eye, and there would be significant contracture of the eyelid as the scarring proceeded. The eye hurt more than anything else: it felt like needles were being pushed through it and into her brain.

The eye was patched, and would remain so even after the other dressings were removed. Already her skin was blistering badly. She had been given lubricant for the eye, as well as antibiotic drops. The boy took care of them all and salved her blistered face, and the physician visited each day and commended him on his efforts, even as he kept his distance from him, his nose wrinkling at the faint odor that seemed to rise from the boy regardless of how many showers he took or how clean his clothes were. His breath was the worst: it stank of decay. Darina had grown used to it from long exposure, but it was still unpleasant, even to her.

But then he was an unusual boy, mostly because he wasn't really a boy at all.

'Hurts,' she said. She still had trouble speaking. If she moved her mouth more than a fraction, her lips bled.

The boy who was more than a boy put some gel on his fingers and gently applied it to her lips. He took a plastic bottle with a fixed straw in its cover, slipped the straw into the undamaged side of her mouth, and squeezed some water through. She nodded when she was done.

'Thank you,' she said.

He stroked her hair. A tear rolled from her uninjured eye. Her face felt as though it were aflame.

'The bitch,' she said. 'Look what the bitch did to me.'

And: 'I'm burned, but she is burning too, and her pain will be greater and longer than mine. The bitch, the burning bitch.'

She was not due another painkiller for a couple of hours, so he turned on the TV as a distraction. Together they watched some cartoons, and a comedy show, and a dumb action movie upon which she wouldn't ordinarily have wasted her time but that now acted as a soporific. The night drew on, and the sun rose. She watched the light change through the crack in the drapes. The boy gave her another pill, then changed into his pajamas and curled up on the floor next to her bed as he saw her falling asleep, his head on a pillow and a comforter covering his body only from the waist down. She felt her eyes begin to close, and prepared to exchange real pain for the memory of pain.

From the floor the boy watched her, unfathomable in his strangeness.

* * *

Messages accumulated. Most were inconsequential. Still, the boy made a careful note of each one, and handed it to her when she was sufficiently alert to understand what she was being shown. Minor tasks were postponed for a time, major ones diverted elsewhere. She willed herself to recover. There was too much that needed to be done.

But for all of the boy's solicitude, and all of the care he took with her phone, some contacts went unexamined for a time. The boy did not have access to the old Darina Flores answering service: it had come into existence before he was born, and there had been no reason to acquaint him with it. Anyway, it had been many years since contact had been made through that number.

And so it was that a message inquiring if she was still interested in news of an airplane that might have crashed in the Great North Woods remained unlistened to for days, and a little time was bought.

But only a little.

15

I called Gordon Walsh, a detective who now worked out of the Maine State Police's Southern Major Crimes Unit in Gray. Walsh was about the closest thing I had to a friend in the MSP, although it would have been stretching the point to call him an actual friend. If Walsh was my friend, then I was lonelier than I thought. Actually, if Walsh was *anybody's* friend they were lonelier than they thought.

'You calling to confess a crime?' he said.

'Anything to help you maintain your unblemished arrest record. You have something in particular you'd like me to 'fess up to, or should I just sign a blank form and leave you to fill in the details?'

'You won't even have to fill in your name because it's already there. Just put your "X" on it and we'll do the rest.'

'I'll think about it. Maybe if you helped me out with something it might encourage me to make the right decision. You have any friends in the New Hampshire MCU?'

'No, but I'll have minus friends there if I set you on them. You're a walking formula for negative friendship equity.'

I waited. I was good at waiting. At last, I heard him sigh.

'Come on, give it to me.'

'Kenny Chan. Killed in his house in Bennington in 2006.'

'How did he die?'

'He was broken up and folded into his own safe.'

'Yeah, I think I remember that one. It was part of a spate of safe-foldings back in the day. Robbery?'

'Only of his *joie de vivre*. Whoever did it left the cash in the safe with him.'

'I take it you pulled up the names of the investigating detectives?'

'Nalty and Gulyas.'

'Yeah, Helen Nalty and Bob Gulyas. Nalty won't talk to you. She's straight edge, and in line for promotion to AUC.' AUC was Assistant Unit Commmander. 'Gulyas is retired. I know him a little. He might talk, as long as you don't interrupt. He's not patient like I am. It'll be the usual deal. If you find out something useful—'

– 'then it goes straight to him, and he whispers it in a sympathetic ear,' I finished. 'And if I get in trouble I don't mention his name. I owe you on this one.'

'You owe me on more than this one, but you can start paying now.'

'Go on.'

'Perry Reed.'

'The auto shop guy. I watch the news. What about him?'

'I heard a story that a couple of members of the Saracens motorcycle gang might recently have been relieved of a delivery of narcotics, at gunpoint. That's a tragedy of course, and they've proved strangely unwilling to file a complaint, but the story has it that one of the guys who robbed them might have been black, and the other white, or whiteish. They were very polite. They said "please" and "thank you". One of them may even have used the words "Would you mind . . .?", and he complimented one of the Saracens on the quality of his boots. The quantity and description of the narcotics in question is pretty similar to what we took from Perry Reed and his guys.'

'So Reed ripped off the Saracens? That doesn't sound wise.'

'Reed did *not* rip off the Saracens. I don't think he burned down his own auto lot and titty bar either, even though we found ethyl alcohol in his garage. I think Perry Reed has been set up, and the kiddy stuff is just the icing on the cake. And the description, however basic, of the two men who stole from the Saracens rings bells that seem to echo in your vicinity.'

'Is Perry Reed a supplier of narcotics?'

'Yes.'

'Is Perry Reed a pimp?'

'Yes, and a trafficker of women. And a suspected rapist, both statutory and otherwise: it's said he and his buddies break in the girls before passing them along.'

'How long has he been doing all this?'

'Years. Decades.'

'And now you have him. What's the problem?'

'You know what the problem is. I want to see him in jail, but for stuff that he did do, not for stuff that he didn't.'

'I can only tell you what I've heard.'

'Which is?'

'The drugs were on their way to Reed anyway, but he always uses middlemen for receipt of deliveries. I've also heard that if you get a court order for the phone records of the numbers found on the cell phones, you'll find that Perry Reed and Alex Wilder were both in touch with known traffickers of underage girls, most of them Chinese and Vietnamese, although they had room for Thai and Laotian too.'

'The gun?'

'Only what I've read in the papers. Pearl grips. Classy, as long as you're not seen in public with them.'

'The auto lot and titty bar?'

'Well, that just looks like arson, but I'm no expert.'

'And the kiddy porn?'

'It was in his possession, and he has a reputation.'

Walsh said nothing for a time. 'Still sounds to me like somebody might have had a personal motive for seeing Perry Reed locked up until his hair turns white. Alex Wilder too.'

I gave him a little: not much, but enough. 'Maybe frightened Asian girls weren't the only women they were raping.'

There was the sound of the phone shifting, and I knew that Walsh was making a note.

'So what am I left with here: that it's not legal, but it's just?'

'Would you prefer it the other way around?'

He grunted. It was as close to acquiescence as Walsh was likely to get. 'I'll tell Bob Gulyas to expect a call,' he said.

'Thank you.'

'Whatever. Just remember: I wasn't kidding about that piece of paper with your name on it. If I don't have it, then somebody else does. It's only a matter of time. Oh, and you tell your friends that I said hello.'

I left a message for Bob Gulyas, and he returned the call within the hour. In the course of a twenty-minute phone conversation during which it became clear that he knew more about me than I might have been comfortable with, which suggested that he'd been talking to Walsh, Gulyas told me as much as he knew, or was willing to share, about Kenny Chan's murder.

A gale force wind had set off the alarm in Chan's home, and his security company had been unable to contact him. His girlfriend was listed as a secondary keyholder: she hadn't heard from him in five days, and it was she who found the body. Whoever killed him had taken the trouble to leave the combination written in lipstick on the safe, along with Kenny Chan's name and the years of his birth and death.

'So you figure a woman was involved?' I said.

'His girlfriend had some cosmetics and clothing in a drawer in his bedroom,' said Gulyas, 'but the lipstick didn't match, so unless it was a guy who killed him and just happened to be the kind who carried lipstick in his pocket, then, yeah, we figured a woman.'

'What about the girlfriend?'

'Cindy Keller. She was a model. She'd been working on a shoot in Vegas, and only got back the night before the body was found. He'd been in there for a couple of days by then, so she was in the clear.'

'Sounds like the end of a run of bad luck for Kenny Chan,' I said. 'First his wife, then his business partner. All he had to console him in his grief was the money he made from the sale of his company. Still, better than being poor and grieving, I guess.'

Gulyas laughed. 'Oh, we looked hard at Kenny Chan after Felice was shot, but there was nothing to connect him to the gas station killings beyond circumstantial evidence. Yeah, it seemed his partner was blocking the sale of the company and, yeah, his murder was a lucky break for Chan, but if he planned it then he planned it well. He was so clean even his shit gleamed.'

'And his wife?'

Gulyas didn't laugh this time. 'She was on the One-Oh-One near Milford. Looks like the car skidded, hit some trees, and burst into flames.'

'Any witnesses?'

'None. It was late at night on a quiet stretch of road.'

'How late?'

'Two thirty a.m.'

'What was she doing out by Milford at two thirty in the morning?'

'We never got an answer to that. There was speculation that she might have been having an affair, but that's all it was. If she was screwing around, then she hid it well.'

'So it all remains one big mystery with three heads?'

'I'll tell you something, Mr Parker. I smelled what you smell, but in the end we were advised to let it lie. The word came from real high up, and that word was "Defense".'

'Because Chan's company had been folded into the Defense Department.'

'Exactly.'

'And Pryor Investments?'

'I had two meetings with them. The first was shortly after Chan died, because we found a batch of papers relating to his dealings with Pryor in a safe deposit box in a bank in Boston.'

'Not in his own safe?'

'No.'

'Odd.'

'Yeah.'

'Anything in the papers?'

'Not that I could see. They seemed pretty straightforward, but what I know about business and investments you could write on a stamp.'

'So you went to Pryor?'

'And got stonewalled by a couple of suits. Oh, they were sweet as pie, but told us nothing.'

'And the second visit?'

'Chan's death led us to re-examine the Felice killing, and to glance again at the accident that killed Chan's wife. Pryor obviously cropped up there too.'

'What happened?'

'Different suits, same result. We even got face time with the big suit himself, Garrison Pryor. He used a lot of words like "tragedy" and "regrettable" without ever looking like he knew what they meant. Shortly after we heard the invocation of national security, and that was it. It wasn't as if we didn't have other major crimes to deal with, and you have to learn when to fade away, either temporarily or permanently. You were a cop. You learn that lesson?'

'No.'

'Good. That's why Walsh said I should talk to you. We done here?'

'I think so.'

'I get to ask what this is about?'

'Not yet. Can I have a raincheck on a beer, and if I find something you can pass on I'll share it with you?'

'I'll make a note of it.'

'Do that. I appreciate you taking the time to talk.'

'Talk? Son, I never said a word to you.'

And he hung up.

16

So: could I have walked away from Marielle Vetters' tale, leaving the plane in the Great North Woods to sink finally into the ground, dragged down, if the testimony of the late Harlan Vetters and Paul Scollay was to be believed, by some intent on the part of nature itself? Possibly, but I knew that it would have come back to haunt me in the end: not simply the nagging knowledge that the plane was out there, nor my curiosity about the nature of the partial list of names that Vetters had taken from the wreckage, but because of Brightwell's involvement in the search. It meant that the plane was part of the pattern of my life, and perhaps within it might lie some inkling of the greater game that was being played, one in which I was more than a pawn but less than a king.

Angel and Louis, too, had elected to become involved, for Brightwell had killed Louis's cousin, and anything that concerned the Believers and their legacy was of interest to Louis. His capacity for vengeance was limitless.

But there was one other who had been intimately involved in the matter of Brightwell and the Believers, one who knew more than anyone else about bodies that decayed but did not die, and migrating spirits, more perhaps than he had even admitted to me. His name was Epstein, and he was a rabbi, and a grieving father, and a hunter of fallen angels.

I called New York, and made arrangements to meet him the following evening.

The kosher diner lay on Stanton, and was situated between a deli that was popular with flies, judging by the number of black corpses in the window, and a tailor who had clearly never met a piece of polyester that he didn't like. Epstein was already at the restaurant by the time I arrived: the sight of one of his goons on the door gave his presence away. This one wasn't wearing a yarmulke, but he fitted the type: young, dark-haired, Jewish, and built from bricks and protein. He would be armed too, which probably explained why his right hand was buried deep in the pocket of his navy coat while his left was not. Epstein didn't carry a gun, but the people who surrounded him and ensured his safety most certainly did. The kid didn't seem surprised to see me approach, but that was probably because I'd passed one of his buddies two blocks earlier, and he'd kept watch on me to make sure nobody was following. Angel, in turn, was a block behind him while Louis shadowed him from across the street. In this way, Epstein and I provided gainful employment for at least four people, and thus ensured that the wheels of capitalism kept turning.

The restaurant was as I remembered it from my last visit: a long wooden serving counter to the right, beneath which was a series of glass cases which would usually have contained overstuffed sandwiches and some carefully created specialties – beef tongue polonaise in raisin gravy, stuffed cabbage leaves, chicken livers sautéed in white wine – but were now empty, and a handful of small, round tables along the left wall, on one of which a trio of candles flickered in an ornate silver sconce. There Rabbi Epstein sat, similarly unchanged. He had always struck me as a man who had probably been old before his time, and so his later years had simply accrued without altering him unduly. Only the death of his son might have added to his white hairs and the fine wrinkles on his face, the young man put to death by those who shared something of the beliefs of Brightwell and his kind, if not their nature.

Epstein rose to shake my hand. He was elegantly dressed in a lightweight black silk suit, and a white shirt with a carefully knotted black silk tie. It was another unseasonably warm evening, but the A/C in the restaurant was off. Had I been wearing something similar to Epstein's suit in this heat I'd have been leaving puddles on chairs, but Epstein's hand was dry to the touch, and there was not even a hint of moisture on his face. By contrast, my shirt was stuck to my back beneath my blue wool sport coat.

From the back of the restaurant a woman appeared, dark-haired, brown-eyed, and silent: the deaf mute who had been present on the first occasion that Epstein and I had met here years before. She placed a glass of ice water in front of each of us, and some sprigs of mint. Her eyes turned to me as she did so, and she looked at me with something like interest. I watched her walk away. She was wearing oversized black jeans belted at her slim waist, and a black camisole top. Her hair hung in a single braid down her tanned back, tied with a length of red ribbon at the end. As when last we met, she smelled of cloves and cinnamon.

If Epstein saw the direction of my gaze, he did not acknowledge it. He fussed with the mint, crumbling it into his water, then stirred it with a spoon. There was silverware on the table. Soon food would start to arrive. It was how Epstein preferred to conduct his business.

Epstein seemed distracted, almost as though he were in some discomfort.

'Are you okay?'

Epstein waved a hand in dismissal. 'An unfortunate incident on my way here, nothing more. I was paying a visit to the Stanton Street Shul, and a man not much younger than I called me a "mockey bastard" as I passed him. It's been many years since I heard that term used. It troubled me: the age of the man who said it, the obsolescence of the insult. It was like stepping back to another time.'

He recovered himself, stretching as though the memory of the insult was a physical thing that he could force from his body.

'Still, ignorance has no sell-by date. It's been a while, Mr Parker. It seems that you've been busy since last we met. I continue to follow your entertaining career with much interest.'

I had a suspicion that whatever Epstein knew about me, he hadn't gleaned from the newspapers. Epstein had his own sources, including the senior FBI agent named Ross at the New York field office, a man whose responsibilities included maintaining a file with my name on it, a file that had come into existence following the deaths of my wife and child. A lesser man might have felt paranoid; I just tried to make myself feel wanted instead.

'I wish that was reassuring to know,' I said.

'Oh, I've tried to help you here and there, you know that.'

'Your help has nearly got me killed.'

'But think of the life-changing experiences that you've had as a result.'

'I'm still trying to avoid the most life-changing one of all: dying.'

'And making a success of it, I see. Here you are, alive and well. I await the reason why with much curiosity, but first, let us eat. Liat has prepared food for us, I believe.'

And although she could not have heard him, and his back was to her so that she could not read his lips, the woman called Liat emerged from the kitchen at that very moment carrying a tray covered with stuffed cabbage and derma, a selection of sweet and hot peppers, three kinds of knishes, and two bowls of salads. She moved another table close to ours so that we would have space to eat.

'No fish,' said Epstein. He tapped a finger to the side of his head. 'I remember these things.'

'My friends think I'm phobic,' I said.

'We all have our peculiarities. I knew a woman once who would faint if someone sliced a tomato in front of her. I have never been able to discover if there is a medical term for it.

The closest I've come is "lachanophobia", which appears to be an irrational fear of vegetables.' He leaned forward conspiratorially. 'I must confess that, on occasion, I have used it as a way to avoid eating broccoli.'

Liat returned with a bottle of Goose Bay Sauvignon Blanc, poured each of us a glass, then a third for herself. She took the glass with her and sat on the counter, her legs crossed before her. She placed on her lap a book, a copy of Norman Maclean's *Young Men and Fire*. She did not eat. Neither did she read, although she opened the book before her. She was watching my lips, and I wondered how large a part she was playing in this particular game of Epstein's.

I tried the wine. It tasted good.

'Kosher?' I asked. I couldn't quite keep the surprise from my voice.

'You could be forgiven for thinking otherwise as it's remarkably palatable, but yes: it's from New Zealand.'

So we ate, and talked of families, and the troubles of the world, and steered scrupulously clear of darker matters until Liat came to clear the table, and coffee was brought with a separate jug of milk for me, and always I was conscious of how she kept her eyes on my lips, all pretense of not watching me now set aside. I noticed that Epstein had turned slightly so that she would be able more easily to see his lips as well as mine.

'So,' said Epstein, 'why are you here?'

'Brightwell,' I said.

'Brightwell is . . . gone,' Epstein replied, leaving the ambiguity to hang between us; not dead, but 'gone'. Epstein knew better than anyone the nature of Brightwell.

'For now?' I said.

'Yes. We might have achieved a more permanent solution had you not shot him to death.'

'It was satisfying nonetheless.'

'I'm sure that it was. So is hitting a cockroach with your

shoe, until it starts to crawl again. But what's done is done. Why bring him up now?'

So I told him the story that Marielle Vetters had passed on to me, leaving out only the identities of those involved, and any reference to the town in which they lived.

'An airplane,' said Epstein, when I was done. 'I know nothing about any airplane. I will need to consult. Perhaps others have heard. What else do you have?'

I had made a copy of the list of names that Marielle had given to me.

'The woman's father took this from the plane,' I said, as I slid the photocopy across the table. 'It was part of a cache of papers in a satchel under one of the pilots' seats. He left the rest in the wreckage, according to his daughter.'

Epstein took his wire-framed spectacles from his pocket and carefully hooked the ends over his ears. He had a way of appearing frailer than he was, a pantomime of squints and grimaces. It was a role he played even with those who knew better than to be taken in by it. Perhaps it was just habit by this point, or maybe even he could no longer separate the deception from the reality.

Epstein was not a man who tended to show surprise. He had seen too much of this world, and something of the next, for them to hold too many secrets from him. But now his eyes widened behind the magnified lenses, and his lips moved as though he were repeating the names to himself as a kind of litany.

'Do those names mean anything to you?' I asked. I had not yet told him about Kenny Chan, and the earlier fates of his wife and former business partner. It wasn't that I didn't trust Epstein, but I saw no reason to give him all that I had learned, not without something in return.

'Perhaps,' he said. 'This one.'

He showed me the paper, his finger resting halfway down the page beneath the name Calvin Buchardt. 'He worked quietly for a number of liberal causes for many years. He was involved with the ACLU, Searchlight, NAACP, as well as anti-authoritarian movements in South and Central America. He was a textbook white male with a conscience.'

'I didn't find his name in any of my searches.'

'You might have found him had you looked for "Calvin Book". Only a handful of people knew his real name.'

'Why the secrecy?'

'He always claimed that it was for protection, but it was also a way of distancing himself from his family legacy. His grandfather, William Buchardt, was a neo-Nazi of the most virulent kind: a supporter of appeasement in his youth, and an ally of segregationists, homophobes, and anti-Semites throughout his life. Calvin's father, Edward, refused to have anything to do with the old man once he reached maturity, and Calvin took that a step further by acting as a discreet supporter of the kind of institutions that his grandfather would have put to the torch. It helped that he had a little wealth to his name.'

'Then what's he doing on this list?'

'I suspect that the answer lies in the manner of his passing: he was found gassed to death in a parking garage in Mexico City. It emerged that Calvin was more like his grandfather than his father after all: he had been betraying his friends and their causes for decades. Labor leaders, civil rights workers, lawyers, all given over to their enemies because of Calvin Buchardt.'

'Are you telling me that he killed himself in a fit of remorse?'

Epstein carefully repositioned his coffee spoon.

'I expect that he did feel remorse at the end, but he didn't kill himself. He'd been tied to his car seat, and his tongue had been removed, along with all of his teeth and the tips of his fingers. He had made the mistake of betraying lions as well as lambs. Officially, his remains were never identified, but unofficially . . .'

He returned his attention to the list, and emitted a small *tsk* of distaste.

'Davis Tate,' he said.

'That one I know something of,' I said.

'A preacher of intolerance and calumny,' said Epstein. 'He's a hatemonger, but like most of his kind he lacks a logical consistency, and any kind of backbone. He's rabidly anti-Islamic but he also distrusts Jews. He hates the president of the United States for being black, but lacks the courage to reveal himself as a racist, so he codifies his racism. He calls himself a Christian, but Christ would disown him. He and his kind should be prosecuted for hate speech, but the powers that be get more exercised about a nipple showing during the Superbowl. Fear and hatred are good currency, Mr Parker. They buy votes in elections.'

He took a sip of wine to wash Tate's name from his mouth.

'And now you, Mr Parker? I can only assume that you did some digging of your own, and found something of interest to yourself among these names.'

'This woman, Solene Escott, was the wife of a man named Kenny Chan,' I said. 'The numbers beside her name correspond to the dates of her birth and death. She was killed in a car accident, but that plane went down before, not after, she died. Her death was planned. Brandon Felice, a little farther down, was Kenny Chan's business partner. He was killed in the course of a gas station robbery not long after Escott died. There was no reason to shoot him. The thieves were masked, and they'd got their money.'

'Declined.' Epstein read the word written beside Felice's name. 'And is that a letter "T" after the word?'

'Looks like it.'

'What does "T" stand for?'

'Terminated?' I suggested.

'Possibly. Probably. Is the husband still alive?'

'He was stuffed into his own safe and left there to rot, surrounded by his wealth.'

'Do you have a narrative in mind?'

'Kenny Chan struck a deal to have his wife and partner killed, but the deal came back to bite him in the end.'

'Poetic justice, perhaps. You say his wife was killed in an accident?'

'Accidents can be made to happen, and there were no witnesses. What do you know about a company called Pryor Investments?'

'I may have read the name, but no more than that. Why?'

'Pryor Investments was closely involved with the sale of Kenny Chan's company. The police investigating Chan's death were discouraged from bothering Pryor. It seems that he may have links to the Defense Department.'

'I'll see what we can find out,' said Epstein.

He carefully folded the list, placed it in the inside pocket of his jacket, and stood. 'Where are you staying tonight?' he asked.

'My ex-partner, Walter Cole, offered me a bed at his place.'

'I'd prefer it if you stayed here. It may be that I'll need to contact you urgently, and it would be easier to do so if you remained with Liat. She keeps an apartment upstairs. You'll be quite comfortable, I assure you. One of my men will remain nearby, just in case. I take it you were shadowed here?'

Epstein was familiar with Angel and Louis.

'They're outside.'

'Let them return to their beds. They won't be needed. You'll be safe. I give you my word.'

I called Angel on my cell phone and told him the plan.

'You happy with the arrangement?' he asked.

I looked at Liat. She looked at me.

'I think I can live with it,' I said, and hung up.

The apartment was more than comfortable. It occupied the top two floors of the building, the rest being given over to storage. It was decorated in a vaguely Middle Eastern style: a lot of cushions, a lot of rugs, the dominant tones of red and orange accented by lamps in the corners instead of a central ceiling light. Liat showed me to a guest bedroom with a small private bathroom next door. I showered to cool myself down. When I came out, the lights were off downstairs, and the apartment was quiet.

I put a towel around my waist and sat by the window, looking out on the streets below. I watched couples pass, hand in hand. I saw a man arguing with a child, and a woman remonstrating with them both. I heard music playing in a building nearby, a piano étude that I could not identify. I thought it was a recording until the player stumbled, and a woman laughed in an easy, loving way, and the man's voice answered and the music ceased. I felt like an outsider here, even though I knew these streets, this city. It was not mine, though. It had never been mine. I was a stranger in a familiar land.

Liat entered the room shortly before midnight. She was wearing a cream nightdress that ended above her knees, and her hair hung loose on her shoulders. I had been sitting in darkness, but now she lit the bedside lamp before coming to me. She took my hand and bid me rise. In the lamplight, she examined me. She traced the scars of old wounds, touching each one with her fingertips, as though taking an account of the toll on my body. When she was done, she placed her right hand against my face, and her expression was one of intense compassion.

When she kissed me, I felt her tears against my skin, and I tasted them upon my lips. It had been so long, and I thought: accept this small gift, this tender, fleeting moment.

Liat: only later did I discover the meaning of her name.

Liat: *You are mine.*

I woke shortly after seven. Beside me, the bed was empty. I showered, dressed, and went downstairs. The apartment was quiet. When I entered the kitchen, a middle-aged man was preparing the day's food, and in the restaurant a woman in her sixties was serving coffee and bagels to a short line of customers. Where Epstein and I had sat the night before, an elderly couple now shared a copy of the *Forward*.

'Where is Liat?' I asked the woman behind the counter.

She shrugged, then fumbled in her apron and produced a note. It was not from Liat, but from Epstein. It read:

Progress being made.
Please stay another night.

E

I left the restaurant. One of Epstein's young men sat at a table outside, drinking mint tea. He didn't glance at me when I appeared, nor did he try to follow. I had coffee at a bakery on Houston, and thought of Liat. I wondered where she was, and I thought that I knew.

I believed that she was telling Epstein of my wounds.

I spent the rest of the morning drifting, browsing in bookstores and what few record stores remained in the city – Other Music at 4th and Broadway, Academy Records on West 18th Street – before meeting Angel and Louis for lunch at the Brickyard in Hell's Kitchen.

'You look different,' said Angel.

'Do I?'

'Yeah, like the cat that got the cream, except maybe a cat that thinks the cream might have been spiked. This woman you were staying with, Liat, what did she look like, exactly?'

'Old,' I said.

'Really?'

'And gray.'

'You don't say? I bet she was a heavy-set woman too.'

'Very.'

'I knew it. So she bore no resemblance to that slim, dark-haired piece of work who was pouring the wine last night?'

'None whatsoever.'

'That's very reassuring. Then I guess we're not celebrating the end of the longest dry spell since the Dust Bowl?'

'No,' I said, 'we're not celebrating anything. You ordering the chicken wings?'

'Yep.'

'Try not to choke on a bone. I'm not sure I could find it in my heart to save you.'

Louis's mouth twitched. It might have been a smile.

'For a man who just got laid by one of the Chosen People, you don't look too happy,' he said.

'That's a large assumption.'

'You saying I'm wrong?'

'I'm not saying anything.'

'Okay, man, be coy.'

'Is telling you that it's none of your damn business either way being coy?'

'Yes, it is.'

'Fine. Then I'm being coy.'

'Well, either you didn't get laid, or you did get laid and it was no good, because you *still* don't look completely happy.'

He was right. I couldn't have explained why, even if I'd wanted to, except that I had learned nothing of Liat beyond the scent of her body, the curve of her spine, and the taste of her, while I felt that she had looked deep into me. It was nothing to do with her silence: even as she came her eyes were wide, and her fingers touched my oldest, deepest wounds while her eyes sought the scars on my soul, and I sensed her memorizing those too so that she might tell others of what she had discovered.

'It was a strange night, that's all,' I said.

'Good sex is wasted on you,' said Angel, with feeling. 'You're a lost cause.'

17

Epstein left a message on my cell phone inviting me to meet him at 'our usual venue' at nine that night. I wasn't sure how comfortable I was staying in Liat's apartment again; it wasn't that I minded being used for sex so much as I minded being used for something else under the pretense of sex. I called my old NYPD mentor and partner, Walter Cole, and told him that I might need that offer of a bed after all. He told me in turn that they'd let the dog sleep outside tonight, and I could have its basket. I think Walter was still sore that I'd once named a dog after him, even if it was a very nice dog.

Once again Angel and Louis drifted along behind me as we approached the diner, and once again I was shadowed by Epstein's people. The same, dour, dark-haired young man was standing outside the restaurant when I arrived, still wearing a jacket that was too warm for the weather and holding on very tightly to the gun beneath it. If anything, he looked even more unhappy than the last time we'd met.

'You should try a loose shirt,' I said. 'Or a smaller gun.'

'Go fuck yourself,' he said. He didn't even look at me when he spoke.

'You learn that language at Hebrew school? Standards are falling.'

'Fuck you, prick,' he said, still not looking at me. He was dumb as well as hostile. If you're going to mouth off at someone then, gun or no gun, it's a bad idea to allow them a free swing at you. I didn't take the opportunity to sock him in the jaw or the kidneys, though. I was afraid that he might shoot his foot off. Worse, I was afraid that he might shoot my foot off.

'Did I do something to upset you?' I said.

He didn't reply, just blinked and scowled some more. It was strange, but I thought he might have been trying not to cry.

'You need to watch your manners,' I said.

I could see his jaw tensing as his teeth clenched. He looked like he might be about to take a swing at me, or even pull that gun, but he brought himself under control and let out a breath.

'The rabbi is waiting for you,' he said.

'Thanks. It's been nice talking to you. Let's not do it again sometime.'

I stepped into the restaurant. Liat was still not present. Instead, the older woman who had handed me the note earlier that day was fussing about behind the counter, and Epstein was seated at the same table as before. When I sat down, Epstein raised an index finger to the woman. She produced two cups of thick, dark Arab coffee, and two small glasses of ice water, then disappeared into the kitchen. A minute or so later, I heard a door slam closed somewhere upstairs. There would be no food and no kosher wine tonight, it seemed.

'I get the feeling I've used up my hospitality quota,' I said.

'Not at all,' said Epstein. 'If you'd prefer wine, there is a cooler behind the counter, and some food has been prepared for you, should you be hungry.'

'Coffee is fine.'

'What were you and Adiv talking about outside?'

'Just exchanging pleasantries.'

Epstein's eyes twinkled.

'You know, his name means "pleasant" in both Arabic and Hebrew; "pleasant", and "grateful".'

'Well, it's very appropriate. He has quite the career ahead of him as a greeter.'

'He has feelings for Liat,' said Epstein.

He was young, much younger than Liat. These things hurt a lot when you're young. Then again, they also hurt like a bitch when you're older.

'And how does she feel about him?'

'She does not say,' he replied. He let the double meaning hang.

'Where is she?'

'Elsewhere. She will join us soon. She has tasks to accomplish first.'

'For you?'

He nodded. 'She told me of your wounds.'

There were to be no secrets here, then. 'I didn't know that you read sign language.'

'I have known Liat for a long time. We have learned to communicate in all sorts of ways.'

'And what did she say of my wounds?'

'She told me that she was surprised you were still alive.'

'I hear that a lot.'

'So many injuries. So many times when you should have died, but you did not. I wonder why you have been spared?'

'Maybe I'm immortal.'

'You would not be the first man to think it. I myself still hope to beat the odds. But, no, I don't think that you're immortal. Someday you'll die: the question is whether you'll come back again.'

'Like Brightwell and his kind?'

'Do you think that you might share something of their nature?'

'No.'

I sipped the coffee. It was too sweet for me. Arab coffee always has been.

'You seem very certain of that.'

'I'm not like them.'

'That wasn't the question.'

'Is this a test?'

'Call it an exploration of ideas.'

'Call it what you want. I don't know what you're talking about.'

'Do you dream of falling, of burning?'

'No.' *Yes.*

'I don't believe you. What do you dream?'

'Is that why you brought me back here, to interrogate me about my dreams?'

'There is truth in them, or an attempt to understand truths.'

I pushed the coffee away.

'Let this go, rabbi. It won't lead us anywhere profitable.'

Behind me, the door opened. I looked back, expecting to see the dark-haired youth with the thwarted feelings. Instead, it was the object of his desire. Liat was dressed in blue jeans and a long coat of sky blue silk. Her hair was braided once again. She looked very beautiful, even with the gun in her hand.

Two of Epstein's young men joined us from the kitchen. They were also armed. One of them walked to the front of the restaurant and pulled the shades, cutting us off from outside, while Liat pulled down another shade on the door. The second gunman kept an eye on me while Epstein removed the cell phone from my pocket. It buzzed in his hand. The number of the caller was blocked.

'Your friends, I assume?' said Epstein.

'They worry about my health in the big city.'

'Answer it. Tell them everything is fine.'

The man who had pulled down the window shades had blond hair and a soft blond beard. It gave him an unfortunate and inappropriate resemblance to a Nazi. He also had a suppressor which he fitted to the muzzle of his pistol before pointing it at my head.

'Answer it,' repeated Epstein.

I did as I was told. Long ago, Angel, Louis and I had agreed a series of red-flag words for circumstances just like this one. I used none of them now, but simply told them that all was well. If I called them in, there would be bloodshed, and nothing would ever be the same again. Better to wait, and see how this played out. I had to believe that Epstein did not want me dead, and I knew that I had done nothing that might cause him to turn against me.

'I thought I could trust you,' I said, once I had ended the call.

'My sentiments exactly. Are you armed?'

'No.'

'That's unusual for you. Are you certain?'

I stood slowly, put my hands up, and turned to face the wall. I smelled Liat's scent, and felt her hands upon me.

'And there I was thinking we had something special,' I said to her.

But she, of course, did not reply.

She stepped back, and I sat down again. This time there were no sly looks as she leaned against the counter. Her face betrayed nothing.

'Why are you behaving like this?' I asked Epstein. 'You know what I've done. I've fought the same fight that you have. Those wounds didn't come out of nowhere.'

'I sacrificed a son,' said Epstein.

'And I a wife and child.'

'They were lost to you before all this began.'

'No, they're part of it. I know they are.'

'You know nothing. You don't even know yourself. The first question one must ask of a thing is, what is its nature? What is *your* nature, Mr Parker?'

I wanted to spring at him for his dismissal of the deaths of my wife and daughter. I wanted to take his throat in my hands and crush it, to pummel him until there was nothing

159

left but a mask of blood. I wanted to put a gun in the mouths of his thugs, his religious soldiers, and watch them squirm. If those whom I had thought of as allies were prepared to turn their guns on me, then I had no need of enemies.

I took a breath and closed my eyes. When I opened them again the anger had begun to fade. If this was a provocation, I would not rise to it.

'You're quoting Marcus Aurelius,' I said. 'Either you've read the *Meditations*, or a serial killer novel. I'll give you the benefit of the doubt and assume the former, in which case you'll know he also warned that each day one would meet violent, ungrateful, uncharitable men, and their actions arose through ignorance of good and evil. If you want to understand a man's nature, he said, look to what he shuns, and what he cleaves to. I think I overestimated you, rabbi. Underneath your cultivated veneer of calm and wisdom, you're a confused, frightened man.'

'And I *know* it,' he replied. 'I will admit to it. But you, you refuse to look too deeply into yourself for fear of what you might find there. What are you, Mr Parker? What *are* you?'

I stood slowly. The man with the suppressor on his gun tracked me.

'I'm the man who killed the one who took your son,' I said, and I saw him flinch. 'I did what you and your people could not. Now what are you going to do, rabbi: shoot me? Bury me somewhere deep along with the others you've found, the ones who think they're fallen angels or risen demons? Do it. I'm tired. Whatever wrong I've done, whatever my failings, I've tried to make reparation for them. I have nothing left to prove to you. If you think I do, then you're a fool.'

For a moment nobody moved, and nobody spoke. Liat's eyes moved from my face to the rabbi's. He glanced at her, and I saw him give her the barest nod. From the pocket of her coat she produced a sheet of paper and tossed it on the table before me.

'What is it?' I asked.

'It's a list of names,' said Epstein. 'It's similar to the one that you gave to me yesterday, but it came from a different source. It's more recent.'

I didn't touch it. I left it where it lay.

'Don't you want to look at it?'

'No. I'm done with you. I'm going to walk out of here, and if one of your knuckle-draggers wants to shoot me in the back along the way, then let him, but you'll all be dead before the night is out. Angel and Louis will tear you apart, and for the next eleven months, rabbi, every time one of your children rises to say Kaddish for you, they'll receive a piece of you in the mail.'

Epstein raised his right hand, then let it fall gently. The guns were lowered, and I heard a click as a hammer was slowly eased down. The fear and anger that had briefly animated Epstein left him, and he was once again as he had always been, or seemed to be.

'If you wish to leave, none here will stop you,' he said. 'But look at the list first.'

'Why?'

Epstein smiled sadly.

'Because your name is on it.'

18

When I was seventeen, and my mother and I were living with my grandfather in Scarborough, Maine, following my father's death, a man named Lambton Everett IV would come visit, and he and my grandfather would share a beer on a seat in the yard or, if the weather was cold, they'd share something stronger: blended Scotch, mostly, on the grounds that they weren't single malt men or, if they were, then they couldn't afford to be so on a regular basis, and therefore there was no point in raising false expectations for their palates.

Lambton Everett IV was a long string of misery, a man who never owned an item of clothing that fitted him correctly. In part this was because his body was so indiscriminately proportioned that no cloth that was not cut to measure could ever have accommodated his limbs without leaving a sock peeping or a forearm exposed halfway to the elbow. Shirts hung from him like collapsed sails from a mast, and his suits appeared to have been stolen randomly from the dead. Yet even had his suits been made from the finest Italian wool, and his shirts spun from silks beloved of kings, Lambton Everett IV would still have looked like a scarecrow that had tired of its frame and wobbled unsteadily from its field to seek pastures new. With his downturned mouth, and his huge ears, and his balding, pointed head, he was a source of genial terror at Halloween, and prided himself on the fact that he didn't have to dress up as a ghoul to scare the children.

There hadn't even been three Lambton Everetts before him: the numeral was an affectation, a private joke that not even my grandfather understood. It lent him a certain gravitas among those who didn't know him well enough to be able to spot the fraud, and gave his friends and neighbors something over which to shake their heads, which is a very important gift to bequeath to others in certain circles.

But my grandfather liked Lambton Everett IV because he had known him for a long time and believed that his flaws were minor, and his decencies major. Lambton Everett IV appeared never to have been married, and it was said that he was a bachelor of the most pronounced kind. He seemed to have little sexual interest in women, and none whatsoever in men. There were those who were convinced that Lambton Everett IV would die a virgin; my grandfather speculated that he might possibly have tried intercourse once, if only to strike it from the short list of things he felt that he should do before he passed away.

But it turned out that my grandfather didn't know Lambton Everett IV at all; or rather he knew only one Lambton, the face that Lambton had chosen to present to the world, but that face bore no more relation to the reality of the man than a mask bears to its wearer. Lambton shared little with my grandfather about his past; my grandfather knew him only in the present, in his Maine existence, and he accepted the fact of this with no rancor. In his bones, he knew Lambton to be a good man, and that was enough for him.

Lambton Everett IV was found dead in his house in Wells on a gray Tuesday morning in December. He had failed to turn up at the Big 20 Bowl for his regular Monday morning session, and telephone messages did not elicit a response from him. Two members of his bowling team visited him shortly after breakfast the next morning. They rang the doorbell with no result, then walked to the back of the house and peered in through the kitchen window, where they saw Lambton lying on the floor, his hand clutched to his chest and his face frozen in an agonized grimace. He had gone quickly, the coroner later said: the pain of the heart attack had been immense, but brief.

My grandfather was one of four men who carried the casket from the church on the morning of the funeral, but he was surprised to be informed by Lambton's lawyer that Lambton had nominated him as executor of his will. The lawyer also gave my grandfather a letter addressed to him in Lambton's messy scrawl. It was short and to the point: it apologized to my grandfather for springing the executorship on him but promised that it would not be an arduous task. Lambton's instructions for the disposal of his estate were relatively simple, mostly involving the dispersal of the proceeds of the sale of his house and possessions among a number of named charities. Ten percent was to be given to my grandfather to do with as he saw fit, along with a gold-and-onyx pocket watch that had been in Lambton's family for three generations. My grandfather was also directed to an album of photographs and newspaper clippings in Lambton's bedroom closet, the contents of which Lambton requested he share only with those who might understand them.

It is difficult for men and women to keep secrets these days, especially concerning matters that might, at some point, have found their way into the media. A quick Internet search can expose even the most personal of histories to the light, and a generation has grown used to being able to access such information with the click of a mouse, but it was not always so. I think now of my grandfather seated at Lambton Everett's kitchen table, the album open before him in the fading winter daylight, and the sense he had that Lambton's shade was somewhere nearby, watching him carefully as his secret pain was exposed at last. Later my grandfather would say that, in looking through the album, he felt like a surgeon lancing a boil, releasing liquid and pus, scouring the infection so Lambton Everett IV might be permitted the peace in death that had been denied him in life.

The album revealed another Lambton Everett, a young man with a wife named Joyce and a son called James. He was still recognizably himself, according to my grandfather: a gangling man, an awkward yet strangely handsome individual, smiling contentedly beside his tiny, pretty wife and his grinning son. In the final picture taken of them, his wife and child were twenty-nine and six respectively. Lambton was thirty-two. The picture was dated May 14, 1965, the place Ankeny, Iowa. Three days later, Joyce and James Everett were dead.

Harman Truelove was twenty-three years old. He had been dismissed from his job slaughtering hogs for undue cruelty to the animals, his sadism exceptional even in a profession where casual brutality was the norm, inflicted by men of subnormal intelligence on animals that were probably smarter than themselves, and certainly more worthy of continuing their existence. Harman Truelove's response to his firing was to set fire to the pens housing the hogs awaiting slaughter, burning two hundred of the animals alive, before hitting the road with only a single change of clothing, sixty-seven dollars, and a set of butcher knives. He hitched a ride as far as Bondurant with a man named Roger Madden, who lied and said that he was going no farther just to get Harman Truelove out of his truck because, as he later told police, 'the boy wasn't right'.

Harman ate a bowl of soup in the Hungry Owl Diner, left a quarter as a tip, and started walking. He had decided that he would stop when the sun began to set, which it did just as he reached the house of Joyce and Lambton Everett, and their son James. Lambton, who had traveled to a conference of insurance adjusters in Cleveland, was not home, but his wife and child were.

And they spent a long night with Harman Truelove and his knives.

*　　*　　*

Lambton got the call in Cleveland the following day. Harman Truelove had been picked up by police as he headed northwest on foot toward, he said, Polk City. He hadn't even bothered to change his clothes, and he was sticky with blood. He had left a trail of it from the Everetts' bedroom, all the way through the house, and halfway down their garden path. Curiously, he had cleaned his knives before he left.

This my grandfather learned from the album at Lambton Everett's kitchen table. He would later recall softly touching the face of the woman and the boy in the picture with his fingertips, and allowing his hand to hover over Lambton's image, just as he might have done if the man were seated before him, seeking to express his sorrow and regret yet conscious that Lambton was a man who had always refrained from unnecessary physical contact. Even his handshakes had been as delicate as the touch of an insect's wings against one's skin. My grandfather had always considered it merely to be another of Lambton's peculiarities, like his refusal to eat meat of any kind and his particular hatred for the smell of bacon or pork. Now the odd details of Lambton's personality began to take a new form, each making a terrible kind of sense in the context of what he had endured in life.

'You should have told me, my friend,' my grandfather said aloud to the listening silence, and the drapes behind him shifted slightly in a cool winter breeze, although the day outside was still as stone. 'You should have told me, and I would have understood. I would never have mentioned it to another soul. I would have kept your secret. But you should have told me.'

And he was overcome by the knowledge of his old friend's suffering, now at an end – no, *almost* at an end, for the story was not yet fully told, and there were more pages to come. Not many, but enough.

Harman Truelove refused to confess to his crime. He declined to speak to the police or even to his own public defender, and did not answer when his lawyer asked him where the bruises on his face and body had come from, for the police had tried hard to make him talk. There was a trial, although few witnesses were called, for Harman Truelove's guilt was never in doubt. Something of Harman Truelove's past was revealed in the course of the police investigation, but more was kept hidden, and only a handful of people were privy to it: years of physical abuse, dating back even to his time in the womb when Harman's father, an alcoholic itinerant laborer and serial despoiler of women, had tried to induce an abortion in Harman's mother by kicking her repeatedly in the stomach; the subsequent death of his mother when Harman was two years old, ostensibly by her own hand in a bath of lukewarm water, although the coroner was heard to wonder why a woman who had been intent upon slitting her arm open with a straight razor might also have bathwater in her lungs; the years spent on the road with his father, beating following beating until Harman Truelove could not speak without stammering; and the death at last of that terrible man who choked on his own vomit while lying unconscious in a drunken stupor, his twelve-year-old son found beside him holding his father's cold hand, gripping it so tightly that the rigor mortis had sealed the child's hand in the father's and the police had to break the dead man's fingers to release his son. By mutual agreement, the prosecutor and defender decided that it was unnecessary to share such information with the jury, and only after Harman Truelove had left this earth did it become public knowledge.

Before sentencing, Lambton Everett requested a moment with the judge, a dour yet fair man named Clarence P. Douglas, who, despite being at least two decades from retirement, tended to inhabit his role in the manner of a man who was set to throw it all in the following day and claim his watch and pension, with subsequent plans for nothing more arduous than fishing, drinking, and reading. He didn't seem to care whom he offended by manner or decision just as long as whatever he did was in accordance, insofar as was possible, with the requirements of both law and justice.

A record of their conversation found its way into the local newspapers following Douglas's eventual retirement, since Lambton Everett had placed no stipulation of secrecy upon him, and Douglas clearly felt that it did not reflect badly on the man: quite the opposite. The article in question was one of the final entries in the album, although my grandfather felt that it had been placed there with a degree of reluctance, as it had not been as carefully cut and pasted as the others, and was separated from the previous cutting by two blank pages. My grandfather took the view that it had been added out of a desire for completeness, but Lambton Everett was somehow embarrassed by it.

In the oak-lined quiet of his chambers, the judge was requested by Lambton Everett to spare Harman Truelove from death by hanging at the state penitentiary in Fort Madison. He did not want 'the boy' to be executed, he said. The judge was surprised, and more. He asked Lambton why Harman Truelove should not be subject to the full vengeance of the law.

'You don't need me to tell you, sir,' said Judge Douglas, 'that what Harman Truelove did was evil, as bad a thing as I ever heard of.'

And Lambton, who knew some but not all of Harman Truelove's past, replied, 'Yes, your honor, what he did was as close to pure evil as makes no difference, but the boy himself isn't evil. He never had the start in life that the rest of us had. What followed wasn't much better, and I think it drove him crazy. Somebody took a child and twisted him until he wasn't even human any longer. I looked at him in that courtroom, and I reckoned that he was in even more pain than I was. Don't misunderstand me, your honor: I hate him for what he did, and I can't ever forgive him for it, but

I don't want his blood on my conscience. Put him away somewhere that he can't hurt anyone ever again, but don't kill him, not in my name.'

Judge Douglas sat back in his leather chair, folded his hands across his belly, and thought that Lambton Everett might well be the most unusual individual who had ever set foot in his chambers. He was more used to hearing the hounds baying for blood, ready to tear apart the accused themselves if the law wasn't prepared to sate them. Few lambs crossed the threshold of his courtroom, and fewer merciful men.

'I hear you, Mr Everett,' he said. 'I even admire you for your sentiments, and it could be you're right in some of what you say, but the law requires that the boy should die. I suggest otherwise, and they'd curse my name right along with his until the day they put me in the ground. If it helps you to sleep any easier, his blood isn't on your hands, nor on mine. And maybe ruminate on this: if that boy is in as much pain as you think, then it could be that the kindest thing anyone could do for him is to put an end to it once and for all.'

Lambton Everett took in his surroundings, the leather furnishings and the book-lined walls, as Clarence Douglas marked the traces of grief upon his face. He had not met Lambton until the case came to trial, but he was well versed in trauma and loss. What kind of man, he wondered, pleads for the life of another who has cut apart his wife and child? Not merely a good one, he decided, but a man who carried something of Christ Himself within him, and Clarence Douglas felt humbled in the man's presence.

'Mr Everett, I can tell the boy that you asked for his life to be spared. Should you choose to do so, it could also be arranged for you to visit with him, and you could tell him yourself. If you had any questions, you could put them to him, and see how he responds.'

'Questions?' said Lambton, looking up at the judge. 'What questions could I have for him?'

'Well, you might want to ask him why he did what he did,' said Clarence Douglas. 'He never told anyone why he murdered your wife and son. He never said anything at all, barring the word "no" when they asked him if it was he who had taken the lives of your wife and boy, even though there's no doubt that it was his hand that did for them. One word, that's all they got out of him. I'll tell you the truth, Mr Everett: there are doctors, psychiatrists and their kind, who are curious as all hell about that boy, but he's as much an enigma to them now as he was when they put the cuffs on him. Even allowing for his history, there's no explanation for what he did. There are folk who've had worse upbringings than him, worse by a country mile, but they never killed an innocent woman and her little boy because of it.'

He shuffled awkwardly in his seat, for there was a dreadful intensity to Lambton Everett's gaze that made Clarence Douglas regret he had ever started talking about the murderer Harman Truelove, that he had ever even agreed to admit Lambton Everett into his chambers.

'There is no "why"', said Lambton, slowly and deliberately. 'There can never be. Even if he came up with some answer for me, it would have no meaning, no weight in this world or the next, so I don't want to talk to him. I don't even want to look at him again after this day. I just didn't want to add to his suffering, or to mine. I didn't want to add to the suffering of the world itself. I figure it has enough to be getting along with. It's never going to run out.'

'I'm sorry, Mr Everett,' said Clarence Douglas. 'I wish there was something more that I could do for you.'

So Lambton Everett returned to the courtroom, and the jury read their verdict, and Judge Clarence Douglas passed sentence, and some time later Harman Truelove took the long drop.

And Lambton Everett eventually traveled northeast, making for the sea, and he came to rest at last in Wells. Although he said nothing of his past, still he brought it with him in his heart, and in his mind, and in an album of old photographs and yellowed newspaper clippings.

My grandfather turned back to the picture of Lambton with his family. Yes, he was still recognizably a younger version of the man that my grandfather had known, but the years had exacerbated his awkwardness, and the flawed dimensions of his limbs. It struck my grandfather that people sometimes spoke of men and women being broken by grief and loss, and they meant by that a psychological or emotional fracturing, but Lambton Everett resembled a man who had been physically broken, one who had been torn apart and then imperfectly reassembled, and he had spent the remainder of his life struggling with the physical legacy of what had been visited upon him.

My grandfather closed the album, and he shut his eyes, and he registered Lambton Everett's presence nearby, could almost smell the scent of pipe tobacco and Old Spice that had been so much a part of him.

'Go on, now,' said my grandfather. 'Go to them. They've waited for you long enough.'

He thought that he heard the drapes flutter once more behind him, and there was a sound that might have been an exhalation, like a second dying, and then the scent faded, and he felt the emptiness of the room, and he opened his eyes again as his ears discerned a soft ticking.

'Ah,' he said. 'Ah.'

On the table before him was Lambton Everett's pocket watch, the one that he had bequeathed to my grandfather in his will. But my grandfather had not taken it from the closet in which he had found it alongside the album. He had left it on Lambton's bed. He was certain of it, as certain as he was of anything in this world.

He slipped the watch into his pocket, and put the album under his arm, and that night, while I watched, he burned the record of Lambton Everett's pain on a pyre behind his house. When I asked him what he was doing he shared with me Lambton Everett's story, and it came to be a foretelling of what was to pass in my own life. For, like Lambton, I would see my wife and child torn apart, and I would travel to this northern state, and there my pain would find its form.

Now, seated at that small, dark table on the Lower East Side, the paper Epstein had given to me held tightly in my hand, I thought again of Lambton Everett, and that bond I had imagined as linking our experiences was severed. What kind of man pleads for the life of one who has taken his wife and child from him, Judge Douglas had asked himself: a good man, was the answer, a man worthy of salvation.

But what kind of man takes the life of one who has murdered his wife and child? A vengeful one? A man driven by wrath, twisted by grief? Lambton Everett had appeared broken in form, but the best of him had remained intact within. It was as if his body had been forced to absorb entirely the impact of the blow in order for his spirit, his soul, to remain unsullied.

I was not Lambton Everett. I had taken many lives. I had killed, over and over, in the hope that it might ease my pain, but instead I had fueled it. Had I damned myself by my actions, or had I always been damned? Was that why my name was on this list?

'Liat, pour Mr Parker a glass of wine,' said Epstein. 'I will take one as well.'

The list contained eight names. Unlike the document given to me by Marielle Vetters it was printed, not typewritten. Davis Tate's name was on this list too but, his apart, my own name was the only one that I recognized. There were no other letters or symbols beside it, no numbers that might be dates or figures. It stood alone, and was printed not in black ink, but in red.

Liat placed two glasses on the table, and filled them both with red wine, not white. She left the bottle.

'Where did you get this list?' I asked Epstein.

'A woman contacted us through an intermediary, a lawyer in our employ,' said Epstein. 'She told him that she had been engaged for decades in a process of blackmail, bribery and solicitation. She had hundreds of names, of which this list was just a taster. She said that she had been responsible for the destruction of families, careers, even lives.'

'On whose behalf?'

'On behalf of an organization with no true name, although some of those like her termed it the "Army of Night".'

'Do we know anything about it?'

'"We?"'

I realized that there were still guns surrounding me, and my life might well be in the balance here, but I would not give them the satisfaction of yielding to their doubts about me.

'Oh, I'm sorry, are "we" still playing that game?'

'You still haven't explained why your name is on that list,' said the blond man.

'And I didn't catch your name,' I said.

'Yonathan,' he replied.

'Well, Yonathan, I don't know you well enough to submit to your questions. Neither do I know you well enough to care if something happens to you when this is all done, so why don't you just keep quiet and let the grown-ups talk?'

I thought that I caught Liat's smile, but it was gone before I could be sure. Yonathan bristled, and his face went red. Had Epstein not been present, he might have lunged for me. Even with Epstein's presence to hold him in check, he still looked like he might take his chances. I was glad Liat had left the wine bottle. I hadn't touched my glass, but the bottle was close by my right hand. If Yonathan or anyone else tried to lay a hand on me, I planned to shred some skulls before I went down.

'Enough,' said Epstein. He scowled at Yonathan before returning his attention to me. 'The question remains pertinent: why is your name on that list?'

'I don't know,' I said.

'He's lying,' said Yonathan. 'Even if he knew, he would not tell us.'

Yonathan clearly had testosterone issues. The hormones were clouding his brain.

'Get out,' said Epstein.

'But—' Yonathan began.

'I told you once to keep quiet, and you did not listen. Go outside and keep Adiv company. You can brood together.'

Yonathan looked like he might be about to start objecting again, but it took only a scowl from Liat to convince him otherwise. He left with as much bad grace as he could muster, even going so far as to nudge me with his shoulder as he passed.

'You need to organize one of those staff training weekends,' I said to Epstein. 'Take them out into the wilderness, then lose them and start all over again.'

'He is young,' Epstein replied. 'They all are. And they're concerned, as am I. You've managed to get too close to us, Mr Parker, and now your very nature is in doubt.'

There was too much tension in the air. I felt like I was taking it in with every breath. I paused for a moment and tried to let myself relax. It was difficult under the circumstances, but somehow I managed.

'Tate apart, who are the others on this list?' I asked.

'Some have been definitely identified: two are members of the Kansas and Texas Houses of Representatives respectively – one liberal, one conservative. Both are tipped for greater things. Another is a corporate lawyer. The rest we're still working on but they appear to be, for want of a better term, regular people.'

'Did this woman give any indication as to why she had chosen to provide these particular names?'

'Our lawyers received a follow-up email from a temporary Yahoo account. It claimed that substantial bribes had been paid to three of those on the list. Two more had been blackmailed: one over hidden homosexual tendencies, the other over a series of affairs with much younger women. Documentary evidence sent as attachments to the email appeared to support her claims.'

'So that accounts for five of the names. Did she say anything about me?'

I saw the possibility of a lie flicker on Epstein's face. He tried to hide it, but he couldn't.

'She didn't mention me, did she?'

'No,' said Epstein. 'Not initially.'

'But when your lawyer passed the list on to you, you instructed him to ask her, right?'

'Yes.'

'And what did she say?'

'She could not confirm if any approaches had been made to you. She said that she had not put your name on the list, and you had not been her responsibility.'

'So who added my name to the list?'

'That doesn't matter.'

'It does to me, because it's left me under the gun. You know. Who was responsible?'

'Brightwell,' said Epstein. 'She said Brightwell insisted that it should be added.'

'When?'

'Shortly before you killed him.'

We were coming close to it now, the point of all this, the nexus of Epstein's doubts about me.

'Do you think I killed Brightwell because I knew he put my name on this list?'

'Well, did you?'

'No. I killed him because he was a monster, and because he would have killed me otherwise.'

Epstein shook his head. 'I don't think that Brightwell wanted to kill you. I suspect he was convinced that you were like him. Brightwell believed you were a fallen angel, a rebel against the Divine. You had forgotten your own nature, or had turned against it, but you might still be convinced to turn again. He saw in you a potential ally.'

'Or an enemy.'

'That's what we're trying to establish.'

'Really? It feels like a kangaroo court. All that's missing is the noose.'

'You're being overdramatic.'

'I don't think so. There are a lot of guns on show, and none of them belongs to me.'

'Just a few more questions, Mr Parker. We're almost done.'

I nodded. What more could I do?

'The woman said something else about you. She said that your name had recently come up again, that there were those within her organization who considered you to be important. It was why she chose to send that particular list of names to us.'

Epstein reached out and took my hands in his. The pads of his index fingers pressed against the pulses on my wrists. To my right, I felt the intensity of Liat's regard. It was like being hooked up to some kind of human lie detector, except this one would not be fooled.

'Did they ever approach you with an offer, or a bribe?'

'No.'

'Did they ever threaten you?'

'People have been threatening me for a decade, Brightwell and his kind among them.'

'And how have you responded?'

'You know how I've responded. I have their blood on my hands. In some cases, so do you.'

'Do you belong to this Army of Night?'

'No.'

176

I heard a buzzing to my left. A wasp was bouncing against the mirror above my head. From the sluggishness of its movements, it looked like it was dying. The sight of it recalled another meeting with Epstein, one in which he spoke of parasitic wasps that laid their eggs in spiders. The spider carried the larvae as they developed, and they in turn altered its behavior, causing it to change the webs that it spun so that, when the larvae finally erupted from its body, they would have a cushioned web upon which to rest while they fed upon the remains of the arachnid in which they had gestated. Epstein had told me that there were entities who did the same to men, dark passengers on the human soul, carried unawares for years, even decades, until it came time to reveal their true natures, and then they consumed the consciousness of their hosts.

I watched Epstein follow the progress of the dying insect, and I knew that he was remembering the same conversation.

'I'd know,' I said. 'By now, I would know if I carried one of them inside me.'

'Are you sure?'

'There have been too many opportunities for it to emerge, too many times when it could have changed the course of events by doing so. If it dwelled within me, it could have shown itself and saved some of its own, but nothing came to save them. Nothing.'

Again, Epstein's eyes flicked to Liat, and I understood it was her response that would determine what happened next. The gunmen watched her too, and I saw them ease their fingers beneath the trigger guards in anticipation. A tiny bead of sweat leaked from Epstein's scalp, like a tear from some hidden eye.

Liat nodded, and I felt myself tense to receive the bullets.

Instead, Epstein released his hold upon my wrists and sat back. The guns vanished, and so did the remaining gunman. Only Liat, Epstein, and I stayed.

'Let us drink, Mr Parker,' said Epstein. 'We are done.'

I stared down at my hands. They were trembling slightly. I stilled them with an effort of will.

'Go to hell,' I said, and I left them to their wine.

III

I rage, I melt, I burn,
The feeble God has stab'd me to the Heart.

'Acis and Galatea', John Gay
(1685–1732)

19

Darina Flores sat in an armchair, the boy sitting, unmoving, at her feet. She stroked his thinning hair, the scalp damp yet curiously cold against her fingertips. It was the first time she had left her bed since what she now thought of as the 'incident'. She had insisted that the dosages of pain medication should be decreased, for she hated the wooziness and the loss of control it brought. Instead she was striving for a balance between tolerable pain and a degree of clarity.

The doctor had come again that morning. He had removed the dressings from her face and she had watched him closely as he did so, seeking some clue in his eyes to the damage that had been inflicted upon her, but his expression remained disinterested throughout. He was a slight man in his early fifties, his fingers long and tapering, the nails professionally manicured. He struck her as mildly effeminate, although she knew that he was straight. She knew everything about him: it was the main reason why he had been chosen to treat her. One of the great benefits of having detailed personal knowledge of an individual was the way in which it deprived that person of the ability to decline an invitation.

'It's healing as well as can be expected, under the circumstances,' he told her. 'How does your eye feel?'

'Like there are needles sticking in it,' she replied.

'You're keeping it lubricated? That's important.'

'Will my sight—?' Her throat felt very dry, and she had trouble enunciating her words. She thought for a moment that there might have been some damage to her tongue, or

181

her vocal cords, until she realized that she had hardly spoken more than a few words in days. When she tried again, speech came more easily. 'Will my sight be restored?'

'I expect so, in time, although I can't guarantee that you'll ever have perfect vision in that eye.' She resisted the urge to lash out at him, so casual was his tone. 'The cornea is also likely to grow opaque in the long term. We could, of course, examine the possibility of a corneal transplant. It's a relatively commonplace procedure now, generally done on an outpatient basis. The main issue is securing a suitable cornea from a recently deceased individual.'

'That won't be a problem,' she said.

He smiled indulgently. 'I didn't mean that we should do it right now.'

'Neither did I.'

His smile faded, and she noticed a slight tremor creep into his fingers.

'I haven't looked at myself,' she said. 'There are no mirrors in the room, and my son has kept the ones in the bathroom covered.'

'Those were my instructions,' said the doctor.

'Why? Am I so terrible now?'

He was good, she gave him that. He did not look away, and he did not betray his true feelings about her.

'It's too early. The burns are still raw. Once they begin to heal, we'll have options. Sometimes, patients will look at themselves in the immediate aftermath of an . . . *accident* like yours, and they will despair. That's true of any serious injury or illness. The early days and weeks are always the hardest. Patients feel that they can't go on, or don't want to go on. In your case, time will heal your wounds, and, as I've told you, what time can't heal, surgeons can. We've come a long way in our ability to treat burn victims.'

He patted her on the arm, a gesture of comfort and assurance that he had probably made to his patients a thousand times before, and she hated him for it, hated him for his lies, and his blank visage, and for even thinking he could get away with patronizing her. He sensed that he had overstepped some mark, so he turned his back on her and began putting away his equipment and dressings. Still, her obvious antagonism seemed to have goaded him, and he could not resist attempting to assert his superiority over her.

'You should have gone to a hospital, though,' he said. 'I warned you at the beginning: had you submitted to proper care, I might be more optimistic about any possible outcomes. Now we'll just have to do our best with what we have.'

The boy appeared beside him. The doctor had not even heard him enter the room, and so it seemed to the older man that he had somehow materialized out of the shadows, drawing black atoms from the ether to reconstitute himself in the gloomy room. In his hand the boy held a photograph of a girl aged sixteen, perhaps a little younger. Her hairstyle and mode of dress indicated that the picture had not been taken recently. He turned the photograph so that it faced the doctor, like a conjuror displaying the crucial card in a sleight-of-hand trick. The doctor paled visibly.

'Remember your manners, Doctor,' said Darina. 'Don't forget who disposed of the evidence of your last botched procedure. Use that tone with me again, and we'll bury you next to that girl and her fetus.'

The doctor said nothing more, and left the room without looking back.

Now here she was, out of bed for the first time since that bitch had scarred her. She wore a loose, open-necked shirt over a pair of sweat pants, and her feet were bare. It was hardly elegant, but wearing a buttoned shirt meant that she did not have to pull anything on over her head, and the sweats were comfortable and nothing more. The boy had brought her a glass of brandy at her request. She sipped it through a straw in order to avoid stinging her damaged lips with liquor. Maybe it wasn't the best idea to mix alcohol and painkillers, but it was only a small glass, and she had been thirsting for a proper drink for days.

The boy began playing with his toy soldiers in their big wooden fort. They were knights on foot and on horseback, made from tin and carefully painted. She had bought them for him at a booth in Prague's Old Town Square. The artisan who sold them also made imitation medieval weapons, and heavy gauntlets and helms, but it was the soldiers that had caught her eye. She bought hundreds of dollars worth of them: sixty or seventy in total. The boy was only a year old then. She had left him in the care of a nanny in Boston, the first time she had been separated from him since his birth, and had traveled to the Czech Republic to retrace his steps. All she knew was that this was the country to which he had departed in his final days, the last place in which he had drawn breath before that stage of his existence was ended, and a new one begun. He had no memory of it, and so could not recall the trauma of his dying. It would come as he grew older, but she had hoped to unearth some clue as to what had occurred there. She found nothing: those responsible had covered their tracks too well.

But she was patient, and the boy would have his revenge.

It surprised her how the old and the new could co-exist inside him. He was so like a regular child now, lost in games of war, but this was the same boy who had helped her to torture Barbara Kelly to death. At times like that his older nature took over, and he seemed almost surprised at the damage that his hands could wreak.

She checked email on her laptop, and began listening to the messages that had been left on her various phones. There was nothing of consequence on the main numbers, and it was with some surprise that she found a message waiting for her at one of the oldest of the numbers, the one that had been earmarked for a very particular cause, and on which she had almost given up by now.

The message began haltingly, the voice slightly slurred. Alcohol, and more: a little toke, possibly, to take the edge off.

'Uh, hey, this is a message for, um, Darina Flores. You don't know me, but a while back you came to Falls End, Maine asking about a plane . . .'

She put down the glass while she listened to the rest of the message. No name left, only a number, but unless the caller had acquired a throwaway phone for the express purpose of calling her, his identity would be easy to establish. She played the message again, concentrating on every word, registering hesitations, emphases, intonation. There had been a lot of pointless calls in the early days, a lot of frustrated men with fantasies of getting her in the sack, and a couple of drunken, anonymous calls from women expressing the opinion that she was a bitch and a slut, and worse. She had responded to none, but recalled them all. She had an extraordinary memory for voices, but she could not remember ever having heard this one on the system before.

And there were details in this message, fragments of knowledge and description, that told her this was worth pursuing, that this would not be a wasted journey. There was *truth* here, small details that could only have come from someone who had actually seen the plane, and one in particular that made her gasp.

A passenger: the caller mentioned a passenger.

She rose and headed for the bathroom. A small nightlight burned in the outlet by the toilet, far from the big mirror which the boy had covered with a towel, but Darina turned on the main bathroom light as she entered. She reached for the towel, and felt the boy's hand on her arm. She looked down at him, and was touched by the expression of concern on his face.

185

Touched, and unnerved.

'It's okay,' she said. 'I want to see.'

He let his hand fall. She removed the towel. Even through the dressings, the appalling damage to her face was clear.

Darina Flores began to cry.

20

Walter Cole sat in his armchair, a beer in his hand and a dog at his feet. He had put on some weight, and there was more white in his hair than I remembered, but he was still recognizably the man who had been my first partner when I made detective, and whose family had consoled me when my own was taken from me. His wife, Lee, had greeted me with a kiss when she answered the door, and an embrace that reminded me there would always be a place for me in their home. Years before, I had found their daughter when, like a child in a fairytale, she got lost in the woods and was taken by an ogre. I think Lee viewed it as a debt that could never be repaid. I looked upon it as some small return for keeping a light in the darkness for a man who had once been forced to look upon the butchered bodies of his wife and daughter. Now it was just Walter and me, and a yawning dog that smelled faintly of popcorn.

I had not spoken to him of Epstein, not yet. Instead I had eaten a late supper of leftover meat loaf and a baked potato. Walter had joined me even though he had already eaten, which probably went some way toward explaining why he was now more than the man I remembered. I had helped him clean up when we were done, and we had taken our coffee into the living room.

'So, you want to tell me about it?' he said.

'Not really.'

'You're sitting there glowering at the rug like it just tried to steal your shoes. Somebody lit your fuse.'

'I misjudged an old acquaintance, or he misjudged me. I'm not sure which. Maybe both.'

'He still alive to tell the tale?'

'Yep.'

'Then he should be grateful.'

'*Et tu, Brute?*'

'It wasn't a judgment, just a statement of fact. I've saved your clippings, but I don't want to know the unofficial details. That way, I can plead ignorance if someone comes knocking. I've reached an accommodation with what you are, even if you haven't.'

'What I am, not what I do?'

'I don't think there's a separation where you're concerned. Come on, Charlie, we've known each other too long. You're like a son to me now. I judged you in the past, and maybe I found you wanting, but I was wrong. I'm on your side here, no questions asked.'

I sipped my coffee. Walter had also opened a beer for himself, but I had declined one. He was singlehandedly keeping the Brooklyn Brewing Company in business. There had barely been room in the refrigerator for food.

So I began talking. I told Walter of Marielle Vetters, and the story of the plane. I told him of Liat, and Epstein, and the second confrontation in the restaurant. I told him more of Brightwell, because Walter had been there when a woman came to my house asking for help in finding her lost daughter, a request that had led, in turn, to Brightwell and his Believers.

'I ever tell you that you keep some strange company?' he said, when I was done.

'Thanks for pointing that out. What would I do without you?'

'Spend money on expensive hotel rooms in New York. You sure you don't want a beer?'

'No, coffee's fine.'

'Something stronger?'

'Not my bag any more.'

He nodded.

'You're going to go back to Epstein, aren't you? You're curious about this list, and the plane. More than that, you're interested in Brightwell. He got under your skin.'

'Yes.'

'Doesn't mean that what Brightwell thought about you was true or right. If you're an angel, fallen or any other kind, then I'm Cleopatra. That stuff is okay if you're Shirley MacLaine, otherwise it starts to sound flaky. But if you want some company dealing with the Chosen People, let me know.'

'I thought you'd signed up for "don't ask, don't tell"?'

'I'm an old man. I forget what I've said as soon as I've said it. Anyway, it'll be an excuse to leave the house that doesn't involve doctors, or a trip to the mall.'

'You know, you're quite the ad for active retirement.'

'I'm going to be a centerfold for the AARP magazine. They promised. It'll be like that Burt Reynolds pic from *Playgirl*, but with more class, and maybe more gray hair. Come on, I'll show you to your bed. If you're not going to drink beer, then you're no good to me awake.'

Epstein called my cell phone before I went to sleep. Somewhere in our brief exchange there was an apology of sorts, perhaps from each of us.

I slept soundly.

I did not dream.

21

I met Epstein late the following afternoon at Nicola's Italian grocery and delicatessen at 54th and First. This part of town was known as Sutton Place, and for much of its history the rich and the poor had lived side by side here, tenements coexisting alongside the homes of socialites, the noise from factories, breweries and wharves providing the soundtrack while artists such as Max Ernst and Ernest Fiene worked in their studios. In the late 1930s, construction began on what was then known as the East River Drive, and subsequently became the FDR. The tenements and wharves began to disappear, and slowly high-rises started to take the place of many of the more civilized, characterful buildings. Still, some of those with long memories remembered a time when the apartments of Sutton Place were occupied mostly by actors and directors, when it was a haven for theatrical folk and, by extension, the gay community. It was said that eighty percent of the population of this small area was gay. Rock Hudson, among others, had an apartment in the 405 building across the street from Nicola's. In those days, if you told a cab driver to take you to 'Four out of Five', he would bring you straight to its door.

The choice of Nicola's as the venue for the meeting was mine. Nick, who owned the store along with his brother Freddy, was ex-military, having served his time in Vietnam. His genius there lay in sourcing whatever was necessary – food, equipment, booze – in order to ensure the continued smooth running of the US military endeavor in Southeast

Asia, but particularly that element of the endeavor which affected the comfort and care of his unit. Whole camps had been sustained thanks to Nick's abilities to scavenge and procure. Given another thousand men like him, the US might even have won the war. Now he had settled comfortably into the role of a store owner in New York, where his undoubted skills in negotiating and appropriating continued to serve him well.

Nick and Freddy were both behind the counter that morning, each dressed in the store's unofficial uniform of check shirt and blue jeans, although on Saturdays Nick eschewed the uniform in favor of a more formal black shirt, a nod to the days when he would hit the town after the store closed. Nicola's was a relic of a better time in New York, when every block had its neighborhood store, and there were personal relationships between shopkeepers and their customers. If you stood still for long enough in Nicola's, either Nick or Freddy would press a fresh espresso into your hand. After that, you were theirs forever. On a crate beside the door sat Dutch, one of their oldest customers, his coffee in his left hand, a blanket across his lap concealing his right, along with the gun that the hand contained on this particular afternoon.

The appearance of the store was deceptive. Although it was compact, with barely enough room for a handful of customers to stand in line, a flight of steps at the back led to a small storage space, and that space in turn opened up into the bowels of the building behind, where Nick and Freddy kept an office. A couple of storefronts to the right of the store, facing the street, was an iron gate that gave access to a large yard at the rear of the block, its footprint massive by the standards of real estate in the city.

Epstein arrived shortly after I did, trailed by Adiv, Liat's would-be suitor, and Yonathan, the older man who had riled me during the previous night's confrontation. When Adiv and

Yonathan tried to follow Epstein into Nicola's, Walter Cole appeared and blocked their way.

'Sorry, boys,' he said. 'Space is at a premium.'

Epstein stared at Walter.

'The ex-policeman,' said Epstein. He emphasized the word 'ex'.

'Once a cop, always a cop.'

'Are you a guarantee of safety?'

'I live to serve. Like I said, once a cop, always a cop.'

'Is there another way in?' asked Adiv.

'Building on 54th, and through the gate to the right,' said Walter. 'Makes you feel better to take one entrance each, then go ahead. As for the store, nobody's going to get past the four of us.' He indicated Nick, Freddy and Dutch. 'Plus we're all so wired on espresso that if the mailman makes a sudden move we might even take him out. Go for a walk, boys. Get some air into your lungs.'

Epstein considered the arrangement, then nodded at his two bodyguards and they moved away, Adiv to the corner of 54th where he could watch both the storefront and the entrance to the apartment block, and Yonathan to the iron gate on First. I led Epstein down the stairs, through the storeroom, and across the hall to Nick's large office where we could talk without clean-shaven young Jewish men with guns threatening the peace.

As we walked, I couldn't help but wonder where Liat might be. Liat troubled me. I hadn't slept with anyone since Rachel left me, and I wasn't entirely sure how I'd ended up in bed with Liat, beyond the fact that I had wanted to, and she had been there and willing, which were pretty good reasons in themselves. But last night, at the restaurant, she'd shown no great desire to repeat the experiment, and Epstein had clearly entrusted her with the task of watching me closely as he confronted me with the list, and assessing my reactions to his subsequent questions. Asking him if he'd also suggested that she sleep with me in order to examine my injuries seemed kind of crass, and I might not have been flattered by the answer; asking what would have happened if she had shaken her head instead of nodding at the end of the questioning might have had a more damaging effect on my feelings toward all concerned.

Nick provided us with more strong Italian coffees on a small tray, and some fresh pastries. Epstein was halfway through a tartlet when Walter Cole wandered in and took his seat at a table in the corner.

'I thought we were going to talk alone,' said Epstein.

'Your mistake,' said Walter.

'I understood this to be neutral territory.'

'No, you *mis*understood this to be neutral territory,' said Walter.

Epstein turned back to me. 'And your guardians, Angel and Louis?'

'Oh, they're around,' I said. 'In fact, I think they may be keeping Adiv and Yonathan company right about now.'

Epstein tried his best not to look unhappy at this news.

Tried, but failed.

Outside, Adiv and Yonathan both found themselves with guns pressed against their sides just as the sun began to set. They could see each other clearly, so Adiv was privy to Yonathan's situation, and vice versa. Adiv saw a tall black man with a shaved head and the graying beard of an aspiring Old Testament prophet, albeit a prophet wearing a thousand-dollar suit, materialize behind Yonathan, the gate opening silently as he emerged, his mouth whispering something softly into Yonathan's ear, his left hand on Yonathan's shoulder, his right driving the gun hard under Yonathan's armpit. Adiv, whose father was a tailor, just had time to adjudge the suit as remarkably well cut before a small, unshaven white man resembling a bum with some access to laundry services was threatening to blow out his insides if he moved, and so Adiv stayed very still indeed while the man disarmed him. Louis was having a similar exchange with Yonathan, with similar consequences, although he took the trouble to add, 'And none of that krav maga shit either. Trigger pull on this is so light a passing breeze could set it off.'

A huge, battered 4WD with smoked glass windows, and driven by a Japanese gentleman, pulled up outside the grocery store. Its rear doors opened to reveal a second Japanese man, and Yonathan and Adiv were bundled inside, Angel following. As the doors closed again, they were forced to the floor and their hands were secured behind their backs with cable ties. Their phones and wallets were taken from them, along with their spare change.

'What are you going to do to the rabbi?' asked Adiv, and Angel was impressed by the fact that the kid was more concerned about the rabbi's safety than his own.

'Nothing,' he replied. 'My friend is going to stay by the store to make sure the rabbi is safe, and we have another man inside, just in case.'

'So what is this about?' asked Yonathan.

'It's about not pointing guns at people who are on your side,' said Angel, then poked Adiv hard in the ribs with the toe of his glitter-covered cowboy boots. 'Oh, and not telling people on your side to go fuck themselves when they try to exchange pleasantries with you just because you're sore about what they may or may not have done with your girl, especially if they didn't know at the time you thought she was your girl, and more particularly when she isn't even your girl to begin with because you're just holding some hidden flame in your heart for her that only you can see. What are you, nine years old? A nice Jewish kid like you should be too smart to be that dumb.'

Yonathan shot a poisonous look at Adiv.

'What?' said Adiv. 'You were the one who pointed the gun at him.'

'Boys, boys,' said Angel. 'Recriminations will get you nowhere, although I will admit that it is entertaining from up here.'

'The rabbi's safety is above such concerns,' said Yonathan, striking for the moral high ground. 'We should be back there with him.'

'You'd have thought, except for the fact that you were taken on a city street in daylight and are now lying in the back of a jeep heading for Jersey. I'm not in the personal protection industry as such, but it suggests to me that the rabbi ought to be contracting for better staff, if you don't mind me saying so. And even if you do.'

'What are you going to do with us?' asked Adiv. His voice didn't crack. Angel had to admit that the kid had balls; not much in the way of manners, but definitely carrying a pair.

'You know what the Pine Barrens are?'

'No.'

'A million acres of trees, reptiles, bobcats, and the Jersey Devil, although I admit the Jersey Devil may not exist. It's a long walk home, even without the devil on your tail.'

'You're going to abandon us in the wilderness?'

'It could be worse: we could be dumping you in Camden County.'

'The city invincible,' said the Japanese driver, speaking for the first time.

'What?' said Angel.

'"In a dream, I saw a city invincible",' said the driver. 'Is the motto of the city of Camden. I learn it in citizenship class.'

'You mean "city invisible",' said Angel. 'Someone probably stole it while the cops weren't looking. Fucking city is so violent even dead people are armed. Personally, I'd take my chances in the Pinelands.'

'But—' Adiv began to say, but Angel aimed another kick at him as he started to protest, silencing him quickly.

'It's a done deal,' he said. 'Quiet now. I do some of my best thinking in the backs of cars.'

We sipped our espressos. They were very, very good.

'So let's start again,' I said to Epstein. 'Tell me what you know about the woman who provided the list.'

'Her name was Barbara Kelly.'

'Was?'

'She died last week.'

'How?'

'She was cut repeatedly with a blade, scourged with a belt of some kind, and partially blinded. Her killer or killers then set fire to the house, probably in an effort to hide the evidence of the attack. They were very careful in how they approached her torture. There were no broken bones, and she was still alive when the fire was started in the kitchen, although probably unconscious. She had quite a sophisticated alarm system, with recessed smoke and heat detectors independent of the main system but running parallel to it. It was also raining heavily, which helped arrest the progress of the conflagration. Nevertheless, by the time the fire department arrived, the blaze had consumed part of the kitchen and spread to the living room, but somehow Kelly had managed to crawl into the hallway. She was badly burned, and died on the way to the hospital. The post-mortem revealed the extent of the injuries she had received prior to burning.'

'You learn anything more since then?'

'She claimed to be an independent consultant. She had very little in her bank accounts, and appeared to be just about keeping her head above water. Her income came from a variety of sources, mostly small businesses. Appearances would suggest that she worked very hard for a modest return, barely enough to cover her mortgage and living expenses.'

'Except?'

'We're looking into the companies, but already two have been revealed as no more than names on mailboxes. We believe there were other sources of income, and other accounts.'

'Did the police find anything at the house?'

'A laptop mentioned in her insurance submission is missing and has not been traced. The hard drive had been removed from her desktop, and her personal files seem to have been carefully harvested.'

'A dead end.'

'We're still looking. And there is an added complication.'

'Isn't there always?'

'We believe that we were not the only ones to whom she sent material. She had cancer, and she felt that she was running out of time. She wanted to make reparation for her sins. She needed to know that the process had begun, that her offer of information was being taken seriously.'

'Who would she have sent it to? The newspapers? A DA somewhere?'

Epstein shook his head. 'Don't you understand? The whole point of this conspiracy was to acquire influence and favors, either now or for the future. From the two extracts we've seen, we know that they own politicians and reporters. Don't you think that they've also wormed their way into the lives of police officers, lawmakers, prosecutors? She couldn't send the list through the usual channels. She had to be more selective.'

'Then how did she decide upon your lawyers?'

'She knew of us because we were her enemies.'

'And she gave no indication of the other recipients?'

'Recipient. There was just one other. The only clue she gave was to warn us to act quickly, because if we did not another less scrupulous than ourselves would take vengeance into his own hands, and through him she would earn her salvation.'

I knew the man she meant. So did Epstein. There was only one individual who fitted that description, who had the resources and, more importantly, the vocation to do as this woman wished.

He called himself the Collector.

22

The envelope had arrived at the offices of the lawyer Thomas Eldritch in Lynn, Massachusetts, by standard mail. Lynn was known in local parlance as 'the city of sin', in part due to its reputation for high crime rates during the peak of its industrial boom but mostly because of the ease of the rhyme. Nevertheless such taunts have a tendency to get under the skin not only of individuals but of entire cities, and at the end of the twentieth century it was suggested that Lynn should change its name to Ocean Park, which gave fewer opportunities to amateur poets for unkind rhymes. The proposal was rejected. Lynn had been Lynn for a very long time, and altering its name would be tantamount to a bullied schoolchild admitting that the bullies had won, and moving to a different school to avoid further confrontation. Also, as any schoolchild will tell you, the more you protest about name-calling, the louder the catcalls become

Eldritch was not troubled by the conjunction of the words 'Lynn' and 'sin': he found it rather apt, for Eldritch was in the sin business, specializing in those of a mortal nature. He was, though, more prosecutor than final arbiter, assembling details of a case, confirming the guilt of the parties involved, and then passing on what he had learned to his private executioner so that the ultimate sentence might be carried out. Eldritch understood the disjunction between the concepts of law and justice. His response was to refuse to accept this fact unconditionally: he was reluctant to wait for justice to be applied in the next world when it could just as easily be dispensed in this one, with a concomitant reduction in the amount of evil and misery contained in this realm. The possibility that he might be a party to that which he hated rarely, if ever, bothered him, and it certainly did not cross the mind of the one who wielded the blade at the final moment.

But the letter was problematical. The return address was a box number that did not exist, and the envelope contained only two sheets of paper. One was a list of names, the other an unsigned covering note which read:

> I have made errors in my life, and I am afraid. I have confessed my sins, and seek to make reparation for them. I believe that the names on this list may be of interest to you and one of your clients. Please believe me when I tell you that it represents only a fraction of the information I have available to me. I know of the Believers. I know of the Army of Night. I can give your enemies into your hands, hundreds and hundreds of them. If you wish to talk further, you can contact me at the number below from November 19 for one twenty-four hour period, beginning at 00.01 a.m. on that date. Should I fail to hear back from you during this period, I will assume that I was mistaken in my approaches. You are not the only ones in a position to act upon this knowledge, and you are not the only ones with whom I have shared it.

Typed below the letter was a cell phone number. When the number was tested, it was discovered not to be in operation. It was still not in operation when November 19 arrived, and passed. This was the source of considerable frustration to Eldritch & Associates, as a cautious investigation of the individuals named on the list, most of whom had not previously come to the firm's attention, revealed that a number were indeed compromised, and had apparently willingly colluded in their own damnation. Some accompanying documentation that followed by mail a few days later, apparently from the same sender, confirmed this view. They had sold themselves in return for influence and advancement, for favors financial and sexual, and sometimes simply for the satisfaction of secretly doing wrong. The letter had promised a treasure trove of further information once contact was made; instead, there was only silence.

The law firm of Eldritch & Associates was an operation that prized documents, as any good law firm should. It knew the value of paperwork because a thing set down on paper was difficult to erase, and the fact of its existence could not be denied. Mr Eldritch liked to say that nothing on a computer screen really existed. He distrusted anything that did not make a noise when it was dropped, but he was no Luddite: he simply prized secrecy and confidentiality, and the success of the firm's mission was predicated on its ability to leave no trace of its actions. Dealings and communications conducted through the Internet left a trail that an idiot child could follow. Thus it was that there were no computers at Eldritch & Associates, and the firm did not accept submissions or messages by email or other electronic means.

Even the firm's phone was rarely answered, and, when it was picked up, assistance of any kind was seldom forthcoming. A caller who contacted that venerable institution in the hope of securing advice or aid relating to difficulties with the law would usually be told that the firm was not accepting new clients at present, and rarely did the name of Eldritch figure in any but the most esoteric of cases: disputes over ancient wills in which some or all of the relevant parties had by then activated wills of their own through the workings of mortality; property dealings that related to houses and plots largely unwanted and generally regarded as unsaleable, often linked by some connection, either peripheral or direct, to crimes of blood; and, most infrequently, offers of representation on a pro bono basis for those involved in the most heinous of crimes, although in each case the defendants had already been found guilty in a court of law, and the approach by Eldritch & Associates typically involved only a carefully worded commitment to investigate the circumstances of the conviction. The interviews would be conducted in person by Mr Eldritch himself, a vision of old world refinement in dark pinstripe trousers, matching waistcoat, black jacket, and black silk tie, all overlaid with a faint patina of dust, as though the lawyer had been roused from the sleep of decades for just this purpose.

Only occasionally did someone comment upon the fact that Mr Eldritch bore a striking resemblance to an undertaker.

Mr Eldritch was a consummate interrogator. His particular interest lay in cases where unanswered questions remained: questions of motivation and, more specifically, of suspicion about the involvement of unknown others in the commission of crimes, men and women who had somehow avoided attracting the attention of the law. He had discovered that self-interest was the great motivator, and the possibility of a sentence reduction, or the avoidance of the needle in a bare room, tended to loosen tongues. True, one had to mine a great weight of lies to uncover a single gem of truth, but that was part of the pleasure for Mr Eldritch: one had to test the acuity of one's processes on a regular basis if one were not to become physically old *and* mentally slow. Being old was bad enough. He couldn't afford to relinquish his faculties as well. Mr Eldritch enjoyed these sessions with the criminal kind, even when he emerged from them without useful information. They kept his mind keen.

Nobody ever won a reprieve from the death chamber, or a reduction in sentence, because Mr Eldritch took an interest in his case, but then Mr Eldritch never made any such specific promises. In fact, those who spoke with him couldn't quite recall why they'd agreed to do so in the first place once Mr Eldritch had gone on his less-than-merry way, and eventually they seemed to forget about him entirely, either of their own volition or through, once again, the actions of mortality, state-sanctioned or otherwise.

But those of whom they spoke with Eldritch – accomplices, employers, betrayers – frequently lived to regret the fact that the old lawyer had taken an interest in their existence, although their regret was destined to be as short-lived as they were. In time a caller would come, trailing nicotine and vengeance. He would have a gun, or more often a blade, in his hand, and as their lifeblood warmed his cold skin, his eyes would scan his surroundings, seeking some small remembrance of the occasion, a token of a sentence carried out, for collecting is an ongoing obsession, and a collection can always be added to.

And so it was that when no response could be elicited from the phone number supplied with the list of names, efforts were made to discover the identity of its owner. Although Mr Eldritch had no fondness for computers, he was willing to employ others to use them on his behalf, just as long as their unnatural glow did not sully his own environment. The number was traced to a cell phone that was part of a batch supplied to a big box store near Waterbury, Connecticut. An electronic search of the store's sales records came up with a date and time of purchase, but no name, indicating a cash payment. Security footage from the premises was stored digitally, and proved to be as easy to access as the store's inventory. An image of the woman was found: fifties, brunette, rather masculine in appearance. She was timed leaving the store, after which footage from the exterior cameras was examined. Her car was identified, and its license plate checked. The plate led, in turn, to her name, address, and Social Security number, since the State of Connecticut required the presentation of a Social Security card to issue a driver's license. Unfortunately, by the time Eldritch & Associates had obtained all of this information, Barbara Kelly was already dead.

But now they had a name, and the Collector could begin his work.

Most smokers have an impaired sense of smell, as smoking damages the olfactory nerves in the back of the nose as well as the taste receptors in the mouth located on the tongue, the soft palate, the upper esophagus, and the epiglottis. The taste buds on the tongue sit on raised protrusions called papillae. Examined in a microscope, they resemble fungi and plants in some exotic garden.

The Collector had noticed some diminution in his capacity to taste in recent years, although since he ate sparingly and unostentatiously he regarded it as only a minor irritant. The ongoing damage to his ability to smell he found more troubling, but as he wandered through the wreckage of Barbara Kelly's home, taking in the damage caused by fire and smoke and water, he was pleased to be able to discern among the conflicting odors the unmistakable porcine stink of roasted human flesh.

He stood in the ruins of the kitchen and lit a cigarette. He was not worried about being seen. The police were no longer concerned with personally securing the scene, contenting themselves with signs and tape to keep away the curious, and the house was sheltered by trees from its neighbors and the road. He twisted the head of his flashlight and commenced a slow and careful examination of each room, starting and ending with the kitchen, his worn but comfortable shoes splashing through puddles of dirty water. His fingers searched dresses and jackets stinking of smoke, underwear and stockings that would eventually be destroyed, towels and medicines and old magazines, all the detritus of a lost life. He found nothing of interest, but then he had expected as much. Still, one never knew.

He went outside. The woman's car had been found fifty miles from her house, burned out. A second vehicle, a red

SUV, was discovered closer to the house, also burned out, and with its plates missing. The chassis number revealed that it had been stolen from Newport two days earlier. Curious. It suggested that Barbara Kelly's killer had arrived in one car and departed in another, perhaps because the first vehicle had broken down.

No signs of forced access, so she had invited her killer in. That suggested it might have been someone known to her. On the other hand, she must have been aware that by sending out the list she was taking a considerable chance. These were not ordinary individuals for whom she worked, and they were very, very careful. They were particularly adept at sniffing out betrayal. She would have been wary of any approaches, whether from strangers or known associates. The background check on Kelly had revealed her sexual orientation. Women in fear tended to be less wary of other women, a small psychological chink in their armor that Kelly's lesbianism might have further compounded.

A woman, then? Perhaps. But then the situation had changed. At some point, Kelly had made a break for her car, but was pulled back inside. No, *dragged* back inside: there was grit embedded in her heels.

He returned to the kitchen. The flames had scoured it of blood, but this was where she was tortured and left to die. The oven and range were electric. A pity: gas would have been so much more effective. Instead, her killer had been forced to use the contents of the liquor cabinet to start the fire. Messy. Amateurish. Whoever was responsible had planned for a different outcome.

The kitchen was surprisingly neat, especially given the damage to the rest of the house. The surfaces were marble, the cabinets polished steel, and all of the kitchen utensils appeared to have been hidden away behind their doors. He reconstructed it in his head, seeing it as it was while its owner was still alive: pristine, sterile, with nothing out of place; apt surroundings for a woman who had hidden so much about herself.

He squatted beside the sink. The coffee pot lay on its side, its glass blackened but unbroken, although the plastic on the rim had become fused to the kitchen tiles. Could the firemen have knocked it over? Possibly, but the fact that it was stuck to the floor suggested otherwise. He looked around. The larger knives were kept on a magnetized board by the oven, directly above the silverware drawer. No reason to be over there, unless you were preparing food.

How did you run? How did you escape, even temporarily? The Collector closed his eyes. He had a good imagination, but more importantly he had a finely honed understanding of the relationship between predator and prey in any range of given situations.

You couldn't go for the knives: that would have been too obvious unless you were cooking, and there was no indication that this was the case. So what do you do? What would be normal behavior, even as your suspicions were perhaps becoming aroused?

You would offer a drink. It was cold and wet on the night that you died. You could have suggested liquor – brandy or whisky – but you would have wanted to stay alert, and liquor would have dulled your responses. The one who was planning to hurt you might have declined for the same reason. Something hot, then: in this case, coffee.

You go to the kitchen. Maybe you're not yet worried – but, no, you probably are. You've made a mistake allowing a potential threat into your home, but you haven't revealed your fear. You're tamping it down because as soon as it's sensed, action will be taken against you. You have to act normal until an opportunity presents itself to strike and defend yourself.

You make that opportunity.

Let's say that you threw the contents of the coffee pot, and you must have hit your target because you bought yourself enough time to get to your car, but not enough to escape. Scalding coffee, probably to the face. Painful. Incapacitating. But you still didn't manage to get away. Not just one attacker, then, but two or more. No, just two: if there were three, you would never have made it so far.

Eldritch & Associates had obtained a copy of the medical examiner's report on Barbara Kelly. It revealed, in addition to the various cuts on her body, a wound to her cheek that appeared to be the result of a bite. Human flesh was a notoriously undependable substance for the recording of bite marks. The reliability of the bite mark record could be affected by the status of the tissue under analysis, the time elapsed between the bite and the creation of an impression, the condition of the skin damaged by the bite pressure and the reaction of the surrounding tissue to it, the size of the wound, and the clearness of the marks. The fact that Kelly's face had been badly scorched by heat caused further difficulties, and meant that there was no possibility of obtaining DNA samples from saliva, or even of making a reasonable comparison based on dental analysis should a suspect be found. What was interesting, though, was the fact that the bite radius was comparatively small, with the first premolars and second premolars absent from both the upper and lower jaws.

Barbara Kelly, it seemed, had been bitten by a child shortly before she died.

The likelihood of a woman being present increased. Yes, it was possible that Kelly might have admitted a man with a young child, but why not take the next logical step and disarm her entirely with a woman and a child?

Why would a child bite a woman?

Because you threatened, or actively hurt, its mother.

That was how you got away, thought the Collector. You used something in the kitchen, in all likelihood the coffee pot, to attack the mother, then ran. It was the child that came after you, distracting you for long enough to allow the woman to recover and drag you back inside. Well done. You must have come close to surviving.

The Collector thought that he might have been quite interested to meet Barbara Kelly. Of course, his interest would have been both personal and professional. If, as he believed, she was responsible for the corruption of so many souls, then he would have been forced to take a blade to her, but he admired her for the battle that she had put up at the end of her life. He knew many people labored under the illusion that they would fight to stay alive under such circumstances, but he had ended too many lives himself to believe that such responses were not the rule, but the exception. Most went to their deaths without a struggle, frozen by shock and incomprehension.

He wondered what she had told them at the end. That was the other thing: nobody resisted torture. Everybody broke. It was nothing to be ashamed of. The difficulty for the torturer lay in figuring out the truth of what one was being told. Scourge a man for long enough, and if you ask him to tell you that the sky is pink and the moon is purple, that day is night and night is day, he will swear to it on the lives of his wife and children. The trick in the early stages was to cause just enough pain, and to ask questions to which the answers were already known, or were easily verifiable. Every study required a baseline.

So what did she have to tell? Well, she had promised in her letter that there were more names to be given, and she had more information to provide, but the kind of people who would inflict that level of pain on another human being and then leave her to burn were hardly on the side of the angels and were therefore unlikely to be sufficiently interested in the identities of those like themselves to kill for them. No, they would be more interested in curbing the supply of such information. They would want to know whom she had approached, and what she had already given them, and she would have told them because the pain would have been too much for her. Her killers now knew, therefore, that Eldritch & Associates had been provided with a list of names. They might move against Eldritch, which would be unwise, or they might seek to limit the damage caused through other means, perhaps by silencing those on that particular list.

Then there was the small matter of who else might have been approached by this woman. There were few candidates who could be trusted enough. In fact, the Collector could think of only one.

But then, the old Jew could take care of himself.

The Collector finished his cigarette and carefully doused the tip in a pool of water before slipping the butt into the pocket of his black coat. The Collector regularly wore a coat, regardless of the weather. Excesses of heat or cold had little effect on him, and anyway, a man always had need of pockets: for cigarettes, a wallet, a lighter, and an assortment of blades. He looked to the north, where Eldritch was probably still sitting in his office, poring over papers. The thought brought him pleasure, even though they had argued earlier that day, and Eldritch and the Collector rarely exchanged a harsh word. On this occasion, the Collector reflected, it was a matter of conflicting philosophies, a belief in preventive measures coming up against the lawyer's requirement for evidential proof of the commission of a crime. In the end, though, it would come down to the blade, for the man with the blade always has the final word.

In his office, a banker's lamp casting soft light across his desk, Eldritch looked up from the list of names as though sensing the thoughts of the other. He and the Collector were almost a single entity, which made their earlier disagreement all the more difficult. Files of varying sizes on most of the individuals named on the list rested by his right hand. All were compromised, but fatally so? Eldritch was uncertain. He approved of the final sanction being used in only the most extreme of cases, and his view was that none of these individuals unconditionally qualified for the Collector's attentions. But he also acknowledged that, like loaded guns or honed blades, they had the potential to do great harm, and it could be argued that some, by their actions, had already committed serious sins. The question remained, though: was their potential to do harm, as yet unrealized in most cases, justification for taking their lives? For Eldritch, the answer was 'no', but for the Collector the answer was 'yes'.

A compromise of sorts had been reached. One name was chosen, the individual whom Eldritch regarded as the most distasteful. The Collector would talk with him, and a decision would follow. Meanwhile, the problem of the final name remained, the only name typed in red.

'Charlie Parker,' whispered the old lawyer. 'What have you done?'

23

Davis Tate slumped in one of the leatherette booths of the bar and looked at his ratings for the fourth time, hoping to find some cause for celebration, or even mild optimism.

His figures should have been through the roof: the economy was still unsteady, the president was hogtied by his own compromised idealism, and the right had succeeded in vilifying unions, immigrants, and welfare cases, making them carry the can for the greed of bankers and Wall Street sharks, thereby somehow convincing sane people that the poorest and weakest in the nation were responsible for most of its ills. What never ceased to amaze Tate was that many of those same individuals – the dirt poor, the unemployed, the welfare recipients – listened to his show, even as he castigated those – the union organizers, the bleeding-heart liberals – who most wanted to help them. Bitterness, stupidity, and self-interest, he had discovered, would win out over reasoned arguments every time. He sometimes asked himself how this generation differed from that of his grandparents when it came to the election of a president, and he had decided that previous generations wanted to be governed by men who were smarter than they were, while today's voters preferred to be led by those who were as dumb as themselves. He knew them well, for he made his living by pandering to their basest instincts. He understood that they were frightened, and he fanned the flickering flames of their fear.

Yet still his figures remained stubbornly plateaued. In some states – Kansas, for crying out loud, and Utah, where being a liberal meant having only one wife – his listenership was actually going *down*. It was unbelievable, just unbelievable. He finished his beer and waved to the waitress for another.

'What the hell is happening?' he asked. 'I mean, is it my voice, my personality, what?'

There were those who might have said that it was all of the above, and more. Strangely, Tate might well have empathized. He knew that he was not particularly talented and not particularly charismatic, but he could rabble-rouse with the best of them. He was also brighter than his enemies gave him credit for, bright enough to understand that most people in America, whether liberal or conservative, just wanted to get along with their lives, and generally didn't wish ill on anyone who had not done them actual harm. They were fundamentally good people, and pretty tolerant to boot. For those reasons, they were of absolutely no use to Tate and his kind. His role in life was to target those who had resentment and animosity simmering inside, and put those base materials to political and social use. Where there is love, he prayed, let me sow hatred. Where there is risk of pardon, a renewed sense of injury. Where there is faith, doubt. Where there is hope, despair. Where there is light . . .

Darkness.

His producer, Becky Phipps, sat across from him, toying with the olive in her dirty Martini; dirty both figuratively and literally. Tate had no idea what she thought she was doing, ordering a cocktail in a dump like this. Tate didn't even want to use the beer glasses, and he'd wiped clean his bottle of beer before drinking from it. Just because this was the kind of dump frequented by regular Joes didn't mean that he had to drink there too, not unless it was going to boost his ratings, and right now he didn't hear anyone applauding.

Tate was also concerned that the bartender might be gay. He was all muscled up, but he was too tanned for Tate's liking, and he seemed to be camping it up some for a couple of the customers who looked like queer bait. The bar had been Becky's choice. She said it was better to have this discussion away from the usual watering holes. There would be fewer distractions, but also fewer ears listening in on their conversation.

'It's not a crisis yet, but it could become one unless we tackle it now,' said Becky. 'There have been some rumblings from advertisers, but assurances are being offered. We're talking, and they're listening.'

'They're not cutting advertising rates, are they?' asked Tate, unable to keep a hint of rising panic out of his voice. That could be the kiss of death. Cutting rates, even temporarily, was a dangerous business. It might be taken as an admission that the slide in listeners couldn't be arrested, and that was like starting a run on a bank.

'No, but I won't lie to you: the possibility has been suggested.'

'How long have we got?'

'A couple of months. We'll get together a focus group next week, do some blue-sky thinking, spitball the whole business.'

Tate hated it when Becky used all of that business school jargon. In his experience, people only spoke that way when they had no idea what they were doing, which was a cause for alarm in the case of his producer, even if Becky was a producer more in name than in practice. She monitored Tate, guided him, suggested targets for his tirades, and he never disagreed with her. He knew better than to do that. He and Becky had been together for five years, and she'd been good for him, but his vanity made him reluctant to attribute too much of his success to her input. On the other hand, Barbara Kelly, the woman who had recommended Becky, had also been responsible for providing seed capital, and for putting him in touch with a whole network of likeminded people: advertisers, syndicators, dealers in influence and information.

But Barbara Kelly was dead. He had to tread carefully here.

'If you think it will help,' said Tate.

He tried not to sound too skeptical. He lived in fear of being dropped, of being sent back to the minors. His third beer arrived. He looked over at the bar and saw the bartender staring back at him. The freak took the empty bottle from the waitress, stuck his finger in the top, and dumped it in the recycling bin. While Tate looked on, he then sucked the finger that had been in Tate's bottle, and winked.

'Did you see that?' asked Tate.

'What?'

'That fag bartender put his finger in my bottle and sucked it.'

'What, that bottle?'

'No, the last one, the one I just drank from.'

'Force of habit.'

'He winked at me while he did it.'

'Maybe he likes you.'

'Jesus. You think he did something with this one too?' Tate eyed the bottle suspiciously. 'Maybe his finger isn't the only thing he tries to put in bottles.'

'I got a wipe, if you want to use it.'

'It'll make the beer taste bad. Maybe not as bad as if the bartender stuck his dick in it, but still bad.'

'You're overreacting.'

'He recognizes me. I'm sure that he does. He did that deliberately because he thinks I'm a homophobe.'

'You *are* a homophobe.'

'That's not the point. I should be able to express my opinions without fear of queer bartenders sticking their fingers, or anything else, in my beer. He could have a disease.'

'You told me he sucked his finger after you drank from the bottle, not before. If anyone's going to catch anything, it's him.'

'What are you, an epidemiologist? And what's that supposed to mean anyway? You implying that I have something he could catch?'

'Paranoia, maybe.'

'I'm telling you, he knows who I am.'

'It would be great if he did,' said Becky, and the sarcasm distracted him from fingers and bottles. 'If every bartender in New York recognized you it would mean that you were a national figure, and all of your problems would be solved.'

'You mean "our" problems, right?'

Becky sipped her drink. 'Of course. I misspoke.'

Tate folded his arms huffily and turned away from her, then quickly reconsidered as he found himself catching the bartender's eye again. Becky swore softly. It was up to her to make some conciliatory gesture. It always was. Sometimes she wished Barbara Kelly had never asked her to take Tate under her wing. He had seemed to be on the verge of breaking through in a big way, at least until recently, but he was a miserable, whiny sonofabitch. It came with the territory. You couldn't spend hours every day spitting out that kind of bile, then more hours working up more bile to spit out the next day, and the day after, and the day after that, and not pollute your spirit. Although she'd never told Tate this, there were times when she muted the volume in the producer's booth to give her a break from his poisonous rants, and she *agreed* with most of what he said. She couldn't have done the job otherwise. At least Tate represented only part of her responsibilities. In a way, being his producer was little more than a cover story for her.

'You smell smoke?' asked Tate. He was sniffing the air like a rat, his head slightly raised. He had even lifted his hands from the bar, and they hung in front of his chest like paws.

'What, like fire?' she said.

'No, tobacco smoke.' He peered over the top of the booth, but there was no one nearby. They'd chosen the table for precisely that reason. 'Stinks like cleaning out time at the lung cancer ward.'

For someone who was ostensibly a libertarian, Tate had

his peculiarities and inconsistencies. Like so many of those who described themselves as pro-life, Tate was only pro the kind of life that was curled up in someone's womb. If it emerged from that same womb and committed a crime, then it was fair game for the needle. Similarly he was inordinately fond of war, as long as that war involved kicking someone's ass in a place far away from decent bars and good restaurants, and was fought by the kind of men and women whom Tate secretly despised when they weren't wearing a uniform. But he was also cautiously in favor of some form of gun control, albeit a control mechanism that allowed him to own guns and kept them out of the hands of the non-white and the non-Christian; and he certainly did not approve of those who smoked in his vicinity, even while advocating the sort of lax environmental policing that in the long run was likely to have a significantly more damaging effect on the quality of the air that he breathed than the occasional breath of secondhand smoke.

In short, Becky thought, Davis Tate was an asshole, but that was why he was so useful. Still, recruiting men such as he required a degree of care, and their continued use involved careful diplomacy. They couldn't be stupid or else they would be unable to perform their appointed role in the media, and they couldn't be too smart in case they began questioning what they were doing, or how they were being used. The easiest way to ensure their continued compliance was to stroke their ego and surround them with those most like themselves. Hatred, like love, needed to be regularly fed and watered.

Tate continued to sniff the air.

'You sure you don't smell it?' he said.

Becky sniffed. There was something, she admitted. It was faint, but unpleasant. She could almost taste it on her tongue, as though she'd just licked a smoker's fingers.

'It's old,' she said. 'It's on someone's clothing.' Their skin and hair too, because you didn't get to smell that way unless the nicotine had ingrained itself upon your system. She could almost hear the cells metastasizing.

She glanced over her shoulder. At the very back of the bar, where the light was at its dimmest, she saw a figure seated in a booth against the wall, a newspaper spread before him, a brandy snifter in one hand, the index finger of the other gently tapping a rhythm upon the table as he read. She couldn't see his face, but his hair looked greasy and untidy. He struck her as unclean, a polluted man, and not just because the tobacco smell was certainly coming from him.

'It's the guy in the corner,' she said.

'There's no excuse for a man smelling that bad,' said Tate. 'At least he won't outlive us.'

Tate was not certain, but for a moment he believed that the rhythm of the man's tapping might have been interrupted, and then it resumed and he forgot about it.

'Ignore him,' said Becky. 'He's not why we're here.'

'Goddamn disloyal advertisers and fat station managers without an original idea in their heads is why we're here,' said Tate.

'It's not just the advertisers and the stations we have to worry about, though,' she replied. 'You realize that? The Backers are concerned.'

Tate's mouthful of beer tasted wrong. It wasn't just his suspicions about the bartender, misplaced or otherwise. He always felt this way when the subject of the Backers was raised. At first, their existence hadn't bothered him so much. The Kelly woman had approached him when he was a minor player broadcasting out of San Antonio, with barely a dozen statewide syndications to his name. She'd arranged to meet him for coffee in the lobby of the Menger Hotel, and he hadn't been impressed with her at first. She was dowdy and plain, and Tate suspected that she was also a dyke. He had no objection to dykes as long as they were pretty – that was probably as close to a liberal viewpoint as he'd ever managed to come – but the butch, masculine-looking ones bothered him. They always seemed so angry, and frankly they scared the shit out of him. Kelly wasn't an extreme case: her hair was shoulder length, and she wasn't making some protest about oppressive male views of women by refusing to wear makeup or avoiding skirts and high heels. No man would have given her a second look in a bar or a mall, though, and most wouldn't even have bothered with the first look.

But when she started speaking he found himself leaning forward, hanging on her every word. She had a soft, melodious voice, one that seemed to him both entirely at odds with her appearance yet also curiously appropriate if you considered her as some kind of mother figure instead of a sexual being. She spoke of how there was a change coming, and voices like his needed to be heard if that change was to become permanent. She said that there were powerful, influential figures with an interest in ensuring this was the case, and they had favors to call in, and money to spend. Davis Tate didn't have to spend the rest of his career broadcasting out of a roach-filled studio in Valley Hi, driving between it and his similarly roach-filled apartment in Camelot in his piece-of-shit Concord hatchback. He could become a big player in syndicated talk radio if he wanted to be. He just had to trust in others to guide him.

Tate might have been a serious hatemonger-in-waiting, but he wasn't dumb. Even back then he was self-aware enough to know that, at best, most of what he said didn't make a whole lot of sense and, at worst, was just damned lies, but he'd been saying it all for so long that even he was starting to believe it. Neither was his ego so out of control as to allow him to think that a northern dyke would come all the way to San Antonio just because of his verbal dexterity and his unerring ability to blame the problems of hardworking white, Christian Americans on niggers, spics, queers and feminists without ever having to go so far as to name them as such. There was always a catch, wasn't there?

'Are we talking about a loan?' he asked. He could barely cover his rent and the repayments on his vehicle as it was, and his credit card was maxed out. The word 'loan' now had the same appeal to him as the word 'noose'.

'No, any money you receive will be offered on an entirely non-repayable basis,' said Kelly. 'Consider it an investment in your career.'

She flicked through the papers on the table before her, and removed a four-page document. It was closely printed, and looked kind of official to Tate. 'This is the initial paperwork for the corporation we propose to set up in your name. Funding would come from a number of 509(a) and 501(c) bodies.'

Tate read through the document. He was no lawyer, but even he could tell that there was a tangle of legalese here. He could also do addition and multiplication, and what he was being offered amounted to many times what he was earning in San Antonio, with further bonuses promised as syndication increased.

'We'd also like to place a separate 501(c) organization under your direct control,' said Kelly. 'As you're probably aware, any such organization is tax-exempt and, as long as it accrues less than twenty-five thousand dollars in gross yearly income, is not required to make an annual return to the IRS. In your line of work, it's often necessary to provide hospitality, and the more hospitable you are, the more friends you'll have. That requires some disposable income, which we're prepared to provide. Sometimes, you may even have to use those funds to put individuals in a position where they become vulnerable to pressure, or exposure.'

'You mean set them up?'

Kelly gave him the kind of look his third-grade teacher used to give him when he failed to master a piece of simple addition, but she masked it with an indulgent smile.

'Not at all,' she said. 'Let's say you heard that a local union organizer was known to cheat on his wife with the occasional waitress, or even with some of the very immigrants whose rights he was ostensibly working to protect. You could take the view that you had a moral and social obligation to expose his behavior. After all, it's hypocrisy, as well as exploitation. In that case, baiting a hook wouldn't be viewed as a set-up. He would be under no obligation to act on his appetites, and you would not be forcing him to do so. It would be a matter of free choice on his part. That's very important, Mr Tate: in all things, the freedom to choose between right and wrong is crucial. Otherwise, well –' Her smile widened. – 'I'd be out of a job.'

Tate still had the uncomfortable feeling that he was missing the point, and the complexity of the legal document in his hand had only increased his suspicion that somewhere a mass of fine print was waiting to come back and bite him in the ass.

'Excuse me, but what is your job, exactly?'

'It's on my business card.' She pointed at the card where it lay next to Tate's coffee cup. 'I'm a consultant.'

'What does that mean?'

'It means that I consult. How much simpler can it be?'

'But for whom?'

'You see, *that's* why we want you, Mr Tate: "for whom." You're bright, and you can speak well, but you never talk down to your listeners. You address them as equals, even if they're not. You give the impression that you're one of them, but you know that you're superior. You have to be. Someone has to guide ignorant men and women. Someone has to explain the reality of a situation in a way that's comprehensible to ordinary people or, if necessary, adjust the nature of that reality slightly so it can *be* comprehended. You're not the only person in the media to receive this approach from us. You're not alone. I'm offering you the chance to become part of a greater purpose, to put your gifts to their optimum use.'

Tate was almost convinced. He *wanted* to be convinced but still he doubted.

'What's the catch?' he said, and he was surprised that Kelly looked pleased he'd asked.

'Finally,' she said.

'Finally?'

'I always wait for that question. It's proof that we have the right person. Because there's always a catch, right? There's always something in the fine print that could come right back to bite you in the ass?'

Tate stared at her. She had used almost exactly the words that he had spoken in his head. He tried to remember if he might have said them aloud, but he was certain that he had not.

'Don't be shocked, Mr Tate,' she said. 'In your position, I'd be thinking the same thing.'

She removed another sheet of paper from her briefcase and placed it before him. There was a single long paragraph at the center of the page. Typed neatly in the middle of an ornate script was his name. It reminded him of a university scroll, not least because it appeared to be written in Latin.

'What's this?' he asked.

'The catch,' she replied. 'In your hand you hold the formal contract, the minor one. This is your private contract, your agreement with us.'

'Why is it written in Latin?'

'The Backers are very old-fashioned, and Latin is the language of jurisprudence.'

'I don't read Latin.'

'Allow me to summarize, then.' Tate noticed that she didn't even have to look at the page. She knew its contents by heart. She rattled off what sounded to him like the pledge of allegiance, except it was loyalty promised not to a country, but to a private body.

'*Excercitus Noctis?*'

'The Army of Night. Catchy, don't you think?'

Tate didn't think it was catchy at all. It sounded like one of those 'Reclaim the Streets' movements. More dykes, he thought.

'And that's it? That's all I have to sign?'

'Nothing else. It will never be publicized, and you will never see the name of our organization written anywhere but here. In fact, the Army of Night doesn't exist. Call it a private joke. Basically, some suitable nomenclature was required, and that one appealed to the Backers. This particular contract is really just to reassure them. We wouldn't want you to take our money and head to Belize.'

Tate didn't even know where Belize was, but he wasn't about to head there even if he did know. He was ambitious, and he'd never get a better opportunity than this one to advance himself in his chosen field.

'Uh, who are these Backers?'

'Wealthy, concerned individuals. They're worried about the direction in which this country is heading. In fact, they're worried about the direction in which the whole world is heading. They want to alter its course before it's too late.'

'When do I get to meet them?'

'The Backers like to keep their distance. They prefer to operate discreetly through others.'

'Like you.'

'Exactly.'

He looked again at the documents before him. One was written in a language that he didn't understand, and the rest were written in a language that he should have understood but didn't.

'Maybe I ought to run these by my attorney,' said Tate.

'I'm afraid that won't be possible. This is a one-time offer. If I leave here with these papers unsigned, the offer will be rescinded.'

'I don't know . . .'

'Perhaps this will be enough to convince you of our bona fides,' said Kelly.

She passed him a plain white envelope. When he opened it, he found that it contained access details for three bank accounts, including the 501(c) organization that Kelly had implied was merely being considered. It was called the American League for Equality and Freedom. Together, the accounts contained more money than he had earned in the last ten years.

Tate signed the papers.

'All this money is mine?' he asked. He couldn't quite believe it.

'Look upon it as your war chest,' said Kelly.

'With whom are we going to war?' he asked.

'Again with the "whom",' said Kelly, admiringly. 'I just love the way you talk.'

'The question remains,' insisted Tate. 'Who are we fighting?'

'Everyone,' said Kelly. 'Everyone who is not like us.'

One week later, he was being introduced to Becky Phipps. One year later, he was a rising star. Now that star appeared to be on the wane, and Becky was alluding darkly to the Backers. The Backers, Tate knew, tended to act when they were displeased. He'd learned that early on. Kelly hadn't just been speculating when she spoke about the union organizer with a taste for skirt: his name was George Keys. He liked to tell people that he was named after George Orwell. Nobody knew if that was true or not, but Keys certainly came from socialist stock. His father had been a union organizer all his life, and his mother continued to be heavily involved with Planned Parenthood. His grandfather, meanwhile, had set up a Catholic Worker camp in California and was personally close to the CW founder, Dorothy Day, who ticked every box on Tate's hate list: Catholic, anarchist, socialist radical, even anti-Franco, which, as far as Tate was concerned, meant that she wasn't even consistent in her own wrongheadedness because the Catholics were supposed to be for the fascists in the Spanish Civil War, right? If the son was one-tenth of the man his grandfather was, then he deserved to be wiped from the earth, even without screwing Mexican factory workers on the side.

It hadn't been difficult to bribe a whore who worked part-time as a waitress – or was she a waitress who worked part-time as a whore? Tate could never quite tell – to come on to Keys with a sad story about her family back in Mexico, and her cousins working in indentured servitude on Texas chicken farms. Keys bought her some drinks, and the whore bought some back, and one thing led to another until Keys and the whore ended up back at Keys' place.

What happened after that Tate didn't know, and didn't care, but he had photographs of Keys and the woman together. He then shared what he knew with his listeners, and made sure the photographs were disseminated to every newspaper in the state, and for an outlay of five hundred dollars he did his part in setting back union activism in the state of Texas. Keys denied everything, and Tate later learned from the wait-ress-cum-whore that all he'd done back at his place was to play her some jazz that she didn't like, talk about his dying mother, and then start crying before calling her a cab. Afterward, Kelly had contacted him personally to say that the Backers were pleased, and he'd received a substantial bonus in cash through Becky. The waitress-whore was shipped back to Mexico on some trumped-up immigration charge, and there she quietly vanished into the sands somewhere around Ciudad Juarez, or so Becky had hinted when she was drunk one evening and he was almost considering making a pass at her, until she told him about what probably happened to the girl in Mexico, and how the Backers had contacts down there. She grinned as she said it, and any desire for Becky on

Tate's part had vanished there and then and had never returned.

Unfortunately, there were other individuals who weren't so pleased with what Tate had done, and he hadn't yet learned to be clever enough to protect himself from his own vices. Tate wasn't above doing a little banging of his own. He wasn't married, but he did have a weakness for colored girls, and particularly the colored whores over at Dicky's on Dolorosa, a hangover from the days when San Antonio's red light district was one of the largest in the state, and the least racially segregated. Anyway, on those nights when a colored whore wasn't available Tate wasn't above dipping in some dark Mexican, and one thing led to another, and somehow it became known that Davis Tate frequented Dicky's, and when he emerged one evening smelling of the disinfectant soap that Dicky's provided for the hygiene needs of its customers he was photographed by a white man in a car, and when he objected, the car doors opened and three Mexicans piled out, and Davis Tate got the beating of his life. But he remembered the number plate of the car, oh yes, and he made the call while he was still waiting for treatment at San Antonio Community Hospital. Barbara Kelly had assured him that the matter would be taken care of, and it was.

The car was registered to one Francis 'Frankie' Russell, a cousin of George Keys who did a little PI work on the side: marital stuff, mostly. Twenty-four hours later, the body of Frankie Russell was found at the eastern edge of Government Canyon. He had been castrated, and it was suggested that he shared some of the weaknesses of his cousin, and the story of the union organizer who liked screwing immigrant women, illegal and otherwise, was dragged up again. No connection was made between Russell's murder and the discovery a week later of the remains of three Mexican chicken farm workers dumped in Calaveras Lake. After all, they had not been castrated, simply shot.

It was, said those who knew about such matters, probably a gang affair.

But Davis Tate knew better, and he was very, very frightened. He hadn't signed up to murder. All he wanted was for one beating to be avenged with another. On the night that the bodies were pulled from Calaveras Lake he got shitfaced drunk and made a call to Barbara Kelly, in the course of which he complained that he had not wanted the men who attacked him to be killed, merely taught a lesson, and Kelly had replied that they *had* been taught a lesson, and Tate had begun shouting, and making threats, and talking about his conscience. He'd hung up, and opened another bottle, and somehow he must have fallen asleep on the floor because he wasn't sure that he was even awake when he opened his eyes and saw the beautiful, dark-haired woman looking down at him.

'My name is Darina Flores,' she said. 'Barbara Kelly sent me.'

'What do you want?'

'I want to warn you about the importance of remaining faithful to the cause. I want to make sure that you understand the seriousness of the document that you signed.'

She knelt beside him and clutched his hair in her left hand, while her right fixed itself on his throat. She was very, very strong.

'And I want to tell you about the Backers, and more.'

She whispered in his ear, and her words became images, and something inside Davis Tate died that night.

That memory came back to him now as Becky spoke. She wasn't on his side. He'd guessed that a long time ago. She represented the interests of the Backers, and those who used them in turn.

'What should I do?' he said. 'How do I get these ratings back up?'

'It has been suggested that you're too subtle, that you're

not being radical enough. You need to stir up some controversy.'

'How?'

'Tomorrow you're going to hear about the disappearance of a teenage girl from upstate New York. Her name is Penny Moss, and she's fifteen years old. You'll be given an exclusive: when Penny Moss's remains are discovered, you'll be supplied with proof that her killer is a Muslim convert who decided to make an example of her for wearing inappropriate dress. Even the cops won't know before you do. The material will be sent to you anonymously. We'll have speakers ready to comment. You're about to become the eye of the storm.'

Tate almost vomited up his beer. He didn't mind tearing meat from the bones of liberals because, say what you liked about liberals – and Tate did, more than most – they didn't tend to voice their objections by pointing a gun at someone, just as they didn't blow up federal buildings in Oklahoma. Muslims were another matter: he was happy to bait them from the safety of his radio station as long as he was just one voice among many, but he didn't want to become a figurehead for anti-Islamic feeling. He owned a nice apartment in Murray Hill, and parts of Marray Hill were becoming like Karachi or Kabul. He preferred being able to walk the streets there without endangering his life, and he certainly didn't want to have to move because of a radio show.

'But how do I know that it's true?'

'Because we'll make it true.'

All of his taste for beer had left him. If this went down the way Becky was suggesting it would, he was going to need a clear head. Only one further detail bothered him.

'This girl, this Penny Moss, I haven't heard anything about her. When did she go missing?'

Later, just as he was about to die, he would realize that he had known the answer already, had guessed it before Becky even opened her lips and began to speak, and he could almost have mouthed the words along with her if he chose.

'Tonight,' said Becky. 'She goes missing tonight.'

24

B ack at Nicola's, Epstein had resigned himself to the absence of his bodyguards, not that he had a whole lot of choice in the matter. Nick's office was warm and smelled faintly of fresh baked bread, and his coffee was very good. At first I felt that I was being more hospitable to Epstein than he probably deserved given the nature of our previous encounter, but it didn't take me long to realize something about the confrontation that my anger had caused me to underestimate at the time: the extent to which Epstein had been frightened, and frightened of me. Even now he remained uneasy, and it wasn't due only to the absence of his protectors. Despite all of my protestations, and Liat's nod of salvation, I was still a troubling figure for the old man. The presence of Louis in the room probably wasn't making him feel any better about the situation. Louis could make the dead nervous.

'Your hand is shaking,' I said, as I watched him sip from his cup.

'It's strong coffee.'

'Really? I could have walked on the surface of that Arab stuff you served me last night if the cup had been big enough, and Nick's coffee is too strong for you?'

He shrugged. '*Chacun à son goût.*'

Louis tapped me on the shoulder

'That's French,' he said.

'Thanks,' I said.

'It means,' said Louis very carefully, as if explaining something to a small, slow child, '"Everyone to his own taste."'

'You done?' Sometimes I wondered if Angel didn't act as some kind of stabilizing influence on Louis. It was a possibility that I found worrying.

'Just helping,' said Louis. He looked at Walter Cole as if to say, 'What's a man to do?'

'I didn't know it was French,' said Walter.

'See?' said Louis to me. 'He didn't know.'

'He's never been further east than Cape May,' I said. 'The closest he's been to France is patting a poodle.'

'What does it mean?' resumed Walter. 'What he said?'

'I just explained what it meant,' said Louis. 'Everyone to his own taste.'

'Oh,' said Walter. 'It sounded different the other way.'

'That's because it was in French,' said Louis.

'I guess,' said Walter. 'French people got a lot of words for stuff, don't they?'

At that point, Louis stopped talking to him, and therefore missed the wink that Walter threw my way.

'So what now?' asked Epstein.

'You speak German, don't you?'

'Yes, I speak German.'

'Jesus,' said Walter, 'it's like Ellis Island in here.'

'Do you know what *Seitensprung* is?' I continued.

'Yes,' said Epstein. 'It is the act of changing partners while one is dancing.'

Walter shifted in his seat and tapped Louis on the arm.

'The Germans got a lot of words for stuff too, don't they?' he said.

'You're fucking with me, man, I know it.'

'No, it's like a whole other language . . .'

I tried to ignore them and concentrated on Epstein. 'I don't know why or how I ended up on that list, but you have no reason to believe that I'd harm you. That's why I brought you here, and that's why you're without your bodyguards. If I'd wanted you dead, then you'd be dead, and these two men wouldn't be here to witness it.' I caught Louis's eye. 'Well, one of them wouldn't be.'

'My fear, as I explained to you last night, is that there may be a presence within you that has not yet revealed itself,' said Epstein.

'And I told you that, if I was like them, whatever was sleeping inside me would have awakened by now. There were so many times when, if I was a host for something foul lying dormant in me, it could have shrugged off its torpor and intervened to save those like it, but it didn't. It didn't because it isn't there.'

Epstein's shoulders slumped. He looked old, older even than he was.

'There is so much at stake,' he said.

'I know that.'

'If we were wrong about you—'

– 'then you'd all be dead, every one of you. There would be no percentage in not killing you.'

Epstein did not answer. He closed his eyes. I thought he might be praying. When he opened them again, he appeared to have reached a decision.

'*Seitensprung*,' he said, and nodded. 'We don't change partners during the dance.'

'No.'

'So what now?'

'What do you think?'

'We need to find that plane,' said Epstein.

'Why?' asked Louis.

'Because there's another version of the list on it,' I said. 'Barbara Kelly was killed because the people she worked for found out that she was trying to repent, to save herself by revealing what she knew. Her list is gone, but that list in the forest remains. It's probably older than Kelly's, but that doesn't matter. It's still worth securing.'

'But we don't know where the plane is,' said Walter.

231

'You could call your friend, Special Agent Ross, at the FBI,' I said to Epstein. 'He could look at satellite images, try to track changes in the forest that might reveal the path of a fallen airplane.'

'No,' said Epstein.

'Don't you trust him?'

'I trust him implicitly, but as I told you yesterday, we don't know who else is on that list. It may be that even the FBI is infected. The risk of alerting them to what we're trying to do is too high.' He leaned forward on the table, clasping his hands together. 'Are you sure that the Vetters woman doesn't know the location of the plane?'

'She told me that her father didn't say.'

'And you believe her?'

'Her father and his buddy were lost when they came across it. It may be that he gave some more specific indication of the area to her before he died, although if he did then she didn't share it with me.'

'You have to go back to her and discover everything that she knows. Everything. Meanwhile, we'll try to trace the movements of Barbara Kelly and find out all that we can about her. It may be that she secreted away a copy of the list before she died.'

I couldn't keep the skepticism from my face. Epstein might have been right about Kelly making a second copy of the list and storing it away from her house, but if she did I was pretty certain that she gave up its location under torture.

'Marielle Vetters,' I said.

Epstein looked confused.

'What?' he said.

'That's the name of the woman who gave me that list. Her father's name was Harlan, and his friend's name was Paul Scollay. They come from a town called Falls End, at the edge of the Great North Woods.'

Epstein's face cleared.

'Why are you telling me this?' he asked, although I think he already knew the answer to the question.

'Because *I* trust *you*.'

'Even after what happened last night?'

'Maybe especially after what happened last night. I didn't like it at the time, and I don't want a repeat of it, but I understand why you reacted the way that you did. We're on the same side, rabbi.'

'The side of light,' he said.

'Lightish,' I corrected him. 'I'll talk to Marielle, and to Ernie Scollay, just in case his brother might have let something slip over the years. You'll keep your people away from them, though.'

'Only Liat will know their names.'

'And Liat doesn't tell, right?'

'No, Mr Parker, Liat doesn't tell. She is very good at keeping secrets.'

He glanced at Louis and Walter. There was more than he wanted to say about this.

'It's okay,' I said. 'Whatever you have to say, you can say in front of them.'

'She spoke to me only of your wounds,' he said. 'Nothing more. And I did not ask her to sleep with you, in case you were wondering. She did that for her own reasons.'

'I *knew* you got laid,' said Louis's voice from behind me. He turned to Walter. 'I knew he got laid.'

'I didn't know he got laid,' said Walter. 'Nobody tells me anything.'

'Shut up, both of you,' I said.

'You might also be interested to know that she believed in you from the start,' said Epstein. 'It was I who had doubts, not her. She had none, but she indulged an old man's fears. She said that she knew from the moment she took you inside herself.'

'God*damn* . . .'

'I told you to shut up.'

'So,' said Epstein. He stood, and buttoned his jacket. 'We move forward. You'll talk to the woman today?'

'Tomorrow,' I said. 'I'd prefer to speak to her in person, her and Scollay. Along the way, though, I may stop off to meet with a lawyer in Lynn.'

'Eldritch,' said Epstein. He didn't look pleased to be speaking that name.

'I'll be careful what I tell him.'

'I suspect that whatever we know, he already knows more: he and his client.'

'My enemy's enemy –' I said.

– 'may be my enemy too,' Epstein concluded. 'We don't share their aims.'

'Sometimes I think we do. We may even share some of their methods.'

Epstein chose not to argue further, and he and I shook hands.

'We have a car waiting for you outside,' I said. 'Louis will escort you back to Brooklyn.'

'And my young friends?'

'They'll be fine,' I assured him. 'Well, mostly fine.'

I planned to fly up to Boston a couple of hours later. Louis and Angel would drive up in a day or two, along with their toys. In the meantime, I went back over what Marielle Vetters had told me, because there was one detail of her tale that stood out, and only because it conflicted with another story I had heard many years before. It might have been nothing, a piece of misremembering on my part or on the part of the man who had shared the tale with me, but if Marielle Vetters genuinely did not know anything more about the location of the plane it was possible that I could find another means of narrowing down the search area.

It would just mean talking to a man about a ghost.

25

A div and Yonathan trudged south through the wilds of the Jersey Pine Barrens. They had been driven for what seemed like hours over rough terrain before eventually being dumped in the woods. The man named Angel had suggested to them the direction in which they should walk if they wanted to get to Winslow or Hammonton, but they had not been sure whether to trust him and, to tell the truth, Angel had seemed a little vague about the directions to begin with.

'I don't like nature,' he told them, as they stood under his gun, birds calling above their heads. 'Too many trees. And garter snakes, and bobcats, and bears.'

'Bears?' asked Adiv.

'*And* garter snakes, *and* bobcats,' said Angel. 'Don't get too hung up on the bears.'

'Why?'

'Because they're more scared of you than you are of them.'

'Really?' said Yonathan.

'Really,' confirmed Angel. He thought for a second. 'Or maybe that's spiders. Well, happy trails.'

The doors closed, and Adiv and Yonathan were abandoned in a spray of dirt and mud and twigs. Now it was growing darker, but at least they had found a road, even if there were no vehicles upon it and they could not yet see any signs of artificial light.

'I thought they were going to kill us,' said Adiv.

'Perhaps you'll be more polite in future,' said Yonathan.

'Perhaps,' admitted Adiv. 'And perhaps you won't go pointing guns at the wrong people.'

They walked on. All was quiet.

'We're bound to find a store or a gas station soon,' said Adiv.

Yonathan wasn't so sure. It seemed like they'd driven far into the wilderness, and it had taken them a while simply to find something that was more than a trail. He just wanted to be out of the woods before night fell in earnest. He hoped that the rabbi was okay. It was one thing to be personally and professionally embarrassed as they had been, but if anything were to happen to the rabbi . . .

'At least they left us with some quarters for the phone,' he said.

Adiv checked his pocket, and came out with the four coins. He clutched them tightly in his fist, kissed the back of his hand, then opened it again. He stopped and examined them more closely, squinting in the poor light.

'What is it?' said Yonathan.

'Sonofabitch,' said Adiv quietly.

He dropped the coins into Yonathan's hand before switching loudly to Hebrew. '*Ben zona! Ya chatichat chara! Ata zevel sheba'olam!*' He shook his fist in the general direction of the southeast, then slapped the back of his right hand hard against his left palm.

Yonathan pushed the coins around with the tip of a finger.

'Canadian quarters,' he said. 'The bastard.'

26

Davis Tate couldn't get the smell of nicotine out of his mouth and nostrils. He felt as though he were coated in filth outside and in, even though by then the man in the corner was long gone from the bar. They hadn't even seen him depart, and only the newspaper and the brandy – largely untouched – confirmed that he had ever been there at all. His presence had made Tate profoundly uneasy. He couldn't have said why exactly, apart from that momentary pause in the tapping of the man's fingers when Tate joked about his mortality, but he was certain that he and Becky had been the focus of the stranger's attention. Tate had even gone so far as to corral their server while she was removing the empty brandy snifter from the booth and wiping the table clean with a cloth that stank of bleach. He could see Becky watching him, puzzled and unamused, but he didn't care.

'That guy,' Tate said to the waitress, 'the one who was sitting at this table: you ever see him in here before?'

The waitress shrugged. If she were any more bored, she'd have been horizontal.

'I don't remember,' she said. 'We're midtown. Half the people who come in here I never see again.'

'Did he pay cash or credit?'

'What are you, a cop?'

'No, I host a radio show.'

'Yeah?' She perked up. 'What station?'

He told her. It didn't register.

'You play music?'

'No, it's talk radio.'

'Oh, I don't listen to that shit. Hector does.'

'Who's Hector?'

'The bartender.'

Instinctively, Tate looked over his shoulder to where Hector was updating the food specials on the chalkboard. Even in the midst of his labors, Hector found time to wink at Tate again. Tate shuddered.

'Does he know who I am?'

'I don't know,' said the waitress. 'Who are you?'

'It doesn't matter. Let's get back to the question. The guy who was sitting here: cash or credit?'

'I get you,' said the waitress. 'If he paid credit, you could ask to see the slip. Then you'd know his name, right?'

'Right. You should be a detective.'

'No, I don't like cops, especially not the kind that come in here. You sure you're not a cop?'

'I look like a cop?'

'No. You don't look like anything.'

Tate tried to gauge if he'd just been insulted, but gave up.

'Cash,' he said deliberately and, he hoped, for the final time, 'or credit?'

The waitress wrinkled her nose, tapped her pen against her chin, and did the worst impression Tate had ever seen of somebody pretending not to remember. He wanted to shove her pencil through her cheek. Instead he took ten bucks from his pocket and watched it disappear into the waitress's apron.

'Cash,' she said.

'Ten bucks for that? You could have just told me.'

'You gambled. You lost.'

'Thanks for nothing.'

'You're welcome,' said the waitress. She picked up her tray, with the brandy snifter and the stranger's copy of the *Post* on top of it. As she tried to pass him, he took her arm.

'Hey!' she said.

'Just one more question,' said Tate. 'Hector, the bartender?'

'What about him?'

'He's gay, right?'

The waitress shook her head.

'Hector's not gay,' she said.

'You serious?' said Tate. He was shocked.

'Sure,' said the waitress. 'Hector's *really* gay.'

As he and Becky prepared to leave, Tate kept thinking about the kid, Penny Moss. Becky couldn't be serious, could she? After all, she was talking about knowledge of a crime yet to be committed, about the abduction and murder of a girl, but to what end: to foment unrest, or to boost his ratings? Both?

'You're part of something much larger than yourself, Davis,' Becky told him. She was paying their tab, the fag bartender chuckling to himself as he ran Becky's credit card, the waitress leaning against the bar, whispering to Hector while he worked, a feral smile on her blunt, graceless face. They'd given up on trying to get her to come over to the table to take Becky's card. Tate was sure that she was telling the bartender about his earlier conversation with her. He hoped that Hector wouldn't think Tate was queer for him. He had enough problems.

The waitress giggled at something Hector said to her, and covered her mouth to reply as she saw Tate watching her. You're trash, Tate thought. You were bred for this work, and you won't be smiling when you see the tip. Not that he ever intended to set foot in this place again, with its stinking customers and its weird vibe, as though the bar were a portal to another realm, one in which men performed unsavory acts on one another and women degraded themselves by association with them.

Tate hated New York. He hated the smugness of the place, the apparent self-assuredness of even the poorest of its citizens,

the minimum wage flunkies who should have kept their eyes
low and their heads down but instead seemed to have been
infected by the city's absurd confidence in its own rightness.
He'd asked Becky to look into the possibility of broadcasting
the show from somewhere – anywhere – else. Well, maybe
not just anywhere. Jesus, he might end up in Boston, or San
Francisco. Becky told him that it wasn't possible, that they
had an agreement with the studio in New York, that if he
moved then she would have to move too and she didn't want
to leave the city. Tate had responded by pointing out that he
was the talent, and maybe his wishes should take priority
over the matter of her own convenience. Becky had given him
a curious look after he said it, equal parts pity and something
close to hatred.

'Maybe you could talk to Darina about it,' she said. 'You
remember Darina, don't you?'

Tate remembered. It was why he took pills to help him
sleep.

'Yes,' he said. 'I remember her.'

He knew then that he would remain exactly where Becky,
and Darina, and the Backers wanted him to be, and they
wanted him here in the city, where they could keep an eye
on him. He'd made a deal with them, but he hadn't been
bright enough to examine the small print on the terms. Then
again, what would have been the point? Had he turned them
down, his career would have been over. They'd have seen
to that, he was sure of it. He would never have progressed,
and he would still be poor and unknown. Now he had
money, and a degree of influence. The drop in ratings was
a temporary glitch. It would be arrested. They'd make sure
of it. They'd invested so much in him that they couldn't just
cut him loose.

Could they?

'You okay?' asked Becky, as they walked to the door. 'You
look ill.'

Like the bitch even cared.

'I don't like this shithole,' said Tate.

'It's just a bar. You're losing touch with your roots. That's part of the problem we're having.'

'No,' said Tate, as sure as he'd ever been about anything. 'I'm talking about this city. These aren't my people. They despise me.'

Somebody at the bar called an order from the stool nearest the entrance – 'Hey, Hector, I'm dying of thirst over here!' – and the bartender ambled toward him, keeping pace with Becky and Tate. Tate felt Hector staring at him. He tried to face him down, and Hector blew him a kiss.

'One for all your listeners,' said Hector. 'You come back, I got something special for you too.'

Tate didn't wait around to hear what it might be, although the way Hector grabbed his crotch and shook it left him with a limited number of possibilities. As they reached the door, his eye happened upon the newspaper rack. All of the papers were already tattered and stained from use, but the stranger's copy of the *Post* stood out as it was cleaner than the rest, and appeared unread. Something had been written across the top of the front page with a black felt-tip. It read:

Hello, Davis

Tate grabbed the paper and showed it to the bartender.

'Did you write this?' he asked. He was shouting, but he didn't care.

'What?' Hector appeared genuinely puzzled.

'I asked you if you wrote these words on the newspaper.'

Hector looked at the paper. He considered it for a time.

'No,' he said. 'If that had been my message, it would have read "Hello, Davis, you homophobic asshole." And I'd have added a smiley face.'

Tate tossed the paper on the bar. He felt very, very tired.

'I don't hate gays,' he said softly.

'You don't?' said Hector.

'No,' said Tate.

He turned to leave.

'I hate everyone.'

He and Becky parted at the corner. He tried to discuss the writing on the newspaper, but she didn't want to listen. She was done with him for the day. Tate watched her go, her tight black skirt clinging to her buttocks and thighs, her breasts high and round under her navy shirt. She was good-looking, Tate would give her that, but he no longer felt any attraction towards her because she scared him so much.

That was the other thing: she might nominally have been his producer, but he had always suspected that she was so much more. She had seemed to defer to Barbara Kelly on the occasion of their first meeting, but in the years that followed he had seen others defer to her, even Kelly herself. Becky had three cell phones, and even when she was in the producer's chair, ostensibly keeping the wheels of the show oiled, one of those phones would be pressed to her ear. Out of curiosity he had followed her once from the hired studio after they had finished recording a show, keeping his distance, trying to blend in with the crowd. Two blocks from the studio he had watched as a black limousine pulled up at the curb beside her, and Becky got in. He had seen nobody else in back, and the driver had not emerged to open the door for her, instead choosing to remain invisible behind smoked glass.

Three times he had followed her, and on each occasion the same car had arrived to pick her up once she was out of sight of the studio. Producer, my ass, thought Tate, but in a way it had been strangely reassuring. It had confirmed that he was involved with serious people, and the wealth that had helped him to rise was not about to vanish any time soon.

Eventually he might even have a limo pickup of his own.

Now here he was, back in the safety of his apartment building but still feeling contaminated by the stink of the bar, both the taint of nicotine and the musky stench of debased sexuality, and tormented by his knowledge of what might be about to happen to Penny Moss. Maybe he could Google her name, or search for her on Facebook. He could send her a message. There had to be a way to do that kind of thing without revealing his identity. He could set up a temporary account under a false name, but wouldn't he have to wait for her to friend him first? And how many Penny Mosses were out there?

It was the same problem with making a telephone call: where could he start? He could notify the police anonymously and tell them what he knew: that a girl named Penny Moss was going to be abducted and killed, except he couldn't say where she lived, or who was going to do the abducting and killing, not without mentioning Becky and, by doing so, giving himself away. He would also lose everything for which he'd worked so hard: his money, his power, his nice apartment, even his life, because there was the small matter of Darina Flores. They'd send her after him, and that wouldn't be good.

He got in the elevator and stared at his reflection in the glass as he ascended. The evening played itself out before him. He would sit in the dark and argue back and forth about the girl while knowing that, in the end, he wouldn't do anything at all. Eventually he'd pour a drink and pretend to himself that nothing was going to happen, not really. No girl named Penny Moss would be abducted the next day, and no butcher's knife with her blood on it would be found on the property of some halal-muncher, some religious fifth columnist who had cloaked himself in suburban normality while secretly hating everything that this country stood for. This would be no innocent, Becky had told him. They had selected a man who was a danger to all, and once attention was drawn to him there would be ample evidence of his involvement in all kinds of viciousness. They were doing the right thing here. And as for Penny Moss, well, it might be possible to achieve their ends without killing her. She didn't have to shed blood, not really.

Or not much.

But Tate had seen the truth in Becky's eyes, and he knew that this was just the latest step on the road to his own damnation, perhaps the final one. His progress along it had been gradual, slow at first, but he'd felt his feet starting to slide as soon as the vitriol he was spewing became directed at specific targets, as soon as he stopped caring about whether what he said was even partly true or not but simply served the purpose of setting Americans against Americans and rendering reasoned debate impossible, as soon as lives were ruined, and careers and marriages were forced into collapse.

As soon as George Keys killed himself, because that's what the dumb bastard went and did. His mother died the week after the union cut him loose, and the combination of the two events broke him. He hanged himself in his mother's bedroom, surrounded by her possessions. And here was the funny thing: George Keys was gay, but he was so tormented by his homosexuality that he'd been afraid to use the fact of it to defend himself against allegations that he'd slept with the Mexican whore-waitress. There were those who blamed Tate for what had happened, but mostly they did so quietly. Davis Tate was by then well on the way to becoming untouchable.

And damned.

Little steps, little increments of evil.

He put his key in the lock and opened his apartment door. He registered the nicotine stench just an instant too late, his reactions slowed by the beers he'd drunk and his senses dulled by the smell and taste of tobacco that he had carried back with him from the bar. He tried to retreat into the hallway, but a blow caught him on the side of the head, knocking him against the door jamb, and a blade pressed itself against his neck, its edge so sharp that he only realized he had been cut when he felt the blood flow, and with it came the pain.

'Time to talk,' said a stinking voice in his ear. 'Time, even, to die.'

27

Walter Cole drove me to the airport to catch the Delta shuttle flight to Boston. He'd been relatively quiet since we left Nicola's. Walter was good at brooding.

'You have something that you want to share?' I asked.

'I'd just forgotten what an interesting life you lead,' he said, as LaGuardia came into view.

'In a good way, or the Chinese way?'

'Both, I guess. I like being retired, but sometimes I get twitchy, you know? I'll read about a case in the newspaper, or see it on the news, and I'll remember what it was like to be part of that, the rush of it, the sense of, I don't know . . .'

'Purpose?'

'Yeah, purpose. But then Lee will come into the room, and she'll have a beer in her hand for me, and a glass of wine for herself. We'll talk, or I'll help her to cook dinner—'

'You cook now?'

'God, no. I tried making stew once and even the dog got ill, and that dog eats deer shit and doesn't blink. I help Lee by not trying to cook, and just making sure her glass is full. Sometimes one of the kids will join us, and the evening stretches into night, and it will be good. Just *good*. You know how many dinners I missed by being a cop? Too many; too many, and more. Now I get to make up for lost time. Contentment is a very underrated feeling, but you only learn that as you get older, and with it comes regret that it took you so long to realize what you'd been missing.'

'So you're telling me that you don't want to trade your life for mine? You'll forgive me if I'm not shocked.'

'Yeah, that's about the size of it. I listened to what was said in back of Nicola's today and I felt the twitch again, but I also felt the fear. I'm too old, too weak, too slow. I'm better off where I am. I can't do what you do. I wouldn't want to. But I'm afraid for you, Charlie, and I get more afraid as the years go by. I used to think that maybe you could stop this, that you'd go to Maine and just be a normal guy doing normal stuff, but now I know that it isn't in the stars for you. I just wonder how it's going to end, that's all, because you're getting older, and so are those two lunatics who walk at your heels. And the people you go up against, they just seem to get worse and worse. You hear what I'm saying?'

'Yes.' And I did.

We were coming to the Delta terminal. Taxis crowded, and farewells were made. Now the time was for leaving, I wanted to stay. Walter pulled up to the curb, and placed a hand on my shoulder.

'They'll take you in the end, Charlie. Eventually there'll be one who's stronger than you, and faster, and more ruthless, or there'll just be too many of them for even Angel and Louis to help you fight. Then you'll die, Charlie: you'll die, and you'll leave your daughter with only the memory of a father. And the thing of it is, you just can't do anything about it, can you? It's like I can see it written already.'

In turn, I placed my hand on his left shoulder.

'Can I tell you something?' I said.

'Sure.'

'You may not want to hear it.'

'It's okay. Whatever it is, I'll listen.'

'You're turning into a miserable old man.'

'Get out of my city,' he replied. 'I hope they kill you slow . . .'

28

Grady Vetters opened his eyes and watched clouds scud across the moon. He had only intended to nap for thirty minutes, but somehow the day had slipped through his fingers. Not that it mattered: it wasn't like he had a job driving an ambulance, or putting out fires. It wasn't like he had any kind of job at all.

He sat up and lit a cigarette, and the paperback book that he had been reading fell to the floor. It was an old Tarzan novel with yellow page edges and a cover illustration that promised more than the book had so far delivered. He'd found it on the shelf in Teddy Gattle's living room, along with a whole lot of other books that wouldn't have chimed with the perceptions of those who didn't know Teddy as well as Grady did. Teddy's place was also a lot neater and cleaner than his yard might have led one to expect, and the bed in the spare room was comfortable enough. It had been good of Teddy to offer Grady a place to stay after Grady and his sister had argued. Grady wasn't sure that, if the circumstances had been reversed, he would have done the same.

Grady's head ached, although he had not been drinking. His head had been aching a lot lately. He put it down to stress, and the fact that he had already stayed too long in Falls End. The town had always had this effect on him, ever since he'd first returned after his initial semester at Maine College of Art in Portland. His mom had already been diagnosed with Alzheimer's by then, although at that stage it was manifesting itself only as a mild disengagement from the world around her, but he knew he had an obligation to return home and see her. There was even a faint nostalgia for Falls End, having been away from it for the first significant period in his life, but then he'd arrived back, and he'd fought with his dad, and he'd felt the town begin to oppress him with its insularity and lack of ambition, the sheer mediocrity of it like a weight upon his chest. Just as with the misleading cover of the Edgar Rice Burroughs novel, the cheerful 'Welcome to Falls End – Gateway to the Great North Woods!' sign at the entrance to the town was the best thing about the place. On his last day in Falls End before returning to MeCA, he and Teddy had vandalized the sign by adding the word 'You're', as in 'You're Welcome to Falls End'. They thought it was funny, or at least Grady did. Teddy had seemed ambivalent about the act, but he went along with it because he wanted to please Grady. Later he told Grady that the sign had been restored to its original state the next day, and the finger of suspicion for defacing it had continued to point at Grady and, by extension, Teddy for many years after. Small towns had long memories.

Facing Grady's bed was a shelf of pictures, medals and trophies, relics of Teddy's time in middle and high school. Teddy had been a pretty good wrestler back then, and there had been talk of scholarships being offered by a couple of colleges further south, but Teddy didn't want to leave Falls End. Truth was, Teddy didn't even want to leave high school. He liked being part of a group, being surrounded by people who, regardless of differences in looks, or academic ability, or physical prowess, shared a common bond, which was the town of Falls End itself. For Teddy, school days really had been the happiest days of his life, and nothing since could compare with them. Grady stared at the photographs. He was in a lot of them alongside Teddy, but he was smiling in fifty percent of them at most. Teddy was smiling in every one.

Teddy Gattle, always orbiting around the sun that was

Grady Vetters; or looked at another way, Teddy was Grady's squat shadow. He was the reality that dogged Grady's dreams.

Grady wondered if he should try calling Marielle again. He'd left one vaguely conciliatory message on her machine, but she hadn't replied, and he figured that she was still pissed at him. He'd woken up dazed and hungover after the latest party at Darryl Shiff's place, Darryl being the kind of guy who felt that a week was wasted if it included only one party at his house. The hangover was bad enough. Worse was the fact that he hadn't woken up alone: there was a girl sleeping next to him, and Grady couldn't remember who she was, or how she got there, or what they'd done together. The girl didn't quite have 'skank' written all over her, but that was mostly because there wasn't much room on her skin to fit it in, what with all of the other stuff that adorned it. There seemed to be a disturbing number of men's names – Grady counted two Franks, and wondered if they commemorated the same guy or two different ones – and when he pulled down the sheet he saw a devil's tail tattooed across the girl's ass, a tail whose origins were lost somewhere between her slim buttocks. Just below the nape of her neck was a wreath of green leaves with berries bright and red. Holly: that was her name. She'd even cracked a joke about the tattoo, he now recalled, something about guys remembering her name from behind.

He suddenly wanted to shower.

He rose to take a leak, hoping that when he returned the girl might have disappeared, but when he emerged from the bathroom Marielle was standing at the bedroom door while a naked, overly tattooed woman asked her for a cigarette, and then followed up by inquiring if Marielle was 'the wife', which suggested she had her priorities all wrong when it came to the possibility that she had just slept with a married man. It was about then that the shouting started, with the result that Grady moved out later in the morning and turned up on Teddy's doorstep carrying his battered suitcase in one hand, his easel in the other, and his paints and brushes stored wherever he could fit them. He had no idea where Holly had disappeared to once she got dressed, but she had seemed pretty mellow about the whole business. Maybe she'd add his name to her list of conquests: possibly in her armpit, or between her toes.

Grady finished the cigarette and stubbed it out on an ashtray stolen from a bar in Bangor, back when bars still had their own ashtrays. He padded to the kitchen, found fresh bread on the table, and ham and cheese in the refrigerator. He made himself a sandwich and ate it standing up, along with a glass of milk. There was cold beer if he wanted it, but he'd fallen out of the habit of drinking beer in recent years, and the amount of it that he'd been putting through his system since he returned to Falls End was playing havoc with his digestion. He preferred wine, but Teddy only had one bottle, and that was the size of a mailbox and smelled like it had been made from a base of cheap perfume and dead flowers.

Once again Grady was feeling trapped in a way that reminded him of his youth, when all he lived for was to head south and leave his parents and his sister and every evolutionary dead-end cell of Falls End far behind. He'd wanted to go to art school in Boston or New York, but settled instead for Portland, where one of his aunts lived. She was his mother's younger sister, regarded as dangerously bohemian by the rest of her family. She provided Grady with a room, and he got a summer job down at one of the tourist places on Commercial, serving up lobster rolls and fries, and beer in plastic glasses. He ate whatever the restaurant gave him, and apart from a few bucks a week to his aunt as a token gesture toward rent, and the occasional beer party in someone's basement, he saved everything that he earned, and he was a good enough employee to be offered additional hours at another bar in town owned by the same guy, and so his first year at MeCA had passed comfortably.

MeCA had been the right choice for him, in the end. The college entrusted its students with a key to the premises so he could work any time that he liked, even sleeping there when he had projects due. He was marked as a student to watch right from the start, a young man with real potential. He'd even realized some of it. Perhaps he'd realized it all, and that was the problem. He was good, but he was never going to be great, and Grady Vetters had always wanted to be great, if only to prove to his family and the doubters up in Falls End how wrong they'd been about him. But the disparity between his desire and his ability, between his reach and his grasp, had quickly become apparent to him when he left the comforting embrace of MeCA and tried to make his way in the big, bad art world. That was when the trouble had started, and now having his picture on the wall of Lester's looked likely to be the best independent testimony to his value as an artist that he was ever going to see.

He wandered back to the bedroom. The temptation to do a little weed was strong, but with it would come the urge to lie down on the couch and flick through the million and one channels on Teddy's cable box. To distract himself, he set out his oils and continued working on the painting that he'd started the day before Marielle had kicked his ass out of her house. 'My' house: that was how she'd described it, and he'd been tempted to argue the point before he realized that she was right: it was 'her' house. Apart from her short-lived marriage, she'd lived there all her life. She loved it, just as she'd loved their father in a way that Grady never had, just as she loved Falls End, and the woods, those damned woods. Everything came back to them. They were the only reason anyone ever came here, the only reason the town thrived.

Grady hated those woods.

So Grady had stopped shouting at his sister, right there and then. He realized that it didn't matter what happened with the banks, or how much the house might be worth and what his cut might be. He wasn't about to put pressure on her to take out a loan that might endanger her hold on the place, not in this economic climate. She wasn't earning much as a schoolteacher, even supplementing it with waitressing on weekends. He'd decided to tell her not to worry, and planned to go over and clear the air the next day. When, or if, the money came through, she could send it on to him. For now he'd stay with Teddy, and paint, and try to figure out where to go next. There were still houses in which he hadn't worn out his welcome, couches and basements where he could crash. He'd put up some flyers offering to do murals, design work, whatever it took.

His old man was dead. What did it matter?

The painting was coming together quickly. It showed the house, and his parents, and was reminiscent of Grant Wood's *American Gothic* except that the couple were happy, not dour, and in the background two children, a boy and a girl, pressed their faces against the inside of their bedroom windows, waving at their parents below. He intended to give it to Marielle as an apology, and as a token of what he felt for her, and their mother and, yes, their father too.

'He went to your show!' Marielle had said, screaming the words at him as the tattooed girl pulled on her jeans, realizing that she was in the middle of a serious domestic meltdown and there was no percentage in her hanging around to see how it all panned out.

'What?' He wished he hadn't drunk so much at Darryl's. He wished he hadn't smoked that second blunt. He wished he'd never even spoken to the Fabulous Tattooed Lady. This was important, but he couldn't get his head clear.

'Your show, your lousy New York show, he went to it,' said Marielle, and she was crying now, the first time he'd seen her cry since the funeral. 'He took the bus to Bangor, and from there to Boston and on to New York. He went in the first week. He didn't want to go on the opening night because he didn't think that he'd fit in. He thought you'd be ashamed of him because he lived out by the edge of the woods, and he couldn't talk about art and music, and he only owned one suit. So he went to your show, and he looked at what you'd done, what you'd achieved, and he was *proud*. He was proud of you, but he couldn't say it and you couldn't see it, because you were too out of it to understand, and when you weren't out of it you were just angry. And it was all fucked up, all of it. You and him, the way it could have been, it was all lost over nothing but pride and booze and drugs and . . . Ah, Christ, just get out. Get out!'

I didn't know, he wanted to say; I didn't know. But the words wouldn't come, and ignorance was no excuse. It wasn't even true. He *had* known that his old man was proud of him, or suspected as much, because how many times had his father tried to reach out to him in his way, and how many times had he been rebuffed? Now it was too late, because it was always too late. Some revelations only came with the sound of dirt falling on a coffin: the ones that mattered, the ones that made for regrets.

So he was painting a picture for his sister, and maybe for himself too. It would be the first such offering he had made to her since they were children, and the most important. He wanted it to be beautiful.

He heard the sound of a vehicle slowing down, and head-lights raked the house as Teddy's truck pulled into the drive. Grady swore softly. Teddy had a heart of gold, and there was nothing that he wouldn't do for Grady, but he liked background noise in his home: the sound of the TV, or the radio, or music on the stereo, usually something from the sixties or seventies sung by men with beards. Grady thought that it came from living alone for too long while being uncomfortable with his own company. Now that Grady was around, Teddy liked being in his presence as much as possible. He'd insist that Grady watch old sci-fi movies with him, or smoke some weed while listening to *Abbey Road* or *Dark Side of the Moon* or *Frampton Comes Alive*.

The engine died. He heard the doors of the truck opening and closing, and footsteps approaching the house. The front door was unlocked. Teddy always left it that way. It was Falls End, and nothing bad ever happened in Falls End.

Doors, Grady realized: Teddy had brought company. Hell, that meant that any small hope Grady had of working for an hour or two had just gone right out the window. Grady put down his brush and walked to the living room.

Teddy was kneeling on the floor, his head bowed and his hands clasped behind his back. He looked like a man bobbing for apples.

'You okay, Teddy?' asked Grady, and Teddy looked up at him. His nose was broken, and his mouth was bloody. Grady wasn't sure, but even through the blood it looked as if some of Grady's teeth were missing because there were gaps where there had not been gaps before.

'I'm sorry,' said Teddy. 'I'm so sorry.'

A boy jumped from behind the couch, like this was all just a big game, a game whose main purpose was to scare Grady Vetters to childhood and back, which the sight of the boy had pretty much done. He had the swollen, unhealthy pallor of a cancer sufferer, and his hair was already thinning. There was bruising around his eyes, his nose was swollen, and his throat was distended by an ugly purple mass. Under other circumstances Grady might almost have pitied him, except the boy wore an expression that was simultaneously blank and malevolent, the way Grady had always imagined concentration camp executioners looked after their victims grew too many to count. The boy was holding a pair of blood-stained pliers in his right hand. He made a throwing motion in Grady's direction with his left, and four teeth landed at Grady's feet, roots and all.

Grady wondered if this was a nightmare. Perhaps he was

still asleep, and if he willed himself awake none of this would be happening. He'd always dreamed vividly: it came with being an artist. But he felt the night air on his face, and he knew that he was not dreaming.

A woman appeared in the doorway behind Teddy, her face partially marred by what at first might have been mistaken for a roseate birthmark but was quickly revealed as a terrible, blistered burn. A patch of gauze covered her left eye. All of these details were incidental, though, next to the gun that she held in her right hand, and the plastic cable ties that dangled from her left.

She pointed the gun at the back of Teddy's head and pulled the trigger. There was an explosion that made Grady's ears ring, and Teddy was no more.

Grady turned on his heel and ran back into the bedroom, slamming the door behind him. There was no lock, so he pushed his bed against the door before he began opening the window. He heard the sound of the doorknob turning, and the bed moving across the floor, but he did not look back. The window was stiff, and he had to punch the frame to force it open. He already had one foot on the windowsill when he felt a weight land on his back and a small arm snake around his neck. He tried to pull himself forward and out, but he was off balance and the boy's full weight was hanging from him. Grady teetered on the windowsill, his arms straining against the frame, and then there were more hands on him, stronger hands, and his fingers lost their grip. He fell back and landed awkwardly on the floor, the boy rolling away from him so that he would not be trapped under the weight of Grady's body. The woman spread herself across Grady's chest, one knee on either side of his body pinning his arms to the ground, and she leveled the gun at the center of his face.

'Stop moving,' she said, and Grady obeyed. There was a sharp pain in his left forearm, and he saw that the boy had injected him from an old metal syringe.

Grady tried to speak, but the woman placed a hand over his mouth.

'No. No talking, not yet.'

A great tiredness came over Grady, but he did not sleep, and when the woman's questions commenced, he answered them, every one.

29

D avis Tate had been forced to secure himself to the heavy radiator in the living room. The intruder had already attached one cuff to the pipe before Tate's arrival, so now only Tate's left hand remained free. At least the radiator wasn't on, which was something, and the mild weather meant that the apartment wasn't too cold. The fact that Tate could joke about his situation, even to himself, suggested that either he was braver than he thought, which seemed unlikely, or he was going crazy from fear, which was more probable.

The man from the bar sat in a chair beside Tate, flicking his butterfly knife open and closed, each *snick* of the blade making Tate wince at the further pain that it promised. The cut on his neck had stopped bleeding, but the sight of his shirt stained red made him queasy, and the smell of nicotine at close quarters had become so strong that it felt as though his nose and tongue were burning.

And the intruder terrified him. It wasn't just the knife in his hand, although that was bad enough. The man conveyed a sense of implacable malice, a desire to inflict hurt that was beyond reason. Tate recalled an evening in a club in El Paso at which he'd been introduced by a mutual friend to some men who claimed to be fans of his show, nondescript figures with sunburned skin and the glassy eyes of dead animals who were either on their way to, or coming back from, the conflict in Afghanistan. As the night wore on, and more alcohol was consumed, Tate worked up enough courage to ask them what it was they did, exactly, and was informed that they specialized in the interrogation of prisoners: they waterboarded, and starved, and froze, and tormented, but they made one thing clear to him: there was a purpose, an end to what they did. They did not torture for the pleasure of it, but to extract information, and once the information was extracted, the torture stopped.

Most of the time.

'We're not like the other guys, the bad guys,' said one, who told Tate that his name was Evan. 'We have a set goal, which is the acquisition of information. Once we're certain that this been achieved, our work is done. You want to hear what's really terrifying? Being tortured by someone who has no interest in what you know, someone for whom torture is an end in itself, so that no matter what you tell him, or who you betray, there's no hope that the pain will stop, not unless he decides to let you die, and he doesn't want to do that; not because he's a sadist, although that's probably part of it, but out of professional pride, like a juggler trying to keep the balls in the air for as long as he can. It's a test of skill: the louder and longer you scream, the greater the vindication of his abilities.'

Tate wondered if here, in his own apartment, he was now looking at just such an individual. His suit was wrinkled and stained, the collar of his shirt as yellowed as his fingers, his hair slick with grease. There was no military bearing to this man, no sense of someone who had been trained to do harm.

But this man was also a zealot. Tate had met enough of them in his time to recognize one when he saw him. In his eyes burned a fierce light, the fire of righteousness. Whatever this man did, or was capable of doing, he would not view as immoral, or an offense against God or humanity. He would hurt, or kill, because he believed that he had the right to do so.

Tate's only hope lay in the man's use of a single word: *perhaps*.

Time, perhaps, to die.

Or, perhaps, to live.

'What do you want?' asked Tate, for what must have been the third or fourth time. 'Please, just tell me what you want.'

He felt and heard the sob catch in his throat. He was getting tired of posing the question, just as he had tired of seeking the man's name. Each time he asked a question the intruder just gave the blade a double flick in reply, as if to say 'Who I am doesn't matter, and what I want is to cut.' This time, though, Tate received an answer.

'I want to know how much you got for your soul.'

His teeth were yellow, and his tongue was stained the dirty white of sour milk.

'My *soul*?'

Snick went the blade. *Snick-snick*.

'You do believe that you have a soul, don't you? You have faith? After all, you speak of it on your radio show. You talk about God a lot, and you speak of Christians as though you know the inner workings of each and every one. You seem very certain about what is right and what is wrong. So what I want to know is, how can a man who has sold his soul speak of his God without gagging on the words? What did they offer you? What did you get in return?'

Tate tried to calm himself, still clinging to the precious *perhaps*. What answer was this man seeking? What answer would keep Tate alive?

And suddenly the intruder was upon him, even as Tate tried to kick out and keep him at a distance. The knife was back at his throat, and this time the *snick* was followed by the drawing of more blood from behind his right ear.

'Don't calculate. Don't think. Just answer.'

Tate closed his eyes.

'I got success. I got syndication. I got money, and influence. I was a nobody, and they made me somebody.'

'Who? Who made you this somebody?'

'I don't know their names.'

'Not true.'

Snick! Another cut, except this one was lower, slicing through his earlobe. Tate shrieked.

'I don't know! I swear to you I don't know. They just told me that the Backers liked what I did. That's what they call them: the Backers. I've never met them, and I've had no contact with them, only with the people who represent them.'

Still he tried to keep back the names. He was scared of this man, scared near to death, but he was more frightened of Darina Flores and the desolation he had experienced as she spoke of all that would follow if he crossed those who were so anxious for him to succeed. But now it was the intruder who was whispering. He held Tate's face in his hand as he spoke, and breathed a fug of fumes and filth and rotting cells into his face.

'I am the Collector,' he said. 'I send souls back to their creator. Your life, and your soul – wherever it may lie – hang in the balance. A feather will be enough to shift the scales against you, and a lie is the weight of a feather. Do you understand?'

'Yes,' said Tate. The manner in which this man spoke left no room for misunderstanding.

'So tell me about Barbara Kelly.'

Tate knew then that there was no point in lying, no point in holding anything back. If the man knew about Kelly, then how much else did he know? Tate didn't want to risk another cut, maybe a fatal one, by being caught out in a lie, and so he told the Collector everything, from his first meeting with Kelly, through the introduction of Becky Phipps and the destruction of the vocation and life of George Keys, right up to the meeting earlier that day concerning the fall in his ratings. He sniveled and wheedled, and engaged in the kind of shameless self-justification that he believed himself to be duty bound to shoot down when his opponents tried to rely on it.

And as he spoke he felt as if he were engaged in a process of confession, even though confession was for Catholics, and they were barely above Muslims, Jews and atheists on the list of folk for whom he reserved a particular hatred. He was listing his crimes. Taken individually they seemed inconsequential, but when recited as a litany they seemed to assume an unstoppable momentum of guilt; or was he merely reflecting the feelings of the man seated opposite him, for although his interrogator's expression never varied – rather it seemed to grow gentler and more encouraging as Tate's lanced conscience spewed out its poison, rewarding him for his honesty with something that might have been mistaken for compassion – there was no escaping the knowledge that Tate's soul was still being weighed against a feather on the Collector's scales, and found wanting.

When he was done, Tate sat back against the wall, and hung his head. His earlobe ached, and his mouth tasted of salt and sour things. For a time there was only silence in the dim room. Even the sound of the traffic outside had faded, and Tate had a sense of the boundlessness of the universe, of stars racing away into the vacuum, colonizing the void, and of himself as a fragment of fragile life, a fading spark from a vital flame.

'What are you going to do?' he finally asked, when his own insignificance threatened to unman him.

A match flared, and another cigarette was lit. Tate smelled the vileness of the smoke, the odor that had first alerted him to the intruder's presence, except now the word 'intruder' had become inappropriate. Somehow, this man *belonged*: here, in this room, in this apartment, on this street, in this city, in this world, in this great dark universe of dying light and distant, spiraling galaxies, while Davis Tate was merely a temporary fault in nature, a stain upon the system, like a mayfly born with one wing.

'Would you like a cigarette?' asked the Collector.

'No.'

'If you're concerned about ruining your health, or becoming addicted, I wouldn't worry.'

Tate tried not to think about what that might mean.

'I asked you what you're planning to do with me,' said Tate.

'I heard you. I've been thinking about the question. Barbara Kelly is dead, so her fate is already decided.'

'Did you kill her?'

'No, but I would have, given the opportunity.'

'So who did kill her?'

'Her own people.'

'Why?'

'Because she was turning against them. She was sick, and frightened, and she feared for her soul, so she set out to make recompense for her sins. By betraying their secrets, she believed that she might save herself. But then there is Becky Phipps . . .'

On the table beside the man lay Tate's cell phone. With the cigarette clamped between his teeth, the Collector flicked through the list of contacts until he found the name that he wanted. A forefinger pressed itself against the screen, and the number was dialed. Tate heard it ringing. The call was answered on the third ring, and Tate knew from the echo that the recipient's phone was on speaker.

'Davis,' said Becky Phipps's voice. She didn't sound particularly pleased to be hearing from him, Tate thought. Bitch. You think you have problems. 'This isn't a good time. Can I call you back later, or tomorrow?'

The stranger indicated to Tate that he should speak. He swallowed. He didn't know what he was supposed to say. In the end, he settled for honesty.

'It's not such a good time for me either, Becky. Something's come up.'

'What now?'

Tate looked at the Collector, who nodded his assent.

'There's a man here with me, in my apartment. I think he wants to talk to you.'

The stranger took a long drag on his cigarette before leaning close to the phone.

'Hello, Ms Phipps,' he said. 'I don't think we've had the pleasure, although I'm sure that we will in the near future.'

Phipps took a couple of seconds to reply. When she did, her tone had changed. She was cautious, and her voice trembled slightly. It caused Tate to wonder if she knew the identity of the caller already, despite her next question.

'Who is this?' she said.

The man leaned yet closer to the phone, so that his lips were almost touching it. He frowned, and his nostrils twitched.

'Is there someone there with you, Ms Phipps?'

'I asked you a question,' said Phipps, and her voice became even less steady, belying her attempt at bravado. 'Who are you?'

'A collector,' came the reply. '*The* Collector.'

'A collector of what?'

'Debts. Regrets. *Souls*. You're stalling for time, Ms Phipps. You know who I am, and what I am.'

There was a pause, and Tate knew that the Collector was right: there was someone else with Becky. He could picture her looking to the other for guidance.

'That was you in the bar, wasn't it?' she said. 'Davis was right to be worried. I thought he was just jittery, but it seems that he was more sensitive than I gave him credit for.'

Tate didn't like his producer's use of the past tense in association with his name.

'He is remarkably sensitive in more ways than one,' said the Collector. 'He screamed very loudly when I sliced through his earlobe. Thankfully, these old brownstones have thick walls. Will you scream when I come for you, Ms Phipps? It won't matter either way, so don't be too concerned. I always bring earplugs. And I really do believe that there is someone with you. That's my particular sensitivity. Who is it? One of your "Backers", perhaps? Put him on. Let him speak. It is a "he", isn't it? I can almost see the price tag on his suit. Be sure, whoever you are, that I'll find you too, and your associates. I've learned a great deal about you already.'

There was an intake of breath before Phipps started shouting.

'What did you tell him, Davis? What did you tell him about us? You keep your mouth shut. You keep it shut or I swear, I swear we'll put you—'

The Collector killed the connection.

'That was all very amusing,' he said.

'You warned her,' said Tate. 'She knows you're coming now. Why would you do that?'

'Because in her fear she'll draw out the others, and then I can take them too. And if they choose to remain hidden, well, she'll give me their names when I find her.'

'But how will you do that? Won't she hide from you? Won't she be protected?'

'I find your concern for her very touching,' said the Collector. 'One would almost think that you liked her, rather than merely being obligated to her. You really should have examined that contract more closely, you know. It made clear your obligations to them, while leaving them with none to you. It is in the nature of their bargains to do so.'

'I don't read Latin,' said Tate glumly.

'Very remiss of you. It's the *lingua franca* of the law. What kind of fool signs a contract written in a language that he can't read?'

'They were very persuasive. They said it was a one-off deal. They told me that if I turned it down, there were others who would accept.'

'There are *always* others who will accept.'

'They told me I'd have my own TV show, that I'd get to

publish books. I wouldn't even have to write them, just put my name to them.'

'And how did that work out?' the Collector asked, and he seemed almost sympathetic.

'Not so good,' admitted Tate. 'They said I had a face made for radio. You know, like Rush Limbaugh.'

The Collector patted him on the shoulder. The small gesture of humanity increased Tate's hope that the word 'perhaps' had become less a piece of driftwood to which he might cling than a life boat to keep him safe from the cold waters that currently lapped at his chin.

'Your friend Becky has a bolt-hole in New Jersey. That's where she'll run to, and that's where I'll find her.'

'She's not my friend. She's my producer.'

'It's an interesting distinction. Do you have any friends?'

Tate thought about the question. 'Not many,' he admitted.

'I suppose that it's difficult to keep them in your line of work.'

'Why, because I'm so busy?'

'No, because you're so unpleasant.'

Tate conceded the point.

'So,' said the Collector. 'What should I do with you now?'

'You could let me go,' said Tate. 'I've told you all that I know.'

'You'll call the police.'

'No', said Tate, 'I won't.'

'How can I be sure?'

'Because I know that you'll come back for me if I do.'

The Collector appeared impressed with his reasoning. 'You may be smarter than I thought,' he said.

'I get that a lot,' said Tate. 'There's something more that I can give you, to convince you to let me go.'

'What would that be?'

'They're going to abduct a girl,' said Tate. 'Her name is Penny Moss. They'll blame whatever happens to her on some raghead.'

'I know. I heard you discussing it.'

'You were right at the other end of the bar.'

'I have very keen hearing. Oh, and I placed a cheap transmitting device on top of your booth as I passed.'

Tate sighed. 'Will they hurt the girl?'

'There is no girl.'

'What?'

'It was a test to see how you'd respond. After what happened with Barbara Kelly, they're worried. Repentance is contagious. They'll administer many such tests in the days and weeks to come. I think they probably figured that they were safe with you, though. After all, you never displayed any signs of being principled before. You were hardly likely to start now.

'The pressing question remains, Mr Tate, what is to be your fate? You've been a bad man: you're a corruptor, a proselytizer for ignorance and intolerance. You thrive on fear, and finding easy enemies for the weak and bitter to hate. You fan the flames, but plead innocence when the ugliness of the consequences becomes apparent. The world is a poorer, more benighted place for your presence in it.'

The Collector stood. From beneath his coat he removed a gun, an old .38 Special, its grips worn, its metal dulled, yet still handsomely lethal. Tate opened his mouth to shout, to scream, but no sound emerged. He tried to worm his way into the corner, covering his face with his arm as though it might shield him from what was to come.

'You're panicking, Mr Tate,' said the Collector. 'You haven't let me finish. Hear me out.'

Tate tried to calm himself, but his heart was beating and his ear throbbed with renewed vigor, and he welcomed the pain of it because he could still feel it, because he was still alive. He peered over his forearm at the man who held his life in his grasp.

'Despite all of your manifest failings,' the Collector continued, 'I feel reluctant to pass final judgment upon you.

You are almost damned, but there is room for doubt: only a little, a scintilla. You do believe in God, don't you, Mr Tate? What you talk about to your listeners, hypocritical and untruthful though it may be, has some roots in a blasted version of faith?'

Tate nodded sharply, and consciously or unconsciously, joined his hands as if in prayer.

'Yes. Yes, I do. I believe in the risen Lord Jesus. I was born again in Christ when I was twenty-six.'

'Hmmmm.' The Collector made no effort to disguise his doubt. 'I've listened to your show, and I don't think your Christ would recognize you for one of His own if He spent an hour in your company. But let's leave it up to Him, as you're such a believer.'

The Collector ejected all six bullets from the gun into the palm of his right hand before carefully reloading three of the chambers.

'Ah Jesus, you got to be kidding,' said Tate.

'Taking the Lord's name in vain?' said the Collector. 'Are you sure that's how you want to start off your greatest test before God?'

'No,' said Tate. 'I'm sorry.'

'I'm sure the deity will put it down to the stressful nature of the situation.'

'Please,' said Tate. 'Not like this. It's wrong.'

'Are the odds too generous?' suggested the Collector. 'Too *ungenerous*?' He looked perturbed. 'You drive a hard bargain, but if you insist.'

He removed one of the bullets, leaving two rounds in their chambers, and spun the cylinder before pointing the gun at Tate.

'If your God wills it,' he said. 'I say "your" God, because He's nobody that I recognize.'

The Collector pulled the trigger.

The clicking of the hammer on the empty chamber was so

loud that Tate was convinced for a moment he had heard the bullet that was to kill him. His eyes were screwed so tightly closed that he had to concentrate just to force them open again. When he did so, the Collector was looking with a puzzled expression at the gun in his hand.

'Strange,' he said.

Tate closed his eyes again, this time as a prelude to a prayer of gratitude.

'Thank you,' he said. 'Jesus Lord, thank you.'

When he finished, the gun was again pointing at his forehead.

'No,' he whispered. 'You said. You *promised*.'

'It always pays to be certain,' said the Collector, as his finger tightened on the trigger. 'Sometimes, I find that God's attention wanders.'

This time, Davis Tate heard no sound, not even God's breath in the exhalation of the bullet.

30

Instead of traveling straight to Portland after arriving in Boston, I stayed at a cheap motel on Route 1 near Saugus and ate a good steak dinner at Frank Giuffrida's Hilltop Steakhouse. When I was a boy, my father would treat my mother and me to an early dinner at the Hilltop when we were heading up to Maine to see my grandfather each summer, and I always associated it with the beginning of our vacations. We would sit at the same table every time, or as near as we could get to it. There would be a view over Route 1, and my father would order a rib steak as big as his head, with all the trimmings, while my mother tut-tutted good naturedly and fretted about his heart.

Frank had died back in 2004, and an investment firm now owned the Hilltop, but it was still a place where regular folk could go for a decent steak dinner without breaking the bank. I hadn't been back there in about thirty years, not since my father took his own life. There was too much of him associated with it, but in recent times I had learned more about my father and the reasons for what he had done, and I had reached an accommodation with the past. It meant that places like the Hilltop were no longer tinged with the same sadness, and I was glad that it remained pretty much as I remembered it, with its illuminated sixty-foot Saguaro cactus outside, and its herd of fiberglass cows. I slipped the hostess ten bucks to give me my family's old table to myself, and ordered the ribeye in memory of my father. The dinner salad was just a little smaller than before, but since the original salad would have fed a small family it meant that there was less to throw away. I drank a glass of wine, and watched the cars go by, and thought about Epstein, and Liat, and an airplane hidden by the woods.

And I thought about the Collector, because one matter had remained untouched upon between Epstein and me, although Louis had raised it before I left with Walter to catch my plane. What Louis suggested was that, if the Collector were in possession of a full or partial list of names, he would almost certainly begin targeting those on it. This begged the question: if my name was on it, would he then also choose to target me? For that reason alone it was necessary to arrange a meeting in Lynn with the lawyer Eldritch, to whom the Collector was linked in ways that I did not fully understand.

I finished dinner, skipped dessert for fear of busting my insides, and headed back to my motel room. I had just turned on the light when my cell phone rang. It was Walter Cole. Davis Tate, the toxic figure on talk radio whose name appeared on the lists, was dead. According to Walter, Tate had been shot in the head, but some knife wounds had been inflicted on him before he died. His wallet, containing his credit cards and 150 dollars in cash, was still in his jacket pocket, but his cell phone was missing and a tan line on his left wrist suggested that his killer might have taken his wristwatch. The theft of the wristwatch, which would later be revealed as a modestly expensive Tudor, puzzled the detectives investigating the killing. Why leave the money but take the watch? I could have told them why, and so could Walter, but we did not.

The man who killed Tate had magpie eyes.

The Collector had just added another trophy to his cabinet of curiosities.

Early the next morning, I drove to Lynn.

If the firm of Eldritch & Associates had been raking in big bucks in recent years, it hadn't seen fit to pump them back into its offices. It continued to occupy the top two floors of a bleak edifice too dull to qualify as an eyesore but still sufficiently ugly to make the neighboring businesses look as though they would have upped foundations and moved if they could, and it wasn't as if they were housed in architectural gems either. The unprepossessing exterior of Tulley's bar, a prime example of fortress design, stood to the right of Eldritch's building. On its left, a telecom store previously run by, and for, Cambodians had been replaced by a telecom store run by, and for, Pakistanis. Short of putting up a sign inviting the American wing of Al Qaeda in for coffee and cookies, it couldn't have advertised itself more as a target for federal surveillance in the current mood of distrust between the US and Pakistan. Otherwise, this stretch of Lynn was still the same accumulation of gray-green condos, nail salons, and ethnic restaurants that I remembered from previous visits.

The gold lettering on Eldritch's upper windows announcing the presence of a lawyer inside was more flaked and faded than before, a graphic representation of Eldritch's own slow physical decline. The first floor of the building remained unoccupied, but its windows were now barred and the filthy old glass had been replaced with dark, semi-reflecting panes. I tapped on one with a finger as I passed. It was strong and thick.

The street-level door no longer opened to the touch. Beside it, a simple intercom panel was set into the wall. There was no visible camera, but I was willing to bet good money that one or more sat behind the dark glass of that first-floor window. As if to confirm my suspicions, the door buzzed before I even had a chance to press the intercom button. Inside, the building remained reassuringly musty, every intake of breath bringing with it the smell of old carpets, impacted dust, cigarette smoke, and slowly peeling wallpaper. The paintwork was a sickly yellow, and marked on the right of the narrow stairway by decades of traffic. On the first landing was a door marked *Bathroom*, and looking down on it, from the second floor, was a frosted glass door with the firm's name written in the same style of gold lettering that adorned the street-facing windows.

It was almost a relief to open the door and discover that the wooden counter remained in place, and behind it the big wooden desk, and behind that the heavily kohled and otherwise cosmeticized presence of Eldritch's secretary, a woman who, if she had a last name, preferred not to share it with strangers, and, if she had a first name, probably never allowed it to be used, even with intimates, assuming anyone was foolhardy or lonely enough to attempt some form of intimacy with her to begin with. Her hair was currently dyed a gothic black, and rose from her head like a pile of coal slack. She had a cigarette burning in the ashtray beside her, smoking away in a pond of butts, and all around her rose teetering piles of paper. She added to the nearest ones as I entered, yanking two sheets from her old green electric typewriter and carefully separating the carbon copy from the original before placing each on the top of its respective tower. She then picked up the cigarette, took a long drag on it, and squinted at me through the smoke. If the memo about the illegality of smoking in the workplace had reached her, I guess she'd burned it.

'Good to see you again,' I said.

'Is it?'

'Well, you know, it's always nice to see a friendly face.'

'Is it?' she repeated.

'Maybe not,' I conceded.

'Yeah.'

There was an uncomfortable silence, but it was still less uncomfortable than actually trying to conduct a conversation. She continued to puff on her cigarette and view me through the fug of the smoke. She produced a lot of smoke, so there was a limit to how much of me she could see through it. I suspected that she liked it better that way.

'I'm here to see Mr Eldritch,' I said, just before I threatened to lose sight of her entirely.

'You have an appointment?'

'No.'

'He doesn't see people without an appointment. You ought to have called ahead.'

'I would have, but nobody ever answers the phone.'

'We're real busy. You could have left a message.'

'You don't have an answering service.'

'You could have written. You can write, can't you?'

'I wasn't thinking that far ahead, and it's urgent.'

'It always is.' She sighed. 'Name?'

'Charlie Parker,' I said. She knew my name. After all, she'd let me in without the aid of the intercom to identify me.

'You got some ID?'

'You're kidding, right?'

'I look like a kidder to you?'

'Not really.' I handed over my license.

'It's the same picture as last time,' she said.

'That's because I'm the same guy.'

'Yeah.' She made it sound as though that represented a regrettable lack of developmental ambition on my part. My license was handed back to me. She picked up the receiver on her beige phone and dialed a number.

'That man is here again,' she said, even though it had been years since my presence had dampened her day. She listened to the voice on the other end of the line, and put the phone down.

'Mr Eldritch says you can go up.'

'Thank you.'

'Wouldn't have been my choice,' she said, and commenced feeding another double sheet of paper into her typewriter, shaking her head and scattering cigarette ash across her desk. 'Wouldn't have been my choice at all.'

I headed up to the third floor, where an unmarked door

stood closed. I knocked, and a cracked voice told me to come in. Thomas Eldritch rose from behind his desk as I entered, a pale, wrinkled hand extended in greeting. He was dressed, as usual, in a black jacket and pinstripe trousers with a matching vest. The gold chain of a watch extended from a buttonhole on his vest to one of the pockets. The bottom button of the vest remained undone. Eldritch adhered to tradition in his modes of attire as in so many other matters.

'Mr Parker,' he said. 'It is a pleasure, as always.'

I shook his hand, expecting it to crumble to pieces in mine. Shaking hands with him was like grasping quail bones wrapped in rice paper.

His office was less tidy than before, and some of those piles of documents from his secretary's lair below had begun to colonize it. Names and case numbers were handwritten on the front of every file in glorious copperplate, the quality of the lettering consistent throughout, even as some of the writing itself had faded over time.

'You seem to accumulate a lot of paper for someone with such a limited client base,' I said.

Eldritch looked around his office as if seeing it for the first time, or perhaps he was just trying to view it as a stranger might.

'A slow, consistent trickle that has grown to form a lake of legalese,' he said. 'It is the lawyer's burden. We throw away nothing, and some of our cases drag on for many, many years. Lifetimes, it often seems to me.'

He shook his head sadly, clearly regarding the propensity of individuals to lead long lives as a deliberate attempt to complicate his existence.

'I suppose a lot of these people are dead by now,' I said, in an effort to provide some consolation.

Eldritch minutely adjusted the neatly ordered stack of files on his desk, flicking the little finger of his left hand along their spines. The finger was missing a nail. I had not noticed its absence before. I wondered if it had simply fallen out, a further manifestation of Eldritch's disintegration.

'Oh yes, very much so,' said Eldritch. 'Very dead indeed, and those that are not dead are dying. They are the dead who have not been named, you might say. We are all walking in their ranks, and in time each of us will have a closed file with our name written upon it. There is great pleasure to be had in closing a file, I find. Please, take a seat.'

The visitor's chair in front of his desk had recently been cleared of paperwork, leaving a clean, rectangular patch in the center of the dust on the leather cushion. It had obviously been some time since anyone had been offered a seat in Eldritch's office.

'So,' said Eldritch, 'what brings you here, Mr Parker? Do you require me to prepare your will? Do you feel the imminence of your mortality?'

He chuckled at his joke. It was the sound of old coals being raked on a cold, ash-laden fire. I didn't join in.

'Thank you,' I said, 'but I have a lawyer.'

'Yes: Ms Price up in South Freeport. You must prove quite a handful for her. After all, you do get up to all sorts of *mischief*.'

He wrinkled his nose, and blew the last word at me as if it were a kiss. In the right light, and the right mood, he might have resembled an indulgent, avuncular figure, except that it was all a pose. Throughout our exchange, not once had an unsettling steeliness left his eyes, and, for all of his obvious ongoing decrepitude, those eyes remained remarkably clear, and bright, and hostile.

'Mischief,' I echoed. 'The same observation might equally be made about your own client.'

I chose the singular carefully. Whatever impression Eldritch's practice gave of even the slightest interest in conventional legalities, I believed that it existed for only one true purpose: as a front for the work of the man who occasionally went by the name of Kushiel, but was more commonly known as the Collector. The law firm of Eldritch & Associates targeted putative victims for a serial killer. It was engaged in an ongoing discourse with the damned.

'I'm afraid I don't know what you're talking about, Mr Parker,' said Eldritch. 'I do hope that you're not implying some knowledge of wrongdoing on our part.'

'Do you want to search me for a wire?'

'I doubt that you would be so crude in your methods. I suspect that it simply amuses you to make accusations you can't possibly prove about suspicions on which you lack the courage to act. If you have questions to ask about the behavior of this "client", then you should put them to him yourself.'

'We've had words about it, but infrequently,' I said. 'He's a difficult man to find. He tends to hide under rocks, waiting to pounce on the unwary and the unarmed.'

'Oh, Mr Kushiel usually hides *much* deeper than that,' said Eldritch, and any pretense of goodwill vanished. The office was very cold, much cooler than the morning outside, but I could find no sign of an air-conditioner. There wasn't even a window to be opened, and yet, as Eldritch spoke, his words found form in plumes of condensation.

And just as my use of the singular about his client had been carefully chosen, so too was his use of his client's name at that particular point in our discussion. I was aware of the derivation of that particular identity.

In demonology, Kushiel was Hell's jailer.

The first time I had approached Eldritch, his client had been waiting for me outside when I left. If that was going to be the case again, I wanted to know. There was an *entente* between us, but it was delicate, and far from *cordiale*. The existence of the list was likely to complicate that relationship further, especially if the Collector had begun to target those on it.

'Where is he now?' I asked.

'Abroad in the world,' came the reply. 'There is work to be done.'

'Is he a fan of talk radio?'

'Somehow, I doubt it.'

'Did you hear that Davis Tate died?'

'I didn't know the man.'

'He was a minor cheese on right-wing radio. Someone shot him in the head.'

'Everyone is a critic nowadays.'

'Some more than others. Usually a bad review on the Internet suffices.'

'I don't see how this concerns me.'

'I believe that you and, by extension, your client, might have been in contact with a woman named Barbara Kelly. She provided you with a document, a list of names.'

'I have no idea what you're talking about.'

I ignored him, and continued. 'Your client may be tempted to act upon that information. In fact, I think he may already have started with Davis Tate. You need to tell him to keep his distance from the people on the list.'

'I don't "tell" him anything,' replied Eldritch acidly. 'You should not presume to do so either. He will do as he sees fit, within, obviously, the limits of the law.'

'And what law would that be, exactly? I'd like to see where serial killing has been enshrined as a legal act.'

'You're baiting me, Mr Parker,' said Eldritch. 'It's uncouth.'

'Your client is more than uncouth: your client is insane. If he is beginning to take action against the individuals on that list, he'll alert others on it, and those who control them, to the fact of its existence. We'll lose them all just to satisfy your client's bloodlust.'

Eldritch's limbs stiffened in anger. It brought out the excessive politeness that was his lawyer's training.

'I would contest your use of the word "bloodlust",' he said, enunciating each syllable slowly and clearly.

'You're right,' I said. 'It implies an emotional capacity to which he can't even aspire, but we can have a semantic discussion about the best definition of his mania on another occasion. For now, all he has to know is that there are larger interests at stake here, and other parties involved.'

Eldritch's hands gripped his desk as he leaned forward, the scrawny tendons in his neck extending so that he looked like a turtle deprived of its shell.

'Do you think he cares about some old Jew squatting in New York, fingering his tassels as he prays for his lost son? My client *acts*. He is an agent of the Divine. There is no sin in his work, for those whom he chooses to confront have forfeited their souls through their own depravity. He is engaged in the great harvest, and he will not, cannot, stop. Files must be closed, Mr Parker. Files must be *closed*!'

Spittle flecked his lips, and his usually bloodless features had bloomed with an unexpected rush of sanguinity. He seemed to realize that he had overstepped his usual boundaries of decorum, for the tension eased out of his body, and he sank back into his chair, releasing his grip upon his desk. He took a clean white handkerchief from his pocket, patted it against his mouth, and looked with distaste at the marks on the material. It was spotted with red. He caught me staring at it, so he folded it quickly and put it away.

'Forgive me,' he said. 'That was uncalled for. I will pass on your message, although I can't promise that it will do any good. He seeks and finds, seeks and finds.'

'There's another risk involved in his actions,' I said.

'Which is?'

'He will force them to act against him, but he's hard to pin down. You're much easier to find.'

'That could almost be interpreted as a threat.'

'It's a warning.'

'To borrow your expression, that's a matter of semantics. Will there be anything else?'

'I do have one last question,' I asked.

'Go on.' He did not look at me, but began writing on a

yellow legal pad in that elegant copperplate. Already he had dismissed me in his mind. I had forced him to shout. I had seen the blood on the handkerchief. He wanted me gone from his presence.

'It concerns the list that you were sent.'

'List, list.' A drop of blood fell from his lips and exploded upon the paper. He continued writing, so that blood and ink combined. 'Again, I know of no such list.'

I ignored him.

'I was wondering if my name was on it.'

The nib of the pen stopped moving, and Eldritch peered up at me like some old, malicious imp.

'Worried, Mr Parker?'

'Interested, Mr Eldritch.'

Eldritch pursed his lips.

'Let us speculate, then, since you seem so convinced of its existence, and my knowledge of it. If my name were on such a list, I might well be worried, for what could one have done to justify one's place upon it?'

He wagged the bloodied nib of his pen at me.

'I think that perhaps you will be meeting my client sooner than you anticipate. I'm sure that the two of you will have a great deal to discuss. If I were you, I would begin preparing my defense now.

'And perhaps,' he added, as I rose to go, 'you might like to think again about that will.'

Eldritch's secretary was standing at her door when I left her boss's office, looking anxiously up the stairs, alerted by the earlier shouting. Despite her concern, a cigarette still dangled securely from her lips.

'What did you do to him?' she asked.

'I endangered his blood pressure a little, although I was surprised he had enough blood in him to manage it.'

'He's an old man.'

'But not a nice one.'

She waited for me to come down before she started up the stairs to check on her employer.

'You'll get what's coming to you,' she said, and she practically hissed the threat. 'You'll vanish from the face of the earth, and when they search your home for clues, they'll find something is missing if they look hard enough: a photograph in a frame, or a pair of cufflinks inherited from your father. It will be an item that had meaning for you, a cherished heirloom, a memory enshrined in a possession, and it will never be found again, because *he* will have added it to his collection, and we will close and burn the file with your name written on it, just as you too will burn.'

'You first,' I said. 'Your dress is smoldering.'

One of her feet was on a higher step than the other, and her dress had formed a neat basket for the cigarette ash that was burning a hole through the fabric. She brushed at it with her hand, but the damage was already done. It was all relative, as the dress had been horrible to begin with.

'Let's talk again soon,' I said. 'You take care now.'

She whispered some obscenity, but by then I was already heading for the door. The night before, I had taken the precaution of removing my gun from the locked box under the spare tire in my car, and I was now armed. Before I left Eldritch's building I took off my jacket, and used it to conceal the gun in my right hand. I kept it there as I walked back to my car, making a slow turn in the middle of the street to make sure that there was nobody at my back. Only when I was driving out of Lynn did I begin to feel even remotely secure, but it was a temporary, compromised thing. My meeting with the old lawyer had unnerved me, but the certainty and venom with which his secretary had spoken had given me the confirmation that I was seeking.

The Collector was in possession of the same list as Epstein.

And my name was on it.

31

G rady Vetters lay unconscious on the floor of Teddy Gattle's living room. The boy had given him a second, stronger dose of sedative after they had finished questioning him, and he would remain out cold for many hours. Darina had closed the drapes and pulled the blinds, and she and the boy had fed themselves from the contents of the refrigerator. Eventually the boy had drifted off to sleep, curled up on the couch with his mouth open and one small fist curled against his chest. One might almost have mistaken him for an innocent.

Darina did not sleep, not yet. Her face hurt, but she made do with swallowing Advil at regular intervals, and watched television with the volume turned down low. Daylight came, but she was not afraid of being discovered. Both Vetters and his friend had confirmed that the house received few visitors during the day, and Vetters' recent argument with his sister meant that even she would be unlikely to trouble her brother until he framed some apology for his actions.

Darina now knew the story of the airplane in the woods, or as much of it as Harlan Vetters had chosen to share with his son, but she was certain that he had told his daughter more. It was clear from what Vetters had said that his father regarded him as untrustworthy, a disappointment. The old man had placed his faith in the sister, Marielle. She had looked after him in his last illness, and who knows what they had spoken of together over those final weeks and months? Darina had been tempted to confront Marielle Vetters immediately, but she and the boy needed to rest. The pain of her burns had debilitated her, and anyway, it would be easier for them to move around once darkness fell. Her ravaged face would attract attention in daylight, and there were those in this town who might remember her from before, when she was still beautiful.

Careful not to wake the boy, she walked to the bathroom and stared at herself in the mirror. Her wounds glistened beneath their layer of ointment, and her damaged eye resembled a drop of milk in a pool of blood. She had loved being beautiful because it was a reminder of her true nature, but she would never be beautiful again, not in this form. She would be scarred forever, even if she consented to grafts. Perhaps she would shed this skin, just as the boy had done, and wander for years before cocooning herself in another body, there to await her emergence.

In time, though, in time. The plane was important. The list had to be secured.

Grady Vetters stirred, and moaned from where he lay beside the cold fireplace. They had only been forced to injure him a little. The sodium thiopental had made him more malleable, but he had still instinctively tried to protect his sister. The boy had been forced to crush the tips of two of Vetters' fingers with a pair of pliers, and after that he had told them everything.

What he could not tell them, though, was whether his sister had spoken to anyone else about the plane. Grady Vetters had been foolish enough to share the story with Teddy Gattle, and Gattle, believing that he was doing his friend a favor, had made the call to Darina. Apparently, Vetters had been reluctant to contact Darina himself. He had been smart enough to realize that it might draw unwanted attention to himself and his sister. Teddy Gattle, unfortunately, had not been quite so smart, which was why he was now dead. Marielle Vetters, according to both her brother and his late friend, was smarter than both of them, but Grady Vetters admitted to Darina that his sister had recently raised the possibility of seeking some professional advice on their situation. Her brother had been less than supportive, and his sister had not brought up the subject again, but she was strong willed, and Grady Vetters knew that she was more than capable of going behind his back if she believed it was the right thing to do. If she had sought counsel, that made finding the plane all the more urgent.

And there was also the matter of the passenger. If what Harlan Vetters had told his children was true, the passenger had survived the impact, as otherwise his body would have been found handcuffed to his seat. Darina wondered if he had caused the crash by escaping from his cuffs while the plane was in flight. He was certainly capable of it, and strong enough to survive anything but the worst of impacts. She believed that he was still alive. She would have known if he was not, would have sensed his pain as he was wrenched from the world, but there had been no communication with him, no contact. She could not understand why. That mystery, too, could be investigated once the plane was found.

Tonight they would speak with Marielle Vetters, and find out all that she knew. They would bring her brother with them, for Darina had learned that the threat of harm to another was often more effective than the threat of harm to oneself, particularly if the individuals in question were linked by bonds of love and blood. Grady Vetters had made it clear to them that he loved his sister. He had even begun painting a picture for her, a picture that neither of them would see completed.

She went back to the living room, glancing down at Teddy Gattle's body as she passed it. He was starting to smell. She dragged him into the main bedroom, and closed the door when she was done. There was no point in making their surroundings any more unpleasant than they had to be while they recovered their strength.

She swallowed two more Advil, then took out her cell phone and dialed a number. A machine picked up, and she left a brief message detailing where she was and what she had discovered so far. She followed it with a second call. She didn't know these woods, and help would be required in finding and securing the plane. The man on the other end of the line didn't sound pleased to hear from her, but people rarely did when their debts fell due. When she was done she lit a cigarette, and let the images on the television screen wash over her. She waited until the boy woke up before she herself slept, and her dreams were filled with visions of beauty lost, and angels falling from the heavens.

Becky Phipps sat on the floor of the safe house in New Jersey. It was little more than a cabin, and sparsely furnished, although it had a land line. She listened to Darina Flores leave her message, and realized that Darina had not been alerted to the latest threat. She did not know that the Collector had begun to hunt them down.

Unfortunately there was little that Becky could do to rectify that situation. Her jaw was broken, and she had received stab wounds to her back and legs. But she had fought hard, and the Collector was still bleeding profusely from his damaged scalp. Nevertheless, she was dying and he was not. Worse, she had told him most of what he wanted to know. Most, but not all. Her only consolation was that, just as he had moved against them, so they would move against him. The thought might have made her smile, had she still been capable of using her mouth.

'Darina Flores,' said the Collector. 'It's good to put a voice to a name, and eventually I'll add her face. I take it that she killed Barbara Kelly? You don't have to speak. Just nod. Actually, a flicker of your eyelids will do.'

Becky blinked once, slowly.

'There was a child with her, wasn't there?'

Becky didn't blink this time. The Collector knelt before Becky, and showed the blade to her. Either Becky didn't know about the child, or even the threat of the blade was not enough to make her acknowledge its existence. No matter: he would discover the truth for himself, eventually.

'And Kelly's copy of the list, does she have it?'

Again, a blink. Becky was not reluctant to confirm this fact. She wanted to point the Collector toward Darina, because Darina would kill him.

'So what is on that plane is an older version? Older, but still dangerous to you if it fell into the wrong hands?'

Blink.

'My hands, for example.'

Blink.

Behind him, Becky saw movement at the window, pale faces pressed against the glass. A gust of wind blew the door open and shapes appeared on the porch. They poured into the house like smoke, these thin, spectral figures.

Hollow Men. She had thought them a myth, even though she had knowledge of matters equally strange. Then again, it was hard for the living to confirm the existence of entities that only the dying could see.

'Only one thing confuses me, Becky,' said the Collector. 'Who was the passenger that Darina mentioned? Who was on that plane? Someone like you? One of the Backers? Should I start trying names?'

Becky managed to shake her head slightly. This, like the child, she would not give him.

'Never mind,' said the Collector. 'I'm sure that it will all become clear in time.'

A look of sorrow crossed his face, and the soulless Hollow Men crowded around him in expectation of another joining their ranks. Tears welled up in Becky's eyes. She tried to speak, her tongue beating weakly inside her ruined mouth like the flutterings of a trapped moth.

'Hush, hush, Becky,' said the Collector. 'There's no more to say.'

With the tip of his blade, he lifted the simple gold chain from around her neck. It had been given to her by her mother, and was her favorite item of jewelry. She watched as it was dropped into a pocket of his overcoat.

'For my collection,' he said. 'Just so that you won't be forgotten.'

The blade came close to her again.

'You have been found wanting,' said the Collector. 'For your sins, I adjudge your life, and your soul, to be forfeit. Goodbye, Becky.'

And slowly, almost tenderly, he cut her throat.

32

Ray Wray was eating breakfast at Marcy's Diner on Oak Street in Portland. He was also reading a copy of the *Portland Press Herald* that someone had kindly left on the next table, minus the sports section, which annoyed Ray Wray more than somewhat. It meant that he was forced to make do with the main paper and the local section, and, in general, Ray Wray couldn't give a damn what happened in Portland. Just because he was a native of the state didn't mean he had to like its principal city or show any interest in its activities. Ray came from the County, and County folk regarded Portland with suspicion.

Ray did like Marcy's Diner, though. He liked the food, and the fact that it was comfortable without being kitsch, and played WBLM, the classic rock station. He liked the fact that it opened early and closed early, and only accepted cash. This suited Ray Wray down to the ground as he had a credit history so bad that he sometimes wondered if he was personally responsible for the collapse of the economy. Ray Wray owed more money than Greece, and whatever cash he had was usually in his pocket. He got by, but only just.

This was his first week back in Maine since taking a 'city bullet' down in New York: eight months on Rikers Island for felonious assault arising out of a disagreement with a Korean restaurateur who believed that Ray should have complained about the quality of the food on his plate *before* he'd eaten it all instead of after, and disputed Ray's right to refuse payment for the meal. There had been some shouting, and a little pushing, and somehow the little Korean lost his balance and banged his head on the corner of a table, and the next thing Ray knew there were Koreans all over him, closely followed by cops and the judiciary of the state of New York. The sentence didn't bother Ray much – he was flat broke anyway, and had been facing the prospect of living on the streets – but the food really had been terrible in that Korean place, and he'd only eaten it because he was so damn hungry.

Now here he was back in Maine with the hunting season almost over, and he hadn't picked up any guide work worth talking about. He'd been forced to stay in Portland, where an ex-girlfriend had an apartment off Congress, not to mention a tolerant attitude to Ray Wray. She'd made it clear to him that her tolerance only extended so far, though, and didn't involve him sharing her bed, or staying in her place beyond the end of November. She worked as a nurse over at Maine Medical so she wasn't around much, which suited him just fine. There was a reason why she was his ex-girlfriend, and he remembered what it was after only a couple of days in her company.

He couldn't stand her, was why.

His inability to secure guide work rankled. He was no longer a registered guide, but he knew those woods as well as anyone, and he still had contacts in some of the lodges and hunting stores. He'd spent time in the warden service before his temper and his drinking combined to have him thrown out on his ass, as that combination is wont to do to a man in any walk of life. Ray had learned his lesson: he didn't drink so much anymore, but it was hard to shake off his history in a state like Maine where everyone knew everyone else, and bad reputations spread like a virus. It didn't matter that Ray was a changed man, his penchant for socking people who crossed him largely excepted, or that he stuck to beer now, not liquor. Coffee had replaced whiskey as his main vice, so that he was rarely without a to-go cup in his hand, and lived off cheap refills at Starbucks. There was a Starbucks at the corner of Oak and Congress, and Ray planned to head over there and fill up once he was done with breakfast. He'd take a seat while no one was looking, stay there for a while, then go to the counter and claim that this was his second coffee, not his first. Nobody ever contradicted him. Say what you liked about Starbucks, but you couldn't fault their staff for their manners. Still, Ray didn't care for those little breakfast sandwiches they sold. For the same price he could get a good meal at Marcy's, which was why he was sitting there now, flicking through his free copy of the *Portland Press Herald* while chewing on egg-smeared toast and wondering just what a man had to do to get a decent break in this life.

He was about to toss the paper aside when an article on the front page, below the fold, caught his eye. He had left the front page until last owing to the half-assed way the paper's previous reader had reassembled it, and because Ray tended toward the view that whatever was in newspapers had already happened, and therefore there wasn't much point in worrying about what they contained, or getting all het up about the order in which you flicked through the pages, except, of course, that sometimes you ended up reading the second half of articles before the first, which could be confusing if you were dumb. Ray Wray was a lot of things – undisciplined, an addictive personality, borderline autistic in his capacity to absorb and recall information – but dumb wasn't one of them. He got into trouble because he was too clever, not because he wasn't clever enough. He was angry at the world because he had never managed to find his place in it, so he lashed out whenever the opportunity arose, and accepted the resulting bruises with equanimity.

He carefully balanced the newspaper against a ketchup bottle and read and reread the front page article, his smile widening as he did so. It was the first piece of good news he'd received in a long time, and he felt that it might presage an upturn in his fortunes.

One Perry Reed, who was facing charges of possession of a class A drug with intent to supply, possession of child pornography, as well as being wanted for questioning in New York in connection with his possible involvement in at least two murders, had been refused bail by a county Superior Court and would remain in custody until his trial began. More to the point, someone had burned Perry's piece-of-shit auto dealership to the ground, along with one of Perry's titty bars. This was a cause for celebration.

Ray Wray raised his coffee cup in salute.

Sometimes, the world just upped and fucked over the right guy.

So this was how Ray Wray come to hate Perry Reed . . .

The car was a piece of shit. Ray knew it, Perry Reed knew it, even the fucking squirrels collecting nuts in the parkland behind the lot knew it. The '02 Mitsubishi Gallant looked like it had been used to transport troops in Iraq, it had so much dust in the engine, and it smelled of dog food, but it wasn't as if automobile salesmen were lining up to offer someone like Ray Wray a credit option. He'd been told that, if he couldn't get Perry Reed to cut him a deal, he might as well resign himself to being the white guy on the bus for the rest of his life, so he convinced his buddy Erik to drive him up to Perry Reed's place and see what could be negotiated. Erik had dropped him off at the entrance to the lot and headed on to Montreal, where he was cutting his own deal for some prime weed that Ray planned to help him offload. The downside was that, if Ray couldn't get Perry Reed to sell him a car, he'd have a long walk home. He would also miss out on a sweet deal with Erik, since pretty much a prerequisite for distributing drugs was the ability to get them from point A to point B, and Ray couldn't see himself getting far on a bicycle with five pounds of cannabis in the basket. Securing a set of wheels was, therefore, a priority if he wasn't to live in penury for the foreseeable future.

Perry Reed came out personally to deal with Ray, which might have been flattering if Reed hadn't been such a nasty fat stocking of shit: brown eyes, brown hair, yellow shirt, brown suit, brown shoes, brown cigar, and a brown nose, just as long as he thought that he might be able sell you something. Ray shook his hand and had to resist the urge to wipe it clean on his jeans. He knew Perry Reed's reputation: the man would fuck a keyhole if there wasn't already a key in it, and it was common knowledge that he had only avoided trial way back on charges of unlawful sexual conduct with a minor because the statute of limitations had been exceeded, hence his nickname of 'Perry the Pervert'. But even a pervert had his uses, and in desperate times people learned to hold their noses when dealing with lowlifes like Perry Reed.

It turned out that Perry Reed had yet to meet a man who didn't meet his less-than-strict customer criteria, which could be summarized as having a down payment and a pulse, although for a time it seemed that Ray Wray might be the man who made even Perry the Pervert think twice about cutting a deal. Ray had scraped together $1,200 to put down, but Reed wanted $3,000 up front, and another $399 per month for the next four years. Ray calculated the interest rate at somewhere around twenty percent, which was mob vig, but he needed that car.

So Ray dug around for the emergency money that he'd been holding back and put a further $300 on the table, and Reed adjusted the monthly payment up to $500 a pop over four years, which made Ray's eyes water, but the deal was struck and Ray drove off the lot in a car that coughed and spluttered and stank but somehow kept moving. Ray figured that with his share of the proceeds from the sale of the weed he could more than cover his payments for the months to come, with enough left over to reinvest with Erik in the wholesale end of the business. He had no intention of stiffing Perry Reed, though. Reed might have looked like a turd squeezed out by a dying dog, but he had a reputation as a man not to be crossed. People who welched on deals with Perry Reed ended up with broken bones, and worse.

As a goodwill gesture, Reed had thrown in free admission to the titty bar next to the lot, which Ray had heard that he owned as well, and a free beer to help make the time pass more pleasurably. Generally speaking, Ray wasn't a man for titty bars. The last time he'd been in one, which must have been a decade before, he'd found himself sharing bar space with his former geography teacher, and Ray had been depressed for a week after. The 120 Club didn't exactly promise good times, resembling as it did the kind of pillbox the Germans had defended during the D-Day landings, but a free beer was a free beer, so Ray pulled up at the side of bar, presented his admission ticket to the bored brunette at the door, and headed inside. He tried to ignore the uric stink, the damp carpets, and what he was pretty sure was the odor of stale male seed, but it wasn't easy. Ray wasn't a fussy guy, but he thought the 120 Club might be as low as a man could sink without licking up spilled beer from cracks in a floor.

The reason for the club's name became apparent to Ray as soon as he looked up at the small mirrored stage, 120 being the combined age of the two women who were currently doing their best to make pole dancing as unerotic an activity as possible. Half-a-dozen men were scattered around the place, trying not to catch one another's eye – or catch anything else, given the standards of hygiene in the place. Ray took a seat at the bar and asked for a Sam Adams, but the bartender told him his voucher was only good for a PBR or a Miller High Life. Ray settled for the PBR, although not happily. He'd never much cared for drinking beer out of cans.

'Perry give you this?' the bartender asked, holding the beer voucher between his fingertips like it might be infected.

'Yeah.'

'You buy a car from him?'

'Mitsubishi Gallant.'

'The oh-two?'

'Yeah.'

'Jesus.' The bartender poured Perry a bourbon from the well, and put the can of PBR beside it. 'You can have the liquor on me. Go ahead, drown your sorrows.'

Perry did. He knew he'd been screwed, but he didn't have much choice. He watched the women gyrate, and wondered how often the poles got cleaned. He wouldn't have touched those poles without a hazmat suit. The bartender came back to him.

'You want, I could arrange for you to spend some time with one of those ladies in a private booth.'

'No thanks,' said Ray. 'I already got a grandmother.'

The bartender tried to look offended on their part, but couldn't put his heart into it.

'Better not let them hear you say that. They'll kick your ass.'

'They can barely lift their legs,' said Ray. 'It wasn't for the poles, they'd fall over.'

This time the bartender scowled. 'You want another drink, or what?'

'Not unless it's free,' said Ray.

'Then get your ass out of here.'

'My pleasure,' said Ray. 'And tell your sisters to find another job.'

It turned out that the Mitsubishi ran pretty good, better than Ray had anticipated. It got him home without any problems, and he spent the weekend working on it, clearing the worst of the crap out of the engine and getting the smell out of the upholstery. He was all set to help Erik move the weed when he learned that Erik had been arrested by the Mounties when he was five miles shy of the border, and he and the weed were now likely to be staying in Canada for the foreseeable future.

So Ray picked up some bar work, and moved some stolen goods, and managed to keep up his payments to Perry Reed for four months, always paying in person and in cash, before he started to fall behind. When the calls began coming in from Reed's people he tried to ignore them, but when they started getting insistent he decided that continuing to ignore them was inadvisable if he wanted to remain in the state of Maine with his limbs intact. He called the lot and asked to speak to Reed, and the big man duly came on the line, and they discussed the matter like gentlemen. Reed said he would find a way to make the loan more affordable for Ray, although it might mean spreading out the payments over two or three more years. Reed told him that he'd have new loan papers drawn up, and Ray could just come by and sign them so everything was above board. Figuring that he had nothing to lose, Ray drove up to the lot, parked outside the main showroom, and headed in to add his initials to whatever needed to be signed. As he took a seat to wait for Reed, a guy in overalls told him that he had to move the car as they were expecting a new consignment of vehicles, and Ray had tossed him the keys without thinking.

That was the last Ray saw of his car. It had just been repossessed.

When he asked to see Perry Reed, he was told that Mr Reed wasn't around. When he started to get loud, four mechanics dumped him on the sidewalk. Ray's mistake was to believe that Perry Reed was in the used car business, but he wasn't. Perry Reed was in the finance business, and the more defaults there were, the better his business was. He could simply sell the same car over again at the same extortionate rates to people who needed a car and couldn't convince anyone else to sell them one.

It was at that point that Ray Wray decided he was going to burn Perry Reed's lot to the ground, along with his titty bar, but then he got sidetracked by the promise of a job in New York that never materialized, and he ate a bad Korean meal, and copped the city bullet, and by the time he got around to taking care of Perry Reed someone else had done it for him.

Which was good, as it saved Ray the trouble of planning and committing a major act of arson, and bad, because it denied Ray the pleasure of planning and committing a major act of arson.

The diner's door opened and Ray's buddy Joe Dahl strolled in, ordered a coffee, and joined Ray at his table. Joe Dahl was a big guy in his forties, which was how he got away with wearing a Yankees cap in Maine. You needed to be big to wear a Yankees cap this far north without someone taking it from your head, and maybe trying to take your head from your shoulders along with it. Dahl claimed that he wore the cap in memory of his late mother, who came from Staten Island, but Ray knew that was bullshit. Dahl wore the cap because he was ornery and peculiar, and because he lived for those times when someone tried to knock it from his head.

'You see this shit?' asked Ray.

'Yeah, I saw it,' said Joe.

'I'd like to shake the hand of the guy that did it. First piece of good news I've had all week.'

'I got some more,' said Joe, as his coffee arrived. 'I found you a job.'

'Yeah? What is it?'

'Guide work.'

'Hunting?'

Joe looked away. He seemed uneasy. Scared, even.

'Kind of. We're going to look for something in the North Woods.'

'Something? What kind of something.'

'I think it's an airplane . . .'

33

I made one small detour before I headed north to Maine: I drove into Boston and found the headquarters of Pryor Investments in Beacon Hill. It occupied a relatively modest-looking, but still absurdly expensive, brownstone not far from the Charles/MGH T-station. There was no sign of activity, and I saw nobody pass in or out of the building while I was parked nearby. So far, Epstein had been unable to find out anything of note about the company, apart from one small detail: the name of Pryor Investments was on documents relating to the formation of a 501(c) body called the American League for Equality and Freedom, and one Davis Tate, now deceased, had been the principal benefactor of the funds channeled through the organization. It was a small thread, but a thread nonetheless. Still, now wasn't the time to pull it and see what would unravel. I drove away from Beacon Hill, and it was only as I passed the Pryor building that I saw the camera systems discreetly mounted in the shadows on the wall, their watchful glass eyes taking in the details of the street and sidewalks surrounding it.

The meeting with Eldritch had not been particularly satisfying, but then meetings with lawyers rarely were. I had no great desire to renew acquaintance with the man who sometimes called himself Kushiel, but was mostly referred to as the Collector. Neither did I want him running loose, indulging his taste for divine justice, or his own interpretation of it, by killing anyone who appeared on his copy of the list, particularly if I was among them. I did not trust the Collector enough to imagine that, if he found my behavior wanting, he would not consider consigning me to his personal retinue of the damned. We had been uneasy allies in the past, but I had no illusions about him: I believed that he, like Epstein, had concerns about my nature, and the Collector tended to err on the side of caution in such matters. He surgically excised polluted tissue.

But there was no reason to believe that the Collector knew about the plane in the Great North Woods, and it was important to secure it before any hint of its existence reached him. Better that Epstein should have the list that Harlan Vetters had seen than have it fall into the hands of the Collector, for Epstein was essentially a good man. Yet even about Epstein I had doubts: I didn't know enough about those who worked alongside him, beyond the fact that the younger ones liked waving guns around, to be certain of their capacity for self-restraint. Epstein appeared to be a moderating influence, but he kept much about himself hidden.

It seemed obvious to say it, but knowing the identity of your enemies was the first step toward defeating them. With their names in his possession, Epstein could begin the task of monitoring their activities, and undermining them when necessary. He would also learn if there were traitors among those whom he had previously trusted, although the list would inevitably be incomplete, dating as it did only to some period prior to the crash of the plane. Who knew how many others had been added to it since then? Nevertheless, obtaining it would be a start. But was there not the possibility that, in some cases, Epstein and his people might choose to act as the Collector had done, and remove from play those on the list who were deemed most threatening?

Those were my thoughts as I drove up to Scarborough, an alternative music station playing in the background on Sirius radio: some Camper Van Beethoven, a double-play of the Minutemen which lasted about three hundred seconds in total, including the DJ's intro, and even a little Dream Syndicate, but I felt compelled to run for cover when some bright spark requested Diamanda Galas, and, in a rush of blood to the head, the DJ obliged.

When I was in my early twenties, and getting to know the kind of girls who would ask you back to their place for coffee and mean it, although with the promise of more than coffee at a later date if you didn't turn out to be a freak, I learned that a surefire way to understand a woman, as with a man, was to flick through her record collection. If she didn't have one then you could largely give up on her right there, because a woman who didn't listen to any music at all didn't have a soul, or anything worthy of the name; if she was loaded up on English alternative music like The Smiths or The Cure, she was probably trying a little too hard to be miserable, but it wasn't likely to be terminal; if she was a fan of hair metal like Kiss, and Poison, and Mötley Crüe, you were faced with the dilemma of staying with her for a while because she might put out, or ditching her before you were forced to listen to any of her music; but if she had Diamanda Galas on her racks, maybe alongside Nico, Lydia Lunch, and Ute Lemper for the quieter moments, then it was time to make your excuses and leave before she dumped powdered sedatives in your coffee and you woke up chained in a basement with the girl in question standing over you, holding a kitchen knife in one hand, a creepy doll in the other, and screaming the name of some guy you'd never met but apparently resembled in psychic form.

So I ditched the alternative station, switched to the CD player, and listened instead to the only album ever released by Winter Hours, which was more tuneful and less frightening, and put me in a better mood as I drove home.

As I parked outside my house, I saw that I had missed a call from Epstein. I returned it from my office phone. The death of Davis Tate was on Epstein's mind.

'Do you believe it was the work of this man, the Collector?' he asked.

'When I heard that he was shot, I thought it might have been your people. The Collector usually prefers to work with a blade.'

'What convinced you otherwise?'

'It seems that there were cuts on Tate's body. He'd lost part of an earlobe. Whoever killed him also took his watch but left his wallet untouched. The Collector likes to acquire souvenirs from his victims. In that sense, he's pretty much your common or garden serial killer. It's the added self-righteousness that makes him special.'

'You spoke to the old lawyer?'

'I did. I got the feeling that Barbara Kelly sent him the same version of the list that you received.'

'With your name on it?'

'So it seems. His secretary was very certain that I was going to get whatever was coming to me.'

'Are you concerned?'

'A little. I like my throat the way it is, and I don't need a smile cut in it. But I think the Collector has the same doubts that you had about me. He won't act until he's certain.'

'And in the meantime, he will continue working through the names on that list. He will bring their protectors down upon himself.'

'I imagine that's what he's hoping.'

Epstein's voice grew muffled for a minute. He had covered the receiver with his hand as he spoke to someone else nearby. When he came back on the line, he sounded excited.

'I have a theory about that plane,' he said. 'The date of the newspaper in the cockpit is close to the date when a Canadian businessman named Arthur Wildon disappeared.'

The name seemed familiar to me, but I couldn't place him. It was left to Epstein to place it for me.

'The Wildon twins, Natasha and Elizabeth, eight years old,

were kidnapped in 1999,' he told me. 'A ransom was demanded, and secretly paid: a simple drop-off on a remote road, the driver instructed not to stop or the girls would be killed. The location of the twins was subsequently communicated by way of a note left by the shore of the Quebec river, its position marked with a rock painted black and white. The note claimed that the girls were being kept at a cabin outside Saint-Sophie, but when the rescue team got to the cabin it was empty, or appeared to be. Five minutes after they arrived, Arthur Wildon received a telephone call. The caller, who was male, gave him a single instruction: "Dig."

'And so they dug. The cabin had a dirt floor. The girls had been bound and gagged, then buried alive together in a hole three feet deep. The medical examiner estimated that they had been dead for days, probably killed within hours of their abduction.'

I held the phone away from my ear for a moment, as though its proximity were somehow causing me pain. I recalled closing a trapdoor on a young girl in an underground cell so that her cries would not alert the man who had put her there, and I heard again the terror in her voice as she had begged me not to leave her in the dark. She had been fortunate, though, because she had been found. Most of them were never found, or not alive.

But the man involved in that case had been a serial abuser and killer of young women, with no intention of ever releasing them. Kidnappers were different. Through Louis, I had once met a man named Steven Tolles, who was a hostage negotiator employed by a leading private security firm. Tolles was a 'sign of life' expert, called in to consult on cases of which not even the FBI or the police ever had any awareness. His primary concern was to ensure the safe return of the victim, and he was very good at his job. It was for others to catch the perpetrators, although Tolles, in his debriefing of victims, often drew from them crucial clues as to the identities of those involved:

stray smells and sounds could be as useful as momentary glimpses of houses, woods and fields, sometimes even more so. From Tolles I learned that the instances of murder in kidnapping cases were comparatively rare. Kidnapping was a crime of greed: those who committed it wanted to pick up the ransom and vanish. Murder upped the ante, and ensured that the victim's relatives would involve law enforcement in the aftermath. There was a very good reason why most instances of kidnapping never made the news: it was because terms were negotiated and ransoms paid without anyone beyond the family and the private negotiators employed by them ever learning anything about what had occurred, and that frequently included the police and the feds.

But if what Epstein was telling me was true, then the people responsible for abducting Arthur Wildon's daughters – and there must have been more than one kidnapper, for two young girls would be difficult for one person to handle – had deliberately set out to extort money when there was no hope of the victims ever being returned alive. Indeed, it appeared that there had never been any intention to release them unharmed, given that they were killed so soon after their abduction. It was possible that something might have gone wrong, of course: one or both of the girls might have seen the faces of those involved, or caught sight of something guaranteed to give away the identity of a captor, in which case their kidnappers could have felt that they had no option but to kill them in order to protect themselves.

But to bury them alive? That was an appalling death to visit on two children, regardless of the ruthlessness of the kidnappers. There was sadism involved here, which suggested that the money was almost an afterthought, or a secondary motivation, and I wondered if Arthur Wildon or someone close to him was being punished for some unspecified offense through the dark suffocation of two little girls.

'Mr Parker?' said Epstein. 'Are you still there?'

'Yes, I'm here. Sorry, I was distracted by my own thoughts.'

'Is there anything that you feel compelled to share?'

'I was considering what the principal motive for the kidnapping might have been.'

'Money. Isn't that what kidnapping is always about?'

'But why kill the girls?'

'To leave no witnesses?'

'Or to torment Wildon and his family.'

Epstein exhaled deeply, then said: 'I knew him.'

'Wildon?'

'Yes. Not well, but we shared certain interests.'

'Any that *you* feel compelled to share?'

'Wildon believed in fallen angels, just as I do, and just as you do too.'

I wasn't sure that was entirely true, despite anything to the contrary I may have said to Marielle Vetters. Most people who talked about angels seemed to picture a fusion between Tinkerbell and a crossing guard, and I remained reluctant to put that name to the entities, terrestrial or otherwise, that I had encountered. After all, none of them had sprouted wings.

Not yet.

'But he also believed that they were infecting others,' continued Epstein, 'acquiring influence through threats, promises, blackmail.'

'For what purpose?'

'Ah, there Wildon and I differed. He talked of the End Times, of the last days, a peculiar mix of millenarianism and apocalyptic Christianity, neither of which I found personally or professionally appealing.'

'And what do you believe, rabbi?' I asked. 'Isn't it time that you shared that with me?'

'Truly?' He laughed: a hollow rattle. 'I believe that somewhere, on earth or below it, an entity waits. It's been there for a long, long time, either by its own will, or, more likely, by the will of another; trapped, perhaps even slumbering, but waiting nonetheless. The worst of these others, these creatures formed in its image, are seeking it. They have always been seeking it, always looking, and while they search they prepare for its coming. That is what I believe, Mr Parker, and I admit that it may well be proof of my madness. Does that satisfy you?'

I didn't answer. Instead I asked, 'Are they close to finding it?'

'Closer than ever before. So many of them emerging in recent years, so much hunting and killing; they are like ants set in motion by the queen's pheromones. And you are involved, Mr Parker. You know this to be true. You *feel* it.'

I stared out of my window at the shapes of trees and the silver channels of the marshes, the pale specter of myself floating against them.

'Did Wildon own a plane?'

'No, but a man named Douglas Ampell did. Ampell went missing around the same time that Wildon disappeared. Ampell and Wildon were acquainted, and Wildon used Ampell's aviation services on an occasional basis.'

'Did Ampell file a flight record in July 2001?'

'None.'

'So if that was Ampell's plane, and Wildon was on it, then where was he heading?'

'I think he was trying to reach me. There had been some contact between us in the months before his disappearance. He had followed up on hundreds of rumors, and was convinced that there was a record in existence of those who had been corrupted. He believed that he was close to finding it, and it seems that he might have done so. I think he was bringing that list with him when the plane went down.'

'And not just the list. Who was the passenger? Who was cuffed to a chair in that plane?'

'Wildon was obsessed with finding those responsible for killing his daughters,' said Epstein. 'It destroyed his marriage, and his business, but he became convinced that he was drawing closer to them. Perhaps on that plane was the man who killed Wildon's daughters: a man, or something worse than a man. You must find that plane, Mr Parker. *Find the plane.*'

34

Darina Flores learned of the deaths of Becky Phipps and Davis Tate shortly before she and the boy moved against Marielle Vetters. Darina had been concerned when she had not immediately heard back directly from Phipps; they had been searching for a definite clue to the location of the plane for so long, yet hours went by with no contact. Darina, always cautious in such matters, was reluctant to disseminate what she had learned any wider than was necessary, but preparations needed to be made.

While she debated what further action to take, she received confirmation from Joe Dahl that he was ready to move when she was. Dahl had been hers for a long time: she and her agents ensured that the inveterate gambler was permitted to fall deeper and deeper into debt until everything he owned was effectively theirs.

And then they let him keep it all: his car, his house, what little of his business remained, all of it. They simply held onto the paper on his debt, and waited. It didn't take long. Dahl was an addict, and he had not yet been cured of his addiction. On the evening that he tried to use his car as security on a cash loan so he could hit Scarborough Downs, Darina paid him a visit, and Joe Dahl was cured of his gambling vice forever. Darina had kept him in her pocket ever since, ready to be used once they had solid information about the plane. Unlike the others, she had not gone on random searches of the woods, chasing wisps of information that dissipated like morning mist in the sunlight. She considered such ventures unwise: they risked drawing attention to the object of the search, and she believed that it was better to wait until a solid lead emerged. True, the plane and its secrets represented a ticking device that could go off at the moment of discovery, but while it remained lost its danger was potential, not actual, and even the list itself was meaningless unless it found its way into the right hands. The mystery of the passenger and his fate troubled her more. He shared her nature, and he was lost.

Grady Vetters, gagged with a scarf and bound with plastic ties, woke just as daylight was fading. He was bleary, but his head began to clear when he took in the boy staring at him from the couch, and the woman cleaning her gun at the kitchen table, and he smelled Teddy Gattle, even through the closed bedroom door. Darina could see Vetters weighing his options. She preferred to keep him alive for as long as possible, but if he proved difficult she would be forced to do without him.

Darina slipped the magazine into the little Colt and approached Grady. He tried to squeeze himself further into the corner of the room, and said something unintelligible through the gag. Darina didn't care to hear what it was, so she left the scarf in place.

'We're going to pay a visit to Marielle,' she said. 'If you do as we tell you, you'll live. If you don't, you and your sister will die. Do you understand?'

Grady didn't respond immediately. He was no fool: she could tell that he didn't believe her. It didn't matter. This was all a game, and he would play his part until an alternative offered itself. The easiest way to ensure that he stayed alive and remained compliant was to make him *want* to stay alive by not doing anything foolish, and so he would do as he was told until they reached Marielle's house. If he died before they got there, he could be of no help to his sister. Alive, he could always hope.

But there was no hope, not really. Darina's entire existence was predicated on that belief.

Grady breathed in deeply against the scarf, and his nose wrinkled as he again took in the smell of Teddy Gattle.

'If it's any consolation, it wasn't an act of betrayal on his part,' said Darina. 'He thought that he was helping you. If you wouldn't use your knowledge of the plane to make some money, then he would do it on your behalf. I think he loved you.' She smiled. 'He must have, since he died for you.'

Grady glared at her. The muscles in his arms tensed as he tried to force the plastic ties apart. His knees were drawn up to his chest, and she could see him preparing to gather his strength to spring at her. Perhaps she had misjudged him. She pointed the gun at his face, said, 'Don't,' and his body relaxed. Darina kept him under the gun as the boy advanced, the syringe once again in his hand.

'Not so much this time,' she warned. 'Just enough to keep him compliant.'

She waited until Grady's eyes grew heavy again before making two more calls. The first was to Marielle Vetters' house to ensure that she was home. When a woman answered the phone, Darina hung up.

The second call she made more reluctantly, not simply because she preferred Becky Phipps to be her primary point of contact, but because the Backers did not like to be drawn into such matters. It was important to them that they should not be linked to acts of blood. It was why they used companies, offshore bank accounts, proxies.

But Phipps always called back within an hour – always, day or night – and so Darina dialed the number of the one that she thought of as the Principal Backer. Darina was not frightened of him; she was frightened of very little to do with men and women, although she found their capacity for self-destruction disturbing, but she was always careful around this Backer. He was so like herself and her kind that sometimes she wondered if he was really human at all, but she could detect no trace of otherness about him. Nevertheless, there was a difference to him, and she had never been able to penetrate his veneer and discover what lay beneath it.

He answered the phone on the second ring. The number was in the possession of only a handful of individuals, and used only when the seriousness of the situation warranted it.

'Hello, Darina,' he said. 'It's been a long time, but I know why you're calling.'

Thus it was that Darina learned of how Becky and Davis had met their ends. Becky had sent out a warning before she fled, but Darina's call had gone to her home number on the assumption that she would still be recuperating: a minor lapse on Becky's part, and understandable if she was running for her life.

The Collector had never moved against them in this way before. Oh, they knew that he suspected their existence, but the Backers had hidden themselves well, and Darina and the others were comfortable in the shadows. Darina understood then that Barbara Kelly had lied to her before she died. She had admitted to reaching out to the lawyer Eldritch and the old Jew, but she had assured Darina that she had offered only the promise of material, and not the material itself. Even when Darina took out her left eye as punishment for what she had done to her own sight, and threatened to leave her blind by cutting out the right as well, still Kelly denied that she had taken more than the first faltering footsteps toward repentance.

But the Collector could not have targeted Davis Tate without the list. On the other hand, Kelly would not have handed over the entire list to their enemies. It was her only bargaining tool. She would have tempted them with part of it, certainly no more than a page or two: a page to the Jew Epstein, perhaps, and a page to the Collector and his handler.

Just as the Collector had never declared outright war upon

them, prevented from doing so by his own caution and their cleverness, they too had kept their distance from him. His was a minor crusade for the most part, a picking off of the vicious and the damned, although his victims had been growing in importance in recent years. The possibility of a strike against him had been mooted, but, as with her ambivalence toward the Principal Backer, the Collector presented a problem. What was he, exactly? What motivated him? He seemed to have knowledge of matters known only to Darina and her fallen brethren, and to share their comfort with the darkness, but he was an unknown quantity. So far, the advantages of removing him from the board had been outweighed by the risk of precipitating a violent reaction, whether from the Collector himself, if he survived such an attack, or from his allies.

And Darina had heard rumors about a detective, one who had crossed paths with those like her, although he remained of little concern to her. Selfishness and viciousness were the curse of her breed, so much so that many of them had forgotten their true purpose on this earth, so lost were they to wrath, and sorrow at all that they had sacrificed in their fall from grace. Even Brightwell had been driven by his own urges, his desire to unite the two halves of the being he worshiped, and he was among the best, and oldest, of them. When he had briefly blinked out of existence, his spirit separating from its host, she had experienced the pain of it so strongly that she had called out to him, willing him to come to her. She had felt his presence near to her, straining to remain close, and she had found a man that night, and in this stranger's act of insemination, Brightwell had been reborn inside her.

But a crucial element was missing. Aspects of his true nature had manifested themselves early, almost as soon as he could walk, but he seemed to have no memory of how his old form had been taken from him, and with that came his silence. He was traumatized, she supposed, but she could as yet find no

310

way to break down the wall that kept him from truly becoming himself once more.

She watched the boy now as the Backer spoke. The Backer sounded worried, as well he might. His final words left it to Darina to take action against those who were moving against them. The death of Becky Phipps had tipped the balance against the Collector, and his fate now lay in Darina's hands.

But the plane was the priority: the plane, the list, and the passenger and his fate. She could not allow herself to be distracted, not now. She flipped through the names in her head, for Darina required no list. She had disputed the need for its existence right from the start, but human evil seemed to have a desire to record, to order. It was, she guessed, a function of mortality: even the worst among them, consciously or not, wanted their deeds to be remembered. Something of that need to record had infected her kind.

So Darina went to work, and the order was given to wipe their enemies from the face of the earth.

And while Darina conspired in his destruction, the Collector paid a visit to a church in Connecticut. The final service of the day had concluded, and the last of the congregation had trailed out into the evening. The Collector looked kindly upon them: they simply worshiped a different aspect of the same God.

When the last of them had gone, he watched as the priest said goodbye to the sacristan at the back of the church, and the two men separated. The sacristan drove away while the priest walked through the church grounds and used a key to unlock a gate in the wall: behind it was a garden, and his home.

The priest saw the Collector approach while the gate was still open.

'Hello?' he said. 'Can I help you?'

He had a faint Irish accent, altered by his years in the United

States. A security light on the wall beside him illuminated his face. He was a middle-aged man with a full head of hair, but no sign of gray. Instead, the light caught unnatural tints.

'Father,' said the Collector. 'I'm sorry to disturb you, but I wish to make a confession.'

The priest looked at his watch. 'I was about to go to dinner. I take confession every morning after ten o'clock mass. If you were to come back then, I'd be happy to listen.'

'It's a matter of some urgency, Father,' said the Collector. 'I fear for a soul.'

The curious formulation of the statement passed the priest by.

'Oh well, I suppose that you'd better come in,' he said.

He held the gate open and the Collector entered the garden. It was carefully arranged as a series of concentric circles, shrubs and hedges alternating with cobbled paths, and winter flowering plants adding color to it all. Between a pair of elegant box trees stood a long stone bench. The priest sat at one end of it, and indicated that the Collector should sit at the other. The priest took a stole from his pocket, kissed the cross, and placed the vestment around his neck. He quickly whispered some prayers, his eyes closed, and then asked the Collector how long it had been since his last confession.

'A very long time,' replied the Collector.

'Years?'

'Decades.'

The priest did not look happy to hear that. Perhaps he thought that the Collector might feel compelled to unburden himself of a lifetime of sins, and he would be forced to sit on the cold bench and listen until breakfast. The priest made the decision to cut to the chase. The Collector suspected that this was not the orthodox approach, but he did not object.

'Go on, my son,' said the priest. 'You said that you had a matter of some seriousness to discuss.'

'Yes,' said the Collector. 'A killing.'

That made the priest's eyes open wider. He started to look worried. He didn't know the Collector from Adam, and now here they were in the garden of the priest's own home, about to discuss the death of another human being.

'You're talking about – what? An accidental death, or something worse?'

'Worse, Father. Much worse.'

'A . . . murder?'

'It might be viewed that way. I couldn't really say. It's a matter of perspective.'

The priest had moved from being worried to actively concerned for his own safety. He saw an out.

'Maybe you should come back tomorrow after all, once you've had a chance to properly consider what it is that you wish to confess,' he said.

The Collector looked puzzled.

'Done?' he said. 'I haven't "done" anything yet. I'm *going* to do it. I was wondering if I could have absolution in advance, as it were. I'm very busy. I have a lot to fit into my days.'

The priest stood. 'Either you're making fun of me, or you're a troubled man,' he said. 'Whatever is the case, I can't help you. I want you to go now, and think hard about yourself.'

'Sit down, priest,' said the Collector.

'If you don't go, I'll call the police.'

The priest didn't even see the blade being drawn. One moment the Collector's hands were empty, and the next there was a flash of light in his hands, and the Collector had risen, the knife pressed hard against the soft flesh of the priest's throat. The priest heard the garden gate swing on its hinges. His eyes moved to the right, hoping to see someone enter, someone who might help him, but instead there were only deeper shadows moving. They took the form of men in hats and dark clothing, their long coats drifting behind them like smoke, but that wasn't possible, was it? Then the shapes became clearer, and he could make out the pale features beneath the old fedoras, the eyes and mouths nothing more than dark holes, the skin around them wrinkled like old, rotting fruit.

'Who are you?' said the priest, as the shapes drew closer.

'You betrayed her,' said the Collector.

The priest was torn between listening to the Collector, and trying to believe what his eyes were seeing.

'Who? I don't know what you're talking about.'

'Barbara Kelly. They put you here to keep watch over her. You befriended her, and as she began to have doubts she shared with you what she planned to do.'

Becky Phipps had told him as much. The Collector liked to think that he had encouraged her to make a full and frank confession.

'No, you don't understand—'

'Oh, but I do,' said the Collector. 'I understand perfectly. And you did it for money: you didn't even have an interesting motive. You just wanted a nicer car, better vacations, more cash in your wallet. What a dull way in which to damn yourself.'

The priest was barely listening. He was terrified by the figures that surrounded him, drifting along the paths of his garden, circling him but drawing no closer.

'What are those . . . *things*?'

'They were once men like you. Now they are hollow. Their souls are lost, as yours will soon be, but you will not join their ranks. The faithless priest has no flock.'

The priest raised his hands imploringly.

'Please, let me explain. I've been a good man, a good shepherd. I can still make recompense for what I've done.'

The priest's hands moved fast, but not fast enough. His nails reached for the the Collector's eyes, raking at them, but the Collector pushed the priest away, and in the same movement flicked the blade at his throat. A small wound opened, and blood began to pour like wine from a tipped goblet. The priest fell to his knees before his judge, who reached down and removed the stole from the priest's shoulders, then folded it into one of his own pockets. He lit a cigarette, and removed a metal canister from inside his coat.

'You have been found wanting, priest,' said the Collector. 'Your soul is forfeit.'

He sprayed the lighter fluid over the head and upper body of the kneeling man, and took one long drag on his cigarette.

'Time to burn,' he said.

He flicked the cigarette at the priest, and turned his back as the man ignited.

IV

For the Angel of Death spread his wings on the blast,
And breathed in the face of the foe as he passed . . .

'The Destruction of Sennacherib',
Lord Byron (1788–1824)

35

The lawyer Eldritch turned the key and opened the door to the basement. The light came on automatically, a piece of electrical engineering that never ceased to give him pleasure, and not a little relief, for the truth was that Eldritch was afraid of the dark.

After all, he knew what the dark concealed.

He carefully made his way down the stairs, one hand on the wooden banister rail, the other trailing along the cool wall. He kept a close watch on his footsteps, taking each step slowly and firmly. Eldritch was no longer a young man; in fact, he could barely remember a time when he was other than he was now. Childhood was a dream, early adulthood a blur, the memories of another man somehow adopted as his own, fragments of love and loss; sepia-tinted, as though soaked in tea and faded by sunlight.

He reached the final step and let out an involuntary sigh of satisfaction; another series of obstacles negotiated without incident, his fragile bones still intact. Five years earlier he had stumbled on the sidewalk and broken his hip: the first serious injury or illness of his senior years. The damage had necessitated a full replacement, and now he was acutely conscious of his own vulnerability. His confidence had been badly shaken.

But more than the pain, and the inconvenience of the long period of convalescence, he remembered the dread of the anesthetic, his unwillingness to surrender himself to the void, his struggle against the fluids that coursed through his body when the anesthetist inserted the needle. Darkness: shadows, and more-than-shadows. He recalled his relief when he awoke in the recovery ward, and his gratitude that he had almost no memory of what had occurred while he slept. Not in relation to the operation itself, of course: that was a separate, purely physical reality, a surrender of the body to the ministrations of the surgeon. No, the phantom images that returned with consciousness were of another realm of existence entirely. The surgeon had told him that he would not dream, but this was a lie. There were always dreams, remembered or unremembered, and Eldritch dreamed more than most, if what he experienced when the need for rest overcame him could truly be termed dreams. It was also why he slept less than most, preferring a low-level lassitude to the torments of night.

And so he had returned to this world with pain in his lower body, dulled greatly by the medication but still terrible to him, a nurse with skin of alabaster translucence asking him how he felt, assuring him that he was fine and all had gone well, and he had tried to smile even as frayed threads of memories caught upon the splinters of another realm.

Hands: that was what he remembered. Hands with hooked claws for nails, tugging at him as the anesthetic wore off, trying to pull him down to the place in which they lay; and above them the Hollow Men, soulless wraiths burning with rage at what had been done to them by Eldritch and his client, desperate to see him punished just as they were being punished. Later, once it was clear that the operation had been a complete success and he was out of danger, the surgeon had admitted to Eldritch that there had been a problem when the final stitches were being put in place. Strange, he had said: most patients emerged easily from the anesthetic as its effects wore off, but for almost two minutes it had seemed as if Eldritch were moving deeper into sleep, and they had feared that he was about to lapse into a coma. Then, in a startling reversal, his heart rate had increased to such a degree that they thought he might be about to go into cardiac arrest.

'You gave us quite a scare,' said the surgeon, patting Eldritch on the shoulder, and his touch had caused the old lawyer to tense with unease, for the pressure on his skin reminded him uncomfortably of those clawed fingers.

And throughout his period of recovery, both inside and outside the hospital, the Collector had kept watch over him, for Eldritch's vulnerability was also his own, and their existences were mutually dependent. Eldritch would wake to find the Collector sitting in the soft light of the bedside lamp, his fingers twitching uneasily, his body temporarily deprived of the nicotine that seemed perpetually to fuel it. The lawyer was never entirely sure how the Collector managed to be omnipresent during those early days, for the hospital, so very private and so very expensive, still had certain rules about the appropriateness of visiting times. But in Eldritch's experience people tended to avoid confrontations with the Collector. He trailed unease just as he trailed the stink and smoke of his cigarettes. That smell: how prevalent it was, how insidious, and how grateful they all should have been for it, for the foul nicotine taint masked a different odor. Even without the cigarettes, the Collector brought with him the smell of the charnel house.

Sometimes, Eldritch himself almost feared him. The Collector was entirely without mercy, entirely committed to his mission in this world. Eldritch was still human enough to have doubts; the Collector was not. There was no humanity left in him; Eldritch wondered if there ever had been. He suspected that the Collector had simply come into the world that way, and his true nature had become more obvious over time.

How strange, thought Eldritch, that a man should fear one to whom he was so closely bound: a client; a source of income; a protector.

A son.

*   *   *

Eldritch had come down to the basement for two reasons. The first was to check the fusebox: there had been two brief interruptions to the power supply that afternoon, and such occurrences were always a source of concern. There was so much information here, so much knowledge, and although it was well secured, there would always be concerns about potential vulnerabilities. Eldritch opened the box and checked it by the beam of a flashlight, but as far as he could tell all appeared to be well. Tomorrow, though, he would contact Bowden, who took care of such things for him. Eldritch trusted Bowden.

His movements on the basement floor had triggered the next set of overhead lights, illuminating shelf upon shelf of files. Some were so old that he was reluctant even to touch them for fear that they would crumble to dust, but the necessity of reaching for them rarely arose. For the most part, these were the closed cases. Judgement had been passed and they had been found wanting.

Someone had once pointed out to him a distinction, real or imagined, between 'judgement' and 'judgment', although to the old man it was largely a matter of preference, the former having more heft and substantiality in his view.

'"Judgment",' the man had said, his voice booming in the confines of the parquet-floored Washington hotel room, 'refers to human justice, but *judgement* with an "e" refers to the Divine,' and he had leaned back and smiled in satisfaction, his teeth perfect and white against the flawless ebony beauty of his skin, his hands clasped upon his small belly, hands with so much hidden blood on them that Eldritch was convinced it might well show up under a combination of luminol and ultraviolet light. Before him lay a document detailing allegations of rape, torture, and mass murder, a product of years of investigation by a group of men who were themselves now dead, killed by this man's agents, and in the fallen leader's eyes Eldritch could see a similar fate being planned for him.

'Really?' Eldritch had replied. 'That is fascinating, although my understanding is that the King James Bible favors "judgment".'

'This is not true,' said the man, with the unalloyed confidence of the truly ignorant. 'I tell you this so you will understand: I will not be judged by a human court but by the Lord God, and He will smile upon me for what I was forced to do to His enemies. They were animals. They were bad men.'

'And women?' added Eldritch. 'And children? Were they all bad? How unfortunate for them.'

The man bristled.

'I told you: I do recognize or accept these allegations. My enemies continue to spread lies about me, to vilify me, but I am not guilty of the accusations made against me. If I were, the International Court of Justice in the Hague would have taken action against me, but it has not. This tells the world that I have no case to answer.'

That was not entirely true. The International Court of Justice was in the process of assembling a dossier on this man, but its progress was being hampered by the ongoing deaths of crucial witnesses, both outside the nation in which he had conducted a genocidal guerilla war for over a decade, and within it, where there were those now in power who had utilized this man and his forces for their own ends, and would have preferred it if the more embarrassing details of the past were forgotten in the rush to embrace something like democracy. Even in the US, there were politicians who had embraced this butcher, this rapist, as an ally in the fight against Islamic terrorists. He was, in every way, an embarrassment and a disgrace: to his allies, to his enemies, and to the entire human race.

'So you see, Mr Eldritch, I do not understand why you have chosen to believe the lies of these men, and to accept them as clients. What is this, this "civil case"? I do not know what this means.' He held up like a dead fish the sheaf of papers that Eldritch had brought with him, with its accounts of butchery and violation, and its names of the dead. 'I agreed to meet you because you told my assistant you had information that might be of use to me in these ongoing attacks on my character, that you might be able to help me in my struggle against the blackening of my name. Instead, you side with these bad men, these fantastists. How can this be of help to me, uh? How?'

He was growing angry now, but Eldritch was not concerned.

'If you were to admit your failings and your crimes, then you might yet save yourself,' said Eldritch.

'Save myself? From what?'

'From damnation,' said Eldritch.

The man looked at him in astonishment, then began to giggle.

'Are you a preacher? Are you a man of God?' The giggles turned to laughter. 'I am a man of God. Look!' He reached into his shirt and pulled out an ornate gold cross. 'See? I am a Christian. That is why I fought God's enemies in my country. That is why your government gave me money and guns. That is why men from the CIA advised me on tactics. We were all engaged in God's work. Now, old man, go with God before you make me mad, and take your ridiculous papers with you.'

Eldritch stood. The window before him looked down on the busy street below. There the Collector waited, his black form like a smudge upon the glass.

'Thank you for your time,' said Eldritch. 'I'm sorry that I couldn't be of more help to you.'

He passed the Collector on the way out of the hotel, but they did not look at each other. The Collector disappeared into a crowd of conference delegates, and later that night the man of God in his high room learned for himself that there was no practical distinction between 'judgment' and 'judgement'.

His file, now closed, was somewhere in this basement.

Eldritch could have placed a hand on it in an instant, but there was no need. His memory was perfect, and anyway he was unlikely to be required to recite chapter and verse of the circumstances of the fallen leader's death, not in this life. Rarely did he trouble courtrooms these days, and he sometimes missed the cut and thrust of legal argument, the pleasure that lay in winning a difficult case, and the lessons to be learned by losing one.

At the same time, he no longer needed to be concerned by the distinction between law and justice. Like every lawyer, he had seen too many cases fail because justice was, in the end, subservient to the requirements of the law. Now he and the Collector were, in their way, restoring the natural order in the most extreme of cases, those from which any reasonable doubt had been excluded to the satisfaction of all but the law itself.

But there were some case files in the basement that were not closed. They were those that Eldritch chose to regard as 'inconclusive' or 'difficult', and for the most part no action had been taken against the individuals named within them. The files had simply increased in girth as more and more details were added, each another ounce of evidence that might yet tip the scales against those concerned.

One of these files concerned the detective, Charlie Parker, and the men who worked alongside him, their files connected to his both figuratively and literally by means of two lengths of black ribbon fed through holes in the top and bottom of each green folder. Eldritch had long counseled that the files should remain as they were: as mere records, not indicators of an intention to pursue a case. Ultimately he believed that Parker was engaged in the same struggle as they were, even if he might not have wanted to accept that it was so. The detective's colleagues, and the ones named Angel and Louis in particular, were more problematical, especially the latter, but Eldritch was convinced that present actions could make up for past sins, even if he had not yet managed to inculcate a similar faith in the Collector. While they might have differed in this crucial aspect, common sense nevertheless dictated that Parker and his acolytes should be left alone insofar as was practical. To damn one would require damning all, or else the survivors would avenge themselves upon everyone involved, and neither age nor sex would be an impediment to their wrath.

But the question of Parker had become increasingly complex, for his name had been on the list sent to them by Barbara Kelly, though with no indication of a reason for its presence. Parker's visit had been troubling to Eldritch. Parker knew of the existence of the list, and he knew that his name was on it, probably because the old Jew had shown it to him. Parker suspected, too, that Eldritch and the Collector had a copy of a similar list, and by coming to Eldritch's office he had been sending a warning to them both: keep your distance from me. I will not be one of your victims.

Only certain conclusions could be drawn from this. Either Parker knew why his name was on the list, and his inclusion was therefore justified, in which case he was secretly in league with everything against which they were fighting, and was worthy of damnation; or he did not know why his name was on it, which opened up two further possibilities: his own nature was compromised, and he was polluted, although the pollution had not yet manifested itself fully; or someone, possibly Barbara Kelly or others known to her, had deliberately added his name to the list in the hope that it would cause his allies to turn against him, thereby ridding his enemies of an increasingly dangerous thorn in their side without risk to themselves.

But Kelly was now dead, killed, it seemed, by her own kind. Her medical records, accessed by Eldritch through his network of informants, confirmed that her body had been riddled with cancer. She was dying, and her efforts at repentance appeared genuine, if ultimately doomed. In a sense, it was apt that lymphoma should have been eating away at her, for she herself had been responsible for a steady, ceaseless corruption, insidiously metastasizing life after life, soul after soul. One act of defiance, born out of fear and desperation, would not have been enough to save her, whatever she might have hoped.

But then Eldritch was not God, and could not pretend to have any understanding of His works. He examined each case on its own merits, but simply from a lawyer's viewpoint. Only the Collector, touched by something that might have been the Divine and transformed into a channel between realms, claimed to have an insight into a consciousness infinitely more complex than his own.

And, if he was to be believed, infinitely more merciless.

Eldritch did not doubt for a moment the veracity of the Collector's claims. Eldritch had seen too much, and knew too much, to try to fool himself into believing that some conventional reason, one unconnected to the existence of a divinity and its opposite, could be found for all that he had learned or witnessed, and the Collector had insights into the matter that were far deeper than Eldritch's. But now the Collector had instructed him to make Parker's file active, even as he began killing the others on the list, and for the first time Eldritch found himself in serious conflict with his son.

Son.

As he stood before Parker's file, his fingers hovering above it like the talons of an ancient predatory bird, a weariness swept over Eldritch. It was easier to think of his son as another: as Kushiel, as the Collector. Eldritch had long ceased wondering if some part of him or his wife had been responsible for the creation of this murderous presence in their lives. No, whatever had colonized his son's spirit had come from outside themselves. A second dwelled within him, and the two were now indivisible, indistinguishable from each other.

But Parker was right: his son's bloodlust was growing, his desire to collect tokens of lives ended becoming ever greater, and his actions with regard to the list represented their latest, and most disturbing, manifestation. There was insufficient proof of guilt to act against most of these people. Some had probably been corrupted without even knowing it, while others might simply have accepted money, or a piece of information that gave them an advantage over others, a small victory against the system which, although wrong in itself, was not enough to render them worthy of condemnation. If a single sin was enough to invite damnation, then the whole human race would roast.

Yet great evils were frequently the product of the slow accumulation of such small sins, and Eldritch knew that, when the time came for the people on the list to keep their side of the bargain they had made, the nature of the harm they would be required to do would be great. They were viruses incubating, according to the Collector's view. They were cancer cells lying dormant. Should they not be eradicated or removed before they could begin to destroy healthy bodies? His son thought so, but to Eldritch these were not viruses, not cancers: these were people, flawed, compromised individuals, and thus no different from the great mass of humanity.

In doing this, thought Eldritch, in killing without just cause, we may well damn ourselves.

He removed Parker's file, heavy because of the weight of the others it carried with it, heavy with the weight of their actions, both right and wrong, and slipped it under his arm. The lights went off behind him as he left the basement, and he ascended the stairs with more confidence than he had descended. Rarely did he take files home with him, but this was an exceptional case. He wanted to re-examine Parker's file, checking every detail for one that he might previously have overlooked, one that would give him confirmation of the man's true aims.

He waited in the hall while his secretary locked the office doors above, and watched as she lumbered down the stairs, the omnipresent cigarette in her mouth. Since the death of his wife nearly three decades before, she had been the sole constant presence in his life, the Collector flitting in and out of it as necessity required like a poisonous moth. Without this woman, he would be lost. He needed her, and at his age need and love were merely the same suitor wearing different coats.

Inside the front door was a locked alarm panel. He put Parker's file on a shelf, opened the panel, and checked the exterior camera on the small embedded screen; there was no one nearby. He nodded at the woman, and she opened the door while he activated the alarm. There was a ten-second delay once it began to beep, which was sometimes barely sufficient for him to get out and lock the door, but on this occasion he managed with a second or two to spare.

He winced as they crossed the street to his car.

'Your hip?' she said.

'Those basement stairs,' he said. 'They kill me.'

'You should have let me go down.'

'What do you know about fuses?'

'More than you.'

Which was true, even if he chose not to admit it.

'Well, I needed—'

He swore. He'd left Parker's file on the shelf beside the alarm panel.

' – the file,' he finished. He lifted his empty hands to her, and she rolled her eyes.

'I'll go back,' she said. 'You stay here.'

'Thank you,' he said, and leaned against the car.

She looked at him with concern. 'Are you sure that it's nothing more serious?'

'I'm fine, I'm fine. Just a little tired.'

But she knew otherwise. He had no secrets from her: not

about the Collector, not about Parker, not about anything. He was worried. She could tell.

'Let's go for dinner,' she said. 'We'll talk about it.'

'The Blue Ox?'

'Where else?'

'My treat, then.'

'You don't pay me enough for it to be mine.'

Which was both true and untrue: he paid her a lot, but he could never pay her enough.

She waited until a car passed, then walked back to the office, her fingers fumbling in her huge purse for her keys. Eldritch looked around. So empty the streets tonight; barely a soul in sight except for themselves. His skin prickled. A man was approaching, his hands buried deep in the folds of a parka jacket, his head down. Eldritch gripped the key fob of his car, the index finger of his left hand poised over the alarm button while his right drifted to the pocket of his overcoat that contained the small derringer. He thought that the man might have glanced at him as he went by, but, if so, it was the slightest shift of his eyes, nothing more, and his head barely moved. Then he was gone, and he did not look back.

Eldritch relaxed. The Collector had made him so wary that he occasionally tipped over into paranoia: justifiable paranoia, perhaps, but paranoia nonetheless. By now his secretary had opened the office door. He heard the alarm beep for a time before going silent as she briefly deactivated it. He could not see her in the gloom of the hallway.

There was movement to his right. The man in the parka had stopped at the corner and was staring back at him. Eldritch thought that he might have shouted something, but whatever he said was lost in the sound of the explosion that blew out the windows of Eldritch's building, deafening him even as it sent plumes of fire and smoke shooting through the gaps, showering him with glass that ripped into his face and body, the wave of heat lifting him up and throwing him to the ground. Nobody came to help him. The man in the parka was already gone.

Eldritch crawled to his knees. He was temporarily deaf, and he hurt all over. For a moment he thought that he was hallucinating as a figure appeared in the doorway of the building, silhouetted against smoke and fire. Slowly the woman walked out, and even from this distance Eldritch could see the dazed look on her face. Her hair was smoldering. She put her hand to the top of her head and patted out the smoke. She stumbled slightly on the curb but kept walking, and she seemed to smile at him as she saw that he was safe, and he found himself smiling back at her in relief.

Then she turned round to take in the sight of the burning building, and he saw that the back of her head was devoid of hair, a deep, terrible wound gleaming wetly in her exposed skull. Her spine showed red and white through her ruined back, and he glimpsed the muscles exposed in her thighs and calves through the shreds of her dress.

She stayed upright just a moment longer before collapsing facedown upon the road, her body unmoving. By then Eldritch was on his feet, running and weeping, but he could not reach her in time to say goodbye.

36

While the lawyer knelt and wept, the rabbi Epstein prepared to catch a flight to Toronto.

Epstein had managed to get in touch with Eleanor Wildon, the widow of Arthur Wildon, and she had agreed to meet with him at her apartment in Toronto, where she had moved following her husband's disappearance. She had never remarried, and had not sought to have her husband declared legally deceased. This had led to speculation in certain quarters that she had some knowledge of where he might be. Some said he had fled to avoid his financial obligations, others that he had committed suicide because of the depth of his money problems, a situation exacerbated by his grief. He had lost focus on his business interests following the deaths of his daughters, driven instead to find the person or persons responsible, and those to whom he had entrusted the care of his principal company and his investments had mismanaged both, with the result that, when he disappeared, he was worth only a fraction of what he once had been, and the Canadian revenue service was about to hit him with a massive tax bill.

Tonya Wildon was due to leave for a short trip to Europe the following evening: her nephew was being married in London, she told Epstein, and she was booked on Air Canada's 6.15 p.m. flight to Heathrow. Rather than wait until the following morning, Epstein decided to catch American Airlines' 9.25 p.m. flight out of LaGuardia and spend the night at the Hazelton Hotel in Toronto. Adiv and Liat would see him safely on to the plane. At Toronto he would be met by another associate, a former major in the Canadian armed forces who now specialized in personal protection details.

While Epstein rarely traveled without security, he was more conscious than ever of his safety and that of the men and women who worked alongside him. The existence of the list offered them a chance to strike at previously hidden enemies, but the actions of the Collector had endangered them all. Davis Tate was dead, and his producer, Becky Phipps, was reported to be missing, which led Epstein to believe that she was also being hunted by the Collector, or had already suffered at his hands.

It was possible that Barbara Kelly had died before revealing to her tormentors the names of those to whom she had sent the partial list. Even so, those who had ordered her death might have suspected that Epstein would be among the likeliest of recipients, and possibly the lawyer too. By starting to work through the list, the Collector would have confirmed those suspicions: if the Collector and the lawyer had received a communication from Barbara Kelly, then their enemies would surmise that Epstein almost certainly had received one as well.

Eldritch and Epstein: men of similar name, of similar age, and with similar aims, yet they had never met. Epstein had once suggested a meeting, and had received in return a handwritten note from the lawyer politely declining his approach. It had made Epstein feel like a spurned suitor. Now the lawyer's pet killer was running loose, assuming Eldritch ever had any real control over the man to begin with, which Epstein doubted. Perhaps it was as well that they had never sat across a table from each other, for they were not really the same. Epstein did no man's bidding, while the lawyer was the Collector's creature.

Adiv, driving his own car, collected Liat and Epstein from the latter's home on Park Slope. They were waiting to turn at the corner of 4th and Carroll when a young man dressed in jeans and an overlong sweater, and wearing worn sneakers, threw a carton of milk at the car, smearing the windshield. His skin was sallow but unhealthy, as though he were suffering from jaundice. Spying Epstein's clothing and Adiv's yarmulka, he then began kicking the side of the car while screaming, 'Fucking Jews! Fucking Jews! You're leeches. The whole country's going to hell because of you.'

Epstein placed a hand on Adiv's shoulder to restrain him. 'Ignore him,' he said. 'It doesn't matter.'

And that might have been the end of it had not the young man struck the windshield a hard blow with something in his right hand. It appeared to be a pool ball, and it cracked the glass instantly. Furious, Adiv got out of the car, slamming his door shut behind him. A shoving match ensued, with the sallow-skinned man seemingly trying to get around Adiv, not away from him. It ended when the sallow-skinned man spat in Adiv's face and tried to run away.

'Leave him, Adiv,' ordered Epstein, but Adiv's blood was up. This had been a bad week for him, and he now had an outlet for his anger. He started running, but his prey was too fast for him, and Adiv's legs still ached from the long walk through the Jersey Pine Barrens. He still managed to grab the strap of the running man's battered satchel, which he was holding in his hand instead of wearing over his shoulder. The bag came away so suddenly that Adiv fell backwards, landing painfully on his coccyx. The young man paused and looked back, as if debating whether it was worth trying to retrieve his satchel and possibly take a beating for his troubles, then decided to sacrifice it.

'Jew bastard!' he shouted once more, before disappearing into the night.

'I have your bag, asshole!' cried Adiv. 'You lose, you prick!'

He got to his feet and dusted himself off. His butt ached. He limped painfully back to the car. Liat had opened the passenger door on the far side and stood on the road, watching him. He could see the gun in her hand.

'I got his bag!' said Adiv, raising the satchel.

Liat shook her head. *No, no*, she mouthed. Her eyes were wide. She waved her arms. *Drop it, Adiv. Drop it and run.* Liat pulled Epstein from the car and began dragging him to safety, keeping her body between Epstein, and Adiv, and the satchel.

Understanding dawned on Adiv. He looked down at the satchel. It was made of soft brown leather, and only one of the buckles on the front was tied. Adiv lifted the unsecured end of the bag and peered inside. There was a package wrapped in aluminum foil, like sandwiches, and beside it a thermos flask.

'I think it's okay,' said Adiv. 'I think—'

And then he was gone.

37

I was anxious to head north to speak with Marielle Vetters again. Once I had done that, I could start figuring out how to get to the plane. For now, though, my daughter, Sam, and her mother, Rachel, were in Portland for an evening, which was good.

Unfortunately, so was Jeff, Rachel's current squeeze, which was bad.

How did I dislike Jeff? Well, let me count the ways. I disliked Jeff because he was so right-wing he made Mussolini look like Che Guevara; because his hair and his teeth were too perfect, especially for a man who was old enough to have started losing most of the former, and some of the latter; because he called me 'big guy' and 'fella' whenever we met, but couldn't seem to bring himself to use my actual name; oh, and because he was sleeping with my ex-girlfriend, and every ex-boyfriend secretly wants his former partner to get herself to a nunnery immediately after their separation, there to rue the day she ever let such a treasure slip through her fingers, and hold herself celibate forever after on the grounds that, having had the best, there really was no call to settle for an inferior product.

Okay, so mostly I didn't like Jeff because of that last part, but the other reasons were pretty important too.

I wanted to see Sam more often, and Rachel and I were agreed that this was a good thing. I had tried to hold my daughter at a distance for too long, perhaps out of some not entirely misguided effort to keep her safe, but I didn't really want things to be that way, and she didn't either. Now we saw each other at least once or twice every month, which was both better and worse than before: better because I was spending time with her, but worse because I missed her more when she wasn't there.

This night, though, was a bonus: Jeff was speaking at a dinner event at the Holiday Inn in Portland, and Rachel had used the trip as an opportunity to let Sam spend an extra night hanging out with me while she played the supportive partner to whatever self-serving bullshit Jeff was spouting about the banking system. According to the *Portland Phoenix*, his speech was entitled 'The Return to Light-Touch Regulation: Making America Wealthy Again.' The *Phoenix*'s columnist had been so stricken by apoplexy over this that the paper had given him an extra half page to vent his spleen, and it still hadn't been enough. He would probably have filled the entire edition if Jeff's appearance in the city hadn't given him an opportunity to tackle the object of his rage in person. It might almost have been worth attending the event just to hear what the *Phoenix* reporter had to say to Jeff if only it wouldn't have required listening to Jeff too.

I took Sam for pizza down at the Flatbread Pizza Company on the Portland waterfront, where she got to create intricate crayon drawings on the paper tablecloth, and then over to Beal's ice-cream parlor for a sundae to finish. Angel and Louis joined us as we were finishing our meal at Flatbread, and the four of us walked up to Beal's together. Sam tended to be slightly in awe of Angel and Louis on the rare occasions she got to meet them. She was comfortable with Angel, who made her laugh, but she had also developed a certain shy fondness for Louis. She hadn't yet managed to convince him to hold her hand, but he seemed to tolerate the way that she clutched the belt of his overcoat. Deep down, I suspected that he even liked it. So we presented quite the picture walking into Beal's, and it was to the server's credit that she recovered herself so quickly when it came time to serve us.

I ordered one-scoop sundaes for us all, except for Angel who wanted two scoops.

'The fu—?' Louis began to say, before he remembered where he was, and the fact that there was a small child holding onto his belt and gazing up at him adoringly. 'I mean,' he went on, struggling to find a way of expressing his disapproval without the use of obscenities, 'maybe one scoop might be, uh, sufficient for your, uh, needs.'

'You saying I'm fat?' said Angel.

'If you ain't, you can see fat from where you're at. You may not be able to see your feet, but you can see fat.'

Sam giggled.

'You're fat,' she told Angel. 'Fat fat.'

'That's rude, Sam,' I said. 'Uncle Angel isn't fat. He's just big boned.'

'Go fu—'. Angel too realized where he was, and with whom. 'I'm not fat, honey,' he told Sam. 'This is all muscle, and your daddy and Uncle Louis are just jealous because they have to watch what they eat, while you and I can order any sundae we want and we only get prettier.'

Sam looked dubious, but wasn't about to argue with someone who said that she was getting prettier.

'You still want the two-scoop?' asked the server.

'Yeah, I still want the two-scoop,' said Angel, then added quietly, as Louis swept by him, trailing Sam, 'but make it with sugar-free ice cream, and hold the cherry.'

The server went to work. Beal's was quiet, with only one other table occupied. It was almost the end of Beal's season. Shortly it would close for the winter.

'Maybe I should have had something with sugar,' said Angel. 'The flavors are better.'

'And you have the fat to worry about anyway.'

'Yeah, thanks for reminding me. I'm making sacrifices and I still feel guilty.'

'Soon you'll have no pleasures left at all,' I said.

'Yeah, I remember pleasures,' said Angel. 'I think. It's been so long.'

'As you get older, they say that certain physical needs grow less urgent.'

'Who the fu—?'

Sam tapped him on the thigh, and handed him a napkin. 'For when you mess up,' she said, then trotted off to join Louis at a table.

'Thank you, honey,' said Angel, before returning to the subject in hand, minus the swearing. 'I mean, who are you calling old?'

'Old*er*,' I corrected.

Our sundaes came, and we carried them over to where Louis and Sam were waiting.

'Like that makes it better,' said Angel. 'Fat, old: you want to add anything else before I go throw myself in the sea?'

'Don't do it,' said Louis.

'Why, because you'd miss me?'

'No, 'cause you'd just float. Bob like a cork until hypothermia took you, or you got eaten by sharks.'

'No!' said Sam. 'Not eaten!'

'It's okay, Sam,' Angel assured her. 'I won't get eaten. Am I right, Uncle Louis?'

Sam looked to Louis for confirmation of this.

'That's right,' said Louis. 'He won't get eaten. Shark's mouth wouldn't be big enough to fit him in.'

Sam seemed content with this, even if Angel wasn't, so she started work on her sundae and forgot about everything else.

'I'm substituting ice cream for affection,' whispered Angel glumly, in deference to Sim's presence. 'I'll be watching *The View* next, and considering male HRT.'

'It'll never get that bad,' I said.

'HRT?'

'Watching *The View*. What are you, gay?'

'I used to be. I'm a sexless being now.'

'That's good. I didn't like thinking of you as a sexual being. It was kind of gross.'

'What, gay sex?'

'No, just you and any form of sex.'

Angel thought about this. 'I guess it kind of was,' he concluded.

Behind us, at the other occupied table, a couple of loud-mouths were discussing a mutual acquaintance in borderline obscene terms. One of them was wearing a Yankees cap even though his accent was Down East. In a town like Portland, a Yankees cap invited harsh words at best, but being a Mainer and wearing one was an act of treachery that made Benedict Arnold and Alger Hiss seem harmless by comparison.

The men moved from borderline to outright obscenity. They smelled of beer. What they were doing in an ice-cream parlor, I couldn't quite figure.

I leaned over. 'Hey, guys, could you keep it clean? I got a kid here.'

They ignored me and kept talking. If anything, the volume increased, and they managed to squeeze in a few more swear words, separating syllables where necessary to accommodate them.

'Guys, I asked you nicely,' I said.

'It's after nine,' said the older of the two. 'Your kid should be at home.'

'It's an ice-cream parlor,' said Angel. 'You ought to watch your fucking language.'

'Was that helpful?' I said to him. 'I don't think so.'

'Sorry.'

I returned my attention to the men nearby.

'I won't ask you again,' I told them.

'And what are you going to do if we don't?' asked the same man. He was tall and broad, and his features had an alcoholic blur to them. His friend, whose back had been

340

to us, turned around, and his eyes widened slightly at the sight of Louis. He looked more sober than his friend, and smarter too.

'My daddy will shoot you,' said Sam. She made a little gun with her fingers, pointed it at the man who had spoken, and said 'Bang!'

I looked at her. Good grief.

'And then I'll shoot you too,' said Louis.

He grinned, and the temperature dropped.

'Bang,' Louis added, for effect. He too had made a gun with his fingers. He aimed it at the big man's groin.

'Bang', he repeated: at his chest.

'Bang': closing one eye to focus, at his head.

Both men visibly blanched.

'Not a Yankees fan,' explained Angel.

'Go find a bar, fellas,' I said, and they left.

'I like bullying people,' said Angel. 'When I grow up, I'm going to do nothing else all day long.'

'Bang,' said Sam. 'They're dead.'

Angel, Louis and I exchanged glances. Angel shrugged.

'She must get it from her mother.'

Sam was staying with me that night. When she had finished brushing her teeth, and her two rag dolls were tucked up to her satisfaction alongside her, I sat on the edge of the bed and touched her cheek.

'You warm enough?'

'Yes.'

'You feel cold.'

'That's because it's cold outside, but I'm not cold. I'm warm inside.'

It sounded plausible.

'Look, I think it might be best if you didn't tell your mom about what happened tonight.'

'About the pizza? Why?'

'No, the pizza's fine. I mean what happened after, when we went for ice cream.'

'You mean about the two men?'

'Yes.'

'What part?'

'The part about you saying that I would shoot them. You can't talk like that to strangers, honey. You can't talk like that to anyone. It's not just rude: it'll get Daddy into trouble.'

'With Mommy?'

'Absolutely with Mommy, but also maybe with the people you say it to. They won't like it. That's how fights start.'

She considered this.

'But you have a gun.'

'Yes. I try not to shoot people with it, though.'

'Then why do you have it?'

'Because sometimes, in my job, I have to show it to people to make them behave themselves.' God, I felt like a spokesman for the NRA.

'But you have shot people with your gun. I heard Mommy say.'

This was new. 'When did you hear that?'

'When she was talking to Jeff about you.'

'Sam, were you listening when you shouldn't have been listening?'

Sam squirmed. She knew that she had said too much.

She shook her head. 'It was a accident.'

'*An* accident.' A spokesman for the Society for Better English too, it seemed. Still, it gave me time to think.

'Look, that's true, Sam, but I didn't like doing it, and those people left me with no other choice. I'd be happy if I never had to do it again, and I hope that I don't. Okay?'

'Okay,' she said. 'Were they bad people?'

'Yes, they were very bad people.'

I watched her face carefully. She was building up to something, skirting the subject warily, like a dog circling a snake, uncertain of whether it were dead and harmless, or alive and capable of striking.

'Was one of them the man who made Jennifer and her mommy dead?'

She always called them that: Jennifer and her mommy. Although she knew Susan's name, she felt uncomfortable using it. Susan was an adult unfamiliar to her, a grown-up, and grown-ups had names that began with Mr or Mrs, Aunt or Uncle, Grandma or Grandpa. Sam had chosen to define her as Jennifer's mommy because Jennifer had been a little girl just like her, but a little girl who had died. The subject held a kind of awful fascination for her, not simply because Jennifer had been my child and, by extension, a half-sister to Sam, but because Sam did not know of any other children who had died. It seemed somehow impossible to her that a child could die – that *anyone* she knew of could die – but this one had.

Sam understood a little of what had happened to my wife and my daughter. She had picked up nuggets of information gleaned from other overheard conversations and hidden them away, examining them in solitude, trying to understand their meaning and their value, and only recently had she revealed her conclusions to her mother and me. She knew that something awful had happened to them, that one man had been responsible, and that man was now dead. We had tried to deal with it as carefully yet as honestly as possible. Our concern was that she might fear for her own safety, but she did not seem to make that particular connection. Her focus was entirely on Jennifer and, to a lesser extent, her mommy. She was, she told us, 'sad for them', and sad for me.

'I—' Speaking of Jennifer and Susan with her was difficult for me at the best of times, but this was new and dangerous territory. 'I think he would have hurt me if I had not,' I said at last. 'And he would have kept on hurting other people too. He gave me no choice.'

I swallowed the taste of the lie, even if it was a lie of omission. He gave me no choice, but neither did I give him a choice. I had wanted it that way.

'So does that make it all right?'

Although Sam was a precocious, unusual child, that was still a very adult question, one that plumbed murky moral depths. Even her tone was adult. This was not coming from Sam. There was the voice of another under her own.

'Is that one of your questions, Sam?'

Again, a shake of the head. 'It was what Jeff asked Mommy when they were talking about how you shot people.'

'And what did Mommy say?' I asked despite myself, and I was ashamed.

'She said that you always tried to do the right thing.'

I bet Jeff didn't like that.

'After that, I had to go pee,' said Sam.

'Good. Well, no more listening to conversations that aren't your business, all right? And no more talking about shooting people. We clear?'

'Yes. I won't tell Mommy.'

'She'd just worry, and you don't want to get Daddy into trouble.'

'No.' She frowned. 'Can I tell her about Uncle Angel saying a bad word?'

I thought about it.

'Sure, why not?'

I went downstairs, where Angel and Louis had opened a bottle of red wine.

'Make yourselves at home.'

Angel waved a glass at me. 'You want some?'

'No, I'm good.'

Louis poured, sipped, tasted, made a face, shrugged resignedly, and filled two glasses.

'Hey,' said Angel, 'Sam's not going to tell Rachel I swore at those guys, is she?'

'No,' I said, 'you're in the clear.'

He looked relieved. 'Thank Christ. I wouldn't want to get in trouble with Rachel.'

While they drank, I called Marielle Vetters. The phone rang four times, then went to the machine. I left a short message to tell her that I'd be heading up there to talk with her the next day, and she should go over all that her father had told her in case she'd forgotten to share with me anything that might be useful. I asked her to give Ernie Scollay a nudge too, on the off-chance that he might recall something that his brother had said. I kept the message deliberately vague, just in case she had company or someone else, like Marielle's brother, happened to hear it.

After an hour of conversation I went to my room, but not before looking in on the strange, beautiful, empathic child fast asleep in her bed, and I felt that I had never loved her more, or understood her less.

38

Marielle heard the phone ring at the same time as her doorbell. For a moment she was torn between the two, but clearly the phone could wait while the doorbell could not.

'You want me to see who it is?' asked Ernie Scollay.

He had come over earlier, seemingly still troubled by the amount they had revealed down at the bar in Portland, but Marielle knew that he was also lonely. A shy man, and one who did not care much for either of the local bars, he had formed a bond with Marielle's father following his brother's suicide, and when Harlan Vetters in turn had died, he had transferred his affection for the father to Marielle. She did not mind. Apart from being kind, if cautious, company, Ernie was good at fixing anything from a stubborn hinge to a car engine, and Marielle's old car needed more attention than most. Her brother's best friend, Teddy Gattle, had frequently offered to look after it for her at no charge, but Marielle knew better than to take him up on it. Ever since they were teenagers, Teddy had eyed her with a mixture of adoration and barely concealed lust. According to her brother, Teddy had cried more than her own mother had on the day Marielle got married, and he had celebrated her divorce with a drunk that lasted three days. No, even if Ernie Scollay had not been around, she would have paid money she could little afford to maintain her car – would, in fact, have set the car on fire and walked to her two jobs – rather than accept a favor from Teddy Gattle.

Marielle stepped out of the kitchen and looked down the hall. Her brother's familiar, rangy figure stood outside, although she could not see him clearly because the exterior light wasn't working. Odd, she thought: I only changed that bulb last week. There must be a fault with the wiring. Another job for Ernie, she supposed.

'It's okay, it's just Grady,' she said.

He'd probably come to apologize, she figured. About time too. He'd had enough of Teddy Gattle's hospitality, and realized what a jerk he'd been for bringing that vacant space in female form into her house. She'd been tempted to burn the sheets once Grady and whatever-her-name was had departed, the skank. Ivy, was that what Grady had said? Holly? What an idiot. What a pair of idiots.

But she loved her brother, for all his flaws, and now they were all that was left of the family. Two failures: he in art, she in marriage, both in life. She didn't want to lose him again. Even when absent, whether at college or trying to make it as an artist in New York, and, finally, lost to his addictions for a time, a part of him had always been with her. They had been so close as children, and although he was her little brother, he had done his best to take care of her. When her marriage finally ended, he had trudged back to Falls End to console her, and they had spent a couple of days drinking, and smoking, and talking, and she had felt better for it. But then he had drifted away again, and when he came back their father was already dying.

The machine picked up the call, and she heard a voice that was kind of familiar, but she wasn't quick enough to catch the caller's name.

The doorbell rang for a second time.

'Coming!' she said. 'I'm coming. God, Grady, you could have a little patience, you know . . .'

She opened the door and the light from the lamp in the hall caught his face. He looked sorrowful and scared. He also looked doped up. He was swaying, and having trouble staying focussed on her.

'Ah, Grady, for crying out loud,' she said. 'No, no. You jerk. You stupid—'

Grady flew at her. She reacted fast enough to step back, one hand instinctively outstretched to ward him off, but he was too big and heavy for her. His weight carried them both to the floor, and her head bounced hard on the boards.

'Jesus, Grady!' she cried, trying to push him from her even as he struggled to find his own footing.

Two people appeared in the doorway, a woman and a child. Even in the soft lamplight Marielle could tell that the woman's face was damaged, and the child, a boy, had a strange, ugly swelling at his neck, and bruising to his nose and eyes.

In the woman's right hand was a gun.

'Who are you?' said Marielle. 'What do you want?'

But as the woman advanced, Marielle knew who she was. Although she had never met her, Marielle had heard her described. She was no longer beautiful, not with her burned, glistening skin, but enough of her former looks remained for Marielle to imagine her as she once had been, drawing men to her, buying drinks in return for stories of lost planes. Her left eye was a different color from her right: most of the color had gone from it, and it reminded Marielle of a raw shellfish dotted with Tabasco sauce.

Ernie Scollay appeared in the hall. He took a single look at the woman and the boy, then turned to run. Darina Flores shot twice him in the back. Ernie fell on his face and tried to crawl to safety, but the third shot stilled him forever.

Darina and the boy stepped inside and closed the door behind them. The boy locked it and pulled down the blind, cutting them off from the world. By now, Marielle had managed to get out from under Grady. She knelt before the intruders, afraid to move. Blood began to spread from under Ernie Scollay, flowing across the boards and dripping between the gaps into the darkness below. Grady lay against the wall, and she could see him trying to overcome whatever drug was in his system.

'I'm sorry,' he said. 'I couldn't . . .'

While Darina and the boy watched, unspeaking, she went to her brother and held him, and she hardly felt the needle as it entered her arm.

They did not inject her with as much of the drug as they had given to her brother. They wanted her to be coherent, but to present no risk to them. They were a woman and a child in a room with two grown adults, and Darina had to ensure that there was no risk of either Marielle or Grady Vetters fighting back. Once again, they secured their captives' hands behind them with plastic ties, just to be certain. Darina poured the boy a glass of milk, and gave him a freshly baked cookie from a tray beside the stove. He sat at the dining table and nibbled the cookie, eating around the edges, his small teeth following the line of the frosting, examining his efforts as he went, just like a normal boy.

Marielle lay supine on the couch with a cushion beneath her head. She was watching all that was taking place, seeking any possible advantage, but there was none. Her eyes were just slightly heavy, her responses dulled, but she was still thinking clearly, if slowly. Grady Vetters sat in an armchair beside the TV, his eyes barely open, a string of spittle connecting his chest to his chin. He glimpsed his own reflection in the mirror on the opposite wall, and wiped his chin on his shirt. The effort seemed to bring him more clarity. He sat up a little straighter and tried to find a smile for his sister, but she took no reassurance from it.

Darina pulled up a chair beside Marielle. She held the gun loosely in her right hand, and with her left brushed some stray strands of hair from Marielle's face.

'Are you comfortable?' she asked.

'What did you inject me with?'

Her words were not remotely slurred. Darina wondered if they shouldn't have given her a bigger dose.

'Just something to help you relax. I don't want you to be uncomfortable, or too frightened.'

Behind Darina, Marielle could see Ernie Scollay's outstretched arm. The rest of his body was hidden by the wall. Darina saw her looking at it, and called to the boy.

'Move that, would you? It's distracting.'

The boy put down the cookie, wiped the crumbs from his hands, and went into the hallway through the alcove beside the kitchen. There was a dragging sound as Ernie Scollay's feet were lifted and his body began to move. The boy was stronger than he looked, and the arm disappeared.

'Better?' said Darina.

'He was just an old man,' said Marielle. 'You didn't have to kill him.'

'Even old men can run,' said Darina. 'Old men can talk. Old men can call the police. So, yes, we did have to kill him, but there doesn't have to be any more killing. If you answer my questions, and answer them honestly, I'll spare you and your brother. That's a basement under the stairs, isn't it?'

'Yes.'

'That's where we'll leave you, then. I'll put water and food in bowls, and you can feed yourselves like dogs, but you'll be alive. We won't be in town for long: a day or two at most. The more you share with me, the easier our task will be, and the sooner we'll be gone. I give you my word.'

Marielle shook her head in dismissal.

'We've seen you,' said Marielle. 'We know who you are. We saw you kill Ernie, saw you shoot him in the back.'

Grady stirred in his chair again.

'They killed Teddy too,' he said. '*She* killed Teddy.'

Marielle flinched. Poor, sad, pathetic Teddy Gattle. He might have been irritating, and besotted with her, but he had been loyal to her brother, and he had meant no harm to anyone.

'He was the one who led us here,' said Darina, 'if it makes his loss any easier to bear. It was Teddy Gattle who alerted us to the truth about your father, and the plane.'

Marielle turned on her brother.

'You told Teddy?' Teddy Gattle couldn't hold a secret for longer than it took to draw another breath. He was a human sieve.

'I'm sorry,' was all Grady could mumble, again.

'But my offer stands,' said Darina. 'I know you don't believe me, but I have no interest in killing you. Once that plane is found, and I get what I want, we'll disappear, and you can tell the police anything you like. You can describe us down to the last hair, and it won't matter. We'll be long gone, and we hide ourselves well. I won't even look like myself any more.' She pointed a finger at her ruined face. 'Would you want to stay like this? No, Marielle, they won't find us. You'll live, and so will we. All you have to do is talk. I know a lot already, but I want to hear it all from you as well: every word, every detail that your father shared with you, anything that might enable me to find that airplane. And don't lie to me. If you lie, there will be consequences, both for you and for your brother.'

The boy returned to the room. Marielle saw that he had trailed a line of bloody footprints across the carpet. He was carrying a backpack illustrated with figures from one of those Japanese animation movies that everyone else seemed to like but for which she didn't much care, all big-eyed children and mouths that didn't match the English dialog. He unzipped the pack and drew from it a pair of pliers, a heavy boxcutter, and three pocket knives of varying lengths. He laid the tools out neatly on the dining room table, then pulled up a chair and sat, his feet dangling a good six inches above the floor.

'Now, Marielle, why don't you begin with the first time you heard your father mention that airplane.'

Marielle told the story, then told it again. Midway between the two tellings, Darina injected her a second time, and her mind grew foggier. She had trouble keeping details straight in her head, and at one point she must have said something wrong, or contradicted herself, because Grady screamed and when she got him in focus she saw that the bottom of his face was bloody and she realized that the boy had sliced off the tip of Grady's nose. She started to cry, but Darina slapped her hard, which made her stop. She was careful after that to tell the truth, because what did it matter? It was only a plane. Her father was dead. Paul Scollay was dead, and his brother Ernie too. Teddy Gattle was gone. Only she and Grady remained.

'Who else have you told?' asked Darina.

'Nobody.'

'The old man,' said Darina. 'Who was he? What was he doing here?'

'Paul Scollay's brother. He knew already. Paul told him.'

'Who else did you tell?'

'No one.'

'I don't believe you.'

'No one,' she repeated, 'I told no one.'

Her mind was clearing – not much, but just enough. She wanted to live. She wanted Grady to live. But if they didn't, if the woman was lying, then she wanted revenge: for her, for her brother, for Ernie and Teddy, for everyone this woman and that terrible child had ever hurt. The detective would find them. He would find them, and he would punish them.

'Nobody,' she repeated. 'I swear it.'

Grady screamed again, but she closed her eyes and her ears to it.

I'm sorry, she thought, but you shouldn't have told. You just shouldn't have told.

Deep darkness without, and darkness within, illuminated only by a lamp on the small table beneath the mirror.

Grady was moaning softly. The boy had sliced vertically through his lips with the boxcutter blade, but they had stopped bleeding, at least for as long as Grady could keep from moving his mouth. They were still alive, though, and Darina Flores had eventually stopped her questions. They had ceased when Marielle had come up with one detail, one small half-remembered piece of information from her father's final days. A fort: her father had mentioned passing a fort as they returned home with the money. She hadn't told the detective about it because she hadn't trusted him enough, not then. Now she wished that she'd told him all as she watched Darina use a laptop to check maps and histories in an effort to confirm the truth of what she had just heard.

Marielle must have slept for a time. She couldn't remember the main lights in the room being turned off, or a blanket being laid over her to keep her warm. She was having trouble breathing. She tried to alter her position, but it didn't help. The boy was staring at her. His pale, washed-out features repelled her, his thinning hair and his swollen throat. He looked like an old man shrunk to the size of a child. She'd dreamed of him, she realized, and the memory of it made her feel ashamed. In the dream, the boy had been trying to kiss her. No, it was not quite a kiss: his mouth had fixed upon hers like a lamprey attaching itself to prey, and he had begun sucking, pulling the breath from her lungs, drawing the life from her, but he hadn't managed to do it because she was still here, still breathing, however poorly.

Just a dream, but as she thought that she felt the tenderness of her lips, and there was a foul taste in her mouth, as though she had eaten a piece of meat that was past its best.

The boy smiled at her, and she began to retch drily.

'Get her some water,' said Darina, but she did not look up from the screen.

The boy went to the kitchen and came back with a glass of water. She was reluctant to accept it, hated having him anywhere near her, but better some brief proximity to him than to reject the water and keep that taste in her mouth, so she drank, and the water dribbled down her chin and fell coldly upon her chest. At last, when she could drink no more, she pulled her head back. The boy removed the glass from her lips but remained standing over her, watching.

Marielle's back ached. She shifted on the couch so that she was sitting upright. A blinking red light caught her eye, hidden before by the table. It was a red number '1' blinking on the telephone answering machine. She remembered the earlier call, and the voice that had sounded so familiar.

It had been the detective's voice.

She turned her head away too quickly. The boy frowned. He looked over his shoulder.

'More water,' said Marielle. 'Please.'

'Do as she asks,' said Darina. 'Give her more water.'

But the boy ignored them both. He put the glass on the dining room table and approached the answering machine. He put his head to one side, like an animal faced with an unfamiliar object. One pale finger reached out and hovered uncertainly above the 'play' button.

'Please!' said Marielle again.

Darina glanced up from her screen.

'What are you doing?' she said to the boy. 'This work is important. If she wants more water, then give her more water. Just shut her up!'

The boy stepped away from the machine. He lowered his hand.

Marielle sank back against the arm of the sofa. She drew in an inadequate, shuddering breath, and closed her eyes.

There was a single beep from the other end of the room, and a voice began to speak, deep and male.

'Hi, Marielle, this is Charlie Parker. I just wanted to let you know—'

The rest of the message was lost in a scream of rage and pain unlike any that Marielle had heard before, made more awful by the fact that it came from a child. The boy screamed a second time. His back arched, his neck straining so far back that it seemed as though his spine must break or the swelling on his throat erupt in a shower of blood and pus. Darina rose to her feet, the laptop falling to the floor, and even over the screaming Marielle could hear the voice of the detective telling her that he was coming up to talk with her, that he just had one or two more questions to ask her and Ernie.

There was a buzzing in the room. Even Grady, immersed in his own misery, heard it. His head moved, trying to find the source of the sound. The house grew colder, as though someone had opened a door, but the air that came through was not filled with the smell of trees and grass but with smoke.

An insect flew across Marielle's line of sight. She shrank away from it instinctively, but it came back, buzzing a foot from her face. Even in the dim light, she could see the wasp's yellow and black striped body, and the curve of its venomous abdomen. She hated wasps, especially those that lived this late into the year. She drew up her knees to her chest and tried to use her feet to flip the blanket at it, but now there was a second insect, and a third. The room began to fill with them, and even in her fear she could not understand how. There were no nests nearby, and how could so many have survived?

Still the boy screamed, and suddenly Grady was screaming too, his voice joining with that of the boy, and her brother's bisected lips burst with the effort, and the sound of pain was added to his fright, for Grady's had been a cry of fear at first.

The mirror: the wasps were pouring out of the mirror. It had ceased to be a reflective surface, or so it appeared to

Marielle, and had instead been transformed into a framed hole in the wall. The dying wasps, once trapped behind it, were now free.

But that was a supporting wall. It was solid concrete, not hollow, and the mirror was just a mirror. Nothing could pass through it. It was simply glass.

She felt a wasp land on her cheek and begin crawling toward her eye. She shook her head and blew at it. It buzzed away angrily, then returned. Its stinger brushed her skin, and she prepared for the pain, but it did not come. The wasp departed, and the others went with it, the little swarm returning to the mirror where they buzzed and roiled in a circular motion, forming a cloud that took on the dimensions of a head with two dark waspless holes for eyes, and another larger slit for a mouth, a face of wasps that stared out at them from the mirror, and its rage was the wasps' rage, and it vented its fury through them.

The wasp mouth moved, forming words that Marielle could not hear, and the boy's screams ceased. Darina clasped him to her, the back of his head against her breasts, and he shuddered in her embrace.

Grady, too, stopped screaming. The only sound in the room was the boy's sobbing breaths, and the buzzing from the mirror.

Darina kissed the top of the boy's head, and laid her cheek on his pale scalp. Her eyes found Marielle staring at her, and Marielle could see that Darina was both smiling and crying.

'He remembers,' said Darina. 'He's back now. He's mine again. My Brightwell. But you shouldn't have lied. You shouldn't have told us lies.'

The boy stepped away from her. He wiped his eyes, and walked to the mirror. He stood before the face of wasps, and he spoke to it in a language that Marielle did not recognize, and it spoke back to him. He stayed that way until the buzzing stopped, and one by one the wasps began to fall to the floor where they crawled sluggishly for a time before dying, leaving only the boy staring at his own reflection.

Grady Vetters had curled in upon himself. He was weeping and shaking, and Marielle knew that something had snapped inside him. When she called his name he did not look at her, and his eyes were those of a stranger.

'He has so many forms,' said Darina to Marielle, 'so many names.' She was pointing to the mirror. 'He Who Waits Behind The Glass, The Upside-Down Man, The God of Wasps . . .'

The boy found a sheet of paper in his bag. On one side was a drawing of a truck, but the other side was blank. He began to write on it with a crayon. When he was done, he handed the sheet of paper to Darina, and she read what was written there before folding the page and placing it in her pocket. She then spoke one word:

'Parker.'

The boy advanced on Marielle, and the sense of an old mind trapped in a younger body was stronger than ever. His lamprey mouth opened, and a pale tongue flicked at his lips. Darina laid a hand upon his shoulder, and he stopped, his face inches from Marielle's.

'No,' she said.

The boy looked up at her questioningly. He tried to say something, but the words just came out as a pair of harsh croaks, like the cawings of a young crow.

'We promised,' said Darina. '*I* promised.'

The boy stepped away from her. He went to the table and began packing his tools in his child's bag. It was time to leave.

Darina stood over Marielle.

'You lied to me,' she said. 'You should have told me about the detective. I could declare our bargain void, and kill you for it.'

Marielle waited. Nothing she could say would make any difference now.

'But perhaps because of your lie something special has been restored to us. Do you know what your detective once did?'

'No.'

'He killed the being that you see here.' She pointed at the boy. 'He stilled his great spirit for a time.'

'I don't understand,' said Marielle.

'No, but Parker will when we confront him. I promised that I would let you and your brother live, and I'll keep my word. We always keep our word.'

The boy went searching in his bag again, and came out with his metal case of syringes. He filled one from a small glass bottle of clear liquid that Marielle had not seen before.

'No more, please,' said Marielle.

'This is different,' said Darina. 'But don't worry: it won't hurt.'

Marielle watched as the boy injected Grady for the last time. Her brother did not react to the needle, or to the boy's presence. His gaze was directed inward, but within seconds his eyes had closed, and his chin fell upon his chest. The boy refilled the syringe from the glass bottle. When he was done, the vessel was empty. He dropped it in his bag, and approached Marielle.

'It's Actrapid,' said Darina. 'Injectable insulin.'

Marielle made her move. Her knees were still drawn up to her chest, her feet flat on the couch. She launched herself at Darina, but the woman was too fast, and Marielle caught her only a glancing blow before she landed hard on the floor, and then the boy was on top of her, the needle was biting, and the world was filling with shadows.

'You'll sleep,' she heard Darina say. 'You'll sleep for a very long time.'

The massive dose flooded Marielle's system, and her mind began to descend into coma.

39

Eldritch woke in a hospital bed and thought, I have dreamed this dream before: a bed; a small, clean room; the pinging of a machine nearby; the sharp chemical odor of antiseptic and, beneath it, all that it was meant to hide; and the clawed fingers pulled at him, trying to keep him forever in the darkness. He lifted his arm and felt a tug as the intravenous drip caught on the sheet. He reached for it, and a hand closed gently but firmly upon his arm.

'No, let me,' said the voice, and he smelled that familiar scent of fire and nicotine, and he knew that his son had come to him; not the Collector but his son, for the Collector was never so gentle. His voice sounded slightly muffled: Eldritch's hearing had been damaged in the blast.

'I dreamed,' said Eldritch. 'I dreamed that she was gone, and then I dreamed that it was but a dream.'

His face hurt. He touched his fingers to it and explored the dressings on the worst of his wounds.

'I'm sorry,' said his son. 'I know what she meant to you.'

Eldritch looked to his left. They had brought his possessions from the scene: his wallet, his keys, his watch. Little things.

But the woman was gone.

'What do you remember?' asked his son.

'The power. We lost power: twice, I think. I went down to the basement, but I could see nothing wrong.'

'And after that?'

'A man. He passed me on the street, and I was concerned, but then he walked on, and I let him go. Seconds before it happened, I thought that he called to me. I think he was trying to warn me of something, but then there was an explosion, and I did not see him again.'

'Do you recall anything about him?'

'He was in his late forties or early fifties, I think. Unshaven, but not bearded. Perhaps six feet tall. Carrying some weight.'

'In which direction did he walk?'

'South.'

'South. On the far side of the street?'

'Yes.'

'Did you tell the police this?'

'No. I don't think I have spoken to anyone until now. I held her in my arms, but she was gone, and I don't remember anything else.'

'The police will want to talk with you. Don't mention the man to them.'

'No.'

The son took a cloth and wiped his father's brow, cooling it while avoiding the wounds.

'How badly am I hurt?' asked Eldritch.

'Cuts and bruises, for the most part. Some concussion. They want to keep you under observation for a few days, though. They're concerned.'

'I have trouble hearing. Your voice, my voice, they don't sound right to me.'

'I'll tell the doctors.'

Eldritch twisted on the bed. There was a pain in his groin. He looked beneath the sheet, saw the catheter, and groaned.

'I know,' said his son.

'It hurts.'

'I'll tell them about that as well.'

'My mouth is dry.'

His son took a plastic beaker of water from the bedside locker and held his father's head while he drank. The old man's skull felt fragile in his hand, like an egg that could be broken with just a tensing of the fingers. It was a miracle that he had survived. Minutes earlier, and he would have been gone too.

'I'll come back later,' said the son. 'Do you need anything?'

Now it was his father's hand that gripped his arm, and his upper body rose from the bed. So strong, this old man . . .

'Parker came. Parker came, and she died. She was getting his file, and then she died.' Eldritch was tiring now, and tears of grief squeezed themselves from the corners of his eyes. 'He warned me, warned you, to back off. He was afraid of the list. He knew that his name was on it.'

'I had doubts. So did you. The woman, Phipps, she told me something—'

But his father was no longer listening.

'The list,' he whispered. 'The list.'

'I still have it,' said his son, and in the soft dawn light filtering through the drapes he was altering in spirit and form, and he was both son and other. 'And I know where I can find the rest of it.'

'Kill them,' said Eldritch, as he fell back on the bed. 'Kill them all.'

He closed his eyes as his son's transformation was completed, and it was the Collector who left the room.

Jeff and Rachel came to pick up Sam shortly after nine a.m. She had been with Angel and Louis in the kitchen since before eight, buttering toast and scrambling eggs, and as a result I had to make her change her sweater before her mother saw her and blew a gasket.

Jeff was driving a Jaguar now. From my office window, Angel and Louis watched him pull up outside, step from the car, and take in the view of the Scarborough marshes with the winter sun shining coldly upon them while Rachel walked to the front door.

'He acts like he owns them,' said Angel.

'Or he made them himself,' said Louis.

'Transference,' I said. 'You know I don't like him, so you don't like him either.'

'No, I just don't like him,' said Angel.

'He got so much money, why's he driving a Jaguar?' asked Louis. 'Jaguar depreciates faster than dollars from Zimbabwe.'

'He drives it because he *has* so much money,' said Angel. 'How old is he?'

'Old,' said Louis.

'Very old,' said I.

'Ancient,' said Angel. 'It's a wonder the man can stand without a stick.'

The front door opened, and Rachel stepped into the hall and called 'Hello!'

'We're in here,' I said.

She came into the office and raised an eyebrow at the sight of the three of us standing there.

'The welcoming committee?'

'Just taking in the view,' said Louis.

She saw where we were looking, and at whom.

'Ha-ha,' she said.

'He's younger than I expected,' said Angel.

'Really?'

'No. He's real old.'

Rachel scowled at Angel.

'You keep saying things like that and you won't live to be his age.'

'I don't want to live to be his age,' said Angel. 'He's, like, Methuselah in pastels. Who dresses like that anyway?'

Rachel, to her credit, seemed determined to fight Jeff's corner.

'He's playing golf later,' she said.

'Golf?' said Louis. It might have been possible to inject more contempt into four letters and one syllable, but I couldn't see how.

'Yeah, golf,' said Rachel. 'Regular people play it. It's a sport.'

'Golf's a sport?'

He looked at Angel. Angel shrugged. 'Maybe we didn't get the memo.'

'You guys are jerks, you know that?' said Rachel. 'Where's my daughter? I need to get her away from here before she contracts jerkdom.'

'Too late,' said Louis. 'She got her father's genes.'

'You guys *are* jerks, you know,' I told him, as I followed Rachel.

'The cool kids are being mean to us,' Louis said to Angel.

'It's homophobia,' said Angel. 'We ought to complain, or write a show tune about it.'

I left them to it.

'Hey,' called Angel to my back, 'does that mean we can't go to the prom?'

In the hallway, Rachel was helping Sam with her bag.

'What happened to your nice new sweater?' asked Rachel, noting that Sam was wearing the old one with holes that I kept in the house for her to use when we worked in the garden.

'It got eggded,' said Sam.

'That figures,' said Rachel. 'Did mean Uncle Louis and Uncle Angel throw them at you and call you names?' She glowered at me.

'I didn't put them up to it,' I said. 'They can be mean without my help.'

'Uncle Angel said a bad word,' said Sam. 'The one beginning with "f".'

There was a cry of shock from my office. 'You promised she wouldn't tell!'

'That doesn't surprise me in the least,' said Rachel. She raised her voice and directed it to the office. 'But I'm very disappointed in Uncle Angel.'

'Sorry.'

Rachel checked that Sam had both socks on, that her underwear was the right way round, and she had her toothbrush and her dolls.

'Okay, say goodbye to your daddy, and then go to the car,' she told Sam.

Sam hugged me, and I held her tight. 'Bye, Daddy.'

'Bye, honey. I'll see you soon, okay? I love you.'

'I love you too.'

She pulled away, and I felt my heart break a little. 'Bye, Uncle Angel who said a bad word,' she called.

'Bye,' said an embarrassed voice.

'Bye, Uncle Louis who promised to shoot that man.'

There was a long, awkward pause before Louis said 'Bye,' and Sam trotted out the door.

Rachel gave me the hard eye. 'What?'

'It was a misunderstanding,' I said. 'He wouldn't really have shot him.'

'Jesus,' she said. 'Can I ask why they're here?'

'Just a thing,' I said.

'You're not going to tell me?'

'Like I said,' and it was my turn to give her the hard eye, 'it's just a thing.'

Her temper was rising now: Angel and Louis's ribbing of her, Sam's sweater, Angel's swearing, and whatever the hell she thought Louis had said, all of it combined to work on her like heat on a pressure cooker. Then again, she hadn't looked too happy when she'd arrived. An evening spent listening to Jeff tell a crowd of wealthy folk that the banking collapse was all the fault of poor people for wanting a roof over their heads probably hadn't helped. Her cheeks were flushed. She looked beautiful, but telling her that wouldn't have helped the situation.

'I hope you get shot in the fucking ass!' she said. She opened the office door wide – 'That goes for all of you!' – then slammed the door shut behind her.

'Come out and say hi to Jeff,' she ordered. 'Be polite and act like a normal guy.'

I followed her outside. Sam was already sitting in the child seat in the back of the car. She waved at me. I waved back.

'Hey, big guy,' said Jeff. He smiled whitely.

Big guy. What an asshole.

'Hey . . . Jeff,' I said.

We shook hands. He did that thing he always did where he held on to my right hand for too long with his right hand while gripping my upper arm with his left hand, and examined my face the way a surgeon will check out a patient who is seriously ill and doesn't appear to be getting any better, and is thus an affront to his caregiver.

'How you doing, fella?' he asked.

Fella: it just got better and better. Rachel grinned maliciously. It was revenge for earlier.

'I'm good, Jeff. And you?'

'Fantastic,' he replied. 'Just fine.'

'Speech went well last night?'

'It went down a storm. There were people asking me to run for office.'

'Wow. Somewhere in Africa would be good. I hear Sudan needs ironing out, or maybe Somalia.'

He looked puzzled, and the smile faltered for a moment, then recovered.

'No, here,' he said.

'Right. Of course.'

'There was a reporter who came along from the *Maine Sunday Telegram*. They're going to report the details of my speech on the weekend.'

'That's great,' I said. If they did, the *Telegram* wouldn't be getting my dollar seventy-five that Sunday. 'Any other reporters there?'

'Some guy from the *Phoenix*, but he was just hanging around to cause trouble.'

'Asking awkward questions? Not accepting the party line?'

'Ordinary people just don't understand deregulation,' said Jeff. 'They think it involves a state of lawlessness, but it simply means allowing market forces to determine outcomes. Once government begins to interfere, those outcomes start to become unpredictable, and that's when the trouble starts. Even light-touch regulation interferes with the natural running of the system. We just want to make sure that it runs right so everyone can benefit.'

'So you're the good guys?'

'We're the wealth generators.'

'You're certainly generating something, Jeff.'

Rachel intervened. 'It's time to go, Jeff. I think you've been baited long enough.' She hugged me and kissed my cheek. 'You'll come see Sam in a week or two?'

'Yes. Thanks for letting her spend the night. I appreciate it.'

'I didn't mean that part about you getting shot,' she said.

'I know.'

'The other two maybe, but not you.'

She looked to the office window. Angel and Louis were dimly visible through the blinds. Angel raised an arm, as if thinking about waving, then thought better of it.

'Jerks,' Rachel said again, as she got into the car, but she was smiling as she said it. Jeff wasn't joining her, though, not yet. Instead he was looking to the road, where a black Cadillac CTS coupe was slowing down before turning into my drive.

'Hey, just in time,' he said.

'In time for what?' I asked. Clearly, someone wasn't being hit too hard by the recession, but it was nobody I knew.

'There's a man I'd like you to meet,' said Jeff. 'He drove up to hear my speech, and he said he might take a look at some new development up on Prouts Neck while he was in town. I told him I'd keep him company, and he should look out for my car.'

The Cadillac pulled to a gentle halt behind Jeff's car. The

man who climbed out looked a couple of years younger than Jeff and glowed with good health, and he couldn't have smelled more of money if he was printing off bills in the back of his car. He had opted for a smart casual wardrobe: tan pants, a black roll-neck sweater, and a black mohair jacket. He was balding, but he hid it well by keeping his hair short, and he wasn't carrying more than a couple of pounds of excess baggage around the waist. He also had the decency to apologize for driving up to my home uninvited, pointing out that the road took a sharp bend and he was concerned about causing an obstruction by leaving his car there. I told him that it was okay, even if I didn't think it was. This guy made my skin prickle.

'I hope I'm not intruding,' he said. He waved at Rachel, and she waved back, but she was careful not to look at me.

'I'd like to introduce you to someone,' said Jeff, but he didn't make it clear to whom he was speaking until his next statement. 'Garrison Pryor, this is Charlie Parker.'

Pryor stretched out a hand, and after only a slight hesitation I shook it.

'Garrison Pryor, as in Pryor Investments?' I said.

'I'm surprised that you've heard of us,' he replied, although he didn't sound surprised. 'We're not one of the big houses.'

'I get the *Wall Street Journal*,' I lied.

'Really?' he said. He raised an eyebrow. 'Know thy enemy, perhaps.'

'Excuse me?' It was an odd thing for him to have said.

'It's just that Jeff has told me a little about you,' he continued. 'From what I could gather, you didn't strike me as a *Journal* reader. Jeff thinks you may be a closet socialist.'

'Compared to Jeff, most people are socialists.'

Pryor laughed, displaying white teeth with slightly elongated canines and sharp incisors. It was like being snarled at by a domesticated wolf.

'How true. I've been very interested to make your

acquaintance for some time,' said Pryor. He maintained steady eye contact, and his smile never wavered.

'Really?' I said.

'I'd read a lot about you, even before Jeff entered your realm of acquaintance. The men and women who you've hunted down, well, it's just frightening that such people could have roamed free for so long. It's quite the service that you're doing for society.'

From where I stood, I could see Rachel. She still wasn't looking at me, but she was biting her lower lip hard. I'd seen that expression before: it was as close as Rachel got to a display of concern in public.

I didn't reply, so Pryor went on talking.

'Do you know what I find most interesting about you, Mr Parker?'

'No,' I said, 'I don't.'

'If I'm correct, when a policeman uses his gun there are committees of inquiry, and paperwork, and sometimes even court cases. But you, a private operator, seem to skate around such obstacles with ease. How do you do that?'

'Good luck,' I said. 'And I only shoot the right people.'

'Oh, I think it's more than that. Somebody must be looking out for you.'

'God?'

'Perhaps, although I was thinking along more terrestrial lines.'

'I try to keep the law on my side.'

'That's funny,' said Pryor. 'So do I, and yet I don't believe we're at all alike.'

Jeff, who had been smiling at the start of our conversation, wasn't smiling any longer. He seemed to realize that this wasn't going the way he might have hoped, whatever that was.

'We'd better be going, Garrison,' he said. 'Rachel and I have to get Sam home, so if you'd like me to take a look at that development with you . . .'

'You know, Jeff, I don't think that will be necessary. Maybe this part of the world isn't for me after all.'

Jeff's face fell faster than a busted elevator. I guessed that he'd been hoping to cut himself in on the deal by acting as a go-between if Pryor started throwing money around in Maine.

'If you're sure,' said Jeff.

'I'm very sure. Goodbye, Mr Parker. I'm sorry again for the intrusion, but I'm happy to have made your acquaintance at last. I look forward to reading more about you in the future.'

'Likewise,' I said.

Pryor said his goodbyes to Jeff, waved again to Rachel but not to Sam, and reversed his car onto the road before heading west toward the Interstate.

'See you, big guy,' said Jeff to me.

As he prepared to get into his car, I leaned in close to him.

'Jeff,' I said softly, 'don't ever bring any of your friends onto my property again, not without asking me first. You understand?'

He smiled thinly, and nodded. Only Sam waved at me again as they drove away.

Angel and Louis joined me on the driveway.

'Who was that?' asked Angel.

'His name's Garrison Pryor,' I replied, 'and I don't think he's one of the good guys.'

Within the hour, I received two messages arising out of that encounter. The first was a text from Rachel. It read only 'Sorry.' The second was an email notifying me of a gift subscription to the *Wall Street Journal*.

It came courtesy of Pryor Investments.

40

The late morning news bulletins detailed the death of a fifty-eight-year-old woman in an explosion at a lawyer's office in Lynn, Massachusetts: I knew nothing about it until then because my focus had been entirely on Sam. The woman, who was not being named until relatives could be informed, was said to be an employee of the business. The principal, Thomas Eldritch, was described only as having suffered injuries in the blast, and was being kept under observation. As yet, the police declined to speculate on the cause of the explosion as investigators remained at the scene, but I knew.

'The list,' I said to Angel and Louis. 'Once the Collector killed Tate, they must have known that he had a copy, either partial or full.'

'And because they couldn't get to him, they tried to take out his lawyer,' said Angel.

I thought about the chain-smoking woman who had guarded the stairs to Eldritch's office, and the look on her face when she believed that I had upset him in some way. I couldn't say that I had liked her, exactly, but she had been loyal to the old man, and she had not deserved to die.

The picture on the screen returned to a view of the exterior of Eldritch's offices. The explosion had started a fire that gutted the building, and it had taken fire department units from adjoining towns to bring it under control. The Pakistani cell phone store was gone too. One of its owners was interviewed on the street. He was weeping. An idiot reporter asked him if he thought the explosion might have been linked to

Islamic extremists. The Pakistani businessman stopped weeping for long enough to look shocked, and hurt, and enraged, and then started crying even more.

I was saved the trouble of contacting Epstein by his call to me. He was at last in Toronto, after spending most of the previous night with the police telling them of the circumstances of Adiv's death. I hadn't liked Adiv much either. It was turning into a bad week for people who had crossed me. While I spoke to Epstein, Louis slipped my delivery copy of the *New York Times* in front of me. Adiv's death had made the front page in what was being described as an assassination attempt on a prominent figure in the Jewish community. The picture of Epstein had been taken a long time before, perhaps a decade or more. Epstein had been doing his best to avoid the limelight ever since the death of his son. The story mentioned that as well. I made the continuation of the story inside, since I was the one who had found his son's killers. That didn't make me happy at all. When I checked my cell phone there were forty missed calls, and my message box was full. I gave the phone to Angel and let him start listening to, and deleting, the messages.

'You're okay?' I asked Epstein.

'Shaken, but otherwise unharmed.'

'I'm sorry about Adiv.'

'I know you are. Had he lived, he might have grown to find that incident of the Pine Barrens amusing.'

'It would have taken some time.'

'Indeed.'

'Did you see hear the news about our lawyer friend in Lynn?'

'I was informed of it this morning,' said Epstein. 'We're assuming that the two attacks are linked?'

'It's a big step up to the majors for coincidence if they're not,' I replied. 'No word on Eldritch's client, though. I figure he was out of town when it happened.'

I was always careful how I discussed the Collector on the phone. It was force of habit, but then I was careful how I discussed the Collector, period.

'And the reason: revenge? An attempt to discourage further investigation? All of these things, and more? After all, it was not my people who killed Davis Tate.'

'Tate's death, and whatever else the client might have been up to, let them know that some version of the list is already out there, courtesy of the late Barbara Kelly. If Eldritch and his client had a copy, then it was logical to surmise that you probably had a copy too. Maybe they hoped to catch Eldritch and his client with the blast at Lynn, or maybe they just wanted to destroy his records. At the very least, it was a way of distracting the client for a time, just as they hoped the attack on you, whether it yielded casualties or not, might be enough to—'

I paused. The word that was on the tip of my tongue was 'delay', but why did it spring to mind?

'Mr Parker?' said Epstein. 'Are you there?'

'It was a delaying tactic, a distraction,' I said.

'But distracting us from what?' said Epstein.

'The plane,' I said. 'Somehow they've found out about the plane, and they know that we're looking for it too.'

'How long before you can start the search?'

'Tomorrow, if we're lucky and we can get a solid lead on its location. I still haven't spoken to Marielle Vetters again. If she can't help us, I have one other idea.'

'Meanwhile, what will the client do?' asked Epstein.

I didn't have to think for long.

'The client will hunt down those he believes were responsible for that explosion,' I said, 'and the client will punish them.'

The Collector stood at the intersection, smoking a cigarette and watching the police go about their business. The gutted buildings were still smoldering, and the street was awash with filthy black water like the aftermath of an oil slick. The curious and the bored lounged behind the cordon, and the news vans had congregated in the parking lot of Tulley's bar, where Tulley himself was charging them three-figure sums for the pleasure, although he was throwing in free coffee which, if the reporters had any sense, they were in turn throwing away.

Behind the Collector stood a pawn shop that extended over four floors, the heaviest and largest items on the ground floor, the rest arrayed over the next two floors in diminishing order of size. The top floor, the Collector knew, contained offices. On the side of the building, overlooking its back door and the parking lot beyond, was a camera. Beside it was a second camera, facing away from the door and toward the street.

The Collector killed the cigarette and left the police to their business. He entered the pawn shop, where the two men seated behind the counter barely glanced at him before returning their attention to a TV screen that was showing the same crime scene that the Collector had just witnessed. Had they walked a couple of feet they could have stood outside and watched it in person, but they were ignorant, lazy men, and they preferred to glean their information from the TV where people who were better-looking than they were could tell them things that they already knew.

The Collector climbed the stairs to the top floor, where there was a red metal door with a spyhole and the words PRIVATE – EMPLOYEES ONLY stenciled on it in white paint. There was no buzzer, but the door opened as the Collector approached, and he was admitted.

A very old, very fat woman, and an even older man, sat in a small outer office. They were the Sister and the Brother. If they had other names – and they must have had, once upon a time – then nobody ever used them. The name on the sign outside came from another business, a drapery store that had closed in the 1970s. Shortly after, the Sister and the Brother had moved in, and they had never left. As she grew larger and larger, the Sister had risen higher and higher in the building in opposition to the items for sale, a great balloon of a woman floating slowly upward until the roof finally arrested her progress.

Arrayed around them on a pair of tables covered in green cloth were various items of jewelry, a half dozen watches, an assortment of coins, and a sprinkling of gemstones. The woman was morbidly obese. The Collector knew that she never left the building, eating and sleeping in the living quarters separated from the office by a pair of red drapes. When she needed medical attention, the doctor came to her. So far, either her health had remained stable enough to require no serious treatment, which seemed unlikely given the strain her system was under, or some combination of the dozens of bottles of prescription and non-prescription medicines on the shelves above her head enabled her to keep functioning for the present. Her tiny head sat on massive folds of fat where her neck had once been, and her arms appeared absurdly small for her body. She was like a melting snowwoman. She wore a pair of black horn-rimmed glasses on a chain. Through them she watched the Collector but said nothing, and her face showed no feeling beyond that of a general weariness at a life lived too long, and in too much pain.

The Brother took the Collector by the hand, a curiously intimate gesture to which the Collector did not object, and walked him into a closet space barely big enough for the two of them. Here there was a giant safe, built by the Victor Safe & Lock Company of Cincinnati, Ohio, at the turn of the last century, virtually an antique in itself. The safe was open, and inside were blocks of bills, and gold coins, and old jewelry boxes containing the store's most valuable pieces. Such an apparently casual attitude to security might not have been considered wise in this day and age, and it was true that the pawn shop had been burgled once, back in 1994. The burglars had beaten the Sister badly, although she presented no threat to them. The attack, more than any other factor, had precipitated her massive gain in weight, and her reluctance to explore an outside world capable of producing such individuals.

The Collector had found those men. They were never seen again.

Actually, this was not entirely true.

Parts of them were seen again.

After that incident, the business of the Sister and the Brother remained untroubled by crime or the fear of crime. Why, then, was there still a need for security cameras? Well, for the same reason that a deserted building at the other end of the street, unoccupied and apparently not for sale or lease, had small, discreet cameras hidden behind bulbs on its façade, and the liquor store down the block operated two surveillance systems running in parallel: because, between them and the cameras in Eldritch's now ruined building, they offered a full panorama of the street.

Just in case.

Now, on a small computer beside the safe, the Collector logged on to the digital recording system linked to the computer, found the feeds for the two cameras on the pawn shop's building, and split the screen between them. He used the mouse to move the cursor back to the minutes before the explosion – and now here was the man, his head down, walking toward the camera, looking over his shoulder, turning, raising his hand. Suddenly a flash, and twin bursts of interference on the screen as the explosion shook the cameras. When the pictures cleared, the man was running, his head no longer down, and he vanished from one screen, then the other.

The Collector rewound and slow-forwarded, back and forth, over and over, until he had one image on the screen. He enlarged it, adjusted the area under examination, and enlarged again. The Brother stood behind him, taking it all in.

'There,' said the Brother.

'There,' said the Collector.

The man's features were revealed to him. The Collector leaned forward, and touched the face on the screen with his fingertips.

I *know* you.

41

Later that mornng, Angel, Louis and I traveled to Falls End with two intentions: the first was to find out if there was anything more that Marielle Vetters could tell us about the location of the plane, anything that she might have remembered, however irrelevant it might seem. If she could not help us further, then there was someone else I might ask, although it would mean leaving Falls End temporarily. Marielle had not returned my call from the previous night, but I had not yet started to worry.

Second, we had to plan for the eventual expedition into the woods. With that in mind, I'd called Jackie Garner and asked him to head up to Falls End as soon as possible, because Jackie knew the woods. Andy Garner, Jackie's old man, had left his wife when Jackie was just a kid. There were irreconcilable differences between them: she thought Jackie's old man was the biggest asshole who ever lived – a serial screwer of women, a deadbeat who had never met a steady job he liked, and an oxygen thief – and he disagreed, but he'd continued to be a part of his son's life until he died, and his wife had continued to love him, despite her better judgment. Andy Garner had that rare gift of charm, a charisma that enabled him to skate over the pain his failings caused others, and inspired a degree of tolerance, and even forgiveness, in those whom he hurt. Jackie's mother, who knew his weaknesses better than anyone, had sometimes been known to take him back into her bed after they had divorced; it was she who had nursed him during his final illness, and she remained his widow in all but name.

Andy Garner kept his head above water by working as a guide in the Great North Woods during hunting season. He was a premium hire, with regular sports who came back to him year after year. They were wealthy businessmen and bankers, and Andy always ensured that they returned to their city lives content with their hunt, and boasting of the animals they had killed. In lean years, where others struggled to find bear or trophy bucks for their clients, Andy Garner would break records, and his bonuses would increase. He was a man who was only truly happy when he was in the forest, a man profoundly in tune with nature but lost in cities and towns. Away from the woods, he found solace in alcohol and women, but during hunting season he was sober and celibate, and happier than at any other time.

As soon as his son was old enough, Andy began taking him into the woods with him, trying to pass on what he knew and develop the instincts for the forest that he was sure lay in the boy. He was right, to a degree: Jackie had his father's understanding of, and empathy with, the natural world, but he was softer than his father, and cared little for hunting.

'You'll never make money from nature walks,' his father would tell him. 'It's hunting that will put bread on your table.'

Jackie Garner found other ways to put bread on his table, some legal and some illegal, but he still returned to the woods whenever he could, sometimes just to escape his mother, who had always been a very demanding woman. He had that in common with his buddies, the Fulcis. It was probably part of the reason why the three of them got on so well together.

Jackie didn't have a camp of his own in the woods, but relied on the generosity of friends. When that was not forthcoming, he was happy to pitch a tent. When I called him from my car and asked him to join us in Falls End, he jumped at the chance. I did not tell him what we were looking for, not yet. That could wait.

'How's your mom doing?' I asked. We still had not yet had the chance to talk properly about her illness.

'Not so good. I ought to have told you about her before but, you know, I think I was in denial.'

'About what exactly, Jackie?'

'I can't even pronounce it, and I've heard it often enough in the last month: Creutzfeldt-Jakob disease. Does that sound right to you?'

I told him that I didn't know. I'd heard of the illness, but I wasn't familiar with its symptoms, or its prognosis. Unfortunately, Jackie now was.

'She'd been acting strange,' he explained. 'Well, stranger than normal. She was getting angry for no reason, and then she'd forget that she'd been angry to start with. I thought it might be Alzheimer's, but the doctors came back to us a couple of weeks ago with a diagnosis of this Creutzfeldt-Jakob thing.'

'How bad is it?'

'She has a year, maybe a little longer. The dementia is progressive, and her vision is starting to suffer. Her legs and arms are spasming. She has to go into a home, and we've started looking at places. Look, Charlie, there's money for this job, right? I need to get some cash together. I have to make sure that she's cared for right.'

Epstein had agreed to cover all expenses. I'd make sure that he paid well for Jackie's guide skills.

'You'll have no complaints, Jackie.'

'And it's a short job?'

'Two days at most, once I get the information that we need. We'll have to be ready to spend a night in the woods if we have to, but I'm hoping it won't come to that.'

'Then I'm good to go,' said Jackie. 'Some time out in the woods will help me to clear my head.'

I told him where to meet us, and the call came to an end. I felt a deep pity for Jackie. He might have been a little screwed up, and with an excessive fondness for homemade munitions, but he was unswervingly loyal to his friends. While he had complained about his mother more than any man I've ever met, he loved her too. Her illness and eventual death would hit him hard.

Angel and Louis were following me to Falls End in their own car. I informed them of my conversation with Jackie when we stopped for coffee along the way. Both of them immediately told me to keep whatever Epstein was paying for their time and expertise, and pass it on to Jackie. I planned to do the same.

It was clear that something was wrong in Falls End as soon as we reached the town. There were patrol cars from the Aroostook County Sheriff's Department parked on the street, along with state police cruisers and the MSP's mobile crime scene unit. Parked on a side road to the east, just at the edge of the forest, I saw a concentration of vehicles, among them one from the Maine medical examiner's office, and standing beside it the medical examiner herself, talking to a couple of detectives whom I recognized.

I knew that Marielle Vetters lived at the northern end of town, and it was there that a second group of law enforcement vehicles had congregated. Because it was still hunting season the town was filled with strangers and their vehicles, so we did not stand out, but I was concerned about being seen by any lawman who might recognize me. I still didn't know for sure that something had happened to Marielle, but I feared the worst.

'Damn,' I said, and I spoke out of concern not only for Marielle but also for myself. My message was on her answering machine, assuming that she hadn't erased it after listening to it. Being connected in any way with what might have happened to her wouldn't be productive. I parked in the municipal lot, and Angel and Louis pulled up alongside me. Angel went scouting for information while Louis and I waited in my car.

Angel returned half an hour later carrying coffees in a cardboard tray. He got in the back of the car and passed them around before speaking.

'Marielle Vetters is alive,' he said. 'So's her brother, but they're both in comas. It's all anyone is talking about in the local diner, which seems to be ground zero for gossip. I just had to sit and listen. Two people are dead, both shot. One is a guy called Teddy Gattle. Marielle's brother was staying with him, and there's speculation that they may have got into an argument at Gattle's place, and maybe Grady Vetters shot Teddy there before heading over to his sister's house to commit the second killing. He and his sister might have had some falling out over money and the house, but the Grady-Vetters-as-killer theory is coming from the cops at the moment, not the locals. Most folk don't believe that Grady Vetters could have shot anyone, but there are rumors that a gun was found beside him, and if it's the murder weapon, well . . .

'But, Charlie, the other dead man is Ernie Scollay. He was found shot in the back in Marielle Vetters' house.'

I said nothing. I had liked Ernie Scollay from the moment I'd met him. In his careful, cautious way, he'd reminded me of my grandfather.

It was a set-up; it had to be. Marielle Vetters might have been having difficulties with her brother, but she had given no indication that she was worried about him becoming violent. Then again, there were a lot of victims of domestic killings who had never seen it coming, never suspected that someone of their own blood would turn against them. If the potential for violence was that easy to spot, there would be far fewer dead people. Was it too much of a stretch to imagine that, on the same evening attacks were launched on two other people connected with the list, the Vetters family, also linked to the list, should become embroiled in a domestic dispute that left two people dead and two others apparently in a coma?

But if Grady Vetters was not, in fact, a killer, how had he and his sister been found by those who had also sought to silence Eldritch and Epstein? Both Marielle and Ernie Scollay had known the risks involved in telling anyone else of what they knew. Ernie hadn't even wanted me to be brought into their little circle. That left Grady Vetters, because he had been with his sister by their father's bedside when the story of the airplane in the woods had been told.

I had to make a decision. Unless Marielle had erased my message after listening to it, it would only be a matter of time before the police came knocking on my door. I could come forward immediately and tell them what I knew, or try to avoid them for as long as possible. The second option sounded best. If I spoke to them I'd have to tell them about the plane, and that would mean the fact of its existence becoming public. I recalled Epstein's refusal to share what he knew even with SAC Ross in the FBI's New York office for fear that it might reach the wrong ears, and Ross was his tame federal agent, a man whom we both trusted, even if I didn't trust him quite as far as Epstein. For now, telling the police anything about that plane was not an option.

I went for the worst case scenario: Grady Vetters had not killed his friend Teddy Gattle, or Ernie Scollay. He and his sister had been found by those who were seeking the plane, and Gattle and Scollay had been killed because they were in the way. Marielle and Grady had probably been forced to share whatever they knew, and then silenced. The decision not to kill them was odd: if someone was trying to frame Grady Vetters, having him shoot his sister and then himself would have left the police with a tidy murder-suicide. Instead, according to gossip – and who knew how true that might be? – there were two potential witnesses still alive, but in comas. On the other hand, leaving them breathing but incapacitated would concentrate the focus of the investigation on the survivors, and muddy the waters for a while. If Marielle or Grady had revealed some new information about the location of the plane, whoever was responsible for what had just occurred in Falls End wouldn't need to distract the police for long: just until the plane was found and the list secured.

'What now?' said Louis.

'Find us a couple of rooms at a motel, and tell Jackie Garner where you're at. I'll be back here by evening.'

'And where are you going?' asked Angel, as they got out of my car.

I started the engine.

'To ask an old friend why he lied to me.'

42

Ray Wray wasn't happy.

He had arrived at Joe Dahl's camp just south-west of Masardis knowing only that there was a job waiting for him, a job that would pay him a couple of grand for a couple of days' work involving an airplane, which meant that the work was probably illegal. Illegal work in that part of Maine generally meant smuggling, and the only thing really worth smuggling was drugs. Hence Ray Wray had decided that what he and Joe Dahl were looking for in the Great North Woods was a crashed plane full of drugs.

Of course, Ray Wray had no trouble with drug smuggling. He'd done enough of it in the past to know how to limit the risk of getting caught, which was the main worry in that line of work. Getting caught caused all kinds of difficulty, and not only with the law: the individuals who paid folk to smuggle their drugs for them often took it amiss when the consignment didn't reach its intended destination. Paying your debt to society was one thing; paying your debt to the bikers, or the Mexicans, or a piece of shit like Perry Reed was another thing entirely.

So the fact of smuggling wasn't the issue for Ray, and neither was securing the plane and its cargo without getting caught. What he did have trouble with was the fact that a woman and a boy were sleeping like vampires in Joe Dahl's place, the drapes drawn on the windows of the little cabin, the woman curled up on the camp bed and the boy sleeping beside her on the floor. Ray could see that the woman's face was badly disfigured when he peered around the thick sheet that separated the sleeping area from the rest of the room, but he'd been troubled more by the kid, who had woken suddenly when Ray appeared and shown Ray the business end of a knife.

Now Ray was sitting on a roughhewn bench overlooking the Oxbow with a cup of coffee in his hand, Joe Dahl beside him, and Dahl was so jittery that he was giving Ray a case of the jitters too.

'This plane?' said Ray.

'Yeah, what about it?'

'When did it come down?'

'Years ago.'

'How many years ago?'

'I don't know.'

'How come nobody's found it before now?'

'They didn't know where to look.' Dahl pointed to the forest beyond with his own cup. 'Come on, Ray, you could lose a jumbo jet in there, you know that. What we're talking about is a small plane. Folk could have passed within feet of it and not have seen it if they weren't already looking for it.'

'What's on it?' asked Ray.

'I don't know.'

'Drugs?'

'I said I don't know, Ray. Jesus.'

This wasn't right. Joe Dahl was hard. Unlike Ray, he'd done some killing. Ray wasn't the killing kind, but he was good in the woods, could hold up his end in a fight, and he knew how to keep his mouth shut. Dahl, on the other hand, had knocked heads with some serious people in the past, and was still standing, but he was giving off bad vibes about this job, and Ray was increasingly inclined to put it down to the woman and her spooky kid.

'So how do we know where it's at?' asked Ray. There was no point in pursuing the subject of the plane's contents any further with Dahl, not now. Maybe later, once he'd calmed down some.

'She says it's near the ruins of a fort, and there ain't but one fort in there,' said Dahl.

Suddenly Ray understood why he was being paid so much money for heading out into the woods for a day or two. It didn't really matter what was on that plane. It wasn't even so much the difficulty in getting to it. But he had heard the stories about that fort, about Wolfe's Folly. It was situated in a part of the forest where hunters didn't go because game stayed away from it; where there were no trails, and the trees hunched like the forms of giants; where the air smelled wrong, and north and south, east and west, got all screwed up, didn't matter how good your compass was, or your own sense of direction. It was a place where a man could get lost, because something in there *wanted* you to get lost, something that maybe looked like a little girl.

Ray had never been out there, and had never intended going. Even the stories about it tended to be kept among locals, just to ensure that no idiot thrill-seekers or hardened skeptics took it into their heads to start exploring to prove some point that only they could understand. There was a time when hikers used to go missing, and it was said that they might have strayed too close to Wolfe's Folly, but that didn't happen so much anymore, not since care had been taken to excise it from the general discourse and ensure, by unspoken agreement, that whatever was out there was left undisturbed. Most of what Ray knew about it he'd learned from Dahl, and Dahl didn't hold with ghost stories, so if you heard it from Joe Dahl's mouth you knew that it was true. Dahl said that nobody with an ounce of sense had been out near Wolfe's Folly in years, and Ray believed him. If the plane had come down near there, it would explain a lot.

'How much is she paying again?' asked Ray.

'Two thousand up front to each of us, and another thousand

each when we find the plane. That's good money, Ray. I could sure use it.'

Amen to that, thought Ray. He'd only managed to get through last winter with cash from the Home Energy Assistance Program, and now that state benefit had been halved because of the recession. Without money for heating oil, a man could die.

'Out there's no place for a woman and a child,' said Ray. 'And that boy looks sick. They ought to stay here, leave the finding to us.'

'They're coming, Ray. There's no discussion about it. I wouldn't worry about her and the boy. They're –' Dahl sought the right word. '*Stronger* than they look.'

'What happened to her face, Joe?'

'She got burned, looks like.'

'Burned bad. She ain't never going to see out of that eye again.'

'You an eye surgeon now?'

'Don't need to be a surgeon to tell a dead eye from a live one.'

'Yeah, I guess.'

'Who does that to a woman?'

'Whoever it was, I don't believe they're around to ask no more,' said Dahl. 'Like I told you, don't misjudge that woman by her appearance. Cross her, and she'll leave you buried in a hole.'

'Is the boy her son?'

'I don't know. You want to ask her, maybe pry into her other affairs while you're about it?'

Ray looked back at the cabin. The drapes moved on one of the windows, and a face appeared. The boy was awake, and watching them, probably with that blade in his hand. Ray shuddered. He shouldn't ought to be scared by a child, but something of Dahl's own unease had communicated itself to him.

'The kid's watching us,' he said.

Joe didn't turn around. 'He looks out for the woman.'

'He's a creepy little fucker, isn't he?'

'Yeah, and he's got real good hearing too.'

Ray shut up.

'This woman, she'll put more work our way if it all goes right for her,' Dahl said. He paused. 'As long as you don't mind getting your hands dirty.'

Ray didn't mind. He'd seen the guns: a pair of Ruger Hawkeyes and two compact 9 mm pistols. So Ray Wray had never killed anyone: that didn't mean he wouldn't, if it came down to it. He'd come close once or twice, and he thought that he could take the final step.

'Are we the only ones looking for this plane, Joe?' he asked.

'No, I don't believe we are.'

'I thought not,' said Ray. 'When do we start?'

'Soon, Ray. Real soon.'

V

Tread lightly, she is near
Under the snow,
Speak gently, she can hear
The daisies grow.

'Requiescat', Oscar Wilde
(1856–1900)

43

When I was a boy, I thought everyone over thirty was old: my parents were old, my grandparents were *real* old, and after that there were just people who were dead. Now my view of aging was more nuanced: there were people in my immediate circle of acquaintances who were younger than I, and people who were older. In time there would be far more of the former than the latter, until eventually I might look around and find that I was the oldest person in the room, which would probably be a bad sign. I recalled Phineas Arbogast as being almost ancient, but he had probably not been more than sixty when I first met him, and possibly even younger than that, although he had lived a hard life, and every year of it was written on his face.

Phineas Arbogast was a friend of my grandfather and, boy, could he talk. There were people who crossed the street when they saw Phineas coming, or dived into stores to avoid him, even if it meant buying an item that they didn't need, just so they wouldn't get drawn into a conversation with him. He was a lovely man, but every incident in his day, however minor, could be transformed into an adventure on the scale of the *Odyssey*. Even my grandfather, a man of seemingly infinite tolerance, had been known to pretend that he wasn't home when Phineas dropped by unexpectedly, my grandfather having been given some warning of his approach by the belchings of Phineas's old truck. On one such occasion, my grandfather had been forced to hide beneath his own bed as Phineas went from window to window, peering inside with his hands cupped against the glass, convinced that my grand-father must be in there somewhere, either sleeping or, God forbid, lying unconscious and requiring rescue, which would have provided Phineas with another tale to add to his ever-expanding collection of stories.

More often than not, though, my grandfather would sit and listen to Phineas. In part he did so because, buried somewhere in every one of Phineas's tales, was a nugget of something useful: a piece of information about a person (my grandfather was a retired sheriff's deputy, and he never quite set aside his policeman's love of secrets), or a little shard of history or forest lore. But my grandfather also listened because he understood that Phineas was lonely: Phineas had never married, and it was said that he had long held a flame for a woman named Abigail Ann Morrison, who owned a bakery in Rangeley that Phineas was known to frequent when he went up to his cabin in the area. She was a single woman of indeterminate age, and he was a single man of indetermi-nate age, and somehow they managed to circle each other for twenty years until Abigail Ann Morrison was sideswiped by a car while delivering a box of cupcakes to a church social, and so their dance was ended.

So Phineas spun his stories, and sometimes people listened and sometimes they did not. I had forgotten most of those that I heard; most, but not all. There was one in particular that had stayed with me: the story of a missing dog and a lost girl in the Great North Woods.

The Cronin Rehabilitation and Senior Living Center was situated a few miles north of Houlton. It wasn't much to look at from the outside – a series of blankly modern buildings built in the seventies, decorated in the eighties, and allowed to remain in stasis ever since, the paintwork and furnishings restored and repaired when required, but never altered. Its lawns were well tended, but there was little color. Cronin's was nothing more or less than a neutral corner of God's waiting room.

Whatever the subtleties of defining the aging process, there was no doubt that Phineas Arbogast was now very old indeed. He lay sleeping on an armchair in the room that he shared with another, marginally younger, man who was reading a newspaper in bed when I arrived, his eyes magnified enormously by thick spectacles. Those owl eyes focused on me with alarm as I approached Phineas.

'You're not going to wake him, are you?' he asked. 'The only peace I get is when that man is asleep.'

I apologized, and said it was important that I spoke with Phineas.

'Well, on your head be it,' he said. 'Just permit me to get my gown on before you go rousing David Copperfield over there.'

I waited while he got out of bed, put on his gown and slippers, and prepared to find somewhere to read undisturbed. I said that I was sorry for a second time, and the old man replied, 'I swear, when that man dies God Himself will move out of heaven and join the devil in hell to get a break from his yammering.' He paused at the door. 'Don't tell him I said that, will you? God knows, I'm fond of the old coot.'

And away he went.

I remembered Phineas as a big man with a gray-brown beard, but the years had picked the meat from his bones just as the fall wind will denude a tree of its leaves before the coming of winter, and Phineas's eternal winter could not be far off. His mouth had collapsed in on itself with the loss of his teeth, and his head was entirely bald, although a little of his beard remained. His skin was transparent, so that I could count the veins and capillaries beneath it, and I thought I could discern not just the shape of his skull, but the skull itself. According to the nursing assistant who had shown me to his room, there was nothing wrong with Phineas: he had no major illnesses beyond an assortment of the various ailments that beset so many at the end of their lives, and his mind was still clear. He was simply dying because it was his time to die. He was dying because he was old.

I pulled up a chair and tapped him lightly on the arm. He woke suddenly, squinted at me, then found his spectacles on his lap and held them to the bridge of his nose without putting them on, like a dowager duchess examining a suspect piece of china.

'Who are you?' he asked. 'You look familiar.'

'My name is Charlie Parker. You and my grandfather were friends.'

His face unclouded, and his smile shone. His hand reached out and shook mine, and his grip was still strong.

'It's good to see you, boy,' he said. 'You're looking well.'

His left hand came out and joined the right, like a man being saved from drowning.

'You too, Phineas.'

'You're a damned liar. Give me a scythe and a hood, and I could play Death himself. If I stumble by a mirror when I'm up to take a piss at night, I think that's the grim old bastard come for me at last.'

He took a brief coughing fit then, and sipped from a can of soda that stood by his chair.

'I was sorry to hear about your wife and your little girl,' he said, when he had recovered. 'I know you maybe don't like folk reminding you about it, but it has to be said.'

He took my hand in his again, there was a final tightening, and the hands withdrew.

I had a box of candy under my arm. He looked at it bemusedly.

'I got no teeth left,' he explained, 'and candy plays hell with my dentures.'

'That's okay,' I told him. 'I didn't bring you any candy.'

I opened the box. Inside were five Cohiba Churchill cigars.

Cigars had always been his vice, I knew. My grandfather would share one with him at Christmas, then complain about the smell for weeks after.

'If you can't have Cuban, I figure the best Dominicans will have to do,' I said.

Phineas took one from the box, held it beneath his nose, and sniffed it. I thought he might be about to cry.

'God bless you,' he said. 'You mind taking an old man for a walk?'

I said that I didn't mind at all. I helped him to put on an extra sweater, and a muffler, then his coat and gloves and a bright red woolen hat that made him look like a marooned buoy. I found a wheelchair, and together we set off for a stroll around those dull grounds. He lit up once we were out of sight of the main building, and happily talked and puffed his way to a small ornamental lake by the edge of a fir copse, where I sat on a bench and listened to him some more. When he eventually had to pause for breath, I took the opportunity to steer the conversation in another direction.

'A long time ago, when I was a teenager, you told my grandfather and me a story,' I said.

'I told you both lots of stories. Your grandfather was still here, he'd say that I told too many for his liking. He hid under his bed from me once, you know that? He thought I didn't see him, but I did.' He chuckled. 'The old fart. I kept meaning to use it against him sometime, but he upped and died before I could, damn him.'

He drew again on the cigar.

'This one was different,' I said. 'It was a ghost story, about a little girl in the North Woods.'

Phineas held the smoke in for so long I was convinced it was going to start coming out of his ears. At last, when he'd had time to think, he let it out and said, 'I remember it.'

Of course you do, I thought, because a man doesn't forget a tale like that, not if he's been a part of it. A man doesn't forget hunting for his lost dog – Misty, wasn't that her name? – in the depths of the forest, and finding her all tangled up in briars with a little barefoot girl waiting nearby, a girl who was both there and not there, both very young and very, very old, a girl who claimed to be lost and lonely even as those briars started snaking around the man's shoes, trying to hold him there so that the girl could have company, so that she could draw him down to the dark place in which she dwelled.

No, you don't forget a thing like that, not ever. There was a truth to the tale that Phineas Arbogast told to my grandfather and me, but it wasn't the whole truth. He had wanted to tell the story, to share what he had seen, but some details needed to be changed, because one had to be careful about such matters.

'You said that you saw the girl somewhere up near Rangeley,' I said. 'You said she was the reason why you stopped going up to your cabin there.'

'That's right,' said Phineas. 'That's what I said.'

I didn't look at him as I spoke, but I kept my voice soft and there was no accusation or blame to my tone. This was not an interrogation, but I needed to know the truth. It was important if I was to find that plane.

'Do you think she roams, this girl?'

'Roams?' asked Phineas. 'What do you mean by that?'

'What I'm wondering is if all of the North Woods is her territory, or if she just sticks to one small area? Because my feeling is that she's linked to a place, that maybe she has, well, a *lair*, for want of a better word. It could be where her body lies, and that's where she returns to, and she can't or won't stray too far from there.'

'I couldn't say for sure,' said Phineas, 'but I guess that sounds about right.'

Now I looked at him. I touched his arm, and he turned his face to me.

'Phineas, why did you say that you were beyond Rangeley

when you saw her? You weren't anywhere near Rangeley. You were farther north, past Falls End. You were deep in the County, weren't you?'

Phineas looked at his cigar.

'You're spoiling my smoke,' he said.

'I'm not trying to catch you out. I'm not blaming you for altering the details of the story. But it's important that you tell me where you were, as best you can, when you saw that girl. Please.'

'How about a story for a story?' said Phineas. 'Suppose you tell me why you need to know?'

So I told him of an old man on his deathbed, and a plane in the Great North Woods, and I told him what linked Harlan Vetters' search for a boy named Barney Shore to the discovery of that plane: the ghost of a girl. The plane lay in her territory, wherever that might be, and despite Harlan Vetters' story about malfunctioning compasses and lost bearings, I believe he did have some notion of where exactly that plane rested. Perhaps he had chosen not to share the location because he didn't trust his son, not entirely, or because he was dying and confused, and couldn't keep all of the details straight in his head.

Or maybe he did share that detail, but only with his daughter, and she had held it back from me for reasons of her own. She didn't know me, and it could be that she wanted to see what I'd do with the information she'd already given me before she entrusted me with that final, crucial element.

When I was finished telling my tale, Phineas nodded his approval. 'That's a good story,' he said.

'You'd know,' I replied.

'I would,' he said. 'Always have.'

His cigar had gone out, so engrossed had he been. He lit it again, taking his time with it.

'What were you doing up there, Phineas?'

'Poachin',' he replied, once the cigar was going again to his satisfaction. 'Bear. And maybe mournin' some.'

'Abigail Ann Morrison,' I said.

'You got a memory almost as good as mine. I suppose you need to, given what you do.'

Now he told the story again, and it was more or less as he had told it before, but the location was changed to deep in the County, and he had a landmark to offer.

'Through the woods, behind that girl, I thought I saw the ruins of a fort,' he said. 'It was all overgrown, more forest than fort, but there's only one fort up in those woods. Wherever she hides, wherever that plane lies, it's not far from Wolfe's Folly.'

It was growing colder, but Phineas did not want to return to his room, not yet. He still had half a cigar left.

'Your grandfather knew that I was lying about where I saw that girl,' said Phineas. 'I didn't want to tell him that I'd been poachin', and he didn't want to be told, and it was none of his business if I was crying for Abigail Ann, but I wanted him to understand that I'd seen the girl. He was the only person I could tell who wouldn't have laughed me away, or turned his face from me. Even back then, people in the County didn't care to hear the fort being brought up in conversation. She still comes to me in my sleep, that girl. Once you've seen something like that, you don't forget it.

'But you were also part of the reason for changing the location. I didn't want to be putting fool ideas into your head. We don't talk about that part of the woods, not if we can help it, and we don't go there. If it hadn't been for that damned dog, *I'd* never have gone there.'

I had brought a copy of the Maine *Gazetteer*, and with Phineas's help I marked the area in which Wolfe's Folly lay. It was less than a day's hike from Falls End.

'Who do you think she is?' I said.

'Not "who",' said Phineas, 'but "what". I think she's a remnant, a residue of anger and pain, all bound up in the form of a child. She might even have been a little girl once: they say there was a child in that fort, the daughter of the commanding officer. Her name was Charity Holcroft. That girl is long gone. Whatever's left bears the same relation to her as smoke does to fire.'

And I knew that what he said was true, for I had seen anger take the form of a dead child, and heard similar stories from Sanctuary Island at the far edge of Casco Bay, and I thought that something of my own lost daughter still walked in the shadows, although she was not composed entirely of wrath.

'I used to wonder if she was evil, and I came to the conclusion that she was not,' said Phineas. 'She'd have done me harm, but I don't think she'd have meant it, not really. She may be angry, and dangerous, but she's lonely too. You might as well call a winter storm evil, or a falling tree. Both will kill you, but they won't consciously set out to do it. They're forces of nature, and that thing in the shape of a little girl is kind of a storm of emotion, a little whirlwind of pain. Maybe there's something so terrible about the death of children, so against the order of things, that this residue, if it sticks around, naturally finds form in a child.'

His cigar was almost done. He stamped it out beneath his foot, then tore apart the butt and scattered the tobacco on the breeze.

'You can tell I've thought on this over the years,' he said. 'All I can say for sure is that's her place, and if you're going in there then you need to watch out for her. Now take me back to my room, please. I don't want a chill to get into my bones.'

I wheeled him back to the center, and we said our goodbyes. His roommate was back in his bed, still reading the same newspaper.

'You brought him back,' he said. 'I was hoping you'da drowned him.'

He sniffed the air. 'Someone's been smoking,' he said. He shook his newspaper at Phineas. 'You smell like Cuba.'

'You're an ignorant old man,' said Phineas. 'I smell like the Dominican Republic.'

He reached into a pocket of his coat, and waved a fresh Cohiba at his rival. 'But if you're good, and you let me nap in peace for an hour or two, maybe I'll let you wheel me out to the lake before supper, and I'll tell you a story . . .'

44

Shielded by looming pines, Wolfe's Folly hid itself from the setting sun; less a fortress than the memory of one constructed by the forest, its lineaments blurred by shrubs and ivy, most of its buildings long collapsed in on themselves and only its log walls still standing intact.

Its proper name was Fort Mordant, after Sir Giles Mordant, an advisor to General Wolfe who had first suggested its construction. It had been intended as a supply depot and a place of refuge, a link in a proposed chain of such small forts stretching from the colonies on the east coast of the British claims to the St Lawrence River by the northwest of the French territories, part of a new front from which to harry Quebec. Unfortunately, the changing fortunes of war had left Fort Mordant unsuited to its purpose, and the signing of the Treaty of Paris in 1763 made the fort redundant. By then Wolfe himself was dead, killed at the Battle of the Plains of Abraham with his enemy Montcalm, and Sir Giles had been shipped home with a chest wound from which he never fully recovered, dying at the age of thirty-three.

In 1764, it was decided that the fort was to be abandoned, and its small garrison sent east. By then, the name Wolfe's Folly had stuck: while the blame for the fort more properly lay with Mordant himself, it was Wolfe's folly to have listened to him in the first place. It was said by some that Wolfe owed a substantial debt of money to Mordant, and was obliged to support his scheme; others took the view that Mordant was a fool, and Wolfe preferred to have him concentrating on his fort than interfering in more important matters of war. Whatever the reason for its construction, it brought no luck to either man, and had no impact on the outcome of the conflict.

The man entrusted with bringing word of the decision to close the fort and supervising its evacuation was a Lieutenant Buckingham, who traveled northwest in April 1764 accompanied by a platoon of infantrymen. They were still three days' march from the fort when the first rumors began to reach them. They encountered a Quaker missionary named Benjamin Woolman, a distant relative of James Woolman of New Jersey, a leading figure in the burgeoning abolition movement. Benjamin Woolman had taken it upon himself to preach Christianity to the natives, and he was known to act as a conduit between the tribes and the British forces.

Woolman informed Buckingham that the garrison at Fort Mordant had carried out a punitive expedition against a small Abenaki village a week or so earlier, killing more than twenty natives, including, it was said, women and children. When Buckingham requested information about the reason for the slaughter, Woolman replied that he had no knowledge of why it was carried out. Such a small native group, scarcely more than a single extended family, could have posed little threat to the fort or its inhabitants, and, as far as Woolman was aware, there had been no particular tension between the soldiers and the natives. The Abenaki considered the fort's construction to be an exercise in foolishness. More importantly, they tended to avoid the area of the forest in which it was located, terming it *majigek*, which Woolman translated as 'wicked'. In fact, that was one of the reasons why Mordant had chosen that location for the fort's construction. One of his sole redeeming qualities was his interest in the traditions of the native population, and he left behind him dozens of notebooks filled with jottings, essays, and sketches on the subject. The French were dependent upon their native guides, and if those guides were reluctant to enter certain areas of the woods, then a fort situated in such a place would enjoy relative immunity from attack. Thus it was that there could be no logical reason why the Abenaki should have been attacked by the British.

Woolman also said that, when he tried to seek further information about what had occurred, he was denied entry to Fort Mordant by its commander, Captain Holcroft, and he was now concerned for the officer's mental state. He was also worried for the safety of Holcroft's wife and daughter. Contrary to advice from all sources, Holcroft had insisted that his family join him when he took command of the fort. Woolman had been traveling east in the hope of communicating his worries to the appropriate authorities, and thus he agreed to accompany Lieutenant Buckingham and his men back to Fort Mordant.

They could see the buzzards hovering while they were still some distance away. When they reached the fort they found its gates open, and everyone inside dead. There were no signs of an Indian attack. Rather, it appeared that some dispute had arisen within the garrison, and the soldiers had fallen to fighting among themselves. Their uniforms were no longer regulation attire but had been accessorized with pieces of bone, both human and animal, and their faces were painted to resemble ferocious masks. Most had died from gunshot wounds, the rest at the point of a sword or a knife. Captain Holcroft's wife was found in their quarters with her heart cut out. Of her husband and her daughter, there was no sign. A subsequent search of the surrounding forest revealed the remains of Captain Holcroft himself, and here, for the first time, there was found some indication of an Abenaki presence: Holcroft had been scalped, and his body mutilated and hanged from a tree.

While Buckingham's men buried the dead, Buckingham and Woolman went in search of the Abenaki. Buckingham was reluctant to meet them without his men to protect him, for the Abenaki had fought on the side of the French, and the memory of their atrocities was still fresh in the minds of the British. Following the siege and subsequent massacre at Fort William Henry in 1757, the ranger commander Major Robert Rogers had found six hundred mostly British, scalps, decorating the Abenaki village of St Francis, and had destroyed it entirely in revenge. Relations with the Abenaki remained uneasy. Woolman assured Buckingham that, with him as a go-between, and with no demonstration of hostile intent, they would be safe. Buckingham grumbled that Holcroft's violated remains gave him little comfort, and he considered the murder of the officer, for whatever reason, an act of war by the natives.

After riding for three hours, during which time Buckingham believed they were always under the eyes, and potentially the knives, of the Abenaki, they were met by a heavily armed party of natives, who quickly surrounded the two men. The leader gave his name as Tomah, or Thomas. He wore a cross at his neck, and had been baptized into the Catholic faith by French missionaries, accepting Thomas as his baptismal name. Buckingham was not sure what troubled him more: that he was surrounded by Abenaki, or surrounded by Catholics. Nevertheless, he and Tomah sat down together, and, with Woolman acting as translator, the Abenaki told them of what had transpired at the fort.

Most of what was said did not pass into the official record. Buckingham's report on what came to be termed 'the incident at Fort Mordant' stated only that a dispute of unknown origin arose there, possibly fueled by alcohol, which led to the deaths of the entire garrison, including its commander, Captain Holcroft, and his wife. The role played by the Abenaki in Holcroft's murder became clear only when Woolman's private diary was discovered after his death, but Woolman also glossed over much of what was disclosed by Tomah, apparently by mutual agreement with Buckingham. Neverthelesss, the contents of Woolman's diary went some way toward explaining why Buckingham allowed the killing of a fellow officer by the Abenaki to go both unreported and unpunished. Buckingham was a professional soldier, and he understood that, sometimes, a lie was preferable to a truth that might tarnish the reputation of his beloved army.

Woolman's diary revealed a few pertinent details. The first was that Holcroft had been discovered by the Abenaki while apparently hunting his own daughter, but despite the Abenaki's own efforts, and a further search by Buckingham and his men, the girl was never found. Second, the Catholic Abenaki told Woolman they had set out to kill the inhabitants of the fort in reprisal for the earlier slaughter. The small band of warriors who had been willing to overcome their fear of the territory were all Catholic converts, although they were additionally armed with totems of their tribe. They arrived at the fort to find that the soldiers had done the job for them, and had to be content with taking their revenge on Holcroft alone, whom Tomah described by using the same word that Woolman had used when Buckingham first met him: *majigek*.

Finally, according to Woolman, the Abenaki claimed that, before he died, Holcroft came to his senses, and begged his tormentors for forgiveness for what he had done. Woolman admitted that he had trouble understanding Tomah's description of Holcroft's final words, and was forced to clarify them in halting French, to little avail. Holcroft, it seemed, had railed in English, of which Tomah knew little; in French, of which Tomah knew slightly more; and in some mishmash of Passamaquoddy and Abenaki that Holcroft had picked up during his postings in the region, for like Mordant himself he was known to be a scholar of languages, and a civilized man.

As Woolman understood it, Holcroft claimed to have committed the slaughter of the Abenaki on the orders of the *tsesuna*, the Raven God who pecked at his window. He also termed him the *apockoli*, the Upsidedown God who spoke to him from behind his shaving mirror, and who sometimes called to him from the depths of the forest, his voice bubbling up from deep beneath the earth. It was this same entity, this demon, who had infected his men with madness, and turned them upon one another.

Holcroft had used another word too in connection with him before the Abenaki set to torturing him: it was *ktahkomikey*, a word that referred to wasps, particularly a certain species that nested in the ground.

Holcroft had died screaming of the God of Wasps.

45

Outside the Cronin home, I rested The *Gazetteer* against the steering wheel while I tried to figure out the journey taken by Harlan Vetters and Paul Scollay on the day they found the plane. Marielle Vetters had told me that her father believed he and his friend had tracked the deer for four hours or more, traveling northwest or north-northwest for the most part, as best they could tell. There was a logging road that ran north from Falls End. It was the one Phineas had used on his illegal bear-hunting trip, and it seemed the most likely route for Vetters and Scollay to have taken as well. It veered northeast after ten miles, as though the road had been specifically designed to discourage anyone from venturing farther northwest: where the road altered direction was probably the closest point to Fort Mordant. From there, we'd move into the forest on foot. I had considered the possibility of using ATVs, but they were cumbersome to transport, and also noisy, and we were not the only ones looking for that plane. The sound of four ATVs moving through the woods might well be enough to get us killed.

I was so lost in the map, as though I were already deep in those woods, that the ringing of my phone came as an unwelcome distraction, and I didn't even glance at the number before I picked it up. It was only when I had pressed the green button that I thought again of the message I had left on Marielle Vetters' answering machine, and the possibility that the police might have listened to it, but by then it was too late.

Thankfully, it was only Epstein on the other end. He was calling from Toronto. I could hear traffic in the background, and then Epstein's words were overcome by the roar of a jet.

'You'll have to repeat that,' I said. 'I couldn't hear you.'

This time, I heard him clearly.

'I said, "I know who was the passenger on that plane."'

Wildon's widow remembered Epstein. They had met once before, she said, at an event to raise funds for the collection of DNA from Holocaust survivors so that the separated members of families might be reunited, and anonymous remains identified, an initiative that eventually became part of the DNA Shoah Project. It was the first time that Wildon and Epstein had come face to face, although each knew of the other's work. Eleanor Wildon recalled the two men shaking hands, and that was the last she saw of her husband for the rest of the evening. Epstein, too, remembered that night, but he had forgotten entirely that Wildon's wife had been present, so pleased was he to meet a kindred spirit.

They were sitting in the drawing room of her apartment, which took up the entire top floor of an expensive condominium in Yorkville. A pair of Andrew Wyeth paintings hung at either side of the marble fireplace: beautiful, tender studies of autumn leaves from his late period. Epstein wondered if, as their lives came to a close, all artists found themselves drawn to images of fall and winter.

Two teacups sat on the table between them. Mrs Wildon had brewed it herself. She lived here alone. She was not a particularly beautiful woman, nor had she ever been. Her features were plain at first glance, her face unremarkable. Had he not been distracted by her husband at their earlier meeting, Epstein would still barely have noted her presence, if he had noted it at all. Even here, in her own home, she seemed to blend into the furniture, the wallpaper, the drapes. The pattern on her dress echoed the textures and colors of the fabrics, rendering a chameleon quality to her. It was only later, when he had already left her, that Epstein understood this was a woman who was hiding herself.

'He thought very highly of you,' said Mrs Wildon. 'He came back that evening more animated than I'd seen him in years. I thought it was all foolishness, his stories about angels, his fascination with the End Times. It wasn't harmless, because it was too odd for that, but I tolerated it. All men have their eccentricities, don't they? Women too, I suppose, but men's are more ingrained: it's something to do with their boyishness, I think. They hold onto the enthusiasm of childhood.'

She didn't sound as though she thought this was a good thing.

'It got worse after he met you, though,' she said. 'I think you fueled his fire.'

Epstein drank his tea. The accusation was clear, but he did not look away, or express sorrow. If this woman wanted someone to blame for what had happened to her children, perhaps her husband too, then he would accept that role as long as she told him what she knew.

'What was he looking for, Mrs Wildon?'

'Proof,' she said. 'Proof of the existence of life beyond this one. Proof that there was an evil beyond human greed and selfishness. Proof that he was right, because he always wanted to be right about everything.'

'But there was a moral component to his work too, was there not?'

She laughed, and as her laughter faded it left a sneer on her face. Epstein realized that he disliked Eleanor Wildon, and he did not know why. He suspected that she was a shallow woman, and he allowed his eyes to take in his surroundings once more, seeking evidence in the furniture and paintings and ornaments to confirm his opinion. Then he saw the small framed photograph of two young girls on a shelf of Lladró porcelain, and was ashamed of himself.

'A moral component?' said Mrs Wildon. The sneer held for a second or two before melting, and when she spoke again she was walking in other rooms, living another life, and her voice came from somewhere far away. 'Yes, I suppose there was. He was making connections between killings and disappearances. He spoke to retired policemen, hired private investigators, visited grieving relatives. When good people died in unusual circumstances, or vanished and were never seen again, he would try to find out all that he could about them, and about their lives. Most were just what they appeared to be: accidents, domestic situations that tipped over into violence, or just the misfortune of meeting the wrong person at the wrong time and suffering for it. But some . . .'

She stopped, and bit her lip.

'Go on, Mrs Wildon. Please.'

'Some he believed were being committed by one man, who moved through the northern states, both in this country and yours. There were police investigators who thought so too, but they could never make the connection, and it was all – what do you call it? – "circumstantial" anyway: a face in the crowd, a half-glimpsed figure on a video screen, nothing more. I saw the pictures. Sometimes there was another with him: a horrible-looking man, bald, with a swelling just here.'

She touched her hand to her throat, and Epstein started.

'Brightwell,' he said. 'That one's name was Brightwell.'

'And the other?' asked Mrs Wildon.

'I don't know.' Wildon had hinted at some of this in cryptic messages to Epstein. He was a man with a love for the gnomic and the hidden.

'That's a pity,' she said, 'as he was the one who killed my children.'

She said it so matter-of-factly that Epstein was convinced for a second that he had misheard, but he had not. Mrs Wildon took a sip of tea, and went on.

'What interested my husband was that these men, or people who looked very like them, seemed to turn up, their features no different, in old photographs and reports of crimes from thirty, forty, even fifty years earlier. There might have been a woman too, he thought, but she wasn't involved as much, or was more careful than the others. He wondered how that could be, and he came up with an answer: they were not men or women but something else, something old and foul. Such nonsense. I'm sure I used that word with him – "nonsense" – but it still frightened me. I wanted him to stop, but he was so single-minded about it, so convinced that there was a truth to it.

'And then they took my girls, and they buried them alive in a hole in the ground, and I knew that it wasn't nonsense. There was no warning, no threats against our family if my husband continued to stick his nose into their business. There was only retribution.'

She put her cup down, and pushed the saucer away from her.

'It was my husband's fault, Mr Epstein. Those others, whoever or whatever they might be, killed my little girls, but my husband drew them down on us, and I hated him for it. I hate him, and I hate you for the encouragement that you gave him. You all share the blame for leaving my daughters to suffocate in a pit of dirt.'

There was that same, neutral voice. There was no anger to it. She might just as easily have been discussing returning a flawed dress to a store, or a movie that had disappointed.

After that, she and her husband had drifted apart, like wreckage from a sinking ship separated by shifting tides. She shared his desire to find and punish those responsible for the deaths of their children, but she did not want her husband in the same house with her, in the same room or the same bed. He left their home and went to live in one of the apartments that he owned, and he lost interest in his business affairs, and in his wife, and she in him. They were united only by memories, and a kind of hatred.

'Then, on the night of July 13, 2001, he called me. He said that he had found the man who had killed our little girls, the man from the photographs. He was living in a place outside Sagueney, in a trailer park surrounded by crows.'

'Did he have a name?'

'He called himself Mr Malphas.'

An interesting choice, thought Epstein: Malphas, one of the great princes of Hell, a deceiver, an artificer.

The Lord of Crows.

'My husband told me that they had him. They'd drugged him, and there was proof of what he had done, or was planning to do.'

'They?'

'There was a man who occasionally assisted my husband in his work. Douglas something – Douglas Ampell. He was a pilot.'

'Ah,' said Epstein. So he had been right about the source of the plane. 'And what proof did your husband find?'

'He was babbling. He was in a hurry. They had to get this man, this Malphas, away before his friends discovered what was happening. He said something about names, a list of names. That's all.'

'Did he say what he planned to do with Malphas?'

'No, just that they were taking him to be questioned by someone else, someone who would understand, someone who would *believe*. That was the last time we spoke, but he warned me that if something happened to him, or if I didn't hear from him again, I was to stay quiet. There was money in trusts, in hidden accounts, and I could sell the house. His lawyers had all of the details. I wasn't to look for him, and I was to send all of the evidence he had collected to you, and you alone.'

Epstein was puzzled. 'But I received nothing from you.

'That's because I burned it all, every last scrap of paper,' she said. 'It killed my daughters, and it killed my fool of a husband. I wanted no more part of it. I did what he told me to do. I stayed quiet, and I lived.'

Now he was certain. 'He was on his way to New York,' said Epstein. 'He was bringing Malphas to me.'

'Yes,' said Mrs Wildon, this empty woman, this shell of grief, brittle as the Lladró figures that stared down from her shelves. 'And I didn't care. My husband didn't understand. He never understood.'

'Understood what, Mrs Wildon?'

Mrs Wildon stood. Their meeting was over.

'That it wouldn't bring them back,' she said, 'that it wouldn't bring my little girls back to me. You'll have to excuse me now, but I have a plane to catch. I'd like you to get out of my home.'

Malphas. I found that I had written the name on the open page of the *Gazetteer*.

'Malphas was the passenger on the plane,' said Epstein. 'Ampell went missing on the same day as Wildon. He owned a Piper Cheyenne aircraft, which that week was based at a small private airfield just north of Chicoutimi. The plane has never been found, and Ampell never filed a flight plan. They didn't want to draw attention to themselves, or their cargo. They didn't want anyone to suspect, but Wildon had to tell his wife. He wanted her to know that he'd succeeded in finding this man, except she didn't care. She blamed her husband for what had happened to their children: Malphas was just the instrument.

'And Malphas survived the crash, Mr Parker. That's why there were no bodies in the wreckage. He removed them, or perhaps they survived too, and he killed them and disposed of their remains.'

'But he left the list, and the money,' I said 'The money

might not have been important to him, but that list was. If he survived, and was strong enough to kill anyone else who had lived, why did he leave the list where it could be found?'

'I don't know,' said Epstein, 'but it's another reason to be careful in those woods.'

'You don't believe that he's still out there?'

'He had been discovered, Mr Parker. They hide themselves away, these creatures, especially when they're under threat. Those woods are vast. They can conceal an aircraft, and so they can conceal a man. If he's alive, where else would he be?'

46

Wolfe's Folly was silent as night fell, and the only movement came from the shifting of the shadows thrown by the trees upon it, or so it appeared until one small shadow separated itself from the rest, moving against the direction of the wind. The crow circled, cawing hoarsely, then resumed its perch with its brethren.

The passenger had no memory of his original name, and little understanding of his own nature. The plane crash, which he had caused by breaking the arms of his seat, freeing him to attack the pilot and co-pilot, had left him with significant injuries to the brain. He had lost the capacity of speech, and he was in constant pain. He retained virtually nothing of his past beyond fragments: scattered recollections of being hunted, and an awareness of the necessity of hiding himself, instincts that he had continued to follow ever since the crash.

And he remembered, too, that he was very good at killing, and killing was his purpose. The co-pilot did not survive the crash, but the pilot did, and the passenger had stared at his face, and one of those shards of memory had glittered in the darkness. This man had hunted him, and therefore the pain in the passenger's head was his fault.

The passenger had pushed his thumbs into the pilot's eyes and kept pushing until the man ceased moving.

He stayed in the wreckage for a number of days, feeding on the candy bars and potato chips that he found in the co-pilot's bag, and drinking bottled water. The pain in his head was so terrible that he would black out for hours. Some of his ribs were broken, and they hurt whenever he moved. His right ankle would not support his weight at first, but in time it healed, although imperfectly, so that he now walked with a slight limp.

The bodies in the plane began to stink. He pulled them from the wreckage and dumped them in the woods, but he could still smell them. He used a broken panel from the plane as a spade and dug a shallow pit in which to bury them. When the snacks from the plane ran out, he salvaged what he could, including the emergency kit and a gun that he found among the pilot's possessions, and started exploring the wilderness, which was how he came upon the fort. He built a temporary shelter for himself inside its walls, and he tried to sleep, even as the girl prowled the woods beyond.

He thought that he might have seen her on the first night after the crash, although he could not be sure. There was a face at the cockpit window, and he might have heard a scratching upon the glass, but he was unconscious more often than he was conscious, and his waking hours were spent in a kind of delirium. The presence of the girl was just another splinter in that cloud of memories, as though his whole life had been part of an intricate painting on a glass wall, and that wall had just exploded.

It was only later, when he began to recover his strength, that he recognized the reality of her existence. He watched her at night as she circled the plane, and he thought that he felt her anger and her desire. His senses were troubled by it just as they had been bothered by the stench of the pilots. Rage was her spoor.

She grew bolder: he woke on the third night to find her inside the plane, standing so close to him that he could see the bloodless scrapes on her white skin. She did not speak. She merely stared at him for a single, long minute, trying to understand him even though he did not understand himself, and then he blinked and she was gone.

That was when he decided to leave the plane. He still could not walk far on his wounded ankle, and when the fort had presented itself to him he had been grateful for it, more so when he found that the girl would not cross its threshold. There he grew stronger. He hunted during the day, while the girl hid herself away. At first he wasted his shots on squirrel and hare until his hunter's instincts led him to a young doe. It took two shots to kill it, and he field-dressed it with the knife from the emergency kit. He ate what he could, and cut the rest into strips to dry; to keep pests away, he covered them with fabric ripped from the seats of the plane, and the deer skin helped to keep him warm as the winter drew in.

In the quiet of the fort, the Buried God began to call to him.

He heard its voice imperfectly, but it was familiar to him. It came to him the way music might come to one who had been struck deaf but retained enough of his hearing to discern muffled chords and rhythms. The Buried God wanted to be released, but the passenger could not find him. He had tried, but the voice was coming from too far away, and he could not understand its words. Sometimes, though, he would stare into the depths of the still, dark pool near to which the plane had come to rest, and he would wonder if the Buried God might not be down there. Once, he reached into it, sinking his forearm up to the elbow, straining his fingers in the hope that his hand might be grasped by whatever waited below. The water was frighteningly cold, so cold that it felt like a burning, but he kept his arm submerged until he could stand it no longer. When he withdrew it, the water dripped slowly from his fingers like oil, and he gazed in disappointment at his numb, empty hand.

He began paying homage to the Buried God. He dug up the bodies in the forest and removed the heads, along with some of the major bones from the arms and legs. It was the beginning of the shrine's creation, the altar of worship to an entity he could not name but whom he understood to be his god. He created impressions of false deities from his fractured memory, carving them from wood with a knife, and he mutilated them in the name of the other.

He was still weak, too weak to explore farther, or seek civilization. He should have died that winter, but he did not. He even wondered if he could die. The Buried God told him that he could not. When spring came, the passenger began to explore his domain farther. He found an old cabin, its walls built from thick logs, but its door long gone and its roof collapsed. He began to restore it.

In March, a man came into his territory: a young hiker, unarmed. The passenger killed him with a spear that he had made, and waited for others to come looking for him, but no one did. He scavenged all that was useful from the man's pack, and a wallet with $320 in cash, although there was still a great deal of money in the plane, along with a satchel of papers that made no sense to him.

Two weeks later, he made his first, careful sortie back to civilization, his damaged skull hidden beneath the dead hiker's cap. He bought food, and salt, and some tools, and ammunition for his pistol, all by pointing at the items that he wanted. He looked at a rifle, but he had no identification. He settled instead for a used hunting bow, and as many arrows as he could afford. He could have found a way to lose himself once again in a city or a town, but he was afraid that his appearance might draw attention. He also knew that he was damaged, and managing anything beyond the simplest of social tasks was beyond him. He was happier in the woods. He was safe there, safe with the Buried God, and perhaps, as he grew stronger, he might find the Buried God, and free him. He could not do that from a city.

And so he hid himself in the woods, and prayed to the Buried God, and tried to limit all human contact. He became adept at avoiding the men from the paper companies, and the wardens. The passenger killed another hiker the following year, but only because the hiker came to the fort and found the shrine nearby. Such trespasses were rare, because there was something about the fort that kept people away, or else most knowledge of it had been lost. Similarly, the cabin had lain undisturbed for decades before the passenger found it: because the ground had been cleared to build it, second-growth foliage had sprung up around it, so the dwelling remained virtually invisible.

Only once had he felt truly threatened. He had gone to the plane to replenish his supplies of cash, for he had to prepare for another winter. He had entered the plane through the canvas hatch at the back, noting once again how far the fuselage had sunk. It might take years, but eventually the plane would be lost entirely. He pulled back a piece of rotting carpet and lifted the panel that it concealed in order to retrieve the money.

He was just about to reach into the bag when he was struck by a blinding flash of white pain, as though a shard of metal had been forced through his right ear and into his brain. They came on him with increasing frequency, these attacks, but this was the worst yet. His body went into seizure, and he spasmed so hard that he broke two teeth on his lower row. The cabin of the plane began to close in on him, and he experienced a terrible sense of falling and burning. Then the world went black, and when he opened his eyes again he had somehow crawled from the plane, and the girl was nearby, circling him but drawing closer. She was angry at the passenger for taking the hiker when she had wanted him for herself. He had to get away from her, but his sense of direction was distorted. He reached for his gun, but it was gone, and he suspected that the girl had taken it. She hated the gun. Its noise troubled her, and she seemed to know that it was important to him, that without it he would be more vulnerable. He was forced to keep the girl at bay with stones until, through sheer luck, he managed to struggle back to his cabin, for in his confused, agonized state he was unable to find the fort. There he barred the door against her, and he listened from his pallet bed as she scratched at the wood, trying to force her way inside.

When at last he was strong enough to leave, he found that the door was scarred by the girl's efforts, and he dug one of her old, twisted fingernails from the exposed white wood. He returned to the plane, and discovered the remains of a fire, and he saw that the interior had been disturbed. The money was gone, although he had retained enough good sense to separate it into three piles, keeping some of it at the cabin and some buried in plastic behind the fort. But it was not the money that concerned him so much as the intrusion, and the imminent risk of discovery.

He stripped the cabin and the fort of his possessions, wrapped them in plastic, and buried them. He hid the shrine beneath a screen of leaves and twigs and moss that he had constructed for just such an eventuality, then retreated many miles to the north where he had built himself a hide. After a month he risked returning to his cabin, and discovered to his surprise that the site was as it had been, and nobody had come to find the plane. He could not understand why, but he was thankful. In the wilderness, he continued his solitary worship, and his solitary search. He subsumed his pleasure in killing because he knew that, if indulged, it would eventually draw people to him.

Until that week, when he had taken the two hikers, and offered up the woman's remains to the Buried God.

That was why he had returned to the fort, at least for a while. The girl always grew angry when he killed, and it would take days for her temper to subside. Just as with the hiker long before, she was angry because she had wanted the couple for herself. She wanted company. By killing those who strayed into her territory, the passenger deprived her of it, and the uneasy truce that existed between them was threatened. On those occasions, the passenger would take refuge in his cabin or, more often, in the fort, and from its safety he would watch the enraged girl stalking outside its walls, casting her whispered threats to the wind. Then the girl would disappear, and he would see no trace of her for weeks.

At those times, the passenger believed that she might be sulking.

So the passenger left the girl to her fury. He climbed into his sleeping bag in the fort and tried to sleep, but sleep would not come. The Buried God's voice had grown louder recently, desperate to communicate something to him, but the passenger could not interpret the message, and so the frustration of both grew. The passenger wished that the Buried God would be silent. He wanted peace. He wanted to reflect upon the man and the woman he had killed. He had enjoyed taking their lives, the woman's in particular. He had forgotten the pleasure that it brought.

He wanted to kill another, and soon.

47

Harlan Vetters and Paul Scollay had headed out on their fateful hunting trip in the afternoon, but it didn't seem like a good idea for us to follow suit: the plane would be difficult enough to find in daylight, and flashlights would mark our position and progress just as surely as the noise of ATVs. Neither did it seem smart to leave at or before dawn, as the likelihood of encountering hunters was greater. I decided that we would leave shortly before ten a.m., which would give us a clear five or six hours of good light before the sun began to set, by which time we would, with luck, have found the plane, obtained the list, and be on our way back to Falls End without incident.

'With luck,' said Louis, without enthusiasm.

'We never have luck,' said Angel.

'Which is why we always need guns,' said Louis.

We were staying at a motel five miles south of Falls End. Next door was a diner that sold only seven types of bottled beer: Bud, Miller and Coors; Bud Light, Miller Lite, and Coors Light; and Heineken.

We were drinking Heineken.

Jackie Garner was back in his room, trying to explain to his mother why he was not joining her for their weekly movie night, especially as she and Lisa, Jackie's girlfriend, had rented *Fifty First Dates* for him because they knew how much he liked Drew Barrymore. Jackie, who neither liked nor disliked Drew Barrymore, and had no idea how this neutral position had been transformed into something close to an obsession, had no satisfactory answer to give other than that a job was a job. He had told me earlier that his mother had seemed more like her normal self these past few days, which meant that she was just inordinately possessive of her only son. But it was also the case that Jackie's mother, who had previously regarded Jackie's girlfriend as a rival for her son's affections, had softened her position over the past year. Having clearly noticed that the relationship between her son and Lisa was not about to fall apart any time soon, despite her best efforts, Mrs Garner had decided it was better to have her as an ally than an enemy, and Lisa had come to the same conclusion. The onset of Mrs Garner's final illness now lent both a poignancy and convenience to this relationship.

The diner was full, and a lot of the conversation revolved around events in Falls End. There appeared to be no change in the condition of Marielle and Grady Vetters. By contrast, judging by the talk in the diner, the focus of the investigation into the deaths of Teddy Gattle and Ernie Scollay had rapidly altered, and Grady Vetters was no longer being treated as a suspect.

'They got injected with somethin', is what I heard,' a big, bearded man had told me in the restroom just minutes earlier. He was swaying as he stood at the urinal, so he resorted to leaning his head against the wall to keep himself steady while he peed.

'Who did?'

'Marielle and Grady,' said the man. 'Somebody stuck a needle in 'em.'

'How'd you hear this?'

'My brother-in-law is a sheriff's deputy.' He belched hard. 'No way Grady injected himself, so he's no killer. I could have told them that. Anyone in town could have. You here to hunt?'

'Yeah.'

'Need a guide?'

'Got one, thanks.'

If he heard me, he decided to ignore what I said. He fumbled in his pocket with his right hand while continuing to aim with his left, and produced a business card for Wessel's Guide Service. Everybody seemed to be a guide in these parts.

'That's me,' he said. 'Greg Wessel. You can call anytime.'

'I'll remember.'

'I didn't catch your name.'

'Parker.'

'I won't shake your hand.'

'I appreciate that. You hear anything about the men who were killed? The folk on the news didn't seem to know any more than I do, and I don't know anything at all.'

'Ernie Scollay and Teddy Gattle,' said Wessel. 'Brother-in-law says Teddy had track marks on his arm too, and Teddy was a pothead. Potheads don't use needles. Old Ernie just took two in the back. What kind of fucking coward shoots an old man in the back, huh?'

'I don't know,' I said.

'You ask a lot of questions,' said Wessel. It was a comment, and I heard no belligerence or suspicion in it. 'You a reporter?'

'No,' I said. 'I'm just here to hunt and, you know, this kind of thing makes a man concerned for his safety.'

'Well, you got guns, don't you?'

'Yes.'

'And you know how to use them?'

'Kind of.'

'Then you got nothing to worry about.'

He finished peeing, and waited his turn while I washed my hands.

'Don't forget,' he said. 'Wessel's Guide and Taxidermy. I'll be sober before dawn. Guaranteed.'

Now, back at the table, the waitress brought three burgers for Angel, Louis and me. They were not big. Around them were scattered a dozen very thin, very brown fries, like the detritus of a destroyed bird's nest. Angel poked at his burger. It oozed a thin trickle of grease.

'Did we order sliders to share?' he asked.

The waitress returned to fill up our water.

'You need anything else?' she asked.

'More food would be a start,' said Angel. 'Any food.'

'It's burger night,' said the waitress. Her hair was very red. So were her lips, her cheeks, and her uniform. If it hadn't been November, and the heart-shaped tattoo on her right forearm had not read 'Muffy's Bitch', she might have seemed festive.

'What's so special about burger night?' asked Angel.

The waitress pointed to a hand-lettered sign behind the register. It read 'Burger Night, Wenedsday! $3 burger and fries!'

'Burger night,' she said. 'Wednesday.'

'It's just that the burgers are kind of small,' said Angel.

'That's why they're three bucks,' said the waitress.

'Right,' said Angel. 'You know, you spelled "Wednesday" wrong.'

'You know, I didn't spell it at all.'

'Right,' said Angel again. 'Who's Muffy?'

'Ex-boyfriend.'

'He ask you to get that done?'

'No, got it done myself, after we broke up.'

'*After* you broke up?'

'To remind myself that I was once Muffy's bitch, and not to let it happen again.'

'Right,' said Angel, for the third time.

'You got any more questions?'

'Too many.'

The waitress patted Angel on the arm. 'Well, you hold onto them. I get you boys another round of beers?'

The diner's front door opened, and Jackie Garner walked in.

'Sure,' I said. 'And one extra for our friend who's just come in.'

'You think he'll want to eat?' asked the waitress. 'Kitchen's closing in five.'

'He can share ours,' said Angel. 'There'll be leftovers.'

Jackie didn't want to eat, and was happy just to sip a beer. The kitchen closed, and gradually the crowd began to thin out, but nobody tried to hurry us along. We clinked our bottles, and toasted to luck, but Angel was right: luck rarely seemed to come our way.

Which was, indeed, why we had guns.

Across the road from the motel and diner stood an abandoned gas station-cum-general store, the pumps long since gone and the windows and front door of the store itself imperfectly boarded up. The back door had disappeared entirely, but the single piece of wood that had failed to deny access to it still remained, although unsecured, providing the illusion of closure.

Scattered inside were empty beer cans and bottles, a box of cheap wine that was still half full, and the odd used rubber. In one corner was a rat's nest of blankets and towels, damp and moldy from the rain that had poured through the hole in the roof above, a consequence of a small fire that had also blackened the walls and left a smell of burning.

A firefly glow appeared in the darkness, its illumination growing quickly until it was entirely consumed by flame. The Collector put the match to his cigarette and stepped closer to the window. The lengths of wood used to block them were imperfectly nailed in place, and he could clearly see through them the four men drinking in the diner.

The Collector was torn. He was not used to experiencing anger or the desire for vengeance. Those whom he hunted had not sinned against him, and the pleasure that he took in removing them from the world was general, not personal. This was different. Someone close to him had been killed, and another injured. The most recent conversation with Eldritch's physician had revealed that he was not recovering as quickly as might have been expected, even for a man of his advanced years, and his stay in hospital was likely to be extended. The physician suggested that the effects of shock and grief were greater threats than his physical wounds, but Eldritch had rejected offers of counseling or the attentions of a psychologist, and when the subject of a priest or pastor had been raised the patient had laughed for the first and only time since his admission.

Kill them. Kill them all.

But they were dangerous, and not only because they were armed. They knew of the Collector, and understood the threat that he posed. He had relearned a painful but valuable lesson from Becky Phipps about confronting someone who was anticipating an attack. He preferred to prey on the unarmed and unwary. He supposed that this might be regarded as cowardice in some quarters, but he saw it simply in terms of practicality. There was no reason to make his task any more difficult than it had to be and, when required, he was prepared to fight for his trophy, just as he had done with Phipps.

Bu he also wanted the rest of the list, and these men could lead him to it. He didn't know where the Flores woman was hiding, and he could only hope that she had not already found the plane. If she had located it and secured her prize, he would have to hunt her down, and that would be time-consuming, and difficult. No, ideally these four men would do his work for him, and he would start killing after.

He watched them finish their drinks and leave the restaurant. They walked to their rooms in two pairs, Parker and Garner in front, the others behind. The Collector's right hand slipped beneath his coat and found the hilt of a knife. He rested his fingers on it but did not draw it from its sheath. Beside it was his gun, fully loaded.

Three rooms, four men. It was risky, but not beyond his capabilities.

Kill them all.

But the list, the list . . .

48

The first sign that luck might not be going our way came when I woke up and went out to get coffee. In the parking lot was a shiny white SUV, obviously a rental, and leaning against it, already drinking a coffee of her own, was Liat. She was wearing a parka over beige canvas combat pants and a green sweater. The ends of her pants were tucked into rubber-soled boots.

'I guess you missed me,' I said.

One corner of her mouth curled up in very slight amusement.

'You didn't want to come in?'

She shook her head.

'Did Epstein send you?'

Nod.

'Doesn't he trust us to bring him the list?'

Shrug.

The door to Angel and Louis's room opened, and Louis appeared. He was already dressed for the woods, but he still managed to make cargo pants look good.

'Who's this?' he asked. 'She looks familiar.'

'This is Liat.'

'Liat,' said Louis. '*That* Liat.'

'The same.'

'Well, I only saw her from a distance, and not from the same angles that you did. She miss you?'

'I don't think so.'

'Then why is she here?'

'To bring the list back to Epstein.'

'She's coming with us?'

'You could try to stop her, but you'd probably have to shoot her.'

Louis considered the possibility, then seemed to discount it.

'You planning on inviting any more ex-girlfriends along? Just asking.'

'No.'

'Well, long as it's just her . . .'

Angel joined Louis. He was also dressed for the woods, and still managed to make cargo pants look bad.

'Who's this?' he asked.

Spare me, I thought.

'Liat,' said Louis.

'*That* Liat?'

'Yep, that Liat.'

'At least we know she exists,' said Angel. 'All I saw was a shape in the distance.'

'You think he made her up?' asked Louis.

'It seemed more likely than him actually being with a woman.'

Liat, who had been following the conversation with her eyes, blushed.

'Nice,' I said.

'Sorry,' said Angel. He smiled at Liat. 'But, you know, it's true.'

Another door opened, and Jackie Garner emerged. He squinted at Liat.

'Who's this?'

'Liat,' said Angel.

Jackie looked confused, as well he might have done.

'Who's Liat?'

It was just after eight. Ray Wray was drinking coffee, eating a protein bar, and, after the events of the night before, wishing he was back in jail.

He and Joe had bedded down in bags on the floor of the cabin, on the other side of the sheet from the boy and his mother, but only Joe had managed to get any real rest. Ray had drifted in and out of sleep, and at some point in the night he had woken to see the boy standing at one of the windows, touching his fingers to the glass, his lips moving soundlessly. His reflection hung like a moon against the night sky, the true moon suspended above it like a second face. Ray had been afraid to move, and kept his breathing regular so that the boy would not suspect he was being watched. After perhaps fifteen minutes, the boy prepared to return to his bed, but he paused at the sheet that divided the room and looked back at Ray. Ray closed his eyes. He heard the padding of the boy's feet as he crossed the room, and then felt his breath on his skin. He smelled it too. It smelled bad. The boy's face was so close to his own that Ray could feel the warmth of it. He forced himself not to pull away, and not to open his eyes, even as he told himself that this was only a kid, and Ray should just tell him to get his ass back to bed where it belonged. But he did not, because the boy frightened him. He frightened him more than his mother, if that's what she was, with her ruined face and that dead eye embedded in it like a bubble of fat on barely cooked meat. Ray willed him to go away. He'd been so careful, but somehow the boy knew that he was awake.

Just a kid, thought Ray, just a kid. So what if I was awake? What's he going to do to me: pull my hair, tell his mom?

The answer came to him without hesitation.

Something bad, that's what he'll do. The feel of the boy's breath shifted. It was on his lips now, as though he were leaning in for a kiss. Ray could taste him in his mouth. He wanted to turn over so badly, except he didn't want his back to the kid. That would be worse than facing him.

The boy moved away. Ray heard the sound of his footsteps as he made his way back to his bed. Ray risked opening his eyes.

The boy was walking backwards, his back to the sheet, so that he could keep watching Ray. The boy grinned when he saw that Ray's eyes were open. He had won, and Ray had lost. He raised his left hand and wagged a finger at Ray.

Ray was tempted to get up and run from the cabin. If there was a forfeit to this game, he didn't want to find out what it was. But the boy just pushed aside the sheet, and Ray heard him climb into the bed behind, and then all was still.

Ray looked at the window. The moon was no longer visible.

That was when Ray realized that there was no moon that night, and he had not closed his eyes again until morning.

Angel, Louis and I rode in Jackie's truck. Liat followed behind in her rental. It was a private road, but one routinely used by locals and hunters. Still, Jackie had secured all the necessary permits, just in case, so we were right with the paper company, the warden service, and probably God Himself.

'You didn't want to ride with your girlfriend?' asked Angel from the back.

'I think she was just using me.'

'Right,' said Angel. He allowed a perfectly timed pause, then said, 'For what?'

'Funny,' I replied, although there was an uncomfortable truth behind Angel's joke.

We passed a couple of trucks and old cars parked by the side of the road: hunters, the ones who had set out before dawn and would return to town by early afternoon if they'd shot anything. Most hunters liked to stay close to a road, and within five miles of Falls End there were a lot of edges where deer came to feed. There was no reason to go very far into the woods, and so we were unlikely to encounter hunting parties where we were going; at least, not the kind that hunt buck. The road was narrow, and at one point we had to pull over to allow a company truck loaded with logs to pass us. It was the only such vehicle we met along the way.

We reached the point where the road made a definite dog-leg east, and there we pulled over. There was still frost on the ground, and the air was noticeably colder than it had been down in Falls End. Liat arrived a minute or two behind us, just as Jackie began unloading our supplies and Louis was checking the rifles. We had a 30.06 each, as well as handguns. Liat had no rifle, but I didn't doubt that she had a gun. She kept her distance from us, watching the woods.

Jackie Garner seemed bemused by her presence.

'She's deaf, right?' he said.

'Yeah,' I said. 'That's why you don't have to whisper.'

'Oh, yeah.' He thought about it, but kept whispering. 'How's a deaf woman going to get by in the woods?'

'She's deaf, Jackie, not blind.'

'I know, but we gotta be quiet, don't we?'

'She's also a mute. I'm no expert, but people who can't speak tend to be quieter than the rest of us.'

'Suppose she steps on a twig, and makes a noise. How will she know?'

Angel joined us. 'What are you, some kind of Buddhist? If a tree falls in the forest, I can tell you now that she won't hear it.'

Jackie shook his head in frustration. We were clearly missing the point.

'She's coming with us, Jackie,' I told him. 'Live with it.'

We didn't plan to be in the woods after dark, but Jackie had still insisted that we bring a groundsheet each. We also had plenty of water, coffee, chocolate, energy bars, nuts, and, courtesy of Jackie, a bag of pasta. Even with the addition of Liat, we had enough to keep us going for a day or more. There were also waterproof matches, cups, one lightweight saucepan, a pair of compasses, and a GPS unit, although Jackie said that we might have trouble getting a signal where we were going. We divided the equipment and supplies between us, and set out. There was no further discussion. We all knew what we were looking for, and what might be out there. I hadn't shared what we suspected of Malphas's possible nature with Jackie, and so Jackie had been skeptical that anyone who had survived the crash might still be out there. I shared something of his point of view, but I wasn't about to bet my life, or anyone else's, on it.

Jackie led, Louis behind him, then Liat, Angel, and I. Jackie's concerns about Liat were unfounded: of all of us, it was she who stepped the softest. While Angel and Louis, unused to the woods, wore leather boots with thick treads, Liat, Jackie and I wore lighter boots with only slight ribbing, the better to feel what lay beneath our feet. Treads could mean the difference between stepping on a branch and bending it, or breaking it entirely. For now we also wore orange vests, and baseball caps with reflective strips. We didn't want some overenthusiastic hunter to mistake us for deer, or raise the suspicions of a warden if we encountered one. Thirty minutes in we heard gunshots to the south, but otherwise we might have been entirely alone in the woods.

The going was relatively easy for the first couple of hours, but then the terrain began to change. There were more ridges to climb, and I could feel the strain in the backs of my legs. Shortly after midday we startled an adolescent buck from a copse of alder, his antlers little more than extended buds, and later there was a flash of brown and white to our left as a doe moved quickly through the trees. She spotted us, seemed to pause in confusion, and changed direction, cutting away from us until we lost sight of her. We noticed the trace of bigger bucks, and there were places where the stink of deer urine was strong enough to make one gag, but those were the only large animals we saw.

After three hours, we stopped and made coffee. Despite the cold, I was sweating under my jacket, and I was grateful for the rest. Louis dropped beside me.

'How you doing, city boy?' I said.

'Yeah, like you Grizzly Adams,' he replied. 'How much farther?'

'Two hours, I reckon, if we keep making this kind of progress.'

'Damn.' He pointed at the sky. There were clouds gathering. 'Doesn't look good.'

'No, it doesn't.'

Jackie finished brewing the coffee and served it up. He gave his cup to Liat, and drank his own by pouring it from the pot into a small thermos. He separated himself from the rest of us, and stood on a small ridge looking back in the direction from which we had come. I followed him up there. He didn't look happy.

'You okay?' I asked.

'Rattled, that's all,' he said.

'By what we're doing?'

'And where we're going.'

'In and out, Jackie. We're not planning on settling there.'

'I guess.' He swished the coffee around in his mouth, and spat. 'And there's the doe we saw.'

'What about it?'

'Something spooked it, and it wasn't us.'

I stared out at the forest. This wasn't first growth, and so the foliage was still thick.

'Could have been a hunter,' I said. 'Even a bobcat or a lynx.'

'Like I said, maybe I'm just rattled.'

'We could hold back, see if anyone comes,' I said, 'but there's rain on the way, and whatever hope we have of finding that plane depends on good light. And we don't want to be stuck out here for a night.'

Jackie shivered. 'I hear that. Come dark, I want to be in a bar with a drink in my hand, and that fort far behind me.'

We returned to the others. Liat approached me. I couldn't have mistaken the questioning look on her face, but she still mouthed the words, just to be sure: *What is it?*

'Jackie was concerned that something might have spooked the doe we saw earlier,' I answered, loud enough for Angel and Louis to hear. 'Something, or someone, following behind us.'

She extended her hand. Another question: *What do we do?*

'It could be nothing, so we keep going. If there is someone following, we'll find out who it is soon enough.'

Jackie poured the rest of the coffee into his thermos, packed away his little Primus stove, and we moved off, but there was a palpable change in our mood. I found myself checking behind me as we walked, and Jackie and I would pause on the higher ridges, seeking movement on the lower ground.

But we saw no one, and at last we came to the fort.

49

My first thought was that Fort Mordant was less the thing itself than the memory of it made manifest. The forest had done its best to blur and disguise its lines as though to discourage closer examination: its walls were covered in poison ivy, like waterfalls of green tumbling over precipices, and hemlock and common juniper had taken advantage of storm damage to mature trees by using them as nurseries. Cairns of stones, perhaps remnants of the original clearance of the land for the fort's construction, had become shadowed by moss, lending them the aspect of funeral markers. Somewhere nearby must have been the actual graves of the fort's original occupants, but I suspected they were long lost to the woods.

In that, I was soon to be proved wrong.

Mordant itself bore some resemblance to the only other such fortification I'd seen in the state: the old Fort Western in Augusta, although on a smaller scale. There were guard towers at each corner, about two stories high, with horizontal slit windows looking over the forest. Inside, although their roofs had long since collapsed, it was possible to see the remains of buildings on three of the four inside walls, with only the wall containing the main gate left free. One had clearly been a stable, because the stalls were still visible, but there was also plenty of room for the storage of supplies. The building opposite seemed to consist of one long single room, and had probably served as a barracks for the men. On the wall facing the gate was a smaller building, but here the division of rooms was obvious: quarters for the commanding officer and his ill-fated family.

'There,' said Jackie. He pointed into the smaller bushes, and when I looked at them from his angle I could see the rough path through them.

'Deer?'

'No, a man did that.'

Angel, Louis and Liat moved into the fort, their weapons ready. Jackie and I remained outside, but Jackie's attention was torn between the fort and the way that we had just come.

'You're making me nervous, Jackie,' I said.

'The hell with you, I'm making myself nervous.'

'Would you rather be in there?'

Perhaps it was our knowledge of its history, but there was a deeply unsettling ambience about the fort. Despite its decay, there was a sense of occupancy about it. That trail between the forest and the gate had been regularly used.

'No, I would not. I'll take my chances out here.'

There was a whistle from inside the fort: Angel. Louis was above whistling.

'At least if there's trouble, you can lock the gate and hide inside,' said Jackie.

'There is no gate. If there's trouble, we're all taking our chances out here.'

Angel appeared at the entrance.

'You need to take a look at this,' he said. 'I'll stay with Jackie.'

Louis and Liat were in the commanding officer's living quarters. The ramparts on the rear wall overhung the interior, creating a natural shelter that had been augmented by a tarpaulin fixed into the wood with nails and supported by two metal bars driven into the ground. I smelled excrement, and urine. A layer of insulating material had been attached to the walls, again held in place by sheets of plastic, to provide further warmth. On the ground was a sleeping bag, along with a half-filled five gallon container of water, a small gas camping stove, and canned food: beans and soups, for the most part. It might have been the temporary home of a down-and-out, or the hardier kind of hiker, were it not for its location deep in the Maine wilderness, and the decorations upon the walls. They were family snaps, but not of any single family: here were a man and a woman and two young girls, all blond, and next to them a man and woman on their wedding day, older and darker than the people in the preceding picture. Around them were photos and drawings culled from newspapers and pornographic magazines, cut and collaged to make new and foul illustrations, all anti-religious in nature, the heads of Christ and the Virgin Mary and Buddha and figures that I couldn't even identify, Asian and Middle Eastern in origin, transposed onto naked bodies bared obscenely. They were concentrated in one corner, for the most part, above a makeshift stone altar adorned with shattered statuary and old bones, animal and human intermingled. Some of the bones looked very, very old. Among them were a handful of tarnished military buttons. If I were to guess, I would have said that someone had dug up the remains of the soldiers who had died here.

'Malphas,' I said.

'Why would he stay out here?' asked Louis. 'Assuming Wildon and the pilot died in the crash, he was free and clear. He could just go back to doing whatever he was doing before Wildon found him.'

'Could be that he didn't want to,' I said.

'You think he liked the outdoor life so much he decided to spend part of his time in a ruined fort making collages from pornography?'

It didn't sound likely. Liat watched us both, following the conversation on our lips.

'Part of the time,' I said.

'What?'

'You said he spent "part of his time" at the fort. This doesn't look like a permanent dwelling, and those pictures on the wall were put there recently. Where does he spend the rest of his time, and why would he hole up in this place anyway if he's made a permanent home somewhere else?'

I looked to Liat, but she had turned her back on us. Now she beckoned us to join her as she examined something carved into the wood, light against dark.

It was a detailed representation of a young girl's head, two or three times normal size, her hair long and curling from her scalp like the bodies of snakes. Her eyes had been cut deeper and larger than the rest of her, the ovals of them so big that I could have placed my fist in them had they not been filled with teeth, the roots of them impaled in the white wood. There were more teeth in her huge mouth, except these ones were root-out, giving them the appearance of fangs. It was terrifying in aspect and effect.

'If you're frightened of something, where better to hide than a fort?' I said.

'A fort with no gates?' said Louis.

'A fort with bad memories,' I replied. 'A fort with blood in its walls and its dirt. Maybe a fort like that doesn't need gates.'

'He was frightened of a little girl?' Louis sounded skeptical.

'If what I've heard about her is true, he had good cause to be.'

'But he stayed out here, even though he was scared of her. I guess that plane must be real important to him.'

Liat shook her head.

'Not the plane?' I said.

She mouthed the word *no*.

'Then what?'

She made it clear that she didn't know. In the fading light, and the shadows of the old fort, I almost missed the lie.

Almost.

50

Ray Wray was running.

He wasn't sure how it had all gone so wrong so fast, but he knew now that he and Joe had been out of their depth right from the start. They should have backed away the first time that the kid and the woman had come near them, except Joe owed them and they were calling in the debt, and Joe had given Ray to understand that these weren't the kind of people on whom one reneged. He was just grateful to Ray for tagging along, even if Ray wouldn't have been anywhere near those woods if he hadn't been so desperate for cash.

They'd made good progress from the start. The kid might have been spookier than a haunted house on Halloween, but the little bastard could move, and there had been no complaints from the woman about the pace that had been set, either on her own behalf or the kid's. While Joe had the map, and a good sense of where they were going, it often seemed to Ray that it was the woman who was guiding them, and not the other way around. When Joe paused to check his malfunctioning compass, the woman would simply keep on walking, the kid trotting behind her, and when Joe and Ray caught up with them there was no need to alter direction.

Ray figured they were less than a mile from the fort when the first arrow struck. His first thought was, Indians! which was absurd and unhelpful but there was no understanding the workings of the human mind. Even as he hit the ground, and heard Joe swear, he'd found himself giggling, and it was only when he looked up and saw the arrow buried in the trunk of a white pine that he stopped laughing and began considering that he might die out here.

Joe was a few feet to his left, trying to find the source of the arrow.

'Hunter?' asked Ray, but he asked more in hope than expectation. They were still wearing their orange bibs. There had been some discussion about it, but Ray and Joe had finally taken the view that, with a woman and a kid in tow, it was better to be safe. It would have to be one dumb-ass bow hunter who'd shoot an arrow at someone in orange.

'No fuckin' way,' said Joe, which was just what Ray had thought.

The Flores woman was using a thick oak for cover. Still searching the forest for the source of the arrow, Joe called back to her.

'Miss Flores, you got any idea who that might be?'

Something darted behind a wind-tipped hemlock, the old tree resembling an animal more than vegetation, its body seemingly poised to rise up on its roots and stride through the forest. The moving figure revealed itself to be a big man, his head misshapen, the bow clearly visible in his hand. Ray didn't think: he just fired. There was an explosion of bark from the hemlock, and then Joe was firing too. The man retreated fast, limping some yet still nimble, but Ray was pretty certain that one or other of them had winged him. Ray had seen him stumble awkwardly on the third or fourth shot: upper body, maybe the right arm or shoulder. It was only when he and Joe stopped shooting that he realized the Flores woman had been shouting. Against the fading echo of the shots, and the ringing in his ears, he heard the word 'No!'

'The hell do you mean, "No"?' asked Joe. He had emptied his rifle, and was reloading from a prone position, lying on his back while Ray provided cover for him.

'I don't want him hurt,' said Flores.

'Miss, I signed up to get you to that airplane, and get you safely out again,' said Joe. He finished reloading and scanned the trees. 'I did not sign up to get myself killed.'

The arrow seemed to materialize in Joe's left leg. One second he was just lying there, preparing to say something else to Flores, and the next the three-blade head had punched its way straight through his thigh, and Joe's mouth was wide open in a scream as the blood began to spill, the wound already hemorrhaging massively. Ray had never seen so much blood pump so quickly from a man. He moved to help as Joe rose up and a second arrow hit him low in the back, and Ray knew instantly that Joe was going to die. He coughed up a great spray of red as Ray crawled to him and, using his friend's body as cover, began shooting into the forest, hoping to hit something, anything. Joe just grunted as the third arrow struck his back. This one must have pierced his heart because his body shook hard once beneath Ray and then went still.

But that final arrow had given Ray an opening. He'd seen the figure again, just as the arrow was loosed, and now he had a target. He got the man in his sights and was about to pull the trigger when a hand yanked his head back and the shot went wild. Ray took a punch to the side of the head. It wasn't much of a blow, but a trailing finger caught his left eye, the pain blinding him for a few seconds. He lashed out, and felt his fist connect with lips and teeth. When he looked around, the boy was lying on the ground, his mouth red from a split lip.

Ray turned the rifle on the child.

'You move and I'll put a bullet in you,' he said, but it wasn't the boy who moved. To his right, Ray saw Darina Flores rise to her feet and begin walking in the direction of the old yellow birch behind which Ray had glimpsed their attacker. She was calling out to him, calling a name.

'Malphas!' she said. 'Malphas!'

The boy crawled away from Ray. Once he was safely distant,

he got to his feet and followed the woman, blood spilling from his damaged gums. He did not look back.

That was when Ray made his decision. He tore off his orange vest and started to run.

We were still in the fort when the first sounds of gunfire reached us. They were coming from the west, as best we could tell. The compasses had ceased to function effectively shortly before we came within sight of the fort, and they now offered differing and constantly changing views on where magnetic north might lie.

I explained to Liat that we were hearing shots, and we joined Jackie outside the fort.

'What do you think?' I asked Louis.

'Hunters?'

'That's a lot of gunfire, and at least some of it is coming from a handgun.'

'You want to wander into somebody else's gunfight?'

'Not particularly. I just wonder who's shooting, and at what?'

We waited. The gunfire stopped. I thought that I heard a bird calling, but it was no birdsong familiar to me. It was Angel who recognized it for what it was.

'That's a woman's voice,' he said.

We looked at one another. I shrugged.

'We go in,' I said.

Ray Wray had no idea where he was running to, or in what direction. He couldn't see the sun, and he was panicking. He kept waiting for the fierce tearing pain of a three-bladed arrow cutting a path through his flesh, but it did not come. He came to an uprooted deadfall oak, and collapsed behind it to catch his breath and find his bearings. He watched the forest. It was very still. He saw no sign of movement behind him, no misshapen head taking aim, no bow flexed and ready to send a shaft his way. He still had his rifle, and about thirty rounds of ammunition, as well as his pistol. He also had water, and food, but no compass. He glanced at the surrounding trees and tried to judge the moss growth upon them: forest lore dictated that it would be thicker on the north side, but it all looked pretty much equal to him. He might as well have tossed a coin.

Once again, he checked the way that he had come, and saw nothing. He wondered if the woman and the boy were dead yet. What was the name that she had called? Malthus? Malphas, that was it. The Flores woman had known the name of the man who killed Joe, sticking him with hunting arrows like a bad child torturing an insect with pins. Maybe Joe's death had been a big mistake, in which case it was just one part of the larger error in agreeing to go into these woods in the first place. At least Ray still had the down payment that the woman had handed over for their services. If there had been time, he'd have searched Joe's pockets for his share as well, but what he had was better than nothing. He took another look at the nearest tree, decided that the moss looked thicker on the side facing the direction in which he had just come, and prepared to head south.

He was just getting to his feet when he caught a pale flash of movement behind him. Instinctively, he fired.

There was a little girl watching him from between two white pines, one older and coarser-barked than the other. He could see a hole in the center of her dress where the bullet had hit. He waited for her to fall, horrified at what he had done but she did not move. She showed no sign of pain or injury, and no blood spilled from the wound. She should have been dead or dying. She should have been lying on her back, bleeding out her life as clouds scudded across her pupils. She should not have been standing and staring at the man who had just put a bullet in her.

Ray had heard the stories, but he'd always hoped that they

were pure foolishness, tall tales like the yarns of lake monsters and hybrid wolves. Now he knew better.

'I'm lost,' said the girl. She reached out a hand, and Ray saw the broken nails, and the dirt upon the fingers. Her eyes were black-gray coals set against the ruined whiteness of her skin. 'Stay with me.'

Ray backed off. He wanted to threaten her, just as he had threatened the boy, but his guns were no good to him here.

'Get away from me,' he said.

'I'm lonely,' said the girl. Her mouth hung open, and a black centipede crawled from between her lips and scuttled down the front of her dress. 'Don't leave me.'

Ray kept retreating, the gun leveled uselessly on the girl. His feet caught in twisted roots, concealed beneath a layer of dead leaves, and he had to glance down to find his footing. When he looked up again, the girl was gone. He turned in a slow circle, and saw her skipping through the shadows. He thought that he heard her laughing.

'Let me be!' he shouted. He fired a shot in her direction. He didn't care if she fell or didn't fall; he simply wanted to keep her at bay. She was circling him like a wolf closing in on wounded yet still dangerous prey. What was it Joe had said? This was her place. If he could just get out of her territory then she might prey on the woman and the boy instead.

She seemed to pause for a moment, and this time he took aim. The bullet struck her head. He saw something explode from her skull, and her hair blew back as if caught by a gust of air. His vision blurred, and he realized that he was crying. This wasn't meant to happen. He wasn't supposed to be shooting at a little girl. He wasn't supposed to be here at all.

'I'm sorry,' he whispered. 'I just want you to leave me be.'

He fired again, and the girl shook her head violently, but still she circled, drawing ever closer to him, before she retreated abruptly into the trees. He could still see her, though. She seemed to be tensing herself for a final attempt at him. He decided that his best chance lay in emptying the gun into her, in the hope that the ferocity of his response might finally send her back whence she came. He watched her buck as the first of the bullets hit her, and this time he felt only satisfaction.

A weight struck Ray in the chest, and he heard another shot, although it did not come from him. He fell back against the trunk of a tree and slowly slid down the bark, leaving a sticky trail of blood as he went. His rifle fell from his hands as he sank to a sitting position, his hands splayed by his sides. He looked down and saw the wound in his chest, the redness of it spreading like a new dawn. Ray's hands hung over the wound, and he sighed like a man who has just spilled soup on himself. His mouth felt dry, and when he tried to swallow the muscles in his throat refused to respond properly. He began to choke.

Two men appeared before him, one tall and black, his face and head hairless but for a neatly-trimmed graying beard at his chin, the other shorter and scruffier. They seemed familiar. He tried to recall where he had seen them before, but he was too busy bleeding out to concentrate on faces. Behind them appeared three other people, one of them a young woman. The black man kicked away Ray's rifle. Ray stretched out a hand to him. He did not know why, except that he was dying, and dying was like drowning, and a drowning man will always reach out in the hope of finding something to save him from sinking.

The black man took Ray's hand and gripped it, as the seconds of Ray's life melted away like snowflakes in the sun. It was the girl, Ray realized: she knew that she wouldn't get him, so she let these others take him instead. By firing at her, he had fired on them, and now they had killed him for it.

'Who is he?' said one of the others, a big, bearded man who looked out of place among these others, yet more at home in the woods.

Ray tried to speak. He wanted to tell them:

My mother gave me my name. The kids used to laugh at me in school because of it. I never had any luck that wasn't bad, and maybe my name was the start of it.

It wasn't supposed to happen like this. I was looking for an airplane.

My name is—

51

We searched the dead man's body. He had two thousand dollars in cash in his pockets, along with some candy bars and a suppressor for the 9 mm pistol he carried under his coat. He bore no identification. Louis had killed him after he fired two shots in our direction, one of which had missed Liat by inches, and seemed set to fire a third. If Louis hadn't shot him then I would have, but I felt shame as I stared down at this unknown man, dead at our hands in the depths of the Maine wilderness, all to secure a list of names from a plane that might already have been consumed by the forest.

'You recognize him?' said Angel.

'I'm not sure,' I said. 'There is something about him.'

'He was in the ice-cream parlor back in Portland. Louis threatened to shoot him and his buddy.'

'I guess it was meant to be,' said Louis.

'I guess so,' said Angel.

'I doubt that he came out here alone,' said Jackie.

'Could be he was the one we heard doing all that shooting earlier,' said Angel.

'Still doesn't answer the question of who he was shooting at before he began taking potshots at us.'

The trail left by the gunman was clear to follow. He had broken branches and trampled shrubs as he made his way through the forest. It was not the careful progress of a hunter, whether of animals or men. This man had been running *from* something.

'You reckon we're still heading northwest?' I said to Jackie.

'Far as I can tell without a working compass, but I'd lay good money on it.'

'That plane came down somewhere near here. We have to keep looking.'

'Jesus,' said Jackie, 'we could pass within feet of it and not even see it. We didn't even spot this guy until he was almost on top of us.'

'We spread out,' I said. 'Form a line, but stay in sight of one another.'

I couldn't see what other choice we had. We needed to cover as much ground as possible, and we had to do it while there was still light. The downside was that we would now present five targets in a row, like ducks at a sideshow shooting range. So we moved on, looking ahead of us, and to either side, and I forgot Jackie's fear that we were ourselves being pursued.

The sun was setting when we found the shrine. Behind it, almost lost to the forest, was the plane. There were crows in the trees, dark and still like tumors on the branches.

And before us stood three figures, one already dying.

Darina had seen the man's head tilt as she called his name. She had no fear of him. They were alike in nature: after all, they had buried the Wildon girls together, neither hesitating as the children squirmed beneath the accumulating dirt, and they both shared a memory of the Fall, the great banishment that had left their kind marooned on a world still forming. The boy followed calmly behind her, picking his way carefully across twisted roots and broken branches. Over and over she repeated the passenger's name, like a mantra, calming him, reassuring him, even though she could not see him.

'Malphas, Malphas. Remember.'

And all around her, a murder of crows seemed to echo her call.

She crested a rise, and before her was the plane. It looked

like a fallen tree, except that there were no other such trees around it, and its body was perhaps too regular, too cylindrical. By now, it was more than half-submerged, as though the forest floor had turned to quicksand beneath it. Beyond it, a pool gleamed darkly.

But between the plane and where she stood was a crazed jumble of broken religious statuary, of skulls and bones arranged in patterns that had no meaning for her, all contained beneath a framework of mud and wood to protect it from the elements. Of Malphas, there was no sign.

They approached the construction and stood before it. The boy reached out a hand to touch one of the skulls, but she stopped him before he could do so. There was a buzzing in her head, and she felt a kind of awe, the closest she had ever come in her long existence to the fervor of a religious zealot. There was a power here, a purpose. She took the boy's hand, and together they tried to understand.

A shadow fell across them. Slowly they turned. Malphas, the passenger, was silhouetted against the setting sun, his distorted head surrounded by a corona of fire. The bow was tensed in his hands, the arrow nocked and ready. Darina stared into his eyes, and the enormity of her mistake became clear to her. There was no recognition, no shared nature. She saw herself reflected only in the blank, hostile gaze of a predator. Blood flowed from a wound in his side.

'Malphas,' she said. 'Know me.'

He frowned at her, and the arrow spoke to Darina's heart. She felt a burning in her chest as the deepening orange of the fading sun was obscured by the deeper red of her own dying. She put her hands close to her chest and caressed the arrow, holding it gently like an offering. She tried to give form to her pain, but no sound came as she collapsed to the ground.

And as she could no longer scream for herself, the boy screamed for her, over and over and over.

*　　*　　*

The man with his back to us was huge. He wore green-and-brown camouflage clothing, and he held a bow in his hand. To his right, a boy stopped screaming as we appeared, and we watched as the woman beside him toppled to the ground with her hands clutched to the arrow in her breast.

The big man turned and I saw the terrible wound to his head, as though a meat cleaver had been taken to the top of his skull, leaving a crevasse along his scalp. This, then, was Malphas: the survivor, the killer of the Wildon girls. He was completely bald, his ears coming to sharp points, his face strangely elongated and very, very pale despite his years in the woods. He resembled a giant albino bat. Yet though his eyes were dark and alien, and he was already reaching for an arrow from the quiver at his side, it was the boy who gripped my attention, the boy whom I feared more than the man. It was Brightwell in miniature, Brightwell in youth, from his pale moist skin to the growing goiter on his neck that would, in adulthood, blight his appearance still further. I saw his face contort with rage as he recognized me, for how often does a man get to confront his own killer?

All that happened next occurred both slowly and quickly. Jackie, Angel and Liat hesitated before firing, fearful of hitting the boy, not recognizing the danger that he posed. Louis was faster to respond, shooting just as Malphas nocked a new arrow to his bow and dropped to one knee to release it. I heard a beating of wings around us, and a murder of crows rose into the sky. Louis's shot struck the shrine, but it was enough to distract Malphas, and his arrow appeared to go wild. He was already rising, preparing to seek cover, when the boy struck. From the folds of his jacket he produced a long knife and used it to slash at the back of Malphas' right thigh, severing the hamstring. Malphas toppled, and the boy buried the blade in his back. Malphas dropped the bow, and tried to reach behind him for the hilt of the knife, but the movement must have forced the blade still deeper into him, the tip of it slowly, insistently, finding his heart. His mouth opened wide in silent agony. The life slowly left him, and he joined the woman who stared lifelessly at him from her single undamaged eye, his blood mingling with hers on the wood-strewn ground.

But he was not the only one to fall. Jackie called my name, and I turned to see Liat stretched in pain upon the ground, an arrow buried in her left shoulder. While we were distracted, the boy ran, disappearing behind the plane and slipping into the woods beyond.

Jackie and Louis helped Liat to sit while Angel examined the arrow.

'It's gone straight through,' he said. 'We break it, take it out, and strap the wound up as best we can until we can get her to a hospital.'

I saw the three sharp blades of the arrow protruding from her upper back. The wound would be bad. Those arrows were designed to create massive trauma. Already Liat was shivering in shock, but she still managed to point at the plane with her right hand.

'I'm going to the plane,' I said. 'The sooner we have that damned list, the sooner we can leave.'

'What about the kid?' asked Angel.

'That was no kid,' I said.

I looked to Louis. 'Go after him,' I said. 'Take him alive.'

Louis nodded, and ran with me as I headed for the plane.

'That thing on his throat,' he said.

'Yes.'

'It looked like the same mark that Brightwell had.'

'It is Brightwell,' I said. 'Like I told you: don't kill him.'

Louis set aside his rifle and took out his pistol.

'I hate these fucking jobs,' he said.

Jackie Garner suddenly moved away from Angel and Liat and began scanning the forest to the south, his rifle raised.

'What now?' said Louis.

Angel called down to us. 'He thinks he saw someone in the woods.'

'Just get the list,' Louis told me. 'I'll check it out, then go after the child, or whatever you say he is.'

The plane had sunk so far that entering it required stepping down into the cockpit, at least once I'd managed to cut away some of the sticky creepers that were coating the door, which was still ajar, even all these years after Vetters and Scollay had first forced it open. It was dark inside, the windows obscured by the vegetation, and I heard something scamper away from me at the back of the plane and flee into the forest through an unseen hole. I turned on my flashlight, and went searching for the leather satchel that Harlan Vetters had described to his daughter. It was still there, the sheaf of typewritten pages safe inside its plastic covering. Scattered beside the bag were various clipboards, soda cans, and a pair of shoes. I went to the back of the plane, for there was light filtering in from somewhere. The plane lay at a slight upward angle, the nosecone facing toward the sky, the rear submerged in the earth, but what had appeared to be just another part of the upper fuselage was revealed, on closer examination, to be a canvas sheet fixed to the metal. It had probably allowed Malphas to enter and leave the plane easily, if he chose to do so.

'Charlie?' It was Louis's voice. 'I think you need to come out here.'

'On my way,' I said.

'Now would be good.'

Another voice spoke, one that I knew well.

'And if you have a gun, Mr Parker, I'd advise you to throw it out ahead of you. I want to see your hands raised as you emerge. If you appear with a weapon there will be blood.'

I did as I was ordered. I emerged from the plane with my hands above my head, the satchel on my left shoulder, and prepared to confront the Collector.

52

I took it all in as soon as I stepped from the airplane: Liat, lying against a tree, her left arm hanging uselessly by her side, her face pale; and Angel and Louis in the clearing below, separated by about twenty feet, their weapons raised and aiming at the rise above that stinking pool of black water.

There, partly hidden by a tree trunk, stood the Collector, the wind causing the tails of his coat to extend behind him like wings but hardly troubling the greased lines of his hair. He appeared to have dressed no differently for an excursion into the wilderness than he would have for a walk in the park: dark pants, worn shoes, a stained white shirt buttoned to the neck and a black suit jacket and coat.

Jackie Garner knelt before him. There was a strange coil of metal around his neck, and silver objects along its length glittered in the dying sunlight. It was only as I drew nearer that their form became clearer. The coil was threaded with razor blades and fish hooks: any movement by Jackie or the man behind him would tear his flesh. Jackie's body blocked a clear shot at what little of the Collector was exposed: just one half of his face, and his right arm, the muzzle of a gun pressed against the top of Jackie's head while the Collector's eyes moved from Angel to Louis and back again. When I appeared, his eyes fixed on me, but even at this distance I could see that they were different. In the past, their bleakness and hostility had been leavened by a kind of dry amusement at the world and its ways, and the manner in which it had forced him to assume the onerous duty of executioner. It was a facet of his madness, but it gave him a humanity that he would otherwise have lacked. Without it, his eyes were windows into an empty, unforgiving universe, a vacuum in which all things were either dead or dying. Here was the Reaper made incarnate, an entity entirely without mercy.

'Let him go,' I said.

Slowly, I shifted the leather satchel from my shoulder and raised it for him to see.

'Isn't this what you came for? Isn't this what you want?'

Liat shook her head, imploring me not to hand the list over to this man, but he said only, 'Is it? If it is, then it is not *all* that I want.'

He looked at the bodies of Malphas and the woman with the burned face.

'Your work?' he said.

'No, their own. Malphas killed the woman, and the boy with her killed Malphas in reprisal.'

'Boy?'

'He has a goiter, here.' I pointed to my neck with my free hand.

'Brightwell,' said the Collector. 'So it's true: he has come back. Where is he?'

'He ran into the forest. We were about to go after him when you appeared.'

'You should fear him. After all, you killed him once. As grievances go, that one's hard to beat. The other two, though, you don't have to concern yourself about. They won't be coming back, maybe not ever.'

'Why?'

'Angels die only at the hands of angels. All gone now. No return, no new forms. *Poof!*'

I considered what he had just told me. Brightwell had once died at my hand, but Brightwell had come back. If what the Collector was saying was true—

But he was ahead of me. He smiled, and his voice was filled with mockery.

'Why? Did you believe that you might be a fallen angel, a shard of the Divine discarded for your disloyalty? You're nothing: you're just an anomaly, a virus in the system. Soon you'll be expunged, and it will be as if you had never existed. Your life is being measured now in minutes – not hours or days, not months or years. You're very close to dying here, because I am very close to killing you.'

I saw Louis and Angel tense, their bodies preparing for the gunfire to come. In response, the Collector jerked on the coil, and Jackie screamed in pain. Lines of blood began to flow down from his neck.

'No!' I said. 'Lower your weapons. Do it!'

Angel and Louis did as I said, but their fingers stayed on their triggers, and their eyes did not leave the Collector.

'And why am I to die: because my name is on that list you received?'

This time, the Collector actually laughed. 'The list? Those names were nothing. They were bait, footsoldiers to be sacrificed. They knew the Kelly woman was faltering. They knew she would betray them. She had never been privy to their deepest secrets, and all she had were the names of those she herself had corrupted. Brightwell may have added your name when your paths first crossed, but others ensured that it ended up on Barbara Kelly's list. It was their hope that its presence on it would convince your own friends to turn against you, that they would cast you out, or kill you. The real list, the important list, is in your hands. It's older, and it's the product of many hands. That list has *power*.'

'How do you know all this?'

'I tortured it from a woman named Becky Phipps before I put her to death. She went hard. By the end, she was confessing in droplets.'

'Who wanted my name to be put on that list?'

'The Phipps woman died before I could get that information from her, but she spoke of Backers, all wealthy and influential men and women, but one of them more important than the rest. It was simple human psychology. They knew Kelly was turning, and they planted your name in her head. They told her it was significant information, that their enemies would place particular value on it, and she used it, just as they knew she would. They've been watching you for a long time, and they were as curious about you as I was, but pragmatism eventually outweighed any interest in your deeper nature. Now, like me, it seems that they'd prefer a world without you in it. So this is my deal, and there will be no bargaining: you give yourself to me, and the woman lives. So too do your belligerent friends down there. One life for many. Consider yourself a martyr to your cause. Otherwise, I'll hunt you all down, and I won't rest until you and everyone you love is dead.'

He tightened the noose around Jackie's neck once again, twisting it as he did so, and Jackie screamed briefly before the constriction reduced it to a pained gurgle.

'You haven't answered my question,' I said. 'Why you, and why now?'

The Collector ground the muzzle of his gun into Jackie's skull.

'No, it's my turn for questions now, and I have only one: why did you send him? Why did you do it?'

I had no idea what he was talking about, and I told him. The Collector pressed his knee into Jackie's back, contorting his body.

'This one!' said the Collector. 'Why did you send him after my – after Eldritch? To destroy his records? To kill him? To kill me? Why? I want to know. *Tell me!*'

And then I understood. 'The explosion? I had nothing to do with it.'

'I don't believe you.'

457

'I did not do it. On my life.'

'It is on your life. It is on all your lives.'

I looked at Jackie. He was trying to talk.

'Let him speak,' I said. The Collector eased the pressure on the noose, and it hung from Jackie's flesh by its hooks.

'I didn't know,' said Jackie, so softly that we could barely hear him. 'I swear, I didn't know.'

'Oh, Jackie,' I said. 'Jackie, what have you done?'

'They told me there would be nobody in the building. They told me that nobody would get hurt.'

He spoke in a monotone. He was not pleading. He was confessing.

'Who, Jackie? Who told you?'

'It was a phone call. They knew about my mother. They knew that she was sick, and I didn't have the money to help her. So I got a call offering me a job, and I was given a down payment in cash, a lot of cash, with the promise of more to come. All I had to do was cause an explosion. I didn't ask any questions; I just took the money, and did the job. But I wanted to be sure that there was going to be nobody in the building when it happened, so I didn't set a timer. I used a cell phone to detonate it instead. I made the call when I saw that the old man and the woman had left the office, but then the woman went back. I'm sorry. I'm so sorry.'

Nobody spoke for a moment. There was nothing to say.

'It seems that I misjudged you, Mr Parker,' said the Collector, 'although I must admit that I'm disappointed. I thought that I'd finally found an excuse to be rid of you.'

'Don't hurt him,' I said at last. 'There must be a way out of this.'

'What will you do?' asked the Collector. 'Will you take his place? Will you hand him over to the law? You're a hypocrite, Mr Parker. You've done bad things. You've used the ends to justify the means. There have even been times when I've considered you for my collection. Have you felt the urge to unburden yourself to the police, to tell them of bodies in swamps, of dead men in bus station restrooms? I do not trust you. I do not trust any of you.'

'I'll trade you,' I said. 'My friend for the list.'

'The list? I have enough names in my head to last me a hundred lifetimes. If I killed one every hour it would still be no more than an echo of the greater reckoning to come. Your crusade is not mine. What I want is vengeance. What I want is blood, and I will have it. But take your friend, then. I release him. See?'

He lifted the end of the noose, and let it fall from his hand. Staying low, and still using Jackie as a shield, he began to retreat into the forest, his blackness becoming a part of the greater dark, until only his voice remained.

'I warned you, Mr Parker. I told you that all those who stood by you would die. It has already begun. It continues now.'

There was the sound of a shot, and Jackie Garner's chest spat a cloud of blood. Angel and Louis both began to move, but a second shot came, then a third, both exploding inches from my feet.

'Stop!' said the Collector. 'Stop, or the girl is next.'

Liat was closer to him than any of us, but she couldn't hear anything that he was saying. She was afraid to move, afraid of what might happen if she did.

So we stood, and we watched Jackie Garner die.

'I can kill her now,' came the shout from the forest. 'I have her in my sights. Now walk toward me, Mr Parker, and throw the satchel up. No tricks, no short throws. I get the list, and you *all* live.'

I held the satchel high by its strap, and threw it hard, but not in the direction of the forest. Instead, I launched it into the dark pool. It seemed to rest on the black, viscous water for too long before disappearing soundlessly into its depths. I saw Liat's eyes widen, and she stretched out her good hand as though somehow hoping to draw the bag back to her by sheer force of will.

I stood and waited for the final shot to come, but there was only that voice, fainter now as the Collector moved deeper into the forest. I heard a noise above my head, and saw a single raven separate itself from the crows and fly north.

'That was a mistake,' it said. 'You know, Mr Parker, I don't think that you and I are going to be friends any more . . .'

53

The boy did not know where he was going. He was angry, and grief-stricken. The woman who had been mother and more to him was lost, and he had seen again the face of the man who had briefly sent him into the void, into the pain of non-being. He wanted to kill him, but he wasn't strong enough yet. He had not even properly regained the power of speech. The words were in his head but he could not form them with his lips or force his tongue to speak them.

So he ran through the woods, and he wept for the woman, and he plotted his revenge.

There was a buzzing in his head, the voice of the God of Wasps, the Reflected Man, but so lost was the boy in his rage and hurt that he was not able to understand it as a warning until he was already aware of being followed. There was a presence among the trees, shadowing him as he unwittingly ran further north. At first he feared that it might be Parker or one of those who stood by him, come to finish him off. He stopped at a copse of low cypress and crouched low behind them, watching and listening.

He glimpsed movement: a flicker of black on green, like burnt paper blown by the wind. He tried to recall if any of those at the plane had been dressed in black, and decided that they had not. Nevertheless, there was danger here: the voice told him so. His right hand searched the ground beside him and found a rock the size of his fist. He clutched it tightly. He would have only one chance to use it, and he would have to make it count. If he could hit his pursuer in the head, then the impact would give him time to pounce. He could use the same rock to beat him, or her, to death.

More movement, closer this time. The figure was small, only a little taller than himself. The boy was puzzled. Could it be an animal of some kind, even a dark wolf? Were there wolves in these woods? He did not know. The thought of being attacked by a carnivorous animal frightened him more than the threat posed by any human being. He feared unreasoning hunger, the sensation of teeth tearing at his flesh, of claws ripping his skin. He feared being consumed.

The girl appeared from behind a tree barely ten feet from where he lay. How she had moved so quickly without being seen he did not know, but he reacted instantly, firing the rock and watching with satisfaction as it struck the girl above her right eye, causing her to stumble but not lose her footing. He prepared to move on her, but the buzzing in his head rose to a crescendo, and he saw that no blood came from the wound in the girl's head. He could discern clearly where the rock had impacted by the abrasion on her skin, but other than the initial shock of the blow she appeared untroubled by hurt. She did not even seem angry. She simply stared at the boy, then raised her right hand and silently beckoned him to her with a crook of a filthy index finger, its nail long gone.

That unreasoning hunger that the boy had feared to find in an animal was now manifested in another, more terrible, form. This was not really a child, no more than he himself was one: this was loneliness and fear, hatred and hurt, all bound up in the skin of a little girl. Cut her open, the boy thought, and biting bugs and poisonous snakes would tumble from her innards. She was neither good nor evil, and was therefore beyond the remit of the boy and those like him, beyond even the God of Wasps himself. She was pure want.

He backed away from her, and she made no move to follow him. She simply kept crooking her finger, as though certain that, if she persisted, he would eventually surrender to her, but he had no intention of succumbing. The boy, in all of his incarnations, had encountered many threats, and understood the nature of most entities. He saw in this one a tethered beast. She was a dog on a chain, free to roam within certain boundaries, but ultimately constrained. If he could move beyond the limits of her domain, he would be safe.

He turned and ran, heedless once more of the direction, caring only that he put as much distance between the girl and himself as he could. It was growing dark quickly, and he wanted to be well beyond her reach before night fell. She moved again, staying with him, a fleeting blur between the trees. He gasped for breath. He was not healthy, had never been healthy, and although he was capable of summoning massive strength when required, he could do so only in short bursts. Lengthy pursuits, either as hunted or hunter, were anathema to him. There was a pain in his side, and the goiter at his neck throbbed angrily. He could not keep up this pace for much longer. He paused to catch his breath, leaning against a tree, and saw the luminous shape of the girl continue north, then pause. She looked around, and he threw himself to the ground. Was it possible that she had trouble seeing in the dark? He watched her slowly retrace her steps, her head slowly twisting left and right, seeking any sign of movement. She was gradually making her way toward where he lay. If he moved again, she would be on him. If he stayed where he was, she would discover him. He was trapped.

The tree behind him was massive and old, some of its roots as thick as the boy's body, its great, spreading branches, now entirely bare, as twisted as arthritic limbs. At the base of its trunk was a vaguely triangular hole, perhaps the lair of a weasel or other small mammal, widened over time by the actions of nature. Beside it lay a broken branch about three feet in length. It was as thick as his wrist, and sharp at one end. The boy gently scuttled backwards until his feet were in the hole. It would be a tight squeeze, but he could make it. Once inside, he could hide from the girl and, if she found him, he could keep her at bay with the stick. The blow from the rock might not have stopped her entirely, but she had clearly felt the force of it. The stick might be enough to torment her and make her keep her distance. All the boy knew was that he could run no longer, and here he must make his stand.

Back, back he went, until the edges of the hole were biting into his sides. There was a moment when he felt sure that he was stuck, incapable of going forward or back, but he wriggled his flabby body and the hole seemed to suck him in. Once inside he stayed quiet and still. He could see nothing except the patch of forest beyond, and even that was growing dimmer as the darkness drew in, but he caught sight of the girl's form as she passed into view. She was crouching as she walked, her upper body slightly extended, her fingers curled like claws. He thought that he heard her sniffing at the air, and her head turned so that she seemed to be looking straight at him. He held tightly to the stick, ready to thrust the point at her if she came. He would aim for one of her eyes, he decided. He wondered if the stick was strong enough to impale her on the ground. He had a vision of her struggling against it like a dying moth. It made him smile.

But she did not approach him, and instead moved on. He realized that he had been holding his breath, and let it out in a gasp of relief. The sound of the God of Wasps subsided a little, for which the boy was grateful. After a few minutes he shifted position, trying to make himself more comfortable. He used the stick to test the limits of the hole and found that it was bigger than he had anticipated. He could not have stood up inside it, but there was room for him to stretch out his legs. If he curled up a little, he might even be able to sleep, but he would not sleep, not with the girl outside, roaming, searching. To pass the time, and keep himself amused, he sorted through his memories, the great rush of them that had returned to him when he heard again the voice of the man who had tried to destroy him, the hated detective. His time would come: once the boy had found more of his own kind, and grown big and strong again, he would take the detective, this man whose nature even the boy did not understand, and in a deep, dark place he would discover the truth about him. First, though, he would kill the detective's woman and his child, just as his first woman and child had been taken from him in blade and blood, but this time the detective would be forced to watch as it happened. There was a circularity about it that appealed to the boy.

The woods grew black, and he heard the scurrying of night creatures. Twice the darkness before him was lit by the passing luminescence of the girl, and he heard her calling to him, coaxing him into revealing himself. She promised to show him the way out of the forest, swore that she would guide him to safety, if only he would play with her for a little while. He did not answer, and he did not move. He stayed where he was, and prayed to the God of Wasps to sacrifice a little of the night so that dawn might come more quickly.

He did not remember sleep coming. There was no instance where his eyes briefly closed only for him to realize what was happening and jolt himself awake. There was only wakefulness, and then sleep. When he opened his eyes again he was slumped against the inside of the tree. It was still dark outside, but the texture of the night had changed, and the woods were silent. Something had caused him to wake, though. He was aware of a disturbance, a sound from close by. He also desperately needed to pee, and he was very, very cold.

The boy listened. Yes, there it was again: a scuffling, a digging. An animal, maybe, some mammal hunting for buried prey. It was coming from nearby, but he could not pinpoint the precise source. The noise echoed inside the tree, further distorting his perception. With it came the warning buzz in his head as the God of Wasps called to him in a voice that he still could not yet fully comprehend.

It was coming from his right, he decided. Now he could hear the scratching of claws against the tree trunk. He leaned over, his ear close to the wood, his face barely six inches from the ground. What are you, he thought. What *are* you?

A small hand exploded from the dirt between his legs, and gripped his face. He felt fingers on his skin, digging deep into his flesh. One found his open mouth and he bit down hard upon it, severing it entirely, but the grip did not weaken. A jagged nail dug into his right eye, and a fierce, intimate pain insinuated itself into his skull. The presence in the dirt rose up still further, now not just a forearm but a head, and a torso. The girl's sickly light infected the gloom as she ascended, her right hand forcing itself deeper and deeper into the boy's face, her left pushing against the ground for leverage. He struggled hard, tearing at her dead flesh with one hand while the other scrabbled in the dirt until he found the stick. He raised it as high as he could before stabbing down, and felt it enter the girl's body. She spasmed, and he struck again, but he was sinking now, and he sensed collapse all around him. The girl was no longer forcing herself up: instead she was dragging him down, deep into that lonely place in which she herself had been interred, with its ceiling of roots and its walls of dirt, where the beetles and the millipedes scuttled over her bones.

The stick caught in the dirt and snapped. The earth rose to the boy's chest, then his neck, and finally his chin. He opened his mouth, but the earth silenced his final scream.

And the girl had her playmate at last.

54

I do not know if all that I have shared with you is true. Some of it I experienced, and some of it was told to me. Some of it, I may have dreamed.

I picked up fragments from Grady Vetters, once he had recovered consciousness. Together we visited his sister at the hospital. She was still deep in her coma. The comatose state into which she had been plunged by the needle had not been alleviated by the coma cocktail of drugs with which she had been treated. In the end, she had not been as strong as her brother, not physically: combined with restrictions on her breathing caused by the position in which she had been left on the couch, the injection had left her with hypoxic brain damage.

Marielle slept, and it seemed that she would never wake again.

We left Jackie Garner's body in the plane to protect it from animals. Later, the wardens retrieved it, and he was brought back to his mother and his girlfriend for burial. The bodies of the woman named Darina Flores, and the man known as Malphas, were taken to Augusta for examination. What happened to them after that, I do not know.

Liat managed to walk out of the forest, with each of us taking turns supporting her. By the end, she was barely conscious. She refused to look at me, or even to recognize my presence beside her while I was helping her. She had been sent to ensure the list's safe retrieval, and she had failed. In the darkness, we came upon the road that we had taken into the wilderness. Louis and Angel stayed with Liat while I went to get the truck. Only when I started driving did I notice that Jackie's totem, the necklace of bear claws that hung from his rear view mirror, was gone, and I wondered when the Collector had added it to his trove: before he killed Jackie, or after?

I took Liat to the local medical center, and explained that she had fallen on an arrow. Stranger things had happened, it seemed, for the doctor on duty barely blinked an eye, and arrangements were made to transfer her immediately to Bangor. I explained that she could neither speak nor hear, but could read lips. I then called Epstein and told him most of what had occurred. When he asked if the list was safe, I answered yes, but nothing more.

After all, it was, in its way.

Shortly before dawn, I drove my own car back up that timber company road, and returned to the forest. This time, I was prepared. I was still two miles from the wreckage of the plane when I picked up the beacon's signal on my cell phone. Twenty feet from the plane, at the base of a white pine, I found the list. I had not thrown it far from the airplane, just far enough. Some small animal had already nibbled at the plastic, but the package remained more or less intact, the little beacon I had placed inside it blinking redly.

Of the boy who was Brightwell, there was no sign, but days later, while the search of the area continued, and the police began gathering and identifying the remains of those killed by Malphas, one of the boy's shoes was discovered near the hollow tree trunk of a massive oak, and it was thought that he might have been taken by a bear.

I told the investigators most of what I knew at that point about the airplane, for I was nothing if not adept at hiding truths. Gordon Walsh was among the police who questioned me, although the north of the state no longer fell into his remit. He had been sent to observe, he said, but I did not ask by whom. I told them that Marielle Vetters had hired me to find the plane, for she believed that her father's silence about its existence might have caused unnecessary pain for the families of those who had been aboard when it crashed, and who still waited for some knowledge of the fate of their loved ones. I left out only the existence of the list, and something of my knowledge of the Collector, although I gave a detailed description of him to the police, and fed them the link to the lawyer, Eldritch. After all, I owed nothing to either of them now. I told the police, too, about Jackie's final sin, the one that had led to his death. One cannot libel the dead, and lying to protect Jackie's reputation, or to spare the feelings of those who loved him, would have caused more problems than telling the truth.

Slowly a narrative began to emerge that was, if not entirely satisfactory, then plausible. The Collector had come seeking revenge for the fatal explosion, and the woman and the boy were searching for the plane for unknown reasons of their own, possibly connected to the man named Malphas but perhaps also in the belief that some money remained hidden in the plane. Meanwhile the process of identifying the remains of Malphas's victims began. Two men, subsequently identified as Joe Dahl and Ray Wray, were added to his list of victims, and I said nothing to contradict that assumption. With so much else to occupy their time, the forces of law and order seemed content to let any holes in my story remain unexplained.

And, in a corner, Gordon Walsh watched, and he listened.

It was Walsh who first asked for more information about Liat, once her connection to what had happened was discovered. I told him that she was eventfully an expert on aviation history, a claim she duly confirmed when it was eventually put to her. As Walsh wasn't about to try to interrogate a deaf and dumb woman about a subject on which he knew nothing, he let that one slide. Before he left Falls End, though, he made it clear to me that, assuming I lived long enough, he expected to hear, at some future date, a more detailed version of events than the one he had just been offered.

By the time the investigators reached the private medical center where the lawyer, Eldritch, was being treated, they found that he had been released from the care of his physicians into the custody of a man who claimed to be his son, and no trace of him could be found. Subsequently, it appeared that the ruined building that had once housed his office was actually owned by an elderly couple who ran a pawnbroking operation nearby, and their agreement with their missing tenant had rested on a handshake, and nothing more. The damaged building was torn down within weeks, and the insurance money, when it came, was swallowed by their pockets.

One month after all this had occurred, Epstein came to visit me. Liat was with him, as well as one of those seemingly interchangeable young men-at arms upon whom he relied for his safety. Epstein and I walked for a time on Ferry Beach, Liat and her companion watching us from a distance.

'Why did you destroy the list?' Epstein finally asked.

'What would you have done with it?' I replied.

'Watched, investigated.'

'Killed?'

He shrugged. 'Perhaps.'

'Before or after those people named upon it could act?'

He shrugged again. 'Sometimes, preventive actions are necessary.'

'*That's* why I destroyed it,' I said.

'In the right hands, it could have proved most useful.'

'In the right hands,' I echoed.

'From what I hear, Liat was at risk of death because of what you did. The Collector threatened her life unless the list was given to him.'

'He wasn't going to kill her.'

'You seem very sure of that.'

'He has a code. It's a twisted, blasted thing, but it's a code nonetheless. He wouldn't have killed her because of something that I did: he would only have killed her for something that she herself had done. I didn't believe that she was guilty of something that would have brought the Collector down upon her.'

'I will try to explain that distinction to her. I fear that, if you were to attempt to do so, she might try to shoot you.'

We reached the end of the beach, and turned back. The sun had begun to set as we turned to the north, the wind breathing winter on our faces.

'What do you think Malphas was doing out there?' said Epstein. 'Liat spoke of an altar, a kind of shrine.'

'Malphas had a dent in his head big enough to hold a book,' I said. 'He was brain-damaged. You think even he knew for sure what he was doing?'

'He certainly had a purpose. Liat said that the altar faced north. A north-facing altar, in a northern state. How far north can one go, do you think, before there is nothing left, nothing to worship, only snow and ice?'

We walked on in silence until we were back at the parking lot.

'This is north,' said Epstein, as his young man started the car, Liat standing by an open rear door, their departure now imminent. 'This place. Planes crash here, and are slowly sucked into the ground. Killers come here, and meet their end. Dark angels spread their wings above its ground, and are brought down by their enemies. And you, you are here. I used to believe that it was you to whom they were drawn in this place, but now I think that I may have been wrong. There is something else here. It called to Malphas, and it tried to hide that plane. It calls to them all, even if they're unaware of its voice. That is what Liat believes, and now that is what I believe.'

We shook hands.

'It is a shame about that list,' said Epstein, and while his right hand clasped mine tightly, he rested his left hand upon both, and his eyes searched my face for any hint that what he suspected might well be true: whatever was in the bag at the bottom of that dark pond, it was not the list. 'You know, I sent some of my people into the interior to search for it, but to no avail. It seems that body of water is very deep. Let's just hope that the list rests in a safe place.'

'I can think we can be sure of that,' I replied.

They left me then. I faced the north, as though, from where I stood, I might see far, far beyond, deep into the darkness of the Great North Woods.

The woods, and whatever lay buried deep beneath them.

Buried, and waiting.

Acknowledgements

As always, I am indebted to a number of individuals who helped to make this book better than it might otherwise have been. I would like to thank my fellow author, Paul Doiron (www.pauldoiron.com), who, in addition to being a very fine writer, is also the editor of *Down East* magazine (www. downeast.com), to which I am a proud subscriber. It was Paul who gave up his time to help me understand the ways of hunters in Maine, and for both his knowledge and the pleasure of his company I am deeply grateful. Meanwhile, Drs Robert and Rosey Drummond kindly advised on medical matters, for which I owe them a good Indian meal, and Rachel Untermon and her sister helped me to swear in Hebrew. Thanks, too, to my good friend Joe Long in New York for introducing me to all at Nicola's fine Italian specialty store in New York. To Nick and Freddy Santilli, my gratitude for letting me hold meetings in your office; and to Dutch, thanks for the books. You should visit them. They're on First Avenue, between 54th and 55th Street. Tell them we sent you.

I am very fortunate to be surrounded by people, most of them women, who are much smarter than I am, and who have taken it upon themselves to look after my odd little books and, by extension, me. I would be very lost without my editors, Sue Fletcher at Hodder & Stoughton and Emily Bestler at Atria, and all who work alongside them: Swati Gamble, Kerry Hood, Lucy Hale, Auriol Bishop, Jamie Hodder-Williams and the fine sales reps at Hodder; and Judith Curr, Louise Burke, Carolyn Reidy, Caroline Porter, David

Brown, and the sales teams at Atria and Pocket. My friend Clair Lamb has made my life immeasurably easier by taking on the thankless role of publicist, assistant, and general organizer of all things book-related, assisted by the patently gifted Madeira James, who looks after my website, and, until recently, Jane Doherty, who has since moved on to sunnier marital climes. My thanks, too, as always, to my agent, Darley Anderson, without whom I would not be in the fortunate position of being published, and his team: Clare Wallace, Mary Darby, Sophie Gordon, Vicki Le Feuvre, Andrea Messent, Camilla Wray, Rosanna Bellingham, Peter Colegrove and, in Los Angeles, my film agent, Steve Fisher.

Finally, the people at home have to put up with a lot. To my lovely Jennie, to Cameron and Alistair, and to the two dogs, Sasha and Coco, who keep me company in my office, my love and thanks.

07 949 451 290

In the best books, the ending often comes as a shock.
Not just because of that one last twist in the tale,
but because you have been so absorbed in their world,
that coming back to the harsh light of reality is a jolt.

If that describes you now, then perhaps you should track down
some new leads, and find new suspense in other worlds.

Join us at www.hodder.co.uk, or follow us on
Twitter @hodderbooks, and you can tap in to a
community of fellow thrill-seekers.

Whether you want to find out more about this book,
or a particular author, watch trailers and interviews, have
the chance to win early limited editions, or simply browse
our expert readers' selection of the very best books,
we think you'll find what you're looking for.

And if you don't, that's the place to tell us what's missing.

We love what we do, and we'd love you to be part of it.

www.hodder.co.uk

@hodderbooks

HodderBooks

HodderBooks